About

Marguerite Kaye has written over fifty historical romances featuring feisty heroines and a strong sense of place and time. She is also co-author with Sarah Ferguson, Duchess of York, of the *Sunday Times* bestsellers, *Her Heart for a Compass* and *A Most Intriguing Lady.* Marguerite lives in Argyll on the west coast of Scotland. When not writing, she loves to read, cook, garden, drink martinis, and sew, though rarely at the same time.

Regency Rebels

Regency Rebels:

Scandalous Secrets

MARGUERITE KAYE

MILLS & BOON

First Published in Great Britain 2024
By Mills & Boon, an imprint of HarperCollins*Publishers* Ltd,
1 London Bridge Street, London, SE1 9GF

www.harpercollins.co.uk

HarperCollins*Publishers*
Macken House, 39/40 Mayor Street Upper,
Dublin 1, D01 C9W8, Ireland

ISBN: 978-0-263-32269-9

MIX
Paper | Supporting
responsible forestry
FSC™ C007454

This book is produced from independently certified FSC™ paper
to ensure responsible forest management.

For more information visit: www.harpercollins.co.uk/green

Printed and Bound in the UK using 100% Renewable Electricity
at CPI Group (UK) Ltd, Croydon, CR0 4YY

THE SOLDIER'S
DARK SECRET

Chapter One

England—August 1815

*The small huddle of women and the bedraggled chil-
dren who clung to their skirts stared at him as one,
wide-eyed and unblinking, struck dumb and motionless with fear. Only the compulsive clutching of their
mother's protective fingers around the children's
shoulders betrayed the full extent of their terror. He
was accustomed to death in combat, but this was
a village, not a battlefield. He was accustomed to
seeing enemy causalities, but these were civilians,
women and young children...*

Jack Trestain's breathing became rapid and shallow
as he tossed and turned in the throes of his recurring
nightmare. He thrashed around on the sweat-soaked
sheets. He knew he was dreaming, but he couldn't
wake from it. He knew what was coming next, but he
couldn't prevent it unfolding in all its horror.

His boots crunched on the rough sun-dried track

as he walked, stunned, around the small village, his brain numb, unable to make sense of what his eyes were telling him. The sun burned the back of his neck. He had lost his hat. A scrawny chicken squawked loudly, running across his path, making him stumble. How had the mission turned into such a debacle? How could his information, his precious, carefully gathered knowledge of the enemy's movements, have been so wrong?

It was not possible. Not possible. Not possible. The words rang in his head over and over. He was aware of his comrades' voices, of orders being barked, but he felt utterly alone.

The cooking fires were still burning. From a large smoke-blackened cauldron the appetising aroma of a herb-filled stew rose in the still, unnaturally silent air. He had not eaten since yesterday. He was suddenly ravenous.

As his stomach growled, he became aware of another, all-pervading smell. Ferrous. The unmistakable odour of dried blood. And another. The sickly-sweet stench of charred flesh.

As the noxious combination seared the back of his throat, Jack retched violently, spilling his guts like a raw recruit in a nearby ditch. Spasm after spasm shook him, until he had to clutch at the scorched trunk of a splintered tree to support himself. Shivering, shaking, he had no idea how long the girl had been looming over him...

It was the fall that woke him. He was on the floor of his bedchamber, clutching a pillow. He had banged his head on the nightstand. The ewer had toppled over and smashed. The chambermaid would think him one of the clumsiest guests she'd ever encountered. His nightshirt was drenched, the contents of the jug adding to his fevered sweat. His head was thumping, his jaw aching, and his wrists too, from clenching his fists. Wearily, Jack dragged himself to his feet and, opening the curtains, checking the hour on his pocket watch. It was just after five. He'd managed to sleep for a total of two hours.

Outside, morning mist wreathed the formal lawns which bordered the carriageway. Opening the casement wide, he leaned out, taking ragged breaths of fresh air. Damp, sweetly herbaceous air, not the dusty dry air of far-off lands, that caught in your lungs and the back of your throat, that was so still all smells lingered, and you carried them with you on your clothes for days afterwards.

Jack swallowed hard, squeezing his eyes tight shut in his effort to block out the unwelcome memory. Slow breaths. One. Two. Three. Four. Open your eyes. Moist air smelling of nothing but dew. More breaths. And more.

Dammit! It had been two years. He should be over it by now. Or if not over it, he should have it under control. He'd been coping perfectly well in the army—more or less. He'd been dealing with it—mostly. Functioning—on the whole. He hadn't fallen apart. He'd been able to control his temper. He'd even been able to sleep, albeit mainly as a result of exhaustion brought on by a punishing schedule of duties. Only now, when he was free of that life, the very life that was responsible for creating his coruscating guilt, it was haunting his every waking and sleeping moment.

Dear God, he must not fall apart now, when it was finally all behind him. He had to get out of the house. He had to get that smell out of his head. Exercise, that's what he needed. It had worked before. It would work again. He would *make* it work again.

His forearm had finally been released just yesterday after weeks in a cumbersome splint. Jack flexed his fingers, relishing the pain which resulted, his toes curling on the rug. He deserved the pain. A damned stupid thing to do, to fall from his horse, even if his shoulder had just been torn open by a French musket. Quite literally adding insult to injury.

Take it easy, the quack had advised yesterday, reminding him that he might never recover his full strength. As if he needed reminding. As if it mattered now. 'As if anything matters,' Jack muttered to himself, pulling off his nightshirt and throwing on a bare minimum of clothes before padding silently out of the house.

The sun was beginning to burn the mist away, drying the dew into a fine sheen as he set off at a fast march through the formal gardens of his older brother's estate. Jack had been on active service in Egypt when their father died, and Charlie inherited. In the intervening years, nearly all of which Jack had spent abroad on one military campaign or another, Charlie had added two wings to their childhood home, and his wife, Eleanor, had redecorated almost every single room. The grounds, though, had been left untouched until now. In a few weeks, the extensive new landscaping programme would begin, and the estate would be transformed. The lake, towards which he now made his way, through the overgrown and soon-to-be-uprooted Topiary Garden, would be drained, dredged, deepened and reshaped into something that would apparently look more natural.

He stood on the reedy bank, inhaling the odours so resonant of childhood: the fresh smell of grass, the cloying scent of honeysuckle and the sweetness of rotting vegetation laced with mud coming from the lake bed. There was never anyone around at this time of day. It was just Jack, and the ducks and whatever fish survived in the brackish water of the lake.

Divesting himself quickly of his few garments, he stretched his arms high above his head, took a deep breath, and plunged head first into the water. Though it was relatively warm on the surface, it was cold enough underneath to make him gasp. Opening his eyes, he could see little, only floating reeds and twigs, the mixture of dead leaves and sludge churned up by his splashy entry. He broke the surface, panting hard, then struck out towards the centre, his weakened right arm making his progress lopsided, forcing his left arm to compensate as he listed to one side like a sloop holed below the waterline by a cannon.

Ignoring the stabbing pain in his newly healed fracture and the familiar throbbing ache in his wounded shoulder, Jack gritted his teeth and began to count the lengths. He would stop when he was too exhausted to continue, and not before.

Celeste Marmion had also been unable to sleep. Attracted by the soft light of the English morning, so very different from the bright blaze of the Côte d'Azur where she had been raised, she had dressed quickly and, grabbing her notebook and charcoals, decided to reconnoitre the grounds of Trestain Manor before facing her hosts at breakfast. Arriving late last night, the brief impression she had had of her new patrons, Sir Charles and Lady Eleanor Trestain, was pretty much as she had expected. He was the perfect gentleman, rather bluff, rather handsome, his smile kind, though his manner veered towards the pompous. His wife, a slender and very tall woman with a long nose and intelligent eyes, reminded Celeste of a highly-strung greyhound. Lady Eleanor was a good deal less welcoming than her husband, giving Celeste the distinct impression that she was placing her hostess in a social quandary, for although Sir Charles had welcomed his landscape painter as a valued guest, Lady Eleanor seemed more inclined to treat her as a tradesperson.

'Which is perfectly fine by me. I am here for my own reasons, not to play the serf in order to placate a social snob. Lady Eleanor is really quite irrelevant in the grand scheme of things,' Celeste muttered to herself as she made her way through a magnificent but dreadfully neglected Topiary Garden.

She could hardly believe that she had finally made

it to England. It had been her goal ever since January, when she had received that fateful letter. It had been a terrible shock, despite the fact that they had been estranged for years, to learn that she would never see her mother again. She had thought herself completely inured to Maman's coldness, but for a few days after learning of her death, Celeste had been left reeling, assailed by a maelstrom of emotions which struck her with a force that was almost physical.

She had, however, quickly regained her equilibrium. After all, her mother had been more of an absence than a presence in her life for as long as she could remember, even before Celeste had been callously packed off to boarding school at the age of ten. It should make no difference to Celeste that the house in Cassis was closed up, for she never visited. It should make no difference that there was now no possibility of any reconciliation. She had never understood her mother's attitude towards her, the cause of their gradual and now final estrangement, but she had long decided not to let it be a cause of hurt to her. Until she had received that blasted letter which hinted at reasons, mysterious reasons, for her mother's heartless indifference.

Celeste had tried very hard in the weeks after that letter to carry on with her perfectly happy, perfectly calm and perfectly ordered and increasingly successful life, but the questions her mother had raised demanded to be answered. Until she knew the whole story, until she knew the truth behind those hints and revelations, Maman's life was an unfinished book.

Celeste had to discover the ending, and then she could close the cover for ever. It was an image she found satisfying, for it explained away quite nicely that churning feeling which kept her awake at nights when she thought of her mother. Guilt? Hardly. Her whole life she had been the innocent victim of a loveless upbringing. And of a certainty it was not grief either. In order to grieve, one had to care. And she did not care. Or, more accurately, she had taught herself not to care. She did feel anger sometimes, though why should she be angry? She did not know, but it did not sit well with the self-contained and independent person she had worked so hard to become. And so she had come to England to find some answers and close an unhappy chapter in her life.

Napoleon's escape from Elba in March earlier in the year had put paid to Celeste's original plans for her trip here. As France and Great Britain resumed hostilities, she waited restlessly for the inevitable denouement on the battlefield, guiltily aware that her impatience was both unpatriotic and more importantly incredibly selfish. She knew nothing of war save that she wished it would not happen. She cared not who won, provided that peace was made. Until Waterloo, like almost every other person of her acquaintance, she managed to close her eyes to the reality of battle. After Waterloo, the full horror of it could not be ignored.

But peace was finally declared, and that, despite the defeat of France, was a cause for celebration. No more war. No more bloodshed. No more death. It also meant that Celeste was finally free to travel. The commission from Sir Charles Trestain to paint his gardens for posterity before he had them substantially altered had come to her by chance. A fellow artist of her acquaintance, who had been the English baronet's first choice, had been unable to accept due to other commitments and had recommended Celeste. She could not but think it was fated.

So here she was, in what she was only beginning to realise was a foreign country. Her command of the language had been the one and only piece of her heritage which her English mother had given her, though they had spoken it only when alone. As far as the world was concerned, Madame Marmion was as French as her husband.

Celeste stopped to remove a long strand of sticky willow which had become entangled in the flounce of her gown. The grass underfoot was lush and green, the air sweet-smelling and fresh, no trace of the southern dry heat of home—or rather the place she was raised, for a home was a place associated with love and affection, something which had been in very short supply in Cassis.

No matter, she had her own home now, her little studio apartment in Paris. The air in the city at this time of year was oppressive. Celeste took a deep breath of English air. She really was here. Soon, hopefully before the summer was over, she would have some answers. Though right at this moment, she wasn't exactly clear how on earth she was going to set about finding them.

A gate at the end of the neglected Topiary Garden revealed a view of a lake. The brownish-green water looked cool and inviting. Frowning, deep in thought, it was only as she reached the water's edge that Celeste noticed the lone swimmer. A man, scything his way through the water in a very odd manner, rather like a drunken fish. Coachman, gamekeeper, gardener or perhaps simply one of the local farmers taking advantage of the early-morning solitude? She could empathise with that. Solitude was a much-underrated virtue. Whoever he was, she ought to leave him to finish his illicit swim in Sir Charles's lake. Had the roles been reversed she would have found the intrusion most offensive. And yet, instead of turning back the way she had come, Celeste stepped behind a bush and continued to watch, fascinated.

He was completely naked. The musculature of his torso was beautifully defined. His legs were long, well shaped, and equally well muscled. He would make a fascinating life study, though it would be a lie to say that it was purely with an artist's eye that she observed him, peering as she did through the straggle of jagged hawthorn branches. Like his swimming, the man's face was far from perfect. His nose was too strong, his brow too high, his eyes too intense and deeply sunk. He looked more fierce than handsome. No, not fierce, but there was a hardness to his features, giving him the air of a man who courted danger.

His swimming was becoming laboured. He slowed and stopped only a few yards from where she stood, staggering slightly as he found his footing. The water lapped around his waist. His chest heaved as he began to make his way towards the bank where his clothes were draped over a branch some distance away. It was too late for her to make her escape. She could only hold her breath, keep as still as possible and hope that he would not spot her.

His torso was deeply tanned. There was an odd puckered hollow in his right shoulder where the flesh appeared to have been scooped out. His entire right arm was distinctly paler than the rest of him, as if he had spent the summer wearing a shirt with one sleeve. A scar formed an inverted crescent on his left side, just under his rib cage. A man who liked to fight or one who was decidedly accident prone? He was panting, his chest expanding, his stomach contracting with each breath. His next step revealed the rest of his flat belly. The next, the top of his thighs, and a distinct line where his tan ended.

And then he stopped. He looked up to the sky, and Celeste's breath caught in her throat as his face almost seemed to crumple, bearing such an expression of despair and grief that it twisted her heart before he dropped his head into his hands with a dry sob. His shoulders were heaving. Appalled, mortified to have witnessed such an intensely intimate moment, Celeste turned to flee. Her gown caught on the hawthorn briar, and before she could stifle it, an exclamation of dismay escaped her mouth.

He looked up. Their eyes met for one brief moment that seemed to last for an eternity. He looked both heartbreakingly vulnerable and volcanically angry. Celeste tore herself free of the thorns and fled.

Back in her room at Trestain Manor, Celeste could not get the image of the man's tortured face out of her head. Nor her deep shame at having spied on him. She, of all people, should respect a person's right to privacy, given how hard she defended her own. It took fifteen minutes for the colour to fade entirely from her cheeks and another fifteen before she was calm enough to face breakfast with her new patrons.

Praying that the man would not turn out to be one of Sir Charles's footmen, she made her way down the stairs to the dining room where one of the austere servants indicated the morning repast was being taken. The very welcome aroma of coffee was overlaid with a stronger one of eggs and something meaty. Hoping that she would not be obliged to partake of either, Celeste opened the door and stopped dead in her tracks on the threshold.

The room was dark, for the windows were heavily curtained, and despite the white-painted ceiling, the overall impression was gloomy. An ornately carved and very highly polished walnut table took up most of the available space, around which were twelve throne-like chairs. Three were occupied. Sir Charles was seated at the top of the table. Lady Eleanor was on his right. And on his left sat another man. A man with damp hair, curling down over his collar. With a coat stretched across a pair of broad shoulders. Her stomach knotted.

'Ah, Mademoiselle Marmion, I trust you slept well. Do join us.'

Sir Charles pushed his chair back and got to his feet. Celeste, her polite smile frozen, could not shift her gaze from the other guest. There was a kerchief knotted around his neck rather than a carefully tied cravat. He had shaved, but somehow he looked as if he had not.

'Jack, this is Mademoiselle Marmion, the artist I was telling you about. She's come all the way from Paris to capture our gardens for posterity before Eleanor's landscaper gets his hands on them. *Mademoiselle*, do allow me to introduce you to my brother Jack, who is residing with us at present.'

Her first instinct, as he rose from his seat, was to run. He was smiling, a thin, cold smile, the sort of smile a man might bestow on a complete stranger, but she was not fooled. Celeste clutched the polished brass doorknob, for her knees had turned to jelly as the man from the lake crossed the room to greet her. The naked man from the lake who was Sir Charles's brother. *Mon Dieu*, she had seen naked men before but what made her cheeks burn crimson was having witnessed that anguished look on his face. She had seen him naked, stripped bare in quite a different way. She felt as if she had violated some unspoken rule of trespass. Forcing herself to let go of the door handle, she met the cold, assessing look in his dark-brown eyes. What had possessed her to watch him? Why on earth had she not fled as soon as she'd seen him?

He bowed over her hand. Did he notice that her fingers were icy? 'Mademoiselle Marmion. *Enchanté*. It is a pleasure to meet you. Again,' he added sotto voce, leaving her in no doubt that he had recognised her.

'Monsieur Trestain.' Her voice was a croak. She cleared her throat. 'It is a pleasure.'

'Indeed?' He ushered her to the table, holding out the chair opposite his own for her. 'For future reference, *Mademoiselle*,' he whispered, 'I am accustomed to taking my morning swim in private.'

His tone was neutral but there was an underlying note of barely controlled fury. Celeste's hand shook as she picked up the silver coffee pot. Though she managed to pour herself a much-needed cup without spilling it, she was acutely aware of Jack Trestain watching her, expecting her to do just that. She had been in the wrong, but she did not like to be intimidated. 'I took the opportunity to explore a little of your beautiful grounds before breakfast,' she said, turning to Sir Charles.

'Excellent, I applaud your sense of enterprise.' Sir Charles rubbed his hands together. 'And did you find anything to inspire you, *Mademoiselle*?'

'Yes, do tell us, did you see anything of interest during your exploration?'

Jack Trestain's curt tone cut across his brother's gentler one. Celeste threw him a tight smile. 'The lake has some interesting views.'

'I'm sure you found it fascinating,' Jack Trestain said, returning her look unblinking, 'though perhaps you will prefer to admire the view in the afternoon sunshine, in future.'

She could not mistake the warning tone in his voice. With some difficulty, Celeste swallowed the spark of temper which it provoked. She had been completely at fault, but this man was taking deliberate pleasure in her discomfort. She nodded curtly and took a sip of coffee to prevent herself from being tempted into a retort.

'Well,' Sir Charles said, casting a sideways glance at his brother, obviously perplexed by the animosity reverberating from him. 'Well, now. Perhaps Jack's right, the afternoon sunshine would provide the best light for capturing the views. What is your opinion, my love?'

The rather desperate look Sir Charles cast his wife intrigued Celeste. The way in which Lady Eleanor commandeered the conversation, launching into a long and detailed description of the various changes which her landscaper planned, and the possible studies Celeste could make, spoke of considerable practice in changing the subject. Jack Trestain, leaning back in his chair, ignoring the plate of ham and eggs set before him, watched with a sardonic smile on his face, obviously perfectly aware of the diversionary tactics being deployed, equally aware that he was being excluded from the conversation lest he cause further offence.

Lady Eleanor, running out of steam on one subject, switched, with barely a moment to take breath, to another. 'You are admiring our dining room, I see,' she said to Celeste, who had actually been staring down at her plate. 'It is quite a contrast to the rest of the house, you were no doubt thinking. Very true, but we did feel, Sir Charles and I, that it was important to preserve at least one of the original rooms when we carried out our refurbishment. The wall covering is Spanish Cordova leather, you know. I believe it dates from the late sixteenth century. When Sir Charles and I decided—'

'You don't look like an artist.'

Lady Eleanor bristled. 'Jack, really, I was in the middle of...'

'...delivering a history lesson,' he finished for her. 'You might at least wait until we've finished eating before you do so.'

Her ladyship looked pointedly at her brother-in-law's full plate. 'So you were, for once, planning on actually eating your breakfast, were you?'

'Eleanor, my love, there is no need to— If Jack is not hungry he need not...'

'Oh, for God's sake, Charlie, there's no need to be perpetually walking on eggshells around me.'

A long, uncomfortable silence greeted this remark, broken eventually by Jack Trestain himself. 'I beg your pardon, Eleanor,' he said stiffly, 'I got out of bed on the wrong side this morning.'

'Happens to us all on occasion. No need for apologies, Brother—that is, I am sure that Eleanor...'

'Apology accepted, Jack,' Lady Eleanor said quickly, pressing her husband's hand.

Celeste took another sip of coffee. Jack Trestain put a small piece of ham onto his fork, though he made no attempt to eat it.

'I confess, Mademoiselle Marmion was not what I was expecting either,' Sir Charles said with another of his placatory smiles. 'Your reputation, you know, I expected someone older, more experienced.'

'I am five-and-twenty, Sir Charles.'

'Oh, please, I did not mean— One must never ask a lady her age.'

'I am not embarrassed by my age, *Monsieur*. My first commission I received seven years ago from the Comte de St Verain. I am proud to say that I have been able to support myself with my painting ever since.'

'And are your commissions all similar in nature to our own?' Lady Eleanor enquired.

Celeste nodded. 'Very similar. In France, many of the great houses were seized during the Revolution and the grounds badly neglected. The families who have managed to reclaim them employ me to paint the gardens once they are restored to their former glory.'

'While you and I, my dear, are rather contrarily commissioning Mademoiselle Marmion to paint our estate before it is enhanced a deal beyond its current state.' Sir Charles beamed, seemingly pleased by the thought of being a little unconventional.

'And you, Monsieur Trestain,' Celeste enquired, turning to his brother, 'will you be remaining here to witness this transformation?'

'I have no idea, *Mademoiselle*. Nor any notion why it should concern you.'

'Until recently, our Jack was in the military, a career soldier at that,' Sir Charles intervened hastily.

Celeste's jaw dropped unbecomingly. 'You are a soldier!'

'A lieutenant-colonel, no less,' Sir Charles said, with a hint of pride, sliding an anxious look at his silent brother.

'Indeed,' Lady Eleanor chimed in with a prim smile, 'Jack was one of the Duke of Wellington's most valued officers. He was mentioned several times in despatches.'

'And Jack has mentioned more than several times that he is no longer a soldier,' Jack Trestain said with a steely look in his eyes. 'In any event, I expect Mademoiselle Marmion is more likely to admire Napoleon than Wellington, Eleanor.'

The scars. She should have realised they were battle scars. And that also explained his animosity towards her. How many years had Britain and France been at war? Celeste pushed her chair back, preparatory to leaving the table. 'I am sorry. It did not occur to me that— I was so delighted to be here in England, so happy that hostilities between our countries had ended, that I did not consider the fact that I am—was until recently—no doubt still am in your eyes, *Monsieur*, the enemy.'

'*Mademoiselle*, please do not distress yourself,' Sir Charles said rather desperately. 'My brother did not mean— You have it quite wrong, does she not, Jack?'

'Entirely wrong. I have no objection to your being French,' Jack Trestain said in a tone that left it clear that he still objected to her having spied on him. 'I repeat, I am no longer a soldier, *Mademoiselle*.'

'But you were until recently?' Appalled, thinking back to the horrific reports she had read in the newspapers, Celeste forgot all about Jack Trestain's rudeness. 'You were at Waterloo? *Mon Dieu*, of course you were. Your arm,' she exclaimed, wondering that she had been so foolish not to have guessed.

'How did you know about Jack's arm?'

Sir Charles was frowning at her. Celeste gaped. She couldn't think of a single thing to say in explanation.

'*Mademoiselle* obviously noticed that I'm favouring my left arm at the moment,' Jack Trestain said, stepping in unexpectedly to cover her gaffe. 'Being an artist, I am sure she is rather more observant than most.'

She was surprised by his fleeting smile. The man's mood seemed to change with the wind. When he smiled, he looked so very different. He did not look as if he smiled often. He was a battle-hardened soldier. Those terrible scars. Realising all three pairs of eyes were on her, Celeste rallied. 'Yes, that's it,' she said, nodding furiously, 'Monsieur Trestain has hit the nail on the head.'

He tilted his head slightly in acknowledgement and flashed her another smile, one that lit his dark-brown eyes this time, and she felt absurdly gratified.

'Well now,' Sir Charles said, after receiving an encouraging nod from his wife, 'the day's getting on. I have a meeting with my lawyer in town at noon, Mademoiselle Marmion, but I thought I could give you a quick run through of our plans for the new gardens, just to give you an idea of where the most extensive changes will be, for it is these areas we wish to have immortalised by you on canvas, so to speak. What do you say?'

'If you are pressed for time, Charlie, then why not let me look after Mademoiselle Marmion.'

It was Sir Charles's turn to gape. 'You, Jack?'

Lady Eleanor pursed her lips. 'I am not sure that would be such a good idea.'

Her husband, however, had recovered from his surprise. 'Come now, my dear, are we not forever encouraging Jack to embark on some gainful enterprise to aid his recuperation?'

His wife looked unconvinced. 'It will take up a deal of Jack's time, and you cannot deny, with all due respect to him, he has not precisely been the most patient of men recently. Every time our little Robert asks him…'

'We have told our son not to pester his uncle. When Jack is good and ready, he will tell his nephew all about Waterloo,' Sir Charles said, rubbing his hands together and slanting his brother a nervous look. 'Jack is still recuperating from some serious injuries, my love,' he reproved gently. 'He is bound to be a little short of—of patience.'

'My point exactly,' Lady Eleanor said. 'Mademoiselle Marmion will have even more questions than Robert, no doubt, about the changes, the estate…'

'Which I am better placed than most to answer,' Jack Trestain interjected, 'having been raised here.'

Sir Charles beamed. 'An excellent point. And

showing *Mademoiselle* around will give you the opportunity to see more of the countryside, for I wish *Mademoiselle* to make a few landscapes of the wider estate. You might even get a taste for country living, see somewhere close at hand that takes your fancy. I can heartily recommend it.'

This last was said with some hopeful enthusiasm, and greeted with some disdain. A bone of contention, obviously.

'Perhaps, Charlie,' Jack Trestain answered, 'stranger things have happened.'

'Excellent! That is settled then, provided *Mademoiselle* has no objection?'

Celeste couldn't fathom Jack Trestain at all. One minute he was furious with her, the next he was covering up for her and the next he was offering to put himself out for her and spend time in her company. He was volatile, to put it mildly, but he also had a delightful smile, and a body which she found distracting, and she had not found the body of any man distracting for a long time. Not since— But she would not think of that.

Realising that they were awaiting an answer from her, Celeste shook her head. 'No, I have no objection whatsoever.'

Chapter Two

'Why did I volunteer?' Jack had not been expecting this to be the first question the intriguing Mademoiselle Marmion asked him, though perhaps he should have. It was obvious she had a sharp intellect and an observant eye. Whether that was because she was an artist, as he had suggested in order to extricate her from her faux pas regarding his arm, he did not know. What was inescapable was that within minutes of meeting her she had already managed to throw his behaviour into sharp relief. He could not be entirely oblivious to the effect his erratic temper was having on Charlie and Eleanor, but his brother's softly-softly approach had allowed them all to be complicit in ignoring it.

Until now. Jack shrugged uncomfortably. 'I have been somewhat out of temper, on account of my injuries. It is the least I can do.' It would suffice as an explanation. It would have to, since he didn't have a better one to offer, being as confused by his recent behaviour as anyone. Which was something he was reluctant to concede, since it implied there was an underlying cause, which there was not. At least not one he cared to admit to Charlie. Or indeed anyone.

As an explanation, it also conveniently excluded the fact that Mademoiselle Marmion herself had influenced his impulsive decision. Had she been a small, balding Frenchman with a goatee beard, would he have been so keen to offer his services? Indeed he would not, but that was another thing to which he would rather not admit. Jack smiled at her maliciously. 'If you would rather have Lady Eleanor's services as a guide…'

'No,' she said hurriedly, just as he had known she would, 'no, I certainly would not. Lady Eleanor cannot decide if I am to be treated as a superior servant or an inferior guest.'

'I'll let you into a little secret about Eleanor,' Jack said. 'She is the youngest of four daughters of the vicar a few parishes over, and though no one gives a fig for that save herself, as a consequence she is inclined to over-play her role of lady of the manor. Don't be too hard on her. She makes my brother happy, which is good enough for me. Or it should be.'

'Have a care, *Monsieur*, or I might think you a sensitive soul beneath that prickly exterior.' Mademoiselle Marmion frowned. 'Which brings me back to my question. Unlike Lady Eleanor, you made your feelings about me perfectly plain at breakfast. I confess I am confused as to why you now voluntarily choose to spend time in my company.'

Unlike Charlie and Eleanor, *Mademoiselle* was not

one to beat about the proverbial bush. 'You are referring to the fact that I took umbrage at your spying on
me this morning,' Jack said.

She flinched, but held his gaze. 'I did not spy. My
intrusion was unwelcome, I can see that, but it was
also unintended. I am, however, very sorry. Had the
roles been reversed, I too would have been...'

She broke off, flushing, but it was too late. Jack
was already imagining her naked, scything through
the waters of the lake, and Mademoiselle Marmion
was clearly perfectly aware of that fact. 'Think nothing more of it,' he said quickly, trying desperately to
do just that. 'Your apology is accepted, provided you
do not repeat the transgression.'

'Thank you. I promise you that in future I will
avoid visiting the lake in the morning.'

She smiled at him, and he caught his breath. She
really was very lovely, with her white-blonde hair, and
those eyes the colour of brandy. Her skin was smooth,
flawless, but not the creamy-white of an English rose;
it was a pale biscuit, sun-kissed and warm. Then there
was her mouth. Luscious pink. Too wide for fashion,
but perfect for kissing. Kissing her would be like biting into the sweet, delicate flesh of a perfectly ripe
peach. The kind which grew in the heat of Spain, not
the hard, bitter little fruits which were espaliered on
the wall of Charlie's garden. Kissing her would be like
bathing in the dry heat of the true south. Kissing her
would be like a taste of another world.

Though he could not for the life of him imagine
why he was thinking of kissing her. He'd had no urge

to kiss anyone since—well, for quite some considerable time. 'I think we should get out into the gardens while the light is good, Mademoiselle Marmion,' Jack said brusquely. 'I'll wait here while you fetch a hat.'

'I was raised in the south of France. I don't need a hat for the pale English sun, Monsieur Trestain.'

'Then thank the Lord, that means I'm not required to wear one either. And since we're dispensing with formalities, I would prefer it if you would call me Jack.'

'Then you must call me Celeste.'

'Celeste.' Jack grinned. 'How very appropriate. An angel sent from heaven to relieve my boredom.'

'An artist sent from France to paint your brother's estate,' she retorted.

'Touché. In that case we should get down to business.'

Celeste followed Jack Trestain down a narrow path through a colourful but uninteresting rose garden. His leather breeches fitted snugly around a taut derrière that was really very pleasant to admire from behind. His jet-black hair, dry now, curled over the collar of his shirt. She couldn't help but remember the muscles, now decently covered in white cambric, which had rippled while he swam.

She cursed softly under her breath and tried to concentrate on the path. And the task in hand. Not the intriguing man ahead of her, with his powerful soldier's body. A frisson of desire made her stomach flutter. Twice today, she had experienced this sudden yearning, for the very first time since—since. She had not missed it. She had not even noted its absence, until now. Perhaps, Celeste thought hopefully, it was a sign that she was starting come to terms with the loss of her mother. Not that she'd been struggling precisely, but she had not been quite herself, she could admit that much now.

'The Topiary Garden.' Jack Trestain opened the gate with a flourish.

Celeste had passed through it this morning, but had not taken the time to study it. Now she did so with delight. 'This is fascinating. I have painted several such places before. I think it is unusual to have such a French garden attached to such a very English house, no?'

'It was first laid out about two hundred years ago,' Jack Trestain replied. 'I think it was originally designed by one of your countrymen, now I come to think about it. To appreciate the symmetry and the scale of it, you'll get a much better view from the top floor of the house, if you were thinking of making this one of your featured landscapes.'

'Absolutely I am,' Celeste said, 'and I think a view from the lake too, through the topiary with the house in the background.'

'When my mother was alive, the borders were a blaze of colour at this time of year. And the parterre too. You'll recognise the lavender that borders it, there. I was once passing through Provence when they were gathering the lavender crop. The scent of it took me straight back to my childhood, escaping down here with Charlie, playing hide-and-seek in this garden. It's well past its best now.'

'Were you in the army for a very long time, Monsieur Jack?'

'Thirteen years. My father bought me a commission when I was sixteen. Why do you ask?'

Celeste shrugged, feigning a casualness she was far from feeling. 'Were you forced to leave because of your injury? Or because there are no more wars to fight?'

'I was not forced to leave. I resigned my commission.'

His clipped tone made it very clear he considered the subject closed. The same tone he had used with Lady Eleanor at breakfast. Thirteen years was a large part of anyone's life to exclude from discussion but then, there was an equally large part of her own life she didn't ever discuss. Celeste smiled brightly. 'Then let us concentrate on my own modest commission, which I have only just started.'

Jack disguised his relief well enough, but she noticed it all the same. As they walked down another path, Celeste prattled on about other gardens she had painted, other topiary she had drawn, aware he was studying her as covertly as she was studying him. Unsettled and distracted by her own interest, unsure whether to be flattered or concerned by his, she decided that she would do better for now to concentrate on her work, and so took out her sketchbook.

The Topiary Garden was divided into two by the long gravelled path which led towards the lake. On either side, the yew hedges had been trained into the most extraordinary shapes. Despite the fact that it had not been pruned, it was still possible to distinguish peacocks, a lion, a crown, and what looked to be several chess pieces, as well as more traditional cones, boxes and cylinders. Holly bordered the low and overgrown beds which had been laid out in the shadow of the yews. No longer feigning interest, Celeste made several rapid sketches.

Looking up some time later, she smiled at Jack watching her now with unalloyed interest, tilting her last sketch to allow him to examine it better. 'In France,' she said, 'this garden would be prized and restored, not cut down to make way for a— What was it Lady Eleanor called it?'

'A little wilderness,' Jack replied, 'whatever conceit that is. Eleanor loathes it as it is, and I have to confess, it is much darker than I remember.'

'With some remedial work, it could be very beautiful.'

'Your sketch certainly makes it look so. Perhaps you should share your thoughts with Eleanor.'

'Oh, no, that would be presumptuous. It is her garden, not mine.'

Jack ushered her towards the welcome of the shade, where a mossy stone bench was positioned under a yew which had been clipped into an arch. He had come out without a coat, and now rolled up the sleeves of his shirt. The contrast between his pale right arm and tanned left was stark. It was not only the colour, but he had clearly lost muscle.

'It must have been a very bad break to have kept your arm in a splint for so long.' Without realising, Celeste had reached out to touch him. She snatched her hand away.

'Why did you stay at the lakeside this morning?' Jack asked. 'You've as much as admitted you should have left the moment you saw me. What made you stay?'

The bench was small. His leather-clad thigh brushed hers, and his knee too, for he had angled himself to face her. 'I am an artist,' Celeste said, her voice sounding odd. 'You made an interesting subject.'

'Did you draw me, then?'

His hand covered hers, which were clasped on her lap. Her heart began to thump. 'There was no time,' she said.

'Yet you insist you were watching me purely with the eye of an artist?'

His thumb was stroking her wrist, so lightly she wondered if he was even aware he was doing it. The tension between them became palpable. Beguiled as much by her own new-found desire as by Jack's proximity, Celeste could think of nothing to say but the truth. 'I watched you because I could not take my eyes off you. I was fascinated.'

His eyes darkened. His hands slid up to her shoulders. She leaned into him as he pulled her towards him. It started so gently. Soft. Delicate. Celeste leant closer. The kiss deepened. She could feel the damp of his shirt and the heat of his skin beneath it. A drop of perspiration trickled down between her breasts, and she felt a sharp twist of pure desire.

She curled her fingers into his hair. Their tongues touched. Jack moaned, a guttural sound that precisely echoed how she felt, filled with longing, and aching and heat. Their kiss became fierce. He bent her backwards on the bench, his body hovering over hers, blocking out the sunlight. He smelt of soap and sweet summer sweat. His legs were tangled in her skirts. Only his arms, planted either side of her, prevented her from falling.

She was also in danger of falling, metaphorically speaking, from a far greater height if she was not extremely careful. Celeste snapped to her senses. Jerking herself free, she sat up. Jack's cheeks were flushed. His hair was in wild disarray. His shirt was falling open at the neck to reveal his tanned throat. The soft linen clung to his frame, revealing tantalising glimpses of the hard body underneath. She wanted more. It was good that she wanted more, but with this man! No, she must be out of her mind.

She edged a little way along the bench, shaking out her skirts. 'I hope you are not expecting me to faint?' she asked more sharply than she intended.

'Despite our extremely brief acquaintance you do not strike me as someone much given to histrionics.'

'You are perfectly correct, I am not. Even when kissing complete strangers.'

'Not quite complete strangers, *Mademoiselle*. We have at least been formally introduced.' Jack shook his head, as if trying to clear the dazed look from his eyes. 'I apologise,' he said tersely. 'I have no idea what came over me. I'm not in the habit of mauling innocent women, especially not when they are my brother's guests.'

'Your brother's landscape artist, not his guest, and I am neither innocent nor inclined to accept an apology for something that was as much my doing as yours,' Celeste snapped, unduly irked by his assumption that it was all his responsibility. She was relieved to discover she could feel this way again, but she really wished it had not been this maddening man who had sparked her back to life. She picked up her sketch pad and charcoals, trying to regain her composure. 'It was just a kiss, nothing more,' she said, because that was all it was, after all.

'Just a kiss?' Jack repeated, still looking stunned. 'Is that what you really think?'

She did not. She thought—not very clearly, admittedly—that it was the most extraordinary kiss she had ever experienced. She thought, looking at him now, that she would very much like to kiss him again, but she was not about to admit that. 'Very well,' Celeste conceded, 'an excellent kiss, though I suspect that abstinence may have contributed to its intensity.'

He flushed dark red. 'What the devil do you mean by that?'

Celeste took a step back. 'Not that it is any of your business, but I have not been inclined to kiss anyone for—for some time.'

His expression softened a little. 'Ah, you are referring to your own abstinence?'

'What else would I have implied?' Celeste said, thoroughly confused. He could not possibly have thought she referred to him? There could be no shortage of women eager and willing to kiss Jack Trestain. Then she remembered. 'Oh, you mean you have been incapacitated by your recent poor health.'

A perfectly understandable explanation, and no reason whatsoever for him to flinch as if she had hit him. Yet that is exactly what he did, before abruptly turning on his heels and marching off. Utterly confounded now, she watched his long legs cover the ground quickly, back through the gate, along the grass walk to the rose garden. He did not look back.

Celeste slumped down on the stone bench. While her mind struggled to make sense of what had happened, her body was very clear in its response. What they had shared had been much more than just a kiss. It had been an awakening, a stirring of something that she hadn't realised had been so utterly dormant.

Her last *affaire* had ended not long before she had received *that* letter. It had ended as her *affaires* always did, without tears or remorse, while it had still been mutually enjoyable, before it could degenerate into boredom, or worse still, the expectation of a future. Not that she'd ever allowed any of her few love affairs to reach that stage. Not that a single one of them had evoked an emotion even close to love in her.

Celeste began to turn the pages of her sketchbook. Love was a subject she knew little about. On the topic of being loveless however, she was something of an expert. It defined her upbringing. It defined her mother's marriage. Or it had. She snapped the leather covers shut. Ever since she'd received that *damned* letter, she'd been losing control in all sorts of odd ways. She snapped at the stupidest of things. She couldn't concentrate on her work. And now this! It was just a kiss, for heaven's sake. She was overwrought. She had not kissed anyone for a long time. Jack was a very accomplished kisser. Jack, for whatever reason, seemed to find the whole process of kissing her even more unsettling than she had. She would very much like to repeat the process of kissing Jack, if only to prove that it was just a kiss, enhanced by abstinence, just as she'd suggested. Her own.

And as for her suggestion regarding his? Why had he taken such umbrage at her perfectly reasonable assumption? Celeste rolled her eyes. Jack Trestain was an enigma, and one that she had no time to decipher.

'There you are, my love. I have been looking for you all over.'

Jack, who had been sleeping on the recessed seat in the nook of the fireplace, woke with a start and looked around him, quite disoriented.

'Charles,' Eleanor was saying, 'I am writing to my mother. We have such a glut of plums and damsons I thought it would be a good idea to pickle some rather than simply bottle them, and Mama has an excellent receipt. How went your meeting with the lawyer?'

Jack had quite forgotten the trick of acoustics between this room and the one below. His head, resting against the fireplace, was in the precise spot which amplified the voices. He and Charlie had discovered it as boys, and had spent hours talking to each other, one of them in each room. The Laird's Lug, their Auntie Kirsty had told them it was known as in Scottish castles, a way for the master of the house to eavesdrop on his family and his servants, though Jack reckoned this one at Trestain Manor existed more by accident than design.

Charlie and Eleanor were discussing estate business now, in that domestic, familiar way Jack remembered his parents doing. His head was thumping. Serve him right for sleeping in the middle of the day, though when he slept so little at night, he had little option but to catnap when he could. While in the army, he used to pride himself on possessing a soldier's ability to sleep whenever and whatever the circumstances. Standing, sitting, marching, he'd slept, and woken refreshed. No, not always refreshed, he thought ruefully, there had been times when he'd felt perpetually exhausted. But the fact remained, until he resigned his commission, sleep had never been a problem.

Was that true? Could his insomnia have been masked by his frenetic army career? He didn't know. He did know that things had gone rapidly downhill after he left. The nightmare which had been sporadic now regularly invaded his dreams. He woke every morning feeling as if he'd been bludgeoned, his limbs weighted with stones. Precisely as he felt at the moment.

It was too much of an effort to move, so he settled back where he was, letting Charlie and Eleanor's voices wash over him. Charlie was uncommonly happy with his estate and his wife and his family. Charlie thought that if Jack could settle down as he had, raise some sheep and cows and pigs, start his own nursery, that Jack would be every bit as contented as he was. Poor delusional Charlie. He meant well, but he had no idea, and his ignorance drove Jack to distraction, though he would never wish it otherwise. He envied Charlie. No, that was a lie. Charlie's placid, uncomplicated life would drive Jack to an early grave, but he envied him the ability to love that placid, uncomplicated life.

Jack couldn't remember a time when he hadn't wanted to be a soldier. He'd been an excellent soldier, and he'd been an exemplary officer. He'd loved being a military man, he'd taken such pride in doing his duty for king and country. There had been times when that duty had required him to see and do some terrible things. Unforgivable things. While he still wore his colours, he had managed to reconcile himself to that. Now, he no longer could. Now, he was being forced to question everything that he'd loved and all that he'd stood for. There were times when he felt as if he were being quite literally torn in two. Times when he raged at the injustice of what was happening to him, times when he was overwhelmed by guilt. There was no right and wrong any more, and his world, which had been one of clear-cut lines for so long, was now so blurred that he was careering around like a compass struggling to find true north. What the hell was happening to him?

Jack ran his fingers through his hair. He ought to have it cut. Just one of many things he ought to do, and had not the gumption to attempt. Every day he swore he would try to be normal. He would take an interest in mundane things like harvests and dressing for dinner and the weather and the king's health. With increasing regularity, he failed. So many things important to Charlie and Eleanor seemed so trivial to him, and so trivial things tended to take on a disproportionate importance. Like that kiss.

Just a kiss, Celeste had said, though he could have sworn she was as unsettled as he had been by it. And then she'd made that comment about abstinence enhancing its intensity. Bloody stupid phrase. Presumptive. Though she had not been referring to him, as he'd assumed. She was no innocent, she claimed, and she certainly didn't kiss like one. He'd never experienced a kiss like it. Was that due to enforced abstinence? It had come as a surprise, certainly. He'd assumed that aspect of his life, like sleeping soundly, was beyond him, at least for the time being.

Jack leant his head back against the hearth. It should be reassuring that it was not. Reassuring that he could still—what? Experience desire, lust? He swore. Most likely the woman was right, and it really had been just a kiss, blown out of all proportion by the circumstances. No mere kiss was that momentous. He wished he hadn't run away now, like a raw recruit retreating under enemy fire. He wished he'd stayed and kissed her again, and proved to himself that it was not a one-off and that his body, unlike his mind, was not completely in limbo.

He closed his eyes and allowed himself to remember the taste of her and the feel of her and the smell of her. She was quite lovely. She was altogether ravishing. She would set any man's blood on fire. He shouldn't have kissed her. As it was, his self-control hung by a fragile thread. He was confused about many thing but the one thing he knew for certain was that maintaining his self-control was crucial. So he could not risk kissing her again. Definitely not picture her lips pressed to his, her hands...

'I wonder how Mademoiselle Marmion is faring?'

Jack's eyes flew open. The name leapt out at him, bringing the background buzz of conversation in the room below to the fore.

Charlie was speaking now. 'I'm sure she fares perfectly well. She seemed to me an uncommonly confident woman for one of her years. Perhaps it comes from being French. And she is a successful artist too. No, my love, we need have no fear for *Mademoiselle*. Jack may be— He has developed something of a temper, but he would never behave with impropriety, I am certain of that.'

'It is not only his temper, Charles. He has a look in his eyes sometimes that frightens me.'

'The things he has experienced on the battlefield would frighten anyone.'

'Yes, but—Charles, you must have noticed, there are times when one may address any number of remarks to him, and it is as if he were deaf or asleep.

I thought he was simply being rude the first time, but—it is very *odd*.'

What was it they said about never overhearing good of oneself? Snooping and listening in to private conversations had been the tools of the trade of his carefully cultivated informants, but this was different. Jack cringed.

'We can be sure of nothing with regard to your brother these days, Charles,' Eleanor continued after a leaden silence. 'He is so very changed.'

'Indeed.' Charlie's voice was wooden, a sure sign that his stiff upper lip was being called into action. No doubt he was wringing his hands.

'He rebuffed poor little Robert again yesterday. I have told the child time and again not to plague his uncle for war stories, but…'

'He is only five years old, and his uncle is a hero to him. Indeed, Jack is a hero to us all, if only he could see it. If only he could *talk* to me, but I fear…'

Jack leapt to his feet. So much for his naive belief that he had been covering his tracks. It was mortifyingly clear that Charlie and Eleanor had merely been pretending not to notice his odd behaviour.

I'm sparing you, he wanted to roar at Charlie. *I'm preserving all your sad, pathetic illusions about me*, he wanted to tell him. He wanted to shake his brother into silence. He wanted to be sick, because he loved Charlie, and he even cared about Eleanor, dammit, because Eleanor loved Charlie too. He wished to hell, for Charlie's sake, that he *could* sit down with Robert and tell him tales of derring-do. He wished that it was true, that he really was the hero mentioned by Wellington in despatches, but it was not the case. Heroes didn't have stains on their soul.

Jack crept from the room. He might not be a hero but he had survived. He would continue to survive. To live, to be truly alive though, that was quite another matter. An aspiration for the future, perhaps. In the meantime, it was a question of enduring.

Chapter Three

Next day, Celeste set to work in the walled garden, the morning sunshine sending fingers of light creeping along the western border. She knew from the landscaper's plans which Jack had shown her that the oldest of the succession houses and the pinery were to be demolished and replaced with modern structures which could be more efficiently heated. There was a charm to the original buildings which she had started to capture in charcoal, the paper pinned to a large board propped on a portable easel.

She had not seen Jack since he so abruptly left the Topiary Garden. He had not appeared at dinner, nor breakfast. According to Lady Eleanor, this was not unusual behaviour, as Jack often skipped meals. Sir Charles had reminded his wife that the remains of his late-night snacks were regularly found by the kitchen maids, so there was no need to worry that Jack had no appetite whatsoever. Which meant that they clearly were worried, and equally clearly set upon pretending to the source of their concern that they were not. Celeste was not, after all, alone in thinking Jack Trestain's behaviour decidedly contrary.

She pinned a fresh sheet of paper on to her easel. She would not speculate as to the cause. She found him intriguing. She found him interesting. She found him very attractive. All of these, she took as positive signs of her own return to normality, but she would not allow herself to dwell on the subject any further. She had more than enough issues to occupy her thoughts without adding Jack Trestain to her list.

She picked up her charcoal, decided to adjust her perspective and set to work.

Half an hour later, deep in concentration, Celeste did not notice Jack's arrival until he was behind her, making her jump, squiggle a line across her drawing, drop her charcoal and swear rather inappropriately in French. 'You gave me such a fright. Look what you've made me do.'

'I didn't mean to startle you, but you were miles away.'

'I was concentrating on my work.'

Jack was looking at her drawing, but Celeste got the impression he was thinking about something else. She had not misremembered how attractive he was. Nor the strength of her reaction to his physical proximity. Her skin was tingling as if the space between them was charged, like the atmosphere prior to a lightning strike. 'What do you think?' she asked, in an attempt to restore some semblance of normality. She was on sure ground discussing art.

He blinked. 'I think I should apologise for my abrupt departure yesterday.'

Celeste too kept her eyes on her drawing. 'I was actually referring to my sketch, but since we are on the subject, I fear we were at cross purposes yesterday. When I said— When I mentioned abstinence— I know nothing of your circumstances. I was speaking for myself.'

'You may as well have been speaking for me,' Jack admitted ruefully. 'I have not— It has also been some time since I...' Their eyes met briefly, then flickered away. 'I was therefore rather taken aback.'

'As was I.' This time their gaze held. Celeste smiled faintly. 'I am sure that was the reason for the— It explains why we allowed ourselves to become somewhat carried away.'

Jack touched his hand to the squiggle Celeste had drawn, tried to rub it out, then stared at the resultant smudge. 'Stupid thing for me to get so aerated about. It was, as you pointed out, just a kiss. We're adults, not flighty adolescents.'

'Yes, exactly.' She nodded determinedly to disguise her disappointment. She should not be disappointed. He was agreeing with her, after all. 'Most likely we would be disappointed if we—if we repeated the experience.'

It came out sounding like a plea to be proved wrong, and for a moment, Jack looked as if he would comply. 'Most likely,' he said as he took a step towards her. She could feel his breath on her cheek. He smelled of grass and sunshine. Her heart was beating hard again, making it difficult to breathe. She stared into his eyes, mesmerised. The gap between them imperceptibly, tantalisingly narrowed. Their lips almost touched before they both leapt back as if they had been singed by a naked flame.

Celeste snatched her sketch from the easel and tore it in half. 'I don't know what is wrong with me today. I am struggling to find the correct perspective for what should be a simple sketch.'

Jack hesitated, then threw himself down on a wooden bench, his long legs sprawled in front of him. 'I doubt either Charlie or Eleanor will care which angle you choose, provided you deliver something that closely matches reality. I'm sure the drawing you have just torn up would have proved perfectly satisfactory.'

'Not to me,' Celeste said indignantly. 'I would have known I could have depicted the scene in a more accomplished manner. You may consider what I do to be a trivial endeavour. My paintings don't save lives or win wars or—or whatever it was you did when you were a soldier, but they are still very important to me.'

'I'm sorry, I didn't mean to patronise you.'

His smile was disarming. Celeste bit her own back, refusing to be so easily won over. 'But you did none the less.'

'I did,' he conceded.

He dug his hands into his pockets. 'You know, life in the military is not as exciting as you might think.

There's far more time spent marching and drilling than waging war. And in the winter, when the campaign season is over, there's a deal more playing cards and making bets and drinking than doing drill.'

'When I am between commissions, I still paint,' Celeste said. 'Not landscapes, but people. I am not so good at portraits, but they are mine, and so it is not like work, you know?'

'Are you often between commissions?'

'In the beginning, regularly.' She chuckled. 'As a result, I was much thinner and not so well dressed as I can now afford to be.'

'No less pretty, though, I'd wager, if I may be so bold as to offer a compliment to compensate for demeaning your sense of professional pride. Did you always aspire to be an artist?'

'I am never going to exhibit at the Académie des Beaux-Arts, and I have no ambition to do so. I am not the type to try to break all the rules and to starve in the process, spending my last sou on paint rather than a baguette. I have a modest talent. I was fortunate enough to study with some excellent teachers in Paris, and I needed to find a way of supporting myself, so…' Celeste shrugged.

'Your parents then, they are dead? You said you needed to support yourself,' Jack explained when she raised her eyebrows at the question, 'so I assumed…'

'Yes, Both dead.' Celeste stared down at her hands, frowning. Despite spending a good deal of time thinking about it, she had not the foggiest idea how to begin the search for answers which had brought her to England. She needed help, but her in-grained habit of trusting no one save herself inhib-ited her from seeking it. Not that, as a foreigner, she thought morosely, she had the first idea of where to start seeking.

'Penny for them?' Jack was looking at her quizzi-cally. 'Your thoughts,' he said. 'You were a hundred miles away again. I fear I'm boring you rather than distracting you.'

'No, it's not that.' Perhaps she could ask him just one simple question to get her search underway? She really did have to make a start because there, tucked away at the back of her sketchbook, was a letter con-taining a puzzle she needed to solve in order to draw a line under the past and get on with her life.

'Jack?'

He looked at her questioningly.

'Jack, if you—if you needed to find something. Or someone. How would you go about it? I mean if you did not know where this person lived, or—or who they were, precisely. Are there people one can employ to discover such things?'

'You mean to track down someone who has gone missing?'

She had his attention now. All of it. Though he was still lounging casually on the bench, though his expression was one of polite interest, his eyes were focused entirely on her. Celeste shifted uncomfort-ably. 'Not missing precisely. Not anything at all, re-ally. I'm speaking hypothetically.'

She risked looking up, and wished she had not. 'Hy-

pothetically,' Jack said, openly sceptical. 'Well, hypothetically, you could employ a Bow Street Runner.'

'Is that what you would do?'

He smiled. 'Good grief, no. Speaking hypothetically of course, I am more than equipped to solve the
problem for myself, but we're not talking hypothetically, are we?'

Realising that she was clenching her hands so
tightly together that the knuckles showed white, Celeste hid them under her painter's smock. She ought
to look him in the eye, but she was sure if she did Jack
would know she was lying. She was not a good liar.
She was good at keeping silent. She was very good
at hiding her feelings, but she was a terrible liar. 'It
doesn't matter,' she said. 'Forget I asked.'

She could have bitten her tongue out, realising only
at the last moment that telling Jack Trestain something didn't matter was a sure-fire way of alerting
him to the fact that it did, though he said nothing for
so long that she began to hope he had done just as
she asked. At least she was a step further forward.
She had no idea what a Bow Street Runner was, but
she could find out. She prepared to get to her feet.
'I should...'

'Sit down.' His grip on her arm was light enough,
but one look at Jack's face, and Celeste thought the
better of resisting him. 'Who exactly is it you're trying to trace? A lover? An errant husband, perhaps?'

'I have no husband, errant or otherwise, and as
to a lover— No, not since before— Since— It has
nothing to do with affairs of the heart.' She sounded

defensive. She was getting upset. And Jack was not missing any of it. 'It is nothing,' Celeste said. 'I regret raising it.'

Jack gave her a neutral look. 'You know, you'd be taking pot luck by employing a Runner. Some of them are excellent chaps, but some— Frankly, I wouldn't trust my sister alone with them. Not that I have a sister. Have you? Or a brother? Is it a sibling you're seeking?'

'I am not so fortunate as to possess either,' Celeste said repressively.

Jack nodded. 'So, it's not your parents or a husband or a sibling you're trying to trace. Who then?'

He was not going to give up. Celeste shook her head and folded her lips.

Once again, Jack failed to get the message. 'Now I come to think about it, you weren't clear if it was a person or a thing. Is it stolen property then, jewellery? Or the family silver?'

'*Mon Dieu*, Jack, I wish you would leave the matter alone!'

'You ask me for advice but now won't tell me why. Don't you trust me, Celeste, is that it?'

'I don't trust anyone. I find it is safer that way.'

'That, if I may say so, is a fairly bleak philosophy.'

'You may, since I suspect it is also yours.'

He looked quite taken aback. 'Irrespective of the veracity of that statement, you would admit it is a philosophy which makes finding your missing person or whatever the hell it is rather problematic.'

'I told you, I was merely speculating.'

'And I told you, I don't believe you,' Jack said, his tone conciliatory. 'Look, it's obviously important to you, whatever it is. It's clear you need help, and I assure you, you can rely on my discretion.'

All of which was most likely true, but it was such a big step to take. Celeste wrapped her arms around herself. What should she do?

'If it's difficult for you to tell me, imagine yourself faced with a complete stranger.'

'Why are you so keen to— Of what possible interest is it to you?' Celeste cursed under her breath and jumped to her feet. 'You wish to know? *Vraiment?* Very well then, I will tell the truth and shame the devil. I have come to England to find out why my mother killed herself! Are you happy now?'

Jack's face was a picture of shock. Celeste, even more shocked than he at her impulsive admission, sucked in great breaths of air.

'I'm sorry,' Jack said after a brief silence. 'Celeste, I'm so very sorry.'

He reached out, as if he would put his arms around her. For a brief moment, she was tempted to accept the comfort of his embrace, and that shocked her almost as much as her blurting out the shameful truth to a man she barely knew. She pushed him away, rather too roughly, though she was beyond caring about that. Then suddenly quite drained, she sank on to the bench beside him.

Suicide. Jack could think of no subject more guaranteed to engage his attention and his sympathy. He clenched his fists. He would try his damnedest to help this woman. That would, at least, be something.

Beside him Celeste was pale, angry and on the verge of tears, though she seemed absolutely determined not to cry. She was looking at him very warily too, most likely already resenting him for forcing her to blurt out something so private and shocking.

'You can trust me,' Jack said once more. 'If I am able to help you, I will.'

'Why would you?' she demanded baldly. 'You're virtually a stranger.'

He pondered how to answer this without arousing her suspicions. It had cost her a good deal to ask for help, which made him wonder that someone so beautiful and so attractive and so talented should be so bereft of confidantes. 'A stranger with too much time on his hands, and not enough to occupy his mind,' he said, which had the benefit of being true. 'A stranger who has had some experience in such matters,' he added, which was, tragically, also true.

'What experience? Jack? I said what experience?'

He realised some time had elapsed since Celeste had posed the question. He dragged his mind back, with some relief, to the present and managed a dismissive shrug, as if he had been merely assembling his thoughts. 'When a man is battle-weary, an extreme melancholy can make him think death offers the only release. No one can persuade him that the melancholy will eventually pass. In extreme cases, the man becomes so desperate as to take matters into his own hands as your mother did. Soldiers are trained not to show their feelings, and very often in such cases, the outcome is totally unexpected and, to those left behind, wholly inexplicable. Like you, they are left with unanswered questions.'

'And how do these bereaved families set about gaining answers?'

They didn't, was the honest answer, in most cases. Jack could no more explain it than the poor unfortunates who took their own lives could. All he could offer was platitudes. He looked at Celeste, no longer distrustful but hanging on his words, the faintest trace of hope flickering in her eyes. He could not bear to douse it with a cold bucket of truth. If he could somehow help her, if he could find the answers for her that he had been unable to provide for others, then perhaps it would help atone. A little. Even a little atonement was better than none. 'Perhaps it would help,' he prevaricated, 'if you could tell me the circumstances of your mother's death first. It must have come as a terrible shock.'

'We were not close.' Perhaps recognising the defensive note in her voice, Celeste made a helpless gesture. 'I live in Paris. My mother lived in Cassis, in the south. I received her letter in January this year. She was already— It was already— I—my mother was already dead. Drowned. She drowned herself.'

Celeste blinked rapidly. Though he could not see, for they were obscured by her smock, Jack was willing to bet that her hands were painfully clasped. Yet there was a defiant tilt to her head, as if she was daring herself to submit to whatever emotions ensnared her in their grasp.

As a soldier, he was well versed in the art of managing grief. An iron will and rigid self-control had vital roles to play in combat. In battle, you put the living before the dead. It was why other soldiers got so uproariously drunk afterwards. It was why they sought out brothels and taverns, to laugh and to lose themselves, because they could not cry, but they could counter death with a lust for life, and they could later blame their tears on an excess of gin.

But Celeste was not a soldier, and the dead woman was her mother, not a comrade. Though like a soldier, she seemed determined not to crack under the strain. Instinctively, he knew any attempt to comfort her would not be welcome. Jack sat up, putting a little distance between them. 'This letter— You said *her* letter? Do you mean…?'

'Yes, my mother wrote to me to inform me she was about to commit suicide. It was, in essence, a letter from beyond the grave.'

Unable to stop himself, Jack reached for her hands. As he had suspected, they were tightly clasped. He covered them with his own. She stiffened, but made no attempt to repel him. He felt a sharp pang of sympathy. It was not just grief she was holding on so tightly to, but a hefty dose of guilt. Anger at her mother's act shook him. He bit back the words of blame, knowing full well they were irrational and undeserved, and unlikely to cause Celeste anything but pain. 'Dear God. I am so sorry.'

'There is no need. It was a shock. I admit it was a shock, but once I had recovered from that, I read the letter in the hope that it would at least provide some sort of explanation for what, to me, was an incomprehensible act.' Now she did pull her hands free. '*Mais non*, nothing so straightforward from my mother. I should have known better than to have expected her to change the habits of a lifetime. It was more of a riddle than an explanation, sent in the full knowledge that by the time I received it, she would not be available to help solve it.'

Her anger simmered, the heat of it palpable. 'Celeste, she would not have been thinking rationally. To take such drastic action, she must have been very desperate,' Jack said, knowing the words were utterly inadequate, though none the less true.

'I don't doubt that. Though not desperate enough to ask for my help.' Her lip quivered. The tension in her shoulders, the gaze fixed on her lap, made it clear that sympathy was the last thing she desired, but the raw pain was there, hidden under a mask of bitterness and anger. 'That letter…' She stopped to take a calming breath. 'It is not only that there is no explanation. That letter raises a list of questions I wouldn't even have known to ask.'

Questions. Such cases always raised more questions than answers. Answers which were so rarely found and which allowed guilt to flourish amid the uncertainty. Jack had written countless letters to the loved ones of his men who died in battle, emphasising the glory, and the valour and painlessness of death.

Lies, all lies, but beneath the glossing over of reality lay one inalienable truth. They had died doing their duty for their country. Their death had a purpose.

The others, though, the families of those thankfully rare cases where death had been self-inflicted, they had no such truths to console them for what he had once, God forgive him, thought the most heinous of crimes. He searched for Celeste's hands once more, gripping them tightly. 'This letter, it's a great deal more than most have in such circumstances. Will you tell me what she said, and then I will be able to see how I might be able to help you?'

She considered it, looking at him earnestly, but eventually shook her head. 'Not yet. I can't.' She slipped from his grasp, getting to her feet with an apologetic look. 'I appreciate you sharing your experience of what is a painful and delicate subject. And for being so careful of my feelings. I do not discount your offer to help—it is most generous, but I must consider it carefully. The emotions involved are intensely private. Do you understand?'

Much as he wished to, he resisted the temptation to press her, because he did understand that, only too well. Jack got wearily to his feet. 'I have no other demands on my time or my services, so please take as much time as you need.'

Following a sleepless night, Celeste felt wrung out like one of her painting rags after washing. In the end, she had decided to trust Jack. She could not imagine having the conversation they'd had yesterday with a complete stranger, and she could not expect that a complete stranger would have demonstrated the tact or level of understanding Jack had of such matters.

It was not really such a leap of faith when she laid it out logically like that, to trust him. But it was not logic which ultimately convinced her. It was only after he had left her, when she had recovered from the dull ache precipitated by speaking of her mother's death, that she realised how difficult it must have been for him to talk so sensitively on such a delicate matter. Soldiers were men of war. Soldiers were tough, and brave and bold. English soldiers were famous for their courage and their staunchness in the face of adversity. They did not cry. They did not fear. They most certainly did not have a conscience. Or so she'd thought. Assumed, she corrected herself, because until she met Jack, Celeste thought shamefully, she hadn't actually thought about it much at all.

She remembered the reports in the newspapers after Waterloo. Death on the battlefield was neither clean nor quick. It was no wonder that the men who fought suffered from—what was it Jack had called it?—an extreme melancholy after witnessing all that horror and suffering. Was Jack suffering from that too? There had been moments yesterday when she thought he spoke from personal experience. But then he did, she reminded herself, thinking of the letters he'd mentioned having to write. The point was he understood and that was why she could trust him.

'May I come in?'

As if she had summoned him, the man himself stood in the doorway of Celeste's temporary studio. Dressed in a pair of tight-fitting pantaloons which showed off his long legs to good effect, and a coat which enhanced his broad shoulders, his cravat was neatly tied, and his jaw freshly shaved.

'You look very—handsomely dressed,' Celeste said, taken by surprise once more by the force of the attraction she felt for him. The clothes of an English gentleman not only accentuated his muscular physique, but they also, somehow, accentuated the fact that the man wearing them was not always a gentleman. In fact he was just a little bit dangerous. And, yes, a trifle intimidating too.

'Which is a polite way of saying I look a lot less shoddy than normal,' Jack said, closing the door behind him. 'You, if I may say so, look as ravishing as usual. And believe me, I have seen my fair share of beauties. A perk of the job, working on Wellington's staff.'

'So his reputation, the French press did not exaggerate it?'

'I doubt it possible.'

Celeste smiled, but the sight of the letter sitting where she had lain it in preparation made it a forced affair. She picked it up, but despite her resolve, found herself surprisingly reluctant to hand it over. 'Are you still— Your offer to help, is it still open?'

'Of course. I want very much to—'

'Only I would not wish to presume,' Celeste interrupted, 'and it occurred to me that perhaps you offered only because you felt a little sorry for me.'

'No. I understand what you are experiencing, that is all, and I wish to prevent you from— Is that the letter?' Jack said, holding out his hand.

'Yes.' Celeste still kept a firm grip on it. 'I don't know what people commonly write in such missives...'

'Most do not write anything,' Jack said, 'as far as I am aware. Or they merely reassure their families that they love them.'

'Well, in that one regard my mother has followed the custom,' Celeste said acerbically, 'though it is the one thing I know for certain to be a lie.' A brief silence met this remark. She flushed, annoyed at having betrayed herself. 'It is more of a puzzle than it is a confession,' she said, gazing down at the letter again. 'I admit it has me baffled. What we need is someone to make sense of it—what on earth have I said to amuse you?'

'Not amused, so much as taken aback, I am sorry,' Jack said, his expression once more serious. 'It's just that solving puzzles is—was—my stock in trade. I have a certain reputation as an expert in acrostics. My brother would be shocked at your ignorance, for he mistakenly delights in my minor fame.' He took her hand. 'Celeste, I was Wellington's code-breaker.'

She looked at him in bewilderment. 'I'm sorry, but I truly am ignorant of these things.' She broke off, staring as the implications of what Jack had said finally dawned on her. 'Code-breaker? Do you mean you were a spy?'

'After a fashion, though not, I suspect, in quite the way you are imagining. Not so much cloak and dagger as pen and paper. Information,' Jack clarified. 'Contrary to what civilians believe, wars are not won on the battlefield. Obviously, the battlefield is where matters are finally resolved, but getting there at the right time, in the correct field positions, having the men and the horses and the artillery all lined up, and knowing your enemy—his strategies, his positions, his plans, his firepower—that's what wins or loses a war. Having a retreat planned if required. And knowing what you're going to do if you break through his ranks—those matter too. You've no idea how many battles are lost when a commander in the field gets too far ahead of himself, or finds himself in retreat when no organised withdrawal has been planned.'

'You are right, I have absolutely no idea.'

Jack laughed. 'Put simply, information is what an army thrives on. My role was to assimilate that information to allow the generals to plot their campaigns and I did that by cracking codes, by piecing together different snippets from different sources and assembling them in an order that made sense. Solving puzzles, in other words.'

'And that, I am pleased to say, does make sense.' Without giving herself the chance to rethink the decision again, Celeste handed Jack the letter.

'Thank you. May I read it now?'

Her nerves jangling, she nodded. Jack sat down on the *chaise longue* which she had positioned in front of her easel. Unable to watch him, she busied herself,

opening her precious box of paints and making an
unnecessary inventory of the powders and pigments
in their glass vials, of her brushes and oils. Behind
her, she could hear the faintest rustle of paper worn
thin by her many readings. A squeak, which must be
Jack's boots as he shifted in his seat. Another rustle.
He was taking an age. He must have gone back to
the beginning. She wondered if she should set about
stretching a canvas, but immediately abandoned the
idea. Her hands were shaking. She began to rearrange
her paints again.

'I'm finished.'

Celeste whirled around, dropping a vial of cad-
mium-yellow which, fortunately for her and the floor
covering, landed softly on a rug without breaking.
Cursing under her breath, she snatched it up and put
it back in her box before joining Jack on the sofa.
'What is your verdict?'

'I think you must have been shocked to the core
when you read this the first time.'

She gave a shaky laugh. 'It was certainly unexpected.'

'Unexpected!' Jack swore. 'You had no inkling of
anything it contained?'

'No. I told you we were not close. *En effet*, my
mother and I were estranged.' She was aware of Jack's
eyes on her, studying her carefully. It made her uncomfortable, for while she refused to become emotional, she suspected that emotional is precisely what
anyone else would be under the circumstances. She
gazed resolutely down at her hands. 'As to the man I

believed to be my father, he was always distant. From the beginning, I sensed he resented me. At least now I know why.'

'You were not his child.'

'So it would seem,' she said with a shrug.

'You're very matter-of-fact about something so important.'

'I have had eight months to become accustomed to it.'

Jack eyed her doubtfully. 'But you're not accustomed to it, are you? Despite your mother's positively begging you not to pursue the questions she raises, here you are in England, doing exactly that. It obviously matters a great deal to you.'

Celeste's hackles rose. 'I am curious, that's all,' she said. Even to her, this sounded like far too much of an understatement. 'Well, would not you be?' She crossed her arms. 'You said yourself only yesterday, people—the ones who are left behind—desire answers. Even when we are advised from beyond the grave not to pursue them. Do not tell me that you would have folded the letter up and forgotten all about it as my mother bids me, Jack Trestain, because I would not believe you.'

'No, I wouldn't do that, but neither would I be sitting here pretending that it was merely a matter of satisfying my curiosity either. For God's sake, Celeste, it's your mother we're talking about, not a distant aunt,' Jack exclaimed. 'She drowned herself. She made sure that this letter wouldn't reach you until she was dead. She then alludes to some tragedy in her past being the reason, and caps it all with the revelation that the man you thought all your life was your father is not actually your father, and fails to inform you of the identity of the man who is."

Jack held the letter out at arm's length. "'Though I write this with the heaviest of hearts,'" he read, "'knowing that I will never see you again, I am thankful that at least this time I have the opportunity to say goodbye.' Your mother's opening words. What about the fact that she denied *you* the opportunity to say goodbye to her? Aren't you upset about that?'

Celeste didn't want him to be angry on her behalf. If anyone was entitled to be angry with her mother it was she, and she was not. In order to be angry she would need to care, and she did not. She didn't want Jack to care either. She wanted him to treat this as an intellectual exercise, devoid of emotion. Like breaking a code. 'You said yourself, she was most likely not in a rational frame of mind. At the end of her tether. Perhaps even a little bit out of her mind. There is no point in my becoming upset. It achieves nothing. Besides, I've told you, we were not remotely close.'

'And if you say that it doesn't trouble you often enough, you think I'll eventually believe you.'

Celeste flinched. 'I don't care what you believe. Next, you will be telling me that my mother loved me despite a lifetime's evidence to the contrary.'

'That is exactly what she claims in her letter.'

'Yes, from beyond the grave, safe from any challenge to the contrary. How am I to believe it when I have nothing, no evidence at all, to support it? All my life—all my life, Jack!—she pushed me away. And now this. I don't believe her. How can I believe her? Of course I don't believe her. *C'est impossible!*'

Celeste jumped to her feet, turning her back on him to stare out at the long, bland stretch of lawn, struggling desperately to get her unaccustomed flash of temper under control. 'You have to understand,' she continued in a more measured tone, 'it was similar when I was growing up. Always, my mother managed to find a way of refusing to answer questions. *Why have I no aunts or uncles? Why must we never speak English except when alone? Why have I no grandparents or even a cousin, as all the other children at school have? Why are you so sad, Maman? Why does Papa hate me?* At least now I have the answer to that last question. Papa was not, in fact, my *papa* at all.'

Tears filled her eyes. Celeste swallowed hard on the jagged lump in her throat, staring determinedly out at the lawn. 'I have endured a lifetime of silences and rejection, so really that letter was in essence one final example. Don't tell me that she loved me, Jack. I know what she wrote, I don't have to read that letter again to see the words dance in front of my eyes, but that's all they are. Just words.'

'If it doesn't matter, if it truly doesn't matter, then why then are you so intent on digging up the past?' Jack put his hands on her shoulders, forcing her to turn and face him. 'You do realise that what you discover might be hurtful.'

'Not to me. My hurt is all in the past. All I am doing is filling in the blanks, the missing pieces of my mother's history. I want to understand why she behaved as she did. I want to know who my real father is. I think I am entitled to know that, but I do not want to meet him, or indeed my mother's family. I'm not expecting anyone to kill the fatted calf and welcome me into their home. I am aware that I am most likely a bastard. Knowing is sufficient for me.'

'Your mother's history is your history too, Celeste. You might be better off not knowing it. Sometimes it's better to leave the past behind you.'

'Or bury it so deeply that you can pretend it never happened, that it can no longer harm you?' She pulled herself free of his hold. 'But what if the ghosts refuse to stay buried, Jack? What if they continue to haunt you?'

His face paled. 'What the devil are you implying?'

She had not meant anything in particular. Intent only on silencing his relentless probing, it seemed she had inadvertently struck a raw nerve. It would be dangerous to push him further but it was time to let him sample a little of his own medicine. 'I have no idea why my mother went to such extremes to make me hate her, but I do know that I need to find out why. I need to understand. I need answers, Jack, while you—you seem so very determined to avoid asking the questions.'

'What questions?'

There was no mistaking the icy tone in his voice, but she ignored it. She was becoming very interested indeed in how he would respond. 'What is it that prevents you eating and sleeping? What is it that makes you stop in the middle of a conversation and—and disappear? As if you are no longer there. What is it that makes—?'

'What is it that stops you from crying, Celeste? What is it that prevents you from admitting that your mother's death affected you? Ask yourself those, more pertinent questions.'

Jack turned towards the door. Furious, uncaring that she had now achieved her objective, Celeste grabbed his arm. 'You see, you are running away from the truth. Why won't you talk about it?'

'Take your hands off me. Now.'

She had gone too far. She knew it would be insane to push him further, but she knew with certainty that was exactly what she was going to do. Celeste tilted her chin and met his stormy eyes. 'No.'

She half-expected him to strike her, but he made no such move. Instead, he pulled her towards him until they stood thigh to thigh, chest to chest. She was still angry, but her body responded immediately to the contact with a shiver of delight. 'I am not afraid of you,' Celeste said, tilting her head at him.

'I know,' Jack said. 'It's part of your appeal.'

Chapter Four

Jack's blood stirred at the first touch of her lips on his. He pulled her tight against him and kissed her more deeply. She returned his kiss with equal fervour. He'd been half-expecting her to slap him. He had kissed her merely to turn the tables on her. Now she was turning the tables back on him, just by reciprocating.

He had been angry. Nay, furious. Now his temper had vanished, burst as easily as a bubble by her touch. A gust of longing twisted his gut. He had not felt desire for such a long time. He could not recall ever feeling desire like this. Nothing to do with abstinence. Everything to do with this woman.

His fingers were shaking as he flattened his hand over her shoulder. This was not what he had intended. She was looking at him, her eyes wide open, watching him. Not afraid of him, though there was something there in her eyes he recognised. Yearning. Yes, and fear of the intensity of that yearning. He ought to stop. She should insist that he stop. He slid his hand down to cup her bottom and kissed her again. He needed, wanted, more. His body demanded it.

Her breathing quickened with his. Her fingers strayed into his hair. Her mouth was on his cheek, her lips warm, soft, little flicks of her tongue on his jaw, the corner of his mouth, licking along his lower lip, nipping, licking, until he could no longer stifle a moan of desire, and she gave an answering sigh.

He abandoned himself to her kisses, to the heat of her touch, to the fever of passion which had him in its iron grip. Their mouths locked. Their tongues thrust and tangled greedily. His hands were on her back, her bottom. Her fingers roamed wildly over him, his back, shoulders, tugging at his coat, clutching at his flanks.

He was achingly hard. He cupped her breasts, frustrated by the layers of her clothing, the impediment of her corsets. He dipped his head to kiss the soft swell of her cleavage, inhaling the sweet smell of her, relishing the shudder of her breath, the rapid beat of her heart, knowing that he had done this to her, that she was doing the same to him.

Their kisses grew ragged. His thirst for her was not remotely quenched. His coat was hanging off by one arm. He shrugged himself free of it, pressing her against the wall of the studio. She moaned, tugging his shirt from his pantaloons, flattening her hands on his back. Her skin on his. He hadn't thought he could get any harder. His erection throbbed. A long strand of her white-blonde hair had escaped its pins to lie against the biscuit-coloured skin of her bosom.

He had never wanted any woman this much. His erection pressed into her belly. He slid his hand inside the neckline of her gown to envelop the fullness of her breast. When he touched the hard peak of her nipple she cried out, the distinctive sound of a woman on the verge of a climax. He felt the answering tingling in the tip of his shaft that precluded his own. Shocked, he pulled himself free, hazily aware that she was pushing him away.

What the hell? It was no consolation at all to see his own question reflected in her face. He couldn't think of a damned thing to say. He could, unfortunately, think of a hundred things he wanted to do. Needed to do. Urgently. Jack swore long and hard under his breath. *Breathe. Don't think about it.* But he couldn't take his eyes of her. She hadn't moved. Head and shoulders against the wall. Eyes closed. Breathing slowly. Measured breaths like his. Hands curled into fists like his. Cheeks flushed with desire, no doubt as his were. That long tendril of hair lying across her breast. He reached for it, caught himself, took a step back and tumbled against the leg of a table.

Celeste opened her eyes. Jack pushed his hair back from his face. They stared at each other for a long moment. Then she stood up, tucked the strand of hair behind her ears, straightened her shoulders. '*Bien*, at least now we know that it was not a product of circumstances, that kiss in the Topiary Garden.' Her voice was shaky, but she made no attempt to avoid his gaze.

'The one you insisted was just a kiss,' he said.

'As I recall, you agreed with me.'

'Because I thought I had exaggerated its effect on me.'

'And what about this time?'

He shook his head. 'No. It would not be possible to exaggerate how that just felt. Frankly, it was almost too much.'

'For both of us,' Celeste said wryly.

Would another woman have denied it? It didn't matter. What mattered was that she did not. It made his own instinct to pretend nothing had happened, or to pretend nothing so—so— No, he would not try to quantify it, and he would not try to deny it. 'Do you regret it?' Jack asked as he self-consciously tucked his shirt back into his pantaloons.

She had been rearranging the neckline of her gown, but at that she looked up. 'Why should I?'

There was an edge in her words that took him aback. He had asked her, he realised now, purely because it was the sort of thing he thought he ought to ask. He knew he ought to regret his actions, but he could not. He was too elated to have the proof that it had not been a fluke, his reaction to that first kiss. Elated to know that whatever was wrong with him, lack of desire was no longer an integral part of it. Frustrated—hell, yes, he was frustrated. But he was also— Yes, he was also still a little bit afraid of the reaction she had provoked in him. And more than a little afraid of the consequences if he had not stopped.

'I have never been one of those women who pretend they have no desires of their own.' Celeste's voice cut into his thoughts. 'Nor am I the kind of woman who pretends that such physical desires represent anything more significant, Jack.'

'You're warning me off. There's no need, I assure you. At this moment in time, my only ambition is to get myself through the day—' He broke off, realising too late what he'd admitted, remembering, suddenly, why he had kissed her in the first place. And now he'd given her the perfect opening to start again.

But to his surprise, her expression softened. 'Yes,' she said. 'That is how I have felt since—since.' She blinked rapidly, and forced a smile. 'It is a good thing, this—this—between us, because now I know that I am recovering myself— No, that is not the correct expression.'

'Slowly getting back to normal?'

'Yes. That is it. That is what this is, yes? We are both adults. We are obviously well suited as regards— kissing,' Celeste said, flushing. 'We need not pretend it is anything else, no?'

He was most likely imagining the pleading note in her voice. It was most likely his male ego that wanted to believe she was much more confused by what had happened between them than she appeared. As confused as he was? 'You're right,' Jack said with a conviction he was far from feeling.

Celeste nodded. 'Yes. It makes sense, what I said.'

It did. Perfect sense. So it was pointless wondering why she sounded as unconvinced as he. 'So,' Jack said in a bracing voice that made him cringe, 'talking of getting back to normal, perhaps we should concentrate on these questions your mother has raised. Do you have any other clues, save the letter?'

If she noticed anything odd in his voice, she chose not to comment on it. 'A couple of things. There is this, for what it's worth, which is not a lot.' Celeste unclasped the locket from her neck and handed it to him. 'It came with the letter. My mother always wore it. I don't think I ever saw her without it.'

Jack turned the oval locket over in his hand, examining it carefully. The metal was slightly tarnished so it was difficult to tell, but it looked like it might be gold or, more likely rose-gold, a cheaper alloy. It was embellished with a fleur-de-lis design. Around the rim were laurel leaves set with clear stones and in the centre was set a larger blue one.

'It's just a trinket,' Celeste said dismissively, 'though a pretty one.'

'I'm no expert,' Jack said, 'but the design is very fine, most intricately worked. See these hinges? They are very high quality indeed and not at all commonplace. I think it may be more valuable than you think.'

In fact, he was pretty sure that the smaller stones were diamonds, and that the blue stone was a sapphire. As a consequence the locket was more than likely commissioned, and indeed, on the back he noted tiny symbols, probably the goldsmith's mark. Which might make it, and the owner's name, traceable. But he could not be certain, and so, as was his custom, he kept his own counsel rather than raise Celeste's hopes prematurely. 'Do you mind if I open it?' he asked.

'If you wish.'

She shrugged, but he was becoming attuned to her many permutations of shrug, and Jack knew this one for feigned indifference. When he eased open the catch, he could understand why. Inside were two miniature portraits, one on each side. The first, of a flaxen-haired child, was obviously Celeste. The second, facing it, was of an older woman, her pale hair pulled tightly back from her forehead. Aside from the eyes, which were blue, the resemblance between mother and daughter was very strong, but when he said so, Celeste frowned.

'Do you think so?'

He was surprised by the uncertainty in her voice. 'She is unmistakably your mother, and clearly the source of your own beauty.'

Celeste touched the miniature with the tip of her finger. 'She was beautiful. I had forgotten.'

'May I ask her name?'

Celeste snatched her hand away. 'Blythe.'

'They seem to me to have been painted as a pair,' Jack said. 'I'm no expert, but...'

'No, you are right. Both are by my mother's hand.' She had herself firmly under control again, and spoke in that cool way of hers he'd initially mistaken for detachment. 'Unusually, actually, for she mostly painted the landscapes around Cassis. The fishing boats, the *calanques*—the limestone cliffs and inlets which punctuate the coast. I have never seen another portrait painted by her.'

Which made this pair all the more touching, Jack

thought. He was tempted to say so, but hesitated, remembering her reaction earlier, when he had pushed her on her feelings. And she had pushed him straight back. A salutary lesson, he reckoned, in how not to go about extracting information. 'Cassis,' he said instead. 'The village where you grew up?'

Celeste treated him to one of her shrugs. The feigned indifference one again. 'Paris has been my home for many years.'

'I remember, you said you were sent there to school when you were—ten?'

'Yes. And stayed on to study art.'

'You were very young to be sent so very far from home.'

'It was a very good school.'

She would not meet his eyes. Another sensitive subject. 'You mentioned there was another clue?' Jack said, once more deciding that the best policy would be to bide his time.

She handed him a small packet of stitched muslin. Inside was a man's signet ring. 'I found it when I went to Cassis to close the house up after—after,' Celeste said. 'I was taking Maman's paintings down. This was sewn to the back of her favourite canvas. It must have been there for years. I have no idea what it signifies. It clearly does not belong to my mother.' She leaned across him to peer down at the ring. 'The markings, I thought perhaps were a family crest. That might lead us somewhere,' she said, looking at him hopefully.

'It looks to me more likely to be a military crest. I'm not sure of the regiment. I would need to check.'

'Military? Why on earth would my mother have such a thing in her possession?'

'It's a good question.'

'As if we don't have enough questions already. Do you think you can help, Jack?'

He studied the ring with an ominous sense of fore-boding. 'I can try.'

The next morning, a soft breeze blew up as Celeste walked with Jack along a path which led from the far end of the lake, over a gentle rise to an ancient oak, underneath the spread of which was a wooden bench. The view was prettily bucolic, bathed in the golden early-morning light. They stood on top of the hill while Jack pointed out the spire of St Mary's Church some five miles away, where Lady Eleanor's father was the vicar, and closer, the many-gabled rooftops of Trestain Manor. Golden fields of half-harvested wheat contrasted with the dark-green tunnels of hops, while the low, thatched roofs of the farm buildings and cottages contrasted with the distinctive, conical roofs of two oast houses where the hops were roasted.

Celeste was entranced, her charcoal flying over page after page of her sketchbook, while Jack, seated on the bench under the tree, filled her in on some of the history of what she was drawing. He was back to his usual garb of leather breeches and boots, a shirt without either waistcoat or coat. The sleeves of his shirt were rolled up. The skin of his right arm was already turning golden-brown. She would like to draw him like this, his long, booted legs stretched out in front of him, his hair falling over his forehead, the curve of his mouth in a lazy smile. That mouth, the source of such intoxicating kisses.

Desire knotted in her belly. She had never before tumbled so perilously close to completion after a few kisses. The rapidity of her arousal had caught her completely unawares. When he had touched her nipple…

Celeste inhaled sharply. Even now, the memory of it was enough to heat her. And to frighten her. All very well to thank Jack for bringing her body back to life as she more or less had, rather embarrassingly, yesterday, but he had brought it to a place it had never been before. Her claim that abstinence had somehow attenuated what Jack's kisses did to her felt faintly ridiculous now. In her whole life, she had taken four lovers, and there had been two years between the first and second, yet she knew with certainty that none had made her feel the way Jack did.

The natural conclusion, that it was not circumstances but this man, this very particular man, was what had kept her awake last night. Clearly there was something, some force, some element, some quirk of nature, which made their bodies so well matched. This explanation, she should have found comforting, but for some reason, she did not. If it had not been so reasonable, she would have been inclined to dismiss it as wrong.

'Is *Mademoiselle* ready to partake of breakfast now?'

Celeste jumped, staring down at blankly her half-finished sketch. Her charcoal was on the grass beside her. How long had she been daydreaming? At least with her back turned to him, Jack would not have noticed. Or if he had, he had decided not to comment, she thought with relief. There was nothing worse than being asked what it was one was thinking, for it was inevitably something one did not wish to share. It had been unkind of her to mention those lost moments of Jack's yesterday. Call it daydreaming, call it disappearing, as she had, wherever they were, they were private. His and his alone.

She gave him an apologetic smile as she joined him on the grass, leaning her back against the bench. 'Thank you.'

He quirked his brow but said nothing, pulling the hamper they had brought with them out from beneath the shade of the tree before spreading a blanket out. There was fresh-baked bread, butter and cheese, a flask of coffee and some peaches. 'Picked fresh this morning, and though they are ripe,' he said, sniffing the soft fruit, 'I don't expect they'll be anything like what you're used to. Our English sun is just not strong enough.'

Celeste stretched her face up to the sky, closing her eyes and relishing the heat on her skin. 'It is a good deal warmer than I expected. I don't think I have seen a drop of English rain yet.'

'You will. One merely has to wait a few days.'

Jack handed her a cup of coffee. Celeste tore off a piece of bread, burying her nose in the delicious, yeasty smell of it. 'Another myth. I was told that the

English cannot bake good bread, but this is most acceptable.'

'A high compliment indeed from a Frenchwoman.' He handed her a slice of cheese and laughed when she sniffed that too, wrinkling her nose. 'Try it, you might be surprised.'

She did, and was forced to admit that, like the bread, it was excellent. 'Though it breaks my French heart to do so,' she added, smiling over her coffee cup.

'But you're half-English, are you not?'

'I suppose I am, though I don't feel it. I think one has to be part of a country before one feels any sense of belonging. All this,' Celeste said, spreading her arms wide at the sweeping view, 'it feels so alien to me.'

'Maybe that's because you're a Parisian.'

Celeste laughed. 'When I first arrived in Paris, I felt such an outsider. It was as if everyone but me knew a secret and they were all whispering about it behind my back. Even after fifteen years, I'm still not considered a genuine Parisian. I don't have that *je ne sais quoi*, that air about me. To the true Parisians, I will always be an incomer.'

'I know exactly what you mean,' Jack said. 'Paris, it's always seemed to me, is a city that only reveals itself at night, and even then, you have to know where to look. I always sense the best elements are just round the next corner, or along the next boulevard. In Paris, I always feel as if I'm on the outside looking in. It's not like London at all.'

'I have never visited London. I hope to go there before I return to France.' Celeste broke off another piece of bread and accepted a second piece of cheese which Jack cut for her. 'You have been away from England a long time,' she said. 'Does it still feel like home?'

He paused in the act of quartering a peach. 'Charlie wants me to buy an estate and settle down. I never did share his love for country life, though he seems to have conveniently forgotten that.'

'Perhaps it would be different if you had been the eldest son, if Trestain Manor belonged to you and not to your brother?'

Jack laughed. 'Lord, no, I'd be bored senseless. It was always the army for me, so it's as well I'm the second son and not the first.' He handed her the peach. 'What about you? Have you never thought of going back to live in your fishing village?'

'No.'

'Don't you miss it? I used to miss all this,' Jack said. 'Even though I wouldn't want to live here, it's my childhood home.'

Celeste stared at the quarter of peach in her hand. 'The house in Cassis was where I lived. It was never a home.' Her voice sounded odd, even to her own ears. She was, yet again, on the brink of tears for no reason. It was Jack's fault. All she wanted him to do was help her unravel the mystery of her mother's past, but for some reason, he persisted in linking that past with her own. He seemed to have the knack of inflaming her emotions as well as her body. She set the peach down. 'Paris is my home,' she said, as if repeating it would make it more true. Not that it needed to be more true. It was true.

She thought of the house where she had grown up. The distinctive creak of the front door. The very different creak of the fifth stair which had a broken tread. The way the floors always seemed to echo when she walked, signalling her presence too loudly. She tried to close her mind to the memories, but they would not stop flowing. It was Jack's fault. This was all Jack's fault.

On her last visit, after receiving the letter, she had packed up every one of her mother's paintings. They lay in crates now, stacked in a corner of her Paris studio. She couldn't bear to look at them but nor could she bear to dispose of them. The rest of the house she had left as it was.

She shook her head. She was aware of Jack, sipping his coffee, pretending not to study her, but the ghosts of the past had too strong a claim on her. Her mother on the cliff top painting, her hair covered by a horrible cap, her body draped in shapeless brown. Her mother's face, starkly beautiful in the miniature inside her locket, strained and sad. Her mother's paintings were all of the coast and the sea which took her. The sea which she had abandoned herself to, without giving Celeste a chance to save her. The beautiful, cruel sea, which her mother had chosen to embrace, rather than her own daughter.

The pain was unexpected. Nothing so clichéd as a stab to the heart; it was duller, weightier, like a heavy blow to the stomach. *At least this time I have the opportunity to say goodbye*, her mother had written, so certain that Celeste cared so little she would not wish to do the same. With good cause, for Celeste had made it very clear, after Henri died...

A tear rolled down her cheek. Her throat was clogged. She couldn't speak. She was filled with the most unbearable sadness. *What was wrong with her!* She never cried. Had never cried. Now, hardly a day went by where she teetered on the verge of stupid, stupid tears.

In the distance, the chime of St Mary's heralded noon. She dabbed frantically at her eyes with her napkin. She never carried a handkerchief.

'Celeste?'

Jack! It was his fault for dredging all this up. His fault for making her so on edge. She jumped to her feet and snatched up her sketchbook. 'I have the headache,' she said. 'I have no more paper. I need to rest. I need more charcoal.'

She was fleeing, just as Jack had, after that first kiss, and she did not care. All that mattered was that he did not stop her. She barely noticed in her anxiety to escape that he made absolutely no attempt to do so.

Chapter Five

'So this is where you're hiding.'

Celeste forced herself to turn around slowly. Jack stood hesitantly in the doorway, dressed in his customary breeches and boots. She willed the flush of embarrassment she could feel creeping up her neck not to show on her face. 'It is safe to come in,' she said. 'I am not going to descend into a fit of hysterics or stamp my feet or even run away again.'

He strode over to her, his relief obvious. 'I'm sorry, Celeste,' he said. 'It was not my intention to cause you upset yesterday.'

'Cassis was not a happy place for me when I was growing up,' she said carefully. 'I don't like to talk of it or even think of those days. *En effet*, I never do. It is in the past where it belongs.'

And she would make sure it remained there. It sounded contrary, considering the accusations she had flung at Jack yesterday, but their cases were not the same, she had decided after another sleepless night. She had come to terms with her past, he had not. What she needed to concentrate on now was dealing with her mother's past. Which was a separate issue.

Slanting a look at Jack, she was not surprised to catch him studying her, but she was relieved when he nodded his acceptance, albeit reluctantly. 'Charlie,' he said, turning his attention to the portrait she had been examining. 'Aged about five, I think. What brings you to the portrait gallery?'

'I was interested to see how the estate had been depicted previously, to avoid the risk of replicating any existing works.'

'Ah, so you're here purely in the name of artistic research and not at all out of curiosity?'

Celeste smiled. 'Naturally.' She turned to the next work, a family portrait, which showed a youthful Jack and Charlie sitting at their parents' feet. 'You looked much more alike as children than you do as adults. You both take after your mother rather than your father, I fancy.'

'So my mother was forever saying. It was a matter of pride to her that Charlie and I bore the McDonald countenance and not the Trestain visage,' Jack said, reaching out to draw the outline of his mother's face on the canvas with his finger. 'She was a Scot, and verrrrry, verrrry proud of the fact,' he said in a ham-fisted attempt at a Scottish burr.

'You miss her?'

'She died when I was in Spain, about six years ago. But, yes, I do miss her. She wanted me to join the Scots Greys, but my father put his foot down on that one. Nevertheless, she always claimed that my fighting spirit as well as my nose came from her side of the family. Here she is, a good deal younger, in her wedding portrait, with my maternal grandfather.'

Celeste eyed the picture of the fierce man in Highland dress. He looked very much like Jack did when he was angry. 'Would you have had to wear one of those skirts if you joined the—the...'

'Scots Greys. No, only the Highland regiments wear kilts.'

'*Tant pis*. That is a pity. It would suit you uncommonly well, I think,' Celeste said. 'You have the most excellent legs for it.'

'You speak merely as an observant artist, of course?'

She felt herself colour slightly. 'Naturally. Is there a picture of you wearing your regimental uniform?'

Jack rolled his eyes. 'In full ceremonial dress, no less, looking like I've a poker up my—looking as if I've swallowed a poker. Charlie commissioned it when I was promoted. Here, take a quick look if you must.'

He put his arm around her shoulders and steered her to the far end of the small gallery, where the portrait, in its expensive gilt frame, was hung to take best advantage of the light. 'Your brother must have spent a small fortune on this,' Celeste said, raising her brows at the artist's signature. 'A full-length study. He is obviously very proud of you, Lieutenant-Colonel.' She waited for Jack's customary glower at any mention of the army, but to her surprise it did not surface.

He looked very forbidding in the portrait. His hair

was cropped much shorter, barely noticeable under the huge crested helmet he wore with its extravagant black horsehair tail. He stood very tall and straight, his hand resting on the hilt of his sabre, his face looking haughtily off into the distance. The scarlet coat was extremely tight-fitting, showing off his broad shoulders and narrow waist, the high, braided collar framing his jaw. White breeches and long, glossy black boots drew attention to his muscular legs. 'Which regiment did you belong to?'

'Dragoons,' Jack said abstractedly. 'Of course we didn't wear those ridiculous helmets or the white breeches when going into battle. What do you think of it?'

'As an artist? It is a technically flawless work. As a viewer, it speaks unmistakably of authority. It depicts you with a—a certain hauteur. I think I would be just a little bit intimidated by the man in the portrait. I would of a certainty obey his orders unquestioningly. If I was one of his men, that is,' she added quickly.

Jack laughed. 'I doubt you would follow even Napoleon's orders.'

'No, I would have made a very bad soldier. But you, you look—*bien*—exactly what you were, a high-ranking British officer, used to unwavering obedience and with the air of a Greek god, gazing down on us mere mortals.'

'Good grief, you make me sound like a pompous ass.'

'No, not pompous, supremely confident. Very sure of yourself.'

'I suppose I was.'

Jack was staring at the portrait as if it were of a stranger, just as she had stared at the miniature of her mother only the other day. She was still struggling to equate the beautiful woman in the portrait with the Maman in her mind's eye. Art could obscure reality as well as portray it. Which was the real Blythe Marmion? Which was the real Jack Trestain? Had the regal, commanding officer in the portrait ever existed? Jack was asking himself the same question, judging by the expression on his face.

'This likeness was taken less than three years ago,' he said. 'I left the army less than three months ago, yet it seems as if a lifetime has passed. I struggle to recognise myself. I can barely remember being the man in the portrait. I thought, you know, that if I re-enlisted, I might— I was fine then. Seeing this—I can't imagine it now.'

He turned away, heading across the room to the farthest point away from the portrait. *I was fine then.* For the first time, he had admitted that he was not fine now. *What had happened to him?* More than ever, she longed to know, but Celeste bit back the questions she was desperate to ask, the answers she would have demanded only a few short days ago. Memories were painful things. Memories were private things. Some memories, as she had learnt only yesterday, were too painful to be shared.

It was like Pandora's box, her memory. Every time the lid creaked open a fraction, it became more and more difficult to close. Things she wanted to forget wriggled free. Things that reminded her she had not always been the person she was so proud of now. She did not want to be reminded of that person. She would never again be that person.

And Jack? With Jack it was very different. The soldier in the portrait had been a respected and admired officer, one mentioned in despatches, whatever that meant. The man he had become was fighting a different battle now. He had his demons, just as she had her ghosts. No doubt she was just a foolish artist, but she admired this man's bravery a great deal more.

She rejoined him in front of another full-length painting. 'And who is this remarkable specimen?' Celeste asked him brightly.

'This is my father's brother, also called Jack,' he replied. 'As you can see, aside from our name, we have precious little in common.'

The man was fat, fair and flamboyant in a claret-velvet suit, gazing winsomely out at the viewer, a silver jug in one hand, a book in the other. 'Household Accounts,' Celeste read in puzzlement. 'How very strange. Usually when a man holds a book in a portrait it is to symbolise his learning.'

Jack smiled wryly. 'In this particular case it symbolises his notorious thriftiness. This next lady now, my Aunt Christina, is my mother's youngest sister, known as Auntie Kirsty. She is married to a real Highland laird and lives in a genuine Highland castle. Charlie and I used to love visiting them. It was a real adventure for us. My mother hated it up there, for it was freezing cold, winter and summer, and Auntie Kirsty is one of those women who hasn't much of an opinion of soap and water. Frankly,' Jack said, grinning, 'Auntie Kirstie smells exactly like her deerhounds when they've been out in the rain. But she's one of the best fishermen I've ever come across, and she can shoot better than almost any trooper I've ever trained. You can see the castle in the background there, and this dog here, that's Calum, her favourite deerhound of the time, though most likely long gone.' His smile faded. 'I've not been there in many years.'

'Now you are no longer tied to the army, you could visit her, if you wished.'

'No. Auntie Kirstie is almost as bad as my mother was for basking in my exploits.'

'You mean she was proud of you?'

'They all were, and I was arrogant enough to think I deserved it.' Jack reached out to touch his aunt's face, the same gesture he'd used on the portrait of his mother. 'I considered myself a good soldier.'

'And the Duke of Wellington agreed,' Celeste reminded him.

'Yes, he did, but it all depends on your perspective.'

He spoke not bitterly, but resignedly. His expression was bleak, the despair not so marked as on that first, unguarded day at the lake, but it was manifestly still there in his eyes. She longed to comfort him, but how? The more he said about the army, the more she realised his relationship with it was complex, perhaps impossible for anyone who was not a soldier to understand. He loved the army, he clearly had loved being a soldier, but he spoke of those days as if it were a different person. As if it was not him. As if he would not allow it to have been him. And so perhaps they were kindred spirits after all.

The door to the portrait gallery burst open, and a small whirlwind of a boy came hurtling in, making a beeline for Jack. 'Please will you take me fishing, Uncle Jack?'

'Robert, make your bow to Mademoiselle Marmion,' Jack said, detaching the grubby little hand which was clutching the pocket of his breeches. 'This, *Mademoiselle*, is my nephew.'

'How do you do?' The child made a perfunctory bow before turning his beseeching countenance back to his uncle. '*Will* you take me fishing? Only Papa was supposed to take me but I think he has quite forgotten, and even though Papa says he always caught the biggest fish when you were little…'

Jack laughed. 'Oh, he did, did he?'

Robert nodded solemnly. 'Yes, and Papa would not lie, Uncle Jack.'

Jack dropped down on to his knees to be level with the child whose eyes were the exact same shade of dark brown, Celeste noted, as his own. 'No,' he said, 'you are quite right. Papa would not lie.'

'But you mustn't feel bad, because he told me you were the much better shot.' Robert patted Jack's shoulder consolingly, making Celeste stifle a giggle. 'Papa said that when you were only six, which is just a little bit bigger than me, you shot a pigeon this high up in the sky,' he said, standing on his tiptoes and stretching his arm above his head. 'Only Papa said that it was very naughty of you, because you weren't supposed to have the gun, and Grandpapa was very angry, and he gave you a sound whipping, and Papa too, even though *he* did not shoot the gun, and I think that's not fair. Do you think that's fair, Uncle Jack, do you?'

'Well, I…'

'Though maybe,' Robert continued, having drawn breath, 'maybe,' he said, plucking at Jack's shirt, 'Papa was whipped because he is the *eldest* and did not show a good example? That is what he said I am to do, when Baby Donal is older. So maybe you would not have stolen the gun and shot the pigeon if Papa had told you not to?'

'Perhaps,' Jack said, his eyes alight with laughter but his expression serious, 'though I was a very naughty boy when I was your age. I tended not to do as I was told, I'm afraid.'

Robert considered this, his head on one side. 'Is that why you are not a soldier any more? Did you disobey orders?'

Jack sat back on his heels, the light fading from his eyes. 'I did not, but I wish to God I had.'

Celeste caught her breath at this, but Robert had already moved on. 'Uncle Jack, will you tell me about the time when you told the Duke of Wellington about that great big fort, and he said that it was a ruin, but you knew better. And there was a big battle and—

and will you tell me, because when Papa tells me, he gets it all mixed up and forgets the regiments, and it is not the same as when you tell it.'

Jack winced. 'Robert, the war is over now.'

'But you were there and you saw it with your own eyes,' the child continued, heedless.

'Robert…'

'Robert, I think perhaps your uncle…' Celeste interjected.

Robert stamped his foot. 'It is not fair! Why must I not ask you? Why won't you tell me, when you have told Papa?'

'Because Papa is a grown up. Because it was a long time ago,' Jack said.

'Well then, why will you not tell me about Waterloo? That was not a long time ago.'

'Robert,' Jack said, getting to his feet, obviously agitated, 'I think it is best…'

'But I only wanted to know what it was like,' the child said, grabbing at his uncle's leg, his face screwed up with temper, 'because Steven, who is my best, best friend in the whole village, his papa fought under Sir Thomas Picton at Waterloo in the Fifth Infantry, and I said that you were much more important than even Sir Thomas Picton, and Steven said you could not be…'

'Enough, child, for pity's sake!' Jack's roar was so unexpected that Robert stopped in mid-flow, his jaw hanging open. Celeste, who felt as if her heart had attempted to jump out of her chest, was also speechless.

Jack pointed at the door. 'Out! You would test the patience of a saint. No war stories, today or ever. Have I made myself perfectly clear?' He glowered at the child.

Robert's lip trembled, but he held his ground. 'I hate you.' He stamped his foot again. 'I *hate* you,' he said and burst into tears, storming from the room, violently slamming the door behind him.

Shaken, white-faced, Jack slumped on to the sofa which was placed in the middle of the room and dropped his head, pinching the furrow between his brows hard. He rubbed his forehead viciously, as if he were trying to erase whatever thoughts lurked behind it. 'I frightened him,' he said starkly. 'He's five years old, for goodness' sake, and I yelled at him as if he'd turned up on the parade ground without his musket. What the hell is wrong with me?'

'Jack, I don't think he was so very frightened. It seemed to me he was more angry than afraid.'

'What blasted difference does it make? He ran away, bawling his eyes out, and that was my fault.' Jack jumped to his feet, his fists clenched. 'I've never upset a child like that before. What on earth is happening to me?'

'Jack, I—'

'No, don't say another word.' He rounded on her. 'You! That is what is behind this. Ever since you— As if I didn't have enough on my mind without having to lie awake thinking of you and your damned kisses and your damned questions. *Why can't I eat? Why can't I sleep? Why do I—* What did you call it?'

'Disappear.' Her voice was no more than a whisper. His anger was not directed at her, but it terrified her, the depths of his anxiety. Though he loomed over her, she stood her ground. 'Jack...'

He threw her hand from his arm. 'Don't pity me. I neither require nor desire your pity, *Mademoiselle*. I want—I want...' He flung himself back on to the sofa and dropped his head into his hands. 'Hell's teeth, I don't know what I want. I'm sorry. I'm better left to my own devices at the moment. Best if you leave.'

Celeste turned to do as he bid her, remembering her own desire yesterday to retire to her bedchamber and lick her wounds, but then she stopped, and instead sat down on the sofa beside him. 'I don't feel sorry for you, Jack. I don't know what I feel for you, to be honest, but I know it's not pity.'

He did not look up, but he did not turn away either.

She wasn't sure what it was she was trying to say. She was reluctant to say anything, especially if it was an unpalatable truth, but she knew she couldn't leave him like this, bereft and seemingly lost. 'You were correct,' she said, though it made her feel quite sick to admit it, 'when you said that Maman's death was— That it meant more to me than I thought. You were right.'

Jack lifted his head. Celeste had to fight the urge to run away. She dug her feet into the wooden floor. 'I blamed you yesterday for what I was feeling. I thought, if it hadn't been for you, I would not be feeling—' She broke off, raising her hands helplessly. 'I don't know what. Something, as opposed to nothing.'

'I'm sorry. I had no right to pry.'

'No more than I did, but it didn't stop me either. I am sorry too.'

'I never used to have such a foul temper, you know.'

'*Moi aussi*, never. Perhaps there is something in the air at Trestain Manor.'

Jack's smile was perfunctory, but it was a smile. 'I don't know what Charlie is playing at, telling Robert those stupid stories, making it sound as if war is some great adventure.'

'Isn't that what you thought at that age?' Celeste asked carefully.

'Precisely.' He ran his fingers through his hair. 'And now I know better.'

'Jack, Robert is just a little boy. He doesn't need or deserve to have his illusions shattered at such a tender age. Why not indulge him a little? What is so different, really, from telling him the kind of stories you once told your brother?'

'I only ever told Charlie the kind of things he wanted to hear.'

'*Exactement.*'

He was silent for a long time. Finally, he shook his head, pressed her hand and got to his feet. 'I need some fresh air, and you are probably wanting to get on with your work. I'm going to try to manage an hour on horseback without falling off.'

'But your arm...'

'Will recover faster if I use the blasted thing. I'm not made of glass. Besides,' Jack added with a grin, 'you've no idea how embarrassing it is for an officer of the Dragoons to fall from his horse. If any of my comrades knew, I'd never be allowed to forget it.'

The next day, as Jack had predicted it would, it was raining. Not the kind of polite, soft rain that Celeste had imagined would fall in an English summer, but a heavy downpour rather like the kind of summer storm in Cassis that turned the narrow streets into raging torrents. Gazing out of the windows of her studio, it was as if the sky consisted of one leaden grey cloud that had been sliced open. Water poured from the gutters on to the paths, cutting new channels into the flower beds. The branches of the trees bent under the weight of the deluge.

Celeste shivered, wrapping the shawl she had fetched after breakfast more tightly around her, for the flimsy sprigged-muslin gown she wore was no protection against the cold, damp air. She looked longingly at the small fireplace, imagining the comfort of a fire. In August! She doubted that the hardy Lady Eleanor would think it necessary.

It was too dark to work, and too wet to go outside. Sir Charles, fretting about the harvest, was planning on a tour of the closest farms, though when his wife had quizzed him on what he thought could be achieved, other than a thorough drenching, he had been unable to supply her with an answer. Lady Eleanor was to spend the morning in the kitchen making jam. A task she and her sisters used to look forward to every year when they were growing up, she had told Celeste over the breakfast table. She hoped to pass her receipts on to her own daughters, when they arrived, but in the meantime, she would be sharing the task with cook. She did not ask Celeste if she wanted to join them in the kitchen.

'And I am glad she did not, for I know nothing at all about making jam or pickles or any of these things the English take such pride in,' Celeste muttered to herself. The truth was, she thought, looking despondently out at the garden, she knew almost nothing about French cooking either. Frowning, she tried to recall if she had ever seen her mother in the kitchen, and could not. They had always had a cook. Her mother planned the meals, she recalled, writing out the menus for the week in the book in which she kept painstaking household accounts, but, no, not once could Celeste recall her actually shopping for food or preparing it. Then, at school, the kitchens were out of bounds, and in her Parisian garret, she could make coffee, but nothing more substantial.

She leafed through her sketches, which were laid out on a large table set against the wall. She didn't even like jam, but when Lady Eleanor talked about sharing the task with her sisters, Celeste had felt quite envious. There had been a softness about her ladyship too, as she speculated about a time when her yet-to-be-born daughter would join her in the kitchen. Celeste cast her sketches aside and returned to the window. Was there nothing, no small domestic task she and her mother had shared?

Painting. Yes, there were the painting and drawing lessons, though there were so many that, to Celeste's frustration, the memory was blurred. She could remember spending hours and hours trying to draw a cat. She could remember struggling to hold her brush in the correct manner. She could remember painting endless bowls of fruit. But her memories were all of her hand, the paper, the paints, the result. She could not recall what her mother had said of any of her work. Could not remember a single occasion when her father—Henri, she corrected herself—had passed any opinion at all on her talent. In fact she could not remember him being present at all.

Outside, the rain was easing. Sir Charles would be relieved. The grass looked much greener, almost too glossy to be real. The trees too looked freshly painted. They reminded her of the idealised pictures in a storybook that her mother used to read to her. She had forgotten that. Returning to the sofa, she sat down and closed her eyes. Her mother was reading the story, her finger pointing to the words so that Celeste could follow along. The book was in English. Where had it come from? Had it been her mother's as a child? The pages had been worn. The book contained several stories, each beautifully illustrated. An expensive book.

Celeste screwed her eyes shut tighter and tried to recall her mother's voice, but though she could see the pictures so clearly, she couldn't hear any accompanying words. Frustrated, she tried to recall other times. Sewing. Her mother had taught her to sew. Not the practical kind that she had been taught at school, but embroidery. Yes, yes, another memory swam into view. She was sitting on a stool at her mother's knee.

'When the first course is served at such a grand dinner,' Maman was saying, 'one must turn to the right, so I had to wait until the second course to speak to him.'

Celeste's eyes flew open. She stared around the room, as if her mother might appear from behind the easel. Her voice had been so clear. '*Mon Dieu*, of all the things, I remember that most useless piece of advice!'

'What most useless piece of advice would that be?'

'Jack.' Celeste jumped to her feet, clutching her shawl. 'You startled me.'

'Sleeping on the job?'

'I was not sleeping,' she said indignantly, 'I was thinking.' She eyed his wet hair, sleeked back on his head, with astonishment. 'You have surely not been swimming in this?'

'Why not?'

She wrapped her arms around herself, giving a mock shudder. 'It is freezing.'

'Nonsense, a little summer rain, that's all. You'll be asking for the fire to be lit next.' She must have looked longingly at the empty hearth, because Jack burst out laughing.

'If you think it is cold now, you should try enduring an English country winter. Which you will not be required to do, since once your business here is concluded I assume you will be anxious to return to your life in Paris.'

'Of course I am.' And she was. Everything she had achieved had been hard-earned and she was looking forward to picking up the threads of her life.

* * *

Jack put the leatherbound folder which he had brought with him down on the table next to her sketches. 'Celeste, have you considered the possibility that whatever we manage to uncover about your mother's past might change things, maybe even change your life, the one you're so keen to reclaim, irrevocably?'

She pursed her lips, shaking her head firmly. 'I thought I'd made myself plain, I have no ambition to claim any family, legitimate or not, if that is what you mean. Clearly, my mother's family disowned her. Equally clearly, my father's family disowned both my mother and me. Frankly, being the unwanted child of one man means I have no wish to repeat the experience as far as my father is concerned, and as to my mother—again, no. Her family rejected her. My mother rejected me. You see the pattern, Jack. Whatever we find will allow me to regain my life, not destroy it.'

She spoke carefully, but coolly. The barriers were well and truly in place once more, but still Jack felt uneasy. She was fragile, she had admitted that much yesterday. He wanted to spare her pain, but he had not that right. All he could do was help her, and hope that the price she paid was worth it.

Jack opened the folder. 'In that case,' he said, 'let us set to work on getting you the answers you need. First things first. Let's take stock of where we are and what we know.'

Chapter Six

Jack took out her mother's letter from his folder, and laid it out alongside a sheet of notes he had made following a detailed analysis of the contents. 'Are you ready for this?' he said.

Celeste nodded, ignoring the fluttering of nerves in her stomach.

'So, to the beginning—or the beginning as we know it. Your mother married Henri Marmion in 1794.'

Again, she nodded.

'At the height of the Terror then, when the blood-letting in the aftermath of the Revolution was at its peak,' Jack said. 'I think that must be significant.'

Celeste frowned. 'I cannot see how. My father—Henri—he was not a member of the aristocracy. He was not a politician, or indeed a man of any influence. Besides, we lived in a tiny fishing village, not Paris, or any other important city. We were just an ordinary family.'

Jack tapped his finger on his notes. 'You were

four when this marriage took place. Do you remember anything from the time before? Anything at all,' he asked. 'Sometimes the most insignificant details are the ones that matter most.'

Celeste shook her head. 'I was thinking only this morning, just before you arrived, how little I can recall of my childhood. An English storybook. Painting lessons. Setting the stitches on a sampler. Maman telling me the etiquette for polite conversation at a dinner party, though why she should think it important to instruct me in *that* I cannot imagine.'

'What's your earliest memory?' Jack asked.

'That is easy,' Celeste said with a smile. 'I found a shell on the beach one day, a huge pink shell, the kind that you put to your ear and can hear the rush of the sea. I remember it was too big for me to hold with one hand. I must have been five, perhaps six. What is yours?'

'That's easy too. Charlie had a toy horse, a wooden one on wheels. He called it Hector. I was forbidden from riding it because I was too little, which Charlie delighted in reminding me, so of course that made me all the more determined. I managed to climb up on Hector, and Charlie caught me and pushed me off, and I split my forehead open on the marble floor. I still have the scar. Here,' Jack said, taking her hand.

It was very faint, right in the middle of his forehead. She ran her finger along it, feeling the tiny notches where it had been stitched, and could not resist pushing back his hair from his brow. It was silky-soft. She snatched her hand away. 'Your first battle scar,' she said. 'Sadly, not your last. How is your arm today?'

Jack shrugged. '*That* wound is healing.'

And so he edged a tiny step closer to admitting there was another, deeper wound. Celeste bit her tongue. Trust, she was learning, was a skittish beast, so she turned the subject to a different sort of animal. 'Hector is a peculiar name for a horse. What age were you when you stole it?'

She was rewarded with a small smile. 'I didn't steal it, I borrowed it. I had to use a stool to climb up on to the saddle, and my legs didn't touch the ground. Three, perhaps?'

'Is it odd, do you think, that I can remember nothing from such a young age?'

'I don't know, but in my experience, people actually take in a great deal more than they can recount. Memory works in different ways for different people. For some, smell is the most evocative sense. I tend to remember things in the form of patterns. As an artist, for you it might be colour. There are tricks that can help flesh out a memory that I used in my days of gathering information professionally,' Jack said.

'You mean when you were interrogating enemy agents?'

'Lord, no, I mean when I was debriefing our chaps after a reconnaissance. No thumbscrews or rack, in case that's what you're imagining either. Simply a case of relaxing the subjects' minds before gently directing their thoughts. We can try it later if you like.'

'No,' Celeste said firmly, 'I will keep my thoughts to myself, thank you.'

Jack raised a quizzical brow, but turned his attention back to his notes. 'I can't help but feel that your mother's marriage to Henri Marmion must be connected somehow with the Terror.' He picked up the letter. '"Without Henri, I do honestly believe we would have perished. I doubt you will believe him capable of heroism, but back in those dark days, that is what he was. A hero." She is convinced that both your lives were in danger. That's too much of a coincidence, don't you think?'

It was hard to disagree with Jack's logic, though difficult to conceive of it being true. Celeste nodded, this time reluctantly.

'Good, then that is our starting premise.' Jack pulled out another sheet of paper. 'So, what else do we know? First, your mother was English. Second, she gave birth to you in France in 1790, so she must have gone there at some point before. I don't suppose you know your place of birth?'

'I'm afraid not.'

'Or your mother's maiden name? Is there a certificate of her marriage to Henri Marmion?'

She shook her head again. 'The number of things I don't know are considerably greater than the number that I do. I don't even know where they were married, so church records aren't available as a source of information.'

'Then you won't know if she was married previously?'

'You need not spare my blushes. I have already said I must assume that I am illegitimate,' Celeste said brusquely. 'That is the only explanation for my mother's insistence that she had no family—everyone has family, hers obviously disowned her, and since she was a woman—' She broke off, struck by a sudden flash of memory. 'My mother once said to me that a woman's reputation was all she had. In her letter she wrote that the love she had for the man who sired me was the source of her downfall. The implications are clear enough.'

'Sired? You speak of your father as if he means nothing to you?'

'I obviously meant nothing to him. I am merely reciprocating his indifference.'

Jack picked up the letter again. '"Your father would have loved you, of that I am sure,"' he read. '"He too would have been proud of you."'

Celeste crossed her arms. 'That is the kind of soft soap a mother would write to console a bastard child, don't you think?'

Jack made no reply.

'You think that I am callous.'

'I think,' he said carefully, 'that perhaps your father never knew of your existence. "Your father *would have* loved you" is what your mother writes. *Would have*, implying he was for some reason prevented from having the opportunity to do so.'

It had not occurred to her to interpret her mother's words thus. A veteran of parental rejection, she had assumed that this was yet another case in point.

Would her father have loved her? It didn't bear thinking about. 'It is hardly relevant,' Celeste said, steeling
herself, 'since he is in all likelihood dead.'

Jack consulted the letter again. 'Your mother mentions "tragic consequences" resulting from the "impossible choice" she had to make?'

'Tragic can only mean a death. I think we must
assume it refers to my natural father.' Saying it aloud
brought a lump to Celeste's throat.

'Talking of fathers, tell me what you know of
Henri Marmion.'

'I don't see what Henri has to do with anything.'

Jack sighed. 'Then it's as well you asked me to
read this letter, because it's perfectly plain to me that
he must have loved your mother a great deal. Think
about the circumstances for a moment, Celeste. Your
mother is in dire straits of some sort. She's alone,
with an infant child and no family, in a strange country. By 1794, simply the fact that she was English
would have put her on a list of suspicious characters,
and it would have been impossible for her to escape
France. To marry her was to take an enormous personal risk, and Marmion not only married her, but
it sounds as though he cut himself off from his own
friends and family in order to keep you both safe. A
man doesn't do that unless he's deep in love or perhaps deep in debt.'

'He was a schoolteacher. He was a very educated
man, but he taught at the village school. He could
read and write Greek and Latin, he could quote so
many of the Classics, but he—he hid his erudition. I

could never understand it. One of the many things I could never fathom.'

'Did he ever mention his family?'

'Not that I remember, but then Henri rarely talked to me. I think he came from Cahors, in the south-west. I don't know how I remember that. His accent, perhaps.' Celeste shook her head, as if doing so would clear the tangled web that her past seemed to have become. 'He was so distant. I can't imagine that he was capable of love. I never saw any sign of affection between them. Besides, my mother claims to have loved my natural father. She made her choice for love, according to her letter.'

'Celeste, do you not think that makes Henri Marmion's behaviour more understandable rather than less so? To love, and never to have that love returned, would that not make a man distant? To see the evidence of his wife's true love in the form of her child—her only child—would that not eventually turn a loving husband into an embittered one?'

Celeste dropped her head on to her hands. 'Stop it! You are turning everything upside down. I don't know! *Dammit, I am not going to cry again.*'

She jumped to her feet, thumping her fist into her open palm, and paced over to the window. 'You know, I could count on the fingers of one hand the number of times I cried before I came to England. Even before boarding school, I learnt that tears were futile, and at school—well, you learn very quickly that it is better not to show weakness. And now I seem to be weeping constantly. Eight months since my mother died, and only now am I beginning to appreciate that she really is gone. It doesn't make sense.

'You can never understand, you with your idyllic childhood here, growing up knowing how much you were loved, you can have no idea what it was like for me. Those miserable days at school, those cold little notes Maman wrote to me there about the weather, and the fishing, and—and nothing about her. Nothing about missing me. She didn't love me, I have known that for a long time.'

'I think she did.'

She jerked her head round to look at him. 'How can you possibly say that?'

'The locket. Worn round her neck every day of her life. Her only possession treasured enough to leave to you. Containing portraits of you and her, so close they are almost touching when the clasp is closed. A mother and her only daughter. Just because she never demonstrated her love doesn't mean it wasn't real. That locket tells me it was very real.'

Celeste dropped her head on to the cool of the window glass. When Jack put his arms around her waist, she resisted the urge to lean back into the comfort of his arms. She did not deserve comfort. This time the urge to confess outweighed the shame of what she must say. 'I had not seen her for a year before she died. The last time—the last time…'

She kept her eyes on the garden through the window glass which was misting over with her breath. 'Yesterday, when I said that she didn't give me a chance, it was a lie. Just after Henri died, Maman came to Paris. She told me that now she had done her duty by Henri, she wanted to heal the rift between us. I—I—I was angry with her. I told her that she had made her choice when she sent me off to boarding school at his behest. She did not protest very much. I presumed that the offer was more of a token than— No, I won't make excuses.'

Celeste turned around, facing Jack unflinchingly. 'I sent her packing. I could not forgive her for choosing Henri over me. When I was ten years old, I begged Maman not to send me away, but she chose to do what Henri wanted. Because she owed him our lives, she did as he asked, the letter says. Perhaps if I'd given her a chance that day in Paris, she would have explained it to me, but I did not. We were estranged for a long time but that last year, our estrangement was my fault alone. I feel such guilt. You would not understand such guilt. There is a part of me, you know, that thinks I deserve to suffer now. A part of me that thinks I do not deserve answers. Jack, I don't want you to be under the misapprehension that I'm an innocent victim.'

'Celeste, for God's sake, you had a lifetime's experience of her not explaining. You can't be thinking that what she did is your fault.'

'Can't I?'

'No.' Jack gave her a gentle shake. 'No. You don't know if it would have made any difference. You cannot know for certain if she would ever have trusted you enough.'

'Yes, I have tried to tell myself that. I am not a

martyr. I have tried.' Celeste shook her head wearily. 'For months, trying, pretending, and until I came here it was working—I thought. But now I can't pretend.'

'Celeste, I repeat, it's not your fault.'

'Jack, you can't know that any more than I can. You don't understand...'

'I understand a damn sight more than you think.'

'Those soldiers you told me about, yes, but they were not your family. You were not directly responsible.' She bit her lip hard enough to draw blood. 'Perhaps this dark secret of Maman's would have sent her to her grave regardless of what I did. But there is the possibility that she might have confided in me if I had given her one last opportunity. It's possible that she might still be alive today as a result.'

'Speculation is pointless, it changes nothing.' Jack's tone was harsh. His fists were clenched. 'You can dig up the skeletons of your mother's past. They might be gruesome, or they might be nothing at all, but whatever they are, they cannot alter what happened. It was her act, not yours. You can't let the guilt destroy you.' His eyes went quite blank. 'You can never know if it would have made a difference. There are so many imponderables. If you had kept your mouth shut. If you had not been so determined to see for yourself. If you had not spilled your guts. If you had not—'

He broke off, staring at her as if she were a spectre. His expression frightened her in its intensity. 'You will never know, but if you keep asking, one thing is for certain. You will tear yourself apart. That much, I most certainly understand.'

Celeste stared at the door as it slammed shut behind him. She sank down on to the sofa. She felt as if she were seeing her life through a shattered mirror. Everything she thought she knew about herself had become distorted. The barrier which her mother had erected between them was bizarrely, in death, beginning to break down. In doing so, it was not only destroying Celeste's idea of her mother, it was destroying her notion of herself.

She curled up, squeezing her eyes closed, but the tears leaked out regardless. Was she tearing herself apart for no purpose? No, she had a purpose. She had to know. And when she did, she would be healed, not broken.

And as for Jack? *If you had kept your mouth shut. If you had not been so determined to see for yourself. If you had not spilled your guts.* He had clearly been talking about himself. What had he been so determined to see? What did it mean, to spill his guts? Had he been ill? Or did he mean he had talked? Given away secrets?

'*Non,*' Celeste muttered. Jack was no traitor, on that she would stake her own life. Then what was Jack? 'I could as well ask, what is Celeste,' she muttered as exhaustion overtook her.

Jack sat at the window of his bedchamber, watching the grey light of dawn appear in the night sky and replaying his conversation with Celeste in his head for the hundredth time.

Guilt. From the moment she had told him that her mother had taken her own life, Jack had known that guilt would eventually overwhelm her. He'd hoped that by helping her quest for answers, he'd postpone its onset but it was already too late. After yesterday's confession, she wouldn't be able to ignore it.

Jack was something of a connoisseur of guilt and all its insidious manifestations. Eating away at you. Keeping you awake. Torturing your dreams. Turning you inside out. He couldn't bear thinking of Celeste suffering the same fate. Celeste, who had worked so hard to escape her miserable childhood and make her own world. Celeste who was so confident, and so independent and so strong.

And now so vulnerable. He couldn't bear to think of what it would do to her, if she did not find the answers she sought. But then he already knew. Guilt would consume her. *As it was consuming him?*

Feeling his chest tightening, Jack pushed open the window and gulped in the fresh air. Outside, the sky had turned from grey to a hazy pink. It was time for his early-morning swim. Pulling off his nightshirt, Jack grabbed his breeches and shirt. As he pulled the window closed, he noticed a flutter of white in the garden below. Celeste, hatless as usual. Her hair was piled carelessly on top of her head, long tendrils of it hanging down, as if she had not even bothered to look in the mirror. Her gown was cream coloured, with short puffs of sleeves and a scooped neck, accentuating the golden glow of her skin.

She was barefoot. He could see tantalising glimpses of her toes as she walked. The deep flounce of her gown was already wet with dew. She paused, lifting her face to the pale sun, closing her eyes. Had she slept? What was she thinking? She was so very lovely, and she looked so very fragile.

She made for the path which would lead her to the lake. Jack watched as she reached the gate, hesitated, then turned away. Giving way to a sudden impulse, he headed out of his bedchamber, descending the stairs three at a time, and ran out into the garden.

'Celeste!'

'Jack.' His bare feet left a line of footprints in the damp grass behind him. He was dressed in only his leather breeches and his shirt. His hair was in disarray and he hadn't shaved.

'I'm going for my swim.'

'Then that is the signal for me to make myself scarce.'

He smiled, pushing his hair back from his face. 'Actually, I wondered if you would care to join me?'

He looked tired. He looked devastatingly dishevelled. He looked as if he had just risen from bed. He made her think of rumpled sheets and tangled limbs. Their tangled limbs. 'Join you?' Celeste repeated, dragging her eyes away from the tantalising glimpse of chest she could see at the opening of his shirt.

'At the lake. To swim. Assuming you can swim, that is?'

'I was brought up on the coast. Of course I can swim,' Celeste said, and then the significance of his offer struck home. The lake at this time of the morning was Jack's private domain, his sanctuary. For him to offer to share it with her was hugely significant. 'No, I would be intruding. After the last time...'

'This is different. I am inviting you as my guest.'

He tucked a strand of her hair behind her ear. His smile made her insides flutter. She was weary of questioning and analysing her thoughts and motives. The urge to just *be*, to surrender to a whim was irresistible. 'Then I accept your kind invitation,' Celeste said. 'I am extremely flattered, since I know how important your privacy is to you. I would very much like to join you for a swim. I should warn you though, I am rather good.'

Jack laughed. 'I am not so very shabby myself,' he said, opening the gate for her. 'I've come on a bit since you last saw me in action.'

'I remember thinking that you swam like a fish that had drunk too much wine.'

'Not so much now. Perhaps one small glass of Madeira.'

The path to the lake was narrow and dark. The earth was cool against her bare feet. She had not swum for so long. She loved the water. She had not allowed herself to miss it. Now, seeing the glint of the lake in the early morning sunshine, Celeste felt her spirits rise in anticipation. The water was a strange colour, nothing like the sea. Golden and greenish, with a hint of brown. She stretched her arms high above her head, lifting her face to the warm English sun, and laughed with delight.

Jack pulled his shirt over his head. His muscles rippled. She caught her breath. He really was magnificent to look at. 'I think I'd best retain these,' he said, indicating his breeches.

Celeste had been so intent upon the swim, she hadn't considered the delicate matter of attire. In Cassis, she had always swum naked. She loved the feel of the ocean on her skin. But in Cassis, she had always swum alone. She had never swum in the company of a man, and this man— She dragged her eyes away again.

'Changed your mind?'

Celeste shook her head. 'Go in. I will follow you but don't look.'

Jack laughed. 'I never make promises I can't keep,' he said, turning his back and beginning to wade into the water.

She watched him dive, and then swim strongly towards the far side. He barely laboured at all. His strength had all but returned. Celeste went behind the very hawthorn bush where she'd hidden that first day, and began to undress, quickly removing her gown, her corset and her petticoats. She was left wearing only her pantaloons and camisole. It was not an ideal outfit for bathing but she could not countenance the alternative.

She picked her way across the pebbles into the

shallows of the lake. Jack was at the far side again, swimming steadily. The water felt warm on her toes, the mud oozed around her feet in a not unpleasant manner. She waded in and gasped as the cool water soaked through her thin camisole and met her skin. Jack turned and began to head back towards her. Hurriedly, Celeste waded out, until the water was waist high, and then she dived into the cool water with relish and began to swim. It was not at all like the waters of Cassis, this English lake, but there was still that marvellous feeling of freedom. She struck out more strongly, heading for the opposite bank, kicking her legs behind her, and just before it became too shallow, she turned and began to swim back, passing Jack on the way.

She swam until her muscles protested, and then she turned over and floated, her eyes closed, careless of the mud and twigs and leaves tangling in her hair. For the first time since Maman had died, she felt relaxed, weightless, free. It was all still there, but it could wait. It could all wait. Rolling over to make her way back to shore, she saw Jack standing waist deep in the water, watching her.

She waded towards him. 'I think I have most of your brother's lake in my hair.'

'Did you enjoy that?'

'Oh—so, so much.' Celeste beamed at him. 'I had forgotten how swimming— It makes you forget everything.' Her smile faded. 'Is that why you...?'

'Yes. And for this.' Jack indicated his arm.

Celeste touched the puckered skin gently. 'Does it still hurt?'

'Not really.'

Sunlight danced on the water and in her eyes. Droplets of lake water clung to the rough smattering of hair on Jack's chest. Her camisole was plastered to her body like a second skin, making it completely transparent. Her nipples were hard and puckered with the cold, and clearly visible. Jack's eyes were riveted on them. She did not feel embarrassed. In fact she felt emboldened. Desire twisted inside her. Jack's eyes met hers. She stepped towards him. His arms went around her waist. His chest was surprisingly warm. It was not like before. No flare of anger to propel them towards each other. This time it was slow, a different kind of heat. She tilted her head. Sunlight dazzled her eyes until Jack's head blocked it, and his lips met hers.

Different. He tasted of lake. Cool. Tentative. Like a first kiss. A gentle tasting, the sweetest of touches. Slow. A kiss with no purpose but to kiss. And to kiss. And then to kiss again. She wrapped her arms around his neck. He pulled her closer. Kissing. Only kissing. Her arousal was languid, melting, none of the fierce flames of before. She could kiss him for ever. This was the kind of kiss that would never end. Lips and tongues in a slow dance. Hands smoothing, stroking. Skin clinging, damp, heating.

Jack traced the line of her throat with butter-fly kisses. He kissed the damp valley between her breasts. His mouth sought hers again, and their lips clung, still slowly, but deeper now. She kissed the pucker of his musket wound. She flattened her palms over the swell of his chest. His hands covered her breasts, making her nipples ache. The sweetest of aches, the gentlest but most insistent tugging of desire, making her sigh, and then making her moan.

She'd thought it was too much before. But this was too different. The dazed look in his eyes, his lack of resistance when she disentangled herself, told her he felt it too.

'Thank you,' she said gently, 'for the swim.' She began to wade ashore. She had hauled her gown over her wet undergarments and was wrapping the rest of her clothing into a bundle when Jack re-joined her. They walked slowly back to the Manor together in silence, words for once superfluous.

Chapter Seven

'A very proper, very English young lady.' Celeste repeated, looking blankly at Jack. They were in the studio, where she had been laying out her preliminary drawings to allow Lady Eleanor and Sir Charles to make their final selections, before she began the task of painting the actual canvases. 'You think that my mother was of genteel stock?'

Jack nodded. He had taken a seat across from her at the table. In the two days which had passed since their early-morning swim, they had both been careful not to mention it or the kiss which had followed. Though as far as Celeste was concerned, it hung in the air, almost palpably, every time she looked at him.

She shuffled a bundle of rejected sketches, quite unnecessarily. 'What makes you come to this conclusion?'

Jack tapped his pencil on the notebook in front of him. 'A number of little things. Hasn't it ever struck you as odd, for example, that the wife of a school teacher would employ a cook?'

'I've never given it much thought. It's just how things were.'

'Then there's this school you attended in Paris. It sounds as if it was a good one.'

Celeste frowned. 'The girls were from good families. Titled, mostly, or very wealthy. Or both. That was one of the problems I had to deal with, being neither.'

'You mean you were bullied?' Jack's hand tightened on his pencil. 'I don't know why, but I assumed that sort of thing was confined to boys.'

'If you mean fighting, then it most likely is. Girls are more subtle,' Celeste said grimly. 'It doesn't matter, I learned to hold my own. Besides, I cannot believe it was really so grand a school,' she rushed on, having no desire to recall how effective the bullying had been. 'We were not permitted a fire except in the dead of winter and then never in the dormitory. And the bedΔsheets were almost threadbare. It was hardly luxurious.'

'Which confirms my point,' Jack said with a tight smile. 'My so-called exclusive prep school had dormitories that would have delighted a Spartan. Such privations don't come cheap. Then there is her knowledge of dinner-party etiquette. And the comment about—what was it—a woman's reputation. Your mother could draw and paint, but she couldn't cook. Could she sew?'

'She taught me to embroider.'

'Precisely.'

Jack looked pleased. Celeste was unconvinced. 'I never thought much about my mother's origins. Why should I, when Maman was so determined that she had none? She would have preferred me to believe she had been baked like dough in an oven.' Blind baked, Celeste added to herself, a brittle pastry with a hard crust.

She pushed back her chair and went over to her favourite spot at the window. Was she being unfair? Maman had been cold, distant, aloof. Certainly stern, and yet at other times she had looked...

Just as Jack had done that first morning at the lake.

Despair? Anguish? Whatever label one put on it, it was obvious now that her mother had indeed suffered. And she, Celeste, had been oblivious to it. All the signs had been right in front of her nose, and she had not noticed them. She shook her head in disgust at herself. 'I have been an idiot! For an artist, quite the blind woman. Thinking I was the poor little schoolgirl, when really it was a case of all the other little schoolgirls being so very rich.'

Her fingers went to the locket around her neck. 'That's another thing,' Jack said almost apologetically. 'I doubt very much that your locket is a trinket. In fact I think you'll find it's made of diamonds and sapphire, not glass. There's a maker's mark. I'll show you.'

Celeste took the locket off obediently. There it was. She looked at the portraits inside, painted in such a way that her mother gazed across at her. Lovingly? Her mother, who had claimed in her last letter, that she had always loved her. Was this locket proof as

Jack said? Celeste found this almost impossible to believe.

Almost? She touched the miniature of her mother with the tip of her finger, an echo of Jack's gesture with his own mother's picture in the portrait gallery, she realised. But his had been one of unmistakable affection and love. Was hers?

She looked up, smiling faintly at Jack. 'You have given me a great deal to think about,' she said, snapping the locket shut.

A rap on the door heralded the arrival of her patrons. Celeste quickly made the final touches to her arrangement of sketches, ensuring the ones she favoured were most prominent, but when the door opened, it was to reveal Lady Eleanor alone.

'My husband sends his apologies, *Mademoiselle*, he will be unable to join us this morning, but he desired me to make some preliminary selections from your work. I trust this is satisfactory?'

Without waiting for an answer, her ladyship made straight for the table where the sketches were laid out and began sifting through them. Jack cast Celeste an eloquent glance, and began unobtrusively to push the preferred drawings towards his brother's wife.

'Of course, these are just very rudimentary sketches to give you an idea of what the finished work would look like,' Celeste said, 'but I hope they are sufficient to allow you to make some decisions on the sequence in which you would like me to paint the formal gardens.'

Lady Eleanor examined the sketches carefully. It had always amused Celeste to witness her patrons' reactions at this stage. Seeing their estates spread out before them on paper almost always made them view their properties afresh, made them somehow grander, more magnificent, which in turn added to their own sense of consequence.

Lady Eleanor was no different. 'I must say, I had not appreciated the epic sweep of the estate. You have managed to cover a great deal of ground in a very short time.'

'Thank you. Monsieur Trestain has been most helpful. He has an excellent eye for the most pleasing views.'

'Well, it is comforting to know that he has managed to occupy himself gainfully,' Lady Eleanor said pointedly. 'I expect you, *Mademoiselle*, being a—a woman of the world are rather more equipped to deal with Jack's outbursts than a child. Robert,' she continued, addressing Jack directly, 'was sobbing his little heart out the other day after his encounter with you.'

Jack blanched. Celeste felt her fists curl. 'If you do not mind me saying,' she said, 'when Jack refused Robert's request in a perfectly reasonable manner, it was the child who threw the tantrum, not Jack.'

'Celeste.' Jack held up his hand to quiet her. 'I am very sorry if I upset Robert, Eleanor.'

'My son, like all small boys, is obsessed with all things military,' her ladyship replied, her stiff manner giving way to a plaintive one. 'He would hang on your every word for a first-hand account of Waterloo. Your brother tells me I must try to stop him bothering you, but Robert is such a naturally inquisitive little chap.'

'He reminds me very much of Charlie at that age,' Jack said. 'Mad keen on fishing.'

'And equally eager to hear his uncle's account of what is our nation's greatest victory. No disrespect intended, *Mademoiselle*. Really, Jack, is that too much to ask? Frankly, I'm at a loss to fathom you these days. I remember a time when you were more than happy to sit up until dawn, regaling Charles with your exploits. I know you are still recovering from your wounds, and that we must all make allowances for your—your— For the anguish you are suffering at having witnessed the deaths of so many of your comrades, but…'

'Is that what Charlie thinks it is?' Jack shook his head when Lady Eleanor made to answer. 'No matter. I am sorry to have upset him, but I cannot— The days of my boasting of my army exploits are over, Eleanor, but I am more than happy to take Robert fishing instead.'

'But I do not see…' Making an obvious effort, Lady Eleanor bit back her remonstration. 'That is kind of you, Jack.'

'It is nothing. I do care for the boy, you know, regardless of how it may appear.' Jack picked up some of Celeste's sketches. 'In the meantime, let us concentrate on your selections. Look at this study of the Topiary Garden. Do you not think that it is a great shame to have it cut down? When you see it afresh like this, through *Mademoiselle*'s clever eye, it really is quite lovely and wants only a little tidying up to bring it back to its former glory.'

'Rather more than a little tidying up,' Lady Eleanor replied, 'and it is so very gloomy.'

Jack picked up another view of the Topiary Garden. 'Look at this, though. Mademoiselle Marmion was telling me that though she's painted some of the grandest estates in France, the Trestain Manor Topiary Garden is one of the finest examples she has ever seen.'

Lady Eleanor looked doubtfully at the sketch. 'Really? I had no idea. Is this true, *Mademoiselle*?'

'Why, yes,' Celeste replied, intensely relieved that Jack had managed to turn the subject. 'In France, the art of topiary is much admired. The best examples attract admirers from all over the country. I think that your garden, with only a few changes, could do the same.'

'You would be leading the way for England,' Jack said. 'Your good sense in preserving the garden will be appreciated by generations of Trestains to come. Think about that, Eleanor.'

Her ladyship did, rewarding Celeste with a tight smile. 'I wonder, *Mademoiselle*, if it is not too much trouble, if you could perhaps give me the benefit of your artistic eye and suggest a few enhancements. I can then discuss them with Sir Charles and our landscaper. Awarding you full credit for your contribution of course.'

Celeste nodded, slanting Jack a complicit smile. Lady Eleanor continued to sift through the drawings, laying a small selection to one side which, Celeste was pleased to note, contained most of her own favourites.

'These are really very good, *Mademoiselle*,' she said, sounding as if she meant it. 'I am most pleased. Sir Charles will make the final selection tomorrow. You will excuse me now, I must go and speak to cook. Your Aunt Christina's long-awaited annual gift of a haunch of prime Highland venison has finally arrived, Jack. Something of a family tradition, *Mademoiselle*,' she added by way of explanation. 'Every year we have a special banquet when it arrives. We will be celebrating the occasion tonight.'

Jack shifted uncomfortably, looking not at all enamoured by the prospect.

'Your brother,' Lady Eleanor said, 'will be very much gratified by your presence. I believe that your aunt, in the accompanying letter, was most eager for you to partake of the beast, and particularly requested that Charles give her an account of the dinner—for it seems she has no hope of a letter from you.'

'I have had my arm in a splint these past two months, Eleanor, in case it has escaped your attention.'

Her ladyship turned to Celeste, ignoring this remark. 'Mademoiselle Marmion, I will entreat you to use any influence you have with Jack. Is it really so much to ask that he joins us *en famille* for a special dinner sent all the way from Scotland by his favourite relative?'

Celeste, taken aback by Lady Eleanor's consulting her on any subject save art, found herself shaking her head.

'You see? Mademoiselle Marmion agrees,' her ladyship said, turning back to Jack.

'I don't think...'

But Celeste's role had, it seemed, been played. 'It is not as if we are even holding the usual grand banquet,' Lady Eleanor said. 'Not a single guest. Not even our closest neighbours. I told Charles that they would be most offended, but he said he cared nothing for any guest save you. So I take it you will not be letting him down?'

'Oh, for God's sake, Eleanor, what a damned— dashed fuss over a bite of dinner. Yes,' Jack said, 'I'll be there. Satisfied?'

'Your brother will be, and that is what matters to me. You too are cordially invited of course, Mademoiselle Marmion. Until tonight, then.'

Lady Eleanor swept from the studio. Jack stared at the door, his jaw working. 'It is just dinner,' Celeste said tentatively. 'Though I am surprised Lady Eleanor thinks me worthy of your aunt's precious venison.'

Jack grimaced. 'Obviously, she assumes that your presence makes the chances of my attendance more likely.'

Celeste coloured. 'Have we been indiscreet?' Her colour deepened. 'You do not think that someone saw us at the lake the other morning?' It was the first time either of them had mentioned it. She wished immediately she had not. Unlike those other kisses, the memory of this one was not inflammatory, but bittersweet.

'No,' Jack said, 'I'm sure no one saw us. It's one of the things I like about that place, it's completely private.'

'Unless someone hides behind a hawthorn tree.'

Jack's smile was twisted. 'As with so many things, you are the exception that proves the rule.'

Their eyes met and held. He reached out to touch her cheek. She turned her head. Her lips brushed his palm.

'Celeste.' His voice was filled with the same longing she felt. He took a step towards her, then halted. 'You must be keen to get to work, now Eleanor has made some decisions. I will see you at this blasted dinner.'

Confused, frustrated, as much by her own reaction as Jack's, Celeste turned her back on the closed door and set about stretching some canvases.

Jack put the final touches to his cravat. It was not perfect, but it would do. At times like this, he missed his faithful army batman, but Alfred was happily ensconced many hundreds of miles away as the landlord of the Bricklayer's Arms in Leeds, and besides, the last thing Jack really wanted was proximity to any of his former comrades. Still, no one could tie a cravat like Alfred.

He pulled on his waistcoat. Grey satin stripes, and one of his best. Quite wasted in the country, but Eleanor would appreciate the effort he was making. As she'd appreciate the formality of his cutaway black coat and silk breeches. They were considerably looser on him than the last time he'd worn them to the now-infamous ball held by Lady Richmond on the eve of Waterloo. He closed his eyes, but it seemed a set of evening clothes, even one with such associations, did not trigger anything other than a vague discomfort, and that was coming from his shoes, which had always pinched.

Perhaps he was on the mend, mentally as well as physically? Perhaps this thing, this nostalgia, whatever the hell it was, would heal, as his shoulder was doing, and his arm.

'Nostalgia,' Jack said viciously as he shrugged himself into his coat. Such a soft, comfortable little word to describe what he felt. Was it all in his head? But the pain, the tearing blackness, the white heat of his uncontrollable fury, the terror that made him run from himself, the sweats and the shakes, and the dull ache in his head, they were all too real.

'I am *not* mad.' He jumped as the porcelain dish containing his cuff-links clattered to the floor. It was not broken, thank the Lord. He picked up the scattered links, replacing the dish carefully. If he was insane he wouldn't recognise or understand what it was that made him feel the way he did. And that, he understood only too well. How could he fail too when he lived through it again and again, almost every night without fail?

Seated at the dressing table, a brush in one hand, he stared at his reflection. What he didn't understand was that for two years he had functioned reasonably well. The dream had been sporadic. He'd carried on doing what he'd always done. True, there had been doubts, but none strong enough to stop him doing his duty, stop him believing that doing his duty was paramount. Only after Waterloo, when peace was indisputable, when war was over, had his symptoms escalated.

And only after Celeste arrived at Trestain Manor, had he had to cope with not only enduring the symptoms, but confronting the fact that they were in danger of ruining his life.

A flicker of rebellion kindled in his heart. He didn't want to spend his life enduring. He wanted to have his life *back*. Not the old one, that was gone for ever, but something preferable to this shadow of a life. Celeste sent his head spinning, she forced him to face a good many unpalatable truths, but she also sent blood rushing to parts of him he'd thought dormant. It frightened him, the thought of giving free reign to the passion she ignited, because he had retained such a tight grip on himself for so long, it was almost impossible for him to think about letting go.

Almost. Jack picked up his other brush and set about taming his hair. Almost was better than completely. Instead of dreading tonight, what he needed to do was to see it as a test. A possible step forward on the road to recovery.

Celeste was nervous, though she couldn't account for it. She stood clutching the obligatory small glass of Madeira wine, half-listening to Sir Charles recount a complicated anecdote which seemed to involve a miller, his wife, the village baker, a neighbouring magistrate and, if her ears were not deceiving her, a wheel of Stilton cheese. Celeste took another sip of the sweet wine and smoothed down her gown. It was one of her plainest, of russet-coloured crêpe with a deep V-shaped neckline and high puffed sleeves, the only embellishment being a corded sash tied around the high waistline. Lady Eleanor was dressed far more elaborately in lilac lace. Sir Charles was in full evening dress for the first time since her arrival. Obviously, Auntie Kirsty's haunch of venison demanded a major effort be made to mark the auspicious occasion. She now regretted her understated choice of attire.

Jack entered the salon just as Lady Eleanor was consulting the clock on the mantel for the third time. He too wore full evening dress. His hair was tamed ruthlessly, his jaw freshly shaved. The deceptively simple cut of his coat, the stark black of the silk suited him. As he strode across the room to bow over Lady Eleanor's hand, Celeste could not help comparing the two brothers, so similarly attired, and so very different. Sir Charles was probably more classically handsome, but Jack's imperfections, his austere countenance, were what made him, in Celeste's eyes, by far the more attractive of the two. She remembered thinking that first day, when she had watched him swimming naked in the lake, that he looked like a man who courted danger.

Heat flooded through her. She should not be thinking of him naked, especially not when he was bowing over her hand. Celeste dipped a formal curtsy, lowering her head to hide her flush. *'Monsieur.'*

'Mademoiselle. You look beautiful as ever.'

'And you too look very handsome.' Though now she studied him, she thought he looked tense. There was no time to pursue the cause of this, however, for at that moment Lady Eleanor's footman sounded a gong, Sir Charles took his wife's hand and led the small procession out into the hall and across into the dining room.

Jack was seated opposite her. Sir Charles led the conversation which was primarily concerned with previous haunches of venison and the large parties at which they had been consumed.

'I hope you've not deprived your neighbours of their annual treat on account of me,' Jack said to Eleanor. 'After all, it's not as if I've been able to attend more than twice in the last dozen years, while they looked forward to it every year.'

'Well, to be honest, Jack, we did not think—'

'What Eleanor means is that we thought it would be cosier to keep it to just the family,' Sir Charles interrupted hurriedly.

Jack put down his wine glass carefully. 'Cosier,' he said with a cold smile. 'I see.'

Sir Charles rubbed his hands together. 'Good. Excellent. It is— You must know, Jack, it is good to see you at the table.'

'You fret about me too much, Charlie.' Jack pushed his glass aside. 'I've heard reports in the village that it's going to be a bumper harvest. What do you say?'

His brother was no fool, but as he was, Celeste had noted several times, most definitely a man who avoided confrontation, he was therefore happy to be diverted. Lady Eleanor's footmen brought in a procession of side dishes. Her ladyship supervised the placing of each, and the brothers chatted about crops. At least, Sir Charles talked, and Jack prompted, saying just enough to keep the conversation ticking over.

The first of the side dishes was already going cold when the door was held open by one footman, and two more entered the dining room bearing an enormous copper platter. Celeste, who was by now rather hungry, felt her mouth watering. The aroma coming from the venison was delicious. The meat looked succulent. Across from her, she caught Jack's hand curling tightly around the stem of his glass, though he quickly put it down when he noticed her watching him.

She couldn't understand what was wrong with him. The platter was placed in front of Sir Charles, who made a great show of sharpening the carving knife on a steel before picking up the fork. Blood and juices trickled from the roast haunch as he began to carve through the charred skin.

A footman placed a side dish in front of Jack. A silver tureen containing vegetable broth of some sort, redolent with the herbs of Provence. Surprised, Celeste turned to Lady Eleanor. 'What is that dish? It smells exactly like home,' she said.

'Indeed,' her ladyship said, gratified. 'I had cook

concoct it as a small gesture to make you feel welcome. I discovered it in a receipt book belonging to Sir Charles's mother. She was Scottish, you know. I believe the Scots have a great affinity with you French. The Auld Alliance, I believe it is—good heavens, Jack, what on earth is the matter?'

He had turned a deathly pale. As he pushed his chair back, he caught the dish of broth and sent it flying from the footman's hand. Jack got to his feet, clutching the table and swaying. His skin now had a greenish hue. He was staring at the venison, his eyes dark with horror.

'Dear lord, I think he is going to be ill, Charles,' Lady Eleanor exclaimed, turning rather green herself. 'Charles. Charles!'

Her husband jumped to his feet at the same time as Celeste pushed back her chair and got to hers. Jack swayed. He looked as if he was about to crumple, but when his brother tried to put his arm around him, he swatted it away and began to lurch for the door, his mouth over his hand. Celeste reached him as he clutched the handle. He pushed her to one side and threw himself out into the hallway and from there out of the front door and into the night air.

Another sleepless night, this one thanks not to his dream but to his lingering and complete mortification. Jack had not actually been physically ill last night. He was trying very hard to see that as some sort of progress, but as he had lain sleepless and sweating in his bed, he replayed the entire hideous scene over and over, to the point where he had thought himself beyond embarrassment. If the dinner had been a test, he'd failed it spectacularly.

Unable to face anyone, knowing he must eventually face them all, he had been wandering aimlessly around the grounds for hours. Exhausted, hungry but unable to contemplate eating, he was instead contemplating retiring to his bed when the sound of voices drifted out through the long French window which gave on to Celeste's studio.

'Yes, yes, these are all excellent, *Mademoiselle*,' he heard Charlie say.

His brother was giving his approval to the selection of sketches to be painted. They would all three of them be there. It was an ideal opportunity for Jack to make himself scarce, but he found himself instead positioned behind a trellis which obscured him, but also afforded a view into the studio. It was inevitable that the subject of the dinner would come up. What would their take on it be? Information was the best of ammunition after all. It seemed old habits died hard.

Charlie, unlike his wife, who had studied each of Celeste's sketches with a great deal of care, gave each a fairly cursory glance, and seemed indiscriminately happy with every one of them. Standing beside him, Celeste, looking pale, with dark circles under her eyes, was struggling to give her patron her full attention. Her gaze drifted over to the window.

Jack froze, though she could not possibly see him. It was ridiculous to be hiding here. He should join them. His feet refused to comply. He wondered fleetingly if this was how Celeste had felt that day—which seemed like months ago—when she had watched him swimming.

Charlie was looking at a view of the lake now. No, he had selected one. Now he was dithering between two views of the Topiary Garden, and Jack could see Celeste making a huge effort not to try to steer him towards the one she herself preferred. She smiled when he opted for it, and pushed the pinery sketches towards him.

'Yes. Excellent.' Charlie rubbed his hands together again, a sure sign he was nervous. 'I wonder if I may be so bold, *Mademoiselle*,' he said, 'as to enquire how you find my brother?'

Jack's hackles rose. Celeste looked wary. 'I am not sure what you mean. He has been most helpful.'

'Yes, yes. I can see that.' Charlie pursed his lips. 'It cannot have escaped your notice, *Mademoiselle*, that my brother is not quite— That he is not— That in short, he is rather out of sorts. On occasion.'

'He has been wounded. I think his arm has given him a great deal of pain. What do you think of this vista, Sir Charles?'

Charlie ignored the proffered sketch. 'It amounts to more than tetchiness, *Mademoiselle*. More than the residual pain from a wound now healed. Last night— for heaven's sake, you witnessed what occurred last night. What in the name of all that's sacred was that about, do you think?'

Celeste blanched. 'I don't know. I was as much— I don't know.'

Charlie threw the sketch down. 'The time has come to stop beating about the bush. My wife and I are at our wits' end. We have tried but we seem singularly ill equipped to help him, *Mademoiselle*, indeed I think we unintentionally exacerbate matters.'

Jack strained forward. Charlie was leaning over Celeste. Celeste, hindered by the table, was bending backwards. 'I am fain to embroil you in a private family matter,' his brother said, 'but it has struck both my wife and myself that you seem to be able to…well, to influence Jack in a way we cannot.'

'*Monsieur*, Sir Charles, I do not…'

'You do. He listens to you. Eleanor says that it was only at your behest that he finally consented to come to dinner last night.'

'No.' Celeste flushed. 'That is, I might have— But it was very wrong of me. Jack was eager to please you too, *Monsieur*—Sir Charles. He is not— He— I should not have—'

'What sparked such an extreme reaction out of the blue like that—that's what I want to know. It can't go on, that much is certain.'

Clearly agitated now, Charlie thumped his fist on the table. Jack felt his own fists curl. Appalled, sick to the stomach and furious, he forced himself to listen.

'He used to be the most even-tempered of chaps,' Charlie was saying, 'and now one must constantly be treading on eggshells around him. He barely eats. He hardly sleeps. I don't know how many times the chambermaid has reported some piece of broken china from his bedchamber. Then there is the way he— He— Our little boy, Robert.'

'You remember, Mademoiselle Marmion was witness to one of those episodes in the portrait gallery the other day, my love.'

'Lady Eleanor, I really do think that your son—'

'I hate to say it,' Charlie interrupted again. 'It pains me a great deal to say it, but I must protect my child from upset or worse. Last night, you will admit, *Mademoiselle*, that Jack was quite out of control?'

'He was— I admit he was not himself.'

Celeste! It was like a punch in the gut. Jack closed his eyes, only to find himself immediately swamped with the smell of that damned soup and the ferrous tang of bloody meat and scorched flesh. He swayed, clutching at the trellis for support. He opened his eyes. Deep breaths. More.

It was as if he was watching a play, the voices booming and fading, his own vision wavering. Celeste was wringing her hands. Charlie was tirading. Celeste was shaking her head. Jack shook his like a dog after a swim.

'We don't know,' Charlie was saying. 'That's the nub of it, we simply don't know. My brother is not the man he was. I hoped we could help him. Fresh country air, good food, that sort of thing. But he is getting worse. We don't know what he will do next, and I'm not sure we can afford to wait and see. I would suggest he see a medical man, one who specialises in matters of the mind, but…but dear God, I cannot contemplate having my brother confined.'

Confined? Stunned, Jack wondered if he'd misheard.

'Confined!' Celeste went quite still. 'Sir Charles, are you saying that you believe Jack—Monsieur Trestain is—is of unsound mind?'

Silence greeted this remark. Jack waited, every muscle clenched so tight his jaw ached. Charlie shuffled his feet. He rubbed his hands together. He cast Eleanor an anguished look. Then he sighed. 'I must confess with a heavy heart that I fear it may be the case,' he said, and Jack, with a growl of fury, launched himself through the French doors and into the studio.

Lady Eleanor screamed. Sir Charles froze in mid-sentence. Jack's expression was thunderous and extremely intimidating, but instead of cowering, Celeste caught herself at the last moment and stood her ground.

He looked wild. His eyes were stormy. His fingers were furling and unfurling into fists. 'I am of a certainty *not* mad, Charlie.'

'I didn't say—'

'You did.' Jack took a menacing step towards his brother. Sir Charles shrank back. '"I must confess... I fear it may be the case" is what you said.'

'Yes, and I also said it was with a very heavy heart I did so,' Charlie countered.

'You should not have been listening in to a private conversation,' Lady Eleanor said primly. 'Eavesdroppers, it is well known, never hear any good of themselves.'

'Eavesdropping is one of the many things I was required to do to protect my country,' Jack said, rounding on her with a snarl. 'A duty I discharged assiduously. Would you rather I had not?'

Her ladyship blanched, but Jack turned his attention back to his brother. 'Tell me I am not mad, Charlie.'

'Well, you must admit, you're not precisely stable, old chap,' Sir Charles said, accompanied by a feeble attempt at a smile, in an utterly misguided attempt to inject humour into the situation.

Jack recoiled, whirling around to face Celeste. 'And you! You must think it too, else you would not have asked the question in the first place. You, of all people! I thought...'

'Jack...' Celeste took hold of his arm and gave it a shake '...Jack, you must know that I don't think...'

He shook her off. He staggered against a gilt-leafed side table. The bowl of dried flowers which sat on it clattered to the ground and smashed. He stared at them all blankly.

Celeste took hold of his arm once again. 'Jack.'

He removed her fingers gently. 'Let me alone.' He straightened his shoulders and marched towards the door. It closed behind him gently.

Chapter Eight

'Why did you say that he was not stable?' Celeste turned furiously on Sir Charles. 'You could not have said anything more damaging had you tried. Jack has not lost his mind, but a part of him is afraid he might. *Eh, bien*, he asks his only brother for a little reassurance and what does he get?'

Sir Charles looked shocked to the core. 'I did not intend— I would never— With respect, *Mademoiselle*, you have been here a matter of days. Eleanor and I have been living with this situation for months. We have tried ignoring him, we have tried pretending nothing is wrong, and now we have tried confronting him. You saw the effect. I am most—most— I am extremely concerned about my brother.'

Lady Eleanor put a comforting hand on her husband's arm. 'Sir Charles has only his brother's best interests at heart. This has been a terrible strain for all of us. I am as shaken as my husband by Jack's decline. We have the advantage over you, *Mademoi-*

selle, of knowing Jack before this—this change. You must believe me when I tell you it is drastic. And then there is our son.'

'Jack loves Robert, *Madame*—Lady Eleanor. That is precisely why he doesn't want to fill his head with the barbarity of war. You asked me how I *found* Jack. Well, I will tell you, for what it is worth. I think he is a deeply unhappy man, and also a very brave one. I think that he has seen and done things that none of us can even imagine. Things so horrific he cannot sleep for thinking of it. All this, he has done unquestioningly in the name of you and your country and your little boy. I think he deserves better than to be told by his own flesh and blood that he is mad. That is what I think. Now, if you'll excuse me, I'm going to find him.'

'But, *Mademoiselle*, Jack made it very clear he wanted to be left alone, I don't think…'

Ignoring Sir Charles, Celeste made her way out of the French window, and quickly across the stretch of lawn. She wondered if she had managed for the first time ever to get herself dismissed from a commission, but she could not, at this moment, bring herself to care. She did not know where Jack had gone but she had a pretty good idea where to start looking.

He was sitting on a rock, casting pebbles into the lake, his expression forbidding. Celeste was tempted, for a moment, to turn tail. Perhaps Sir Charles was right, and it would be best to leave him alone. She had no idea what to say. She had no idea what was wrong with Jack, but she had missed the chance once before, to try to comfort a person in torment, and she was not going to repeat the mistake by running away from a similar situation.

'Did Charlie send you to check on me?' he demanded as she sat down cautiously on the boulder beside him. 'Not brave enough to come himself, I suppose.'

'He thought you would be best left alone.'

Jack threw another pebble into the water. 'He was right.'

Celeste forced herself to remain seated.

Jack threw another pebble forcefully into the water. 'I won't harm myself, if that's what you're worried about. I would not inflict *that* on Charlie, on top of everything else, so you can leave with a clear conscience.'

He was angry. He was embarrassed, no doubt. He was obviously much more hurt than he cared to let on. He didn't mean it. Still, his barb hit painfully home. Celeste flinched.

Jack swore. 'I'm sorry. God, I'm sorry. That was a foul thing to say to you, of all people.'

'Yes, it was.'

Jack cast another pebble. 'Is that why you're here? Do you think I would…?'

'No. And nor does Sir Charles, before you ask.'

'Small compensation, when my own brother thinks I need to be locked up in Bedlam.'

'Your brother is *worried* about you. He doesn't know how best to help you.'

Jack threw the small bundle of remaining pebbles he had into the lake and jumped to his feet. 'Do you not think that if I knew of some cure for what ails me I'd have taken it by now? Do you think I enjoy being like this? Have you any idea what it's like for me to be so—so at the whim of emotions I can't control? Me! Discipline and order is what my life's been about until now. Men and information, that's what I deal in. I turn men into soldiers. I turn meaningless jumbles of letters and numbers into sequences and patterns. That's what I do, Celeste—that's what I did. Not any more. Now I can't make sense of anything.'

He turned away from her, pinching the bridge of his nose viciously between his thumb and forefinger. What he said resonated so strongly with her, she was tempted to tell him so, but what good would it do, to tell him that she too felt as if the world made no sense any more? 'I think you do understand some things, though,' she said. 'Whatever it was at dinner that made you sick, you knew it would. That's why you avoid dinner.'

'And would have avoided it again last night were it not for you.' He turned on her, his eyes flashing fury.

'That's not fair. I did not know you…'

'No, you didn't, but you smiled that winsome smile of yours, and you looked at me with those big brown eyes and you made it impossible for me to say no.'

She knew he was simply trying to hurt her, lashing out like a wounded animal, but the injustice of this was too much. 'I did no such thing!' Celeste jumped to her feet. 'I don't have a winsome smile. I am not a fool. I look in the mirror, and I see I have the kind of face men find attractive, but I am not— I have never, ever, been one of those women who use a mere quirk of nature to manipulate people. *Never*.'

Jack swore again. 'I'm sorry,' he snapped, sounding anything but. 'Very well, you did not force me into that damned dinner, but if it had not been that, it would have been something else.'

'What do you mean by that?' Celeste folded her arms and glared at him.

'You,' Jack said. 'From the moment I first saw you, you've tormented me. Spying on me. Kissing me. Goading me. Tempting me. As if I didn't have enough to keep me awake at nights without torturing myself with visions of you, of us. I can barely keep my hands off you. I've never been that sort of man before. I've never lost my temper with Robert before. I've never come so near to spilling my guts on the dinner table before. And what is the common factor in all this? You.'

'That is completely outrageous! I could say the exact same thing of you. You make me feel as if I am some sort of—of insatiable temptress,' Celeste exclaimed. 'And look at me now, screeching like a fishwife. I never shout. I never cry. I never have any difficulty whatsoever in keeping my hands and my lips and my body to myself. I am a calm person, I am a cold person, even, and yet with you...' She threw her hands into the air.

'You realise how ridiculous you sound,' Jack said.

Even through her temper, she did. Celeste bit her lip and tried to glower.

He sighed. 'How ridiculous we both sound.'

She took a tentative step towards him. 'I didn't come here to harangue you. I'm sorry.'

'I deserved it.' Jack managed a wry smile. 'You are most definitely not the kind of woman who uses her charms to get her own way. I went to dinner last night of my own accord. It was a sort of test. Which I failed rather spectacularly.'

Celeste took another step towards him. 'What happened, Jack?'

He stared out over the lake. He picked up a stone, then let if fall. 'It's just— There are smells. Certain smells.'

'The blood! You mean the blood from the meat?'

'No. No, it's not the blood. I've seen too much blood for it to be— Not on its own.' He picked up another stone and began to turn it over and over in his hands. 'I thought it might be. Eleanor is very fond of serving up roast beef, charred and bloody in the English tradition, so I do tend to avoid that, just in case...' He closed his eyes momentarily. 'But I would have been fine last night, I think, if it hadn't been for the stew she had specially made for you.'

'The Provençal dish?' Celeste's face fell. 'So it was my fault?'

'No. I did blame you, but I wasn't exactly rational. Don't ask me, I can't explain. Given my spectacular outburst back there. I'm not surprised Charlie thinks I'm mad.'

Celeste caught his hand. 'Jack, you know you are not.'

'I do know that much, actually.' He gently disengaged himself. 'You know, if Robert is hoping to catch a trout here, I reckon he'll be disappointed. I saw a heron take one this morning. If it's been here awhile, there will be precious little left.'

'I think they will be draining it very soon. You will have to find somewhere else to swim.'

'I'm thinking of going to London.'

Celeste swallowed hard. 'London?'

'I'm sick of kicking my heels here, and I'm becoming an embarrassment to Charlie and Eleanor—they didn't even feel they could risk inviting their friends to dinner, for God's sake. And as it turns out, they were right.'

'Jack…'

'Celeste, I need to get away from here. And from you. You are far too much of a distraction—as I fear I am, for you. You need to concentrate on your painting, and I need to be doing something. I will take your locket and ring with me, if I may, do some digging, lean on my contacts a bit,' Jack said with a tight smile, 'I do still have some.'

'But you will be coming back?' she could not stop herself from asking.

'In a week or so. I promised I'd do my best to help you find answers. I have no intention of breaking that promise.'

'And I will be here. My commission will take me several more weeks.' Unless Sir Charles had her bags packed. Or more likely his wife had, Celeste thought, wearily contemplating the necessity for an apology.

'Good. That's settled then. So, if you could hand it over—the locket? I've still got the signet ring.'

'You mean right now?'

'I'm heading off first thing in the morning,' he said briskly. 'Turn around.'

She did as he asked. It was a good thing, Jack's wanting to go to London, she told herself. She did need to work. And he was right, he was too much of a distraction. She still, more than ever, wanted to re-solve the issue of her mother's letter. She would not miss him at all. Not a bit.

His fingers were cool on the nape of her neck as he undid the clasp. If she leaned back only a fraction, she would feel his chest on her back, his legs against hers.

He turned her around, tucking the necklace into his waistcoat pocket.

'I am very grateful for all your help.'

'There's no need. I am glad to have a purpose again.'

'Still, I am grateful.'

Jack nodded. 'I should go.'

'Yes.'

'Early start.'

'Yes.'

He leaned forward to brush her cheek with his lips just as she stepped towards him to do the same. He caught her as she stumbled, his arms tight around her waist, her body pressed firmly to his chest. He looked down into her eyes, and she raised her mouth to his.

Their lips brushed for the merest second. Enough for her to close her eyes. Enough for the attraction between them to spark to life and send them jumping awkwardly apart. For the second time in the space of a few days, they walked back together from the lake in silence.

London—two weeks later

Jack completed what had become his daily circuit of Hyde Park, then decided on impulse to walk through Green Park to St James's. He found a bench at the opposite end from Horse Guards, and sat back, closing his eyes and enjoying the early-evening sunshine on his face. The change of scene seemed to be having a positive effect on his melancholia. Only three times had he woken in the last two weeks after enduring the nightmare, though a good many of the other nights had been spent awake, his brain churning in an endless circle of questions.

Here in London, Jack could have easily stayed out on the town, but he'd never been a carouser, not even when he was a young colt. Instead, he took the opportunity to catch up on his reading. There was a German mathematician called Gauss who had published several fascinating papers, which Jack was methodically working his way through. Complex stuff, and much of it in Latin, which kept him occupied through the long hours of darkness. He was having to pay extra for candles at his lodgings, and the piles of paper covered in scribbled equations were most likely in-

terpreted by his landlord as evidence he dabbled in
the black arts.

A barked order issued from the direction of Horse
Guards shattered the silence of the park. Jack smiled
wryly to himself. Someone was getting a rollicking.
One thing he did not miss, the army's obsession with
spit and polish. His slapdash approach to his own appearance, after all those years of having to appear immaculate, surprised him. He'd had his hair cut here
in London, but he had felt no temptation to blow any
of the considerable wealth he had amassed over the
years on anything other than a couple of pairs of boots
and some new breeches. To be bang up to the mark
interested him not one jot.

Nor had he felt any urge to blow his cash on wine,
women or any other vice for that matter. London,
even out of Season, offered many opportunities to do
so. He'd attended far too many parties and balls in
Wellington's entourage to find them anything other
than a duty call. And women—Jack had always liked
women, but for that reason, he'd never been interested
in bawdy houses. Not that he condemned them, or
judged the men and women who frequented them—
a combination of war and absence made such places
necessary to an army. But for Jack, the notion of sex-
ual congress with a woman he did not know was repugnant.

Until he met Celeste, in the two years since that
fateful day, all thoughts of intimacy were repugnant.
His celibacy hadn't been a conscious decision at first.
He had barely noticed the complete absence of desire,

because he had at the time been between affairs. It was only later, when the opportunity arose and he—literally—did not. He'd dismissed it on that occasion as exhaustion. It was only now, thinking back, that he could see he'd simply—and without any regrets—taken to avoiding any social occasions where he would be confronted with his apathy.

He sat up on the bench, rubbing his eyes. Away from Trestain Manor, alone in the city, awake during the long night hours, he had had plenty of time to think. He had no name for it, his condition, he doubted that any medical doctor would recognise it, but he could no longer deny its existence. Army life had kept it at bay. The pressure, especially after Napoleon escaped from Elba, to find ever more clever ways to keep one step ahead of the French, had forced him to work ever longer hours, deep into the night, not sleeping so much as passing out from exhaustion. It had been there, catching him unawares in his rare moments of inactivity, but only then.

Finding a new occupation was surely the key to containing his melancholia again. This mystery of Celeste's was merely a stop-gap, though it was a useful one, if only because it had been the kick up the backside he needed to stop putting up and start getting on with life.

Though it had been Celeste, rather than her unanswered questions, who had done the kicking, Jack thought ruefully. Celeste, with her sharp mind and her determination not to be cowed, as Charlie and Eleanor had been, by Jack's inexplicable behaviour. She was the reason he'd finally admitted to the problem. She was the reason the admission had led to action. She was the reason he was determined to find a way out of the morass he'd been sinking in.

He was grateful to Celeste. He was missing her like hell. He wanted her more than ever. Absence, instead of dulling his desire, had made it impossible to ignore. Well then, he must do the impossible.

Jack checked his watch and got to his feet. He was due to meet Finlay in an hour at a tavern over near Covent Garden for a spot of dinner. He wondered how she was faring with her painting. He pictured her in her studio, in that paint-stained smock, gazing critically at her day's work. Her hair would be coming out of its chignon by now. He pictured her, putting a hand to her throat, missing her mother's locket, and perhaps thinking about him.

He gave himself a mental shake, as he strode out of the park and made his way on to the Mall. Aside from the fact that Celeste had made it very clear she was not interested in any future but an independent one without ties and aside from the fact that admitting he had a problem did not necessarily mean there was a cure, there was one basic and fundamental reason why Jack had no right at all to dream of happiness. He might be able to manage his symptoms, but he could never rid himself of their cause, and he had no right to try. Like Blythe Marmion, he would carry his burden of guilt to the grave. And like Blythe Marmion, Jack believed her daughter deserved a lot better. Celeste was better off without either of them. What he needed to focus on was proving that.

Finlay had reserved a private room in the tavern, and was waiting for Jack when he arrived. 'Claret,' he said, pouring them each a glass. 'Not a particularly fine vintage, but not the worst we've had either. Dear God, man, we've drunk some awful gut-rot in our time.'

'Most of it that illicit whisky you insist on bringing back after every visit home to Scotland,' Jack said with a broad smile.

'I'll have you know my father is very proud of his wee home-made still,' Finley replied with mock indignation. 'Although I'm not so sure the excise man is quite so enamoured.'

'Still no uniform, I see,' Jack said.

Finlay laughed. 'Do you have any idea how curious these Sassenachs are about what a good Scot wears under the kilt? And to add to it, this mane of mine,' he said, referring to his distinctive auburn hair, 'makes them stare at me like I'm a specimen in the menagerie at the Tower.'

'More likely they're wondering how best to get you home and into their bed, if you're talking about the females of this city. And every other city we've visited, come to think of it.'

'Spare my blushes, man. You draw them in and I pick up the scraps is the truth of it. Used be, at any rate.' Finlay's smile faded. 'If only it was still that easy, to lose yourself in a lass—any lass. But we've both of us always been picky. A mite too picky, in my case.'

'Good God, don't tell me that you've finally met the one woman on this earth who isn't taken in by that Gaelic charm of yours?'

Finlay shook his head, the teasing glint gone from his dark-blue eyes. 'I know, it's unbelievable. And it is also of no consequence.'

Obviously, it mattered a good deal, but Jack knew his friend of old and forbore from questioning him. They were alike in that way, the pair of them, preferring always to keep what mattered most close to their chests.

'Any road,' Finlay said, picking up his glass, 'I'm on leave, and unlike some, I prefer to walk the streets of London without being accosted by all and sundry begging me to tell them what it was really like, the great triumph of Waterloo, and whether this was true or that, and have I ever met the great Duke. I leave the swaggering to the man himself. Though Wellington will need to get a bigger hat if his head swells any more.'

'You realise you're mocking England's saviour.'

'You realise that we fought at Waterloo for Scotland and Wales as well as England,' Finlay retorted.

Jack raised his glass. 'As you never fail to remind him at every opportunity.'

'The more he dislikes it the more I am minded to do it.' Finlay grimaced. 'Strictly speaking, my next opportunity should arise next Saturday. He's hosting some grand dinner before he goes back to Paris, and

I'm expected along with a lady friend, and I've other much more important plans. I've tried excusing myself on the grounds I've no lady friend—or at least none fit for that company—but I'm getting pelters for not attending, let me tell you.'

'What are these other plans of yours, then?'

Finlay looked uncomfortable. 'They'll likely come to nought.'

But they were clearly very important, for Finlay, much as he might mock the pomp and ceremony of regimental life, was also very much aware of its importance to a career he'd worked bloody hard to forge. The parlour maid arrived with a loaded tray, before Jack had the chance to pursue this interesting train of thought.

The food was very good, and very much to Jack's taste, with roasted squab, game pie and a dish of celery. He made a better fist of it than Finlay, he was surprised to notice. His friend was distinctly out of sorts. Were they all, Wellington's men, changed utterly?

'So, to business.' Finlay pushed his half-empty plate aside. 'This ring that you asked me to investigate. I have to tell you, the ownership of it caused quite a stramash.' He placed Celeste's signet ring on the table. 'As you suspected, it's a regimental crest, though the dragon is misleading. Not Welsh, but the Buffs, from Kent.'

'The Third Foot.' Jack frowned. 'Do you happen to know where they were while the French were slaughtering each other in the Terror?'

Finlay pulled out a sheet of paper from his pocket. 'Here you are,' he said, 'the official deployment records, though you won't be needing them.'

'You've found something of interest,' Jack said, recognising the familiar gleam in his friend's eye.

'Ach, did you expect any less of me?' Finlay picked up the signet ring. 'You see here, what looks like part of the marking of the dragon's wing? Take a closer look.'

Jack went over to the window, but the light had faded. 'No, I can't make it out.'

Finlay shook his head, grinning. 'Tut tut, Wellington's favourite code-breaker, and you've overlooked something vital. You should be ashamed of yourself, laddie.'

'Haud your wheesht, as my own Scots mother would say, and don't talk to your superior officer like that or I'll have you up on a charge.'

'Aye, you would an' all, if it weren't for the fact that you're not actually wearing the colours any more. Give it here.' Finlay lit a candle and held the ring close to the flame. 'See here,' he said, pointing to the tip of the dragon's wing. 'You have to know what to look for, but once you do, it's obvious. It looks a wee bit like that Egyptian writing we saw on the pharaoh's tombs, remember?'

Jack frowned, screwing up his eyes to examine the ring more closely. 'You're right. I see it now. What does it signify?'

'Aye, well, here's the thing.' Finlay put the candle down and took a sip of wine. 'I had to do quite a bit of digging on that one, and pull in a good few favours. Your man here,' he said, tapping the ring, 'was assigned to the Buffs as a cover. He wasn't your run-of-the-mill infantry man at all. He was a spy. A real spy, not your kind, that works out what to do with the secrets that are uncovered, but the kind that uncovers the secrets. An infiltrator, if you like.'

'Hell and damnation!' Jack stared at his friend in disbelief. 'Are you sure?'

Finlay nodded. 'Certain. If I wasn't a persistent bugger, I'd have hit a brick wall. Honestly, it's a whole other world that these boys inhabit. Makes yours look like an open book.'

'I had a bad feeling about this,' Jack said, picking up the ring and turning it over in his hand. 'How the devil did it end up hidden away at the back of a painting in the south of France?'

Finlay whistled. 'Is that where she found it, this wee painter lassie of yours?'

'She's not my wee painter lassie, she's my brother's landscape artist.'

'Mmm-hmm. You're going to an awful lot of bother for her.'

It was Jack's turn to look uncomfortable. 'You know me. I can't resist a mystery.'

'I do know you, a mite too well for your own comfort, I reckon.'

Jack snorted. 'I could say the exact same thing to you, Finlay Urquhart.'

Finlay lifted his glass. 'Well, here's to the bonds of friendship keeping both our traps shut.'

'I'll gladly drink to that.' Jack sipped his wine, then picked up the signet ring once again. 'Another dead end. I'm almost relieved. I'll just have to hope that Rundell and Bridge turn up something on the locket.'

'It's not quite a dead end, actually, though if you would rather…'

'Finlay, you devil, what else…?'

His friend grinned. 'Did I not say I'm a persistent bugger, and are you not the oldest friend I have in the world! Each ring issued to this elite squad was unique. The hieroglyph denotes a serial number assigned to each man. I've established that this ring belonged to one Arthur Derwent. Born 1773 to Lord and Lady Derwent, youngest of four sons. Commissioned aged sixteen. Served two years with the Buffs. And then, in 1791, his military record becomes a complete blank. Other than to record his death.'

'How did he die?'

'That, I can't tell you, Jack. There's nothing. Well, no, that's not true, the full story will be there, but I couldn't get at it. That's the strangest thing. Any time I tried to find out more, the door was slammed in my face. It's as if this chap never existed and the army wants to make sure it stays that way. All I know is that he died on active service. Don't know where, but I take it the date means something.'

'I don't know. Possibly, but without proof I'd be loath to speculate. Celeste—Mademoiselle Marmion—she's had enough unpleasant truths to deal with as it is without adding this to the mix. I can't talk about it, she only confided in me out of desperation—and to be honest, because I pushed her just a bit. She would be mortified if—'

'No, there's no need,' Finlay interrupted. 'I've enough on my plate myself without— Never mind. I just wish I could have been of more help.'

'You have been an enormous help and I'm very grateful.'

'Nothing you couldn't have done yourself, if you'd wanted. You know that, Jack, this is much more up your street than mine. I know you feel you're not one of us any more, but that feeling, I promise you, is entirely one-sided. The powers that be would welcome you back with open arms.'

'No,' Jack said firmly. 'Those days really are behind me.'

Finlay picked up the claret bottle and poured the dregs of it into their glasses. 'Be that as it may, there is one way of unlocking the key to what it was the mysterious Arthur Derwent was involved in when he died,' he said diffidently.

'You mean Wellington?'

'He's the one man in England with enough clout to provide you with that information, Jack. And I reckon he would if he thought there was the slightest chance of you coming back into the fold. In fact, knowing the man's eye for the long game, he'd pull strings for you just in the hope of it. But as I mentioned, he's away back abroad next week so you'd have to be quick off the mark. Did I mention that I have an invitation to his dinner party going a-begging?'

'Which would also conveniently get you off the hook.'

Finlay laughed. 'A fortuitous side-benefit, nothing more. Anyway, I'm bloody certain Wellington would rather have you there than "Urquhart the Jock Upstart", as he never fails to call me. Seriously, Jack, if you want to unravel this puzzle any further, you're going to have to take the bull by the horns. Shall we get another bottle while you mull it over?'

Jack nodded abstractedly. Finlay embarked on one of his infamous anecdotes about life in the Highlands. His friend, who had had to fight harder than anyone to attain his current rank of major, took great pleasure in spinning fantastic tales of his 'wee Highland hame'. He recounted them in the officers' mess with the purely malicious purpose of insulting those who considered their blood too blue to mix with a commoner, but he was in the habit of recounting them to Jack first, in order to refine them for maximum effect.

Jack listened with half an ear. Though he was utterly appalled by the notion of facing not only Wellington but any number of his former comrades, part of him was already working out a strategy. Having failed what he'd come to think of as the venison test, part of him was still deeply ashamed. Dinner with Wellington would be the antidote he needed, and this time, he would make sure he could not fail. He would prepare properly. He would plan this like a campaign, with not one but two objectives, Celeste's and his own. It would be quite a coup to persuade the Duke to grant him access to this Derwent's file without making any actual promises. He'd need to think his tactics through very carefully. He found he relished the challenge.

'I'll do it!'

'You know you'll have to wear your regimentals?' Finlay cautioned him.

He had not thought of that. Jack swore, then braced himself. One more test. 'So be it.'

Only now did Finlay let his relief show on his face. 'I owe you, Jack,' he said, lifting his glass. 'I really do need to be somewhere else.'

Jack tilted his own glass and took a small sip, torn between anxiety and excitement. He had forgotten that tingling feeling, of being on the brink of something, of all the pieces of a complex puzzle not quite forming into a pattern, but promising that they might. He hadn't realised how much he missed it.

He couldn't quite believe what he'd agreed to, but he had no option now, and he was glad. No more enduring, he was ready to fight. For Celeste, and for himself. He'd better make bloody sure he didn't fail this time.

Chapter Nine

Celeste stepped back and assessed the completed painting of the Topiary Garden with a critical eye. She was still not completely happy with the quality of light, but the sun had moved from the top-floor room where she had set up her easel and she would be foolish to do any further tinkering until the morning.

She was drained and a little bit edgy, the way she always was when one of her paintings refused to be finished. The view from this window was one Jack had suggested to her the very first day she arrived here at Trestain Manor. Down there, and depicted on the canvas behind her, was the stone bench where they had first kissed. Sir Charles and Lady Eleanor would be shocked to their very respectable cores if she included that in her painting.

Though perhaps they saw more than they revealed. Perhaps the notion of his French artist kissing his soldier brother was one of those things which Sir Charles knew all about, but chose not to mention. Not because it was shocking, but because it was unimportant. A French artist could have no role to play in the future of a baronet's brother, save the obvious one as his mistress. Celeste perched on the windowsill. Why was it that being a mistress seemed so much more demeaning than being a lover? '*Bien*, it is obvious,' she muttered. 'A question of property, bought and paid for. Always, it comes to this, in France and in England. I will never be anyone's mistress.'

She would, however, very much like to be Jack's lover. In the two weeks that had passed since he had left for London, Celeste had been forced to accept that her feelings for him were a great deal stronger than she had ever experienced before. She missed him. The problem was, she missed him a great deal too much. She longed to make love to him. She knew he felt the same. One of the reasons he'd gone to London was because he was determined not to let that happen. Not that either of them had acknowledged the depth of their attraction, but they had not had to. That kiss in the lake had been evidence enough.

Sir Charles had made no reference to her intemperate outburst the day before Jack's departure. Another thing swept under the carpet, no doubt because the opinion of the hired artisan meant as little as the fact that the hired artisan had been kissing her patron's brother. Perhaps she was being unfair. Perhaps.

Jack had left his brother a note. It had been handed to Sir Charles at breakfast the morning of his departure, and the peer had been so surprised, he had read it aloud, quite forgetting Celeste's presence.

'So you see, my dear,' Sir Charles had said to his wife, 'he knows full well that his behaviour was somewhat extreme. I think we must take comfort in the fact that he feels well enough to venture alone to the metropolis.'

'I am not entirely convinced,' Lady Eleanor had replied, 'that he ought to be let loose in London in his fragile state of mind.'

Sir Charles however had fully recovered his optimistic spirit. 'We must regard that as a positive sign. He is no doubt looking to take up the reins of his life again. A cause for rejoicing, not worry.'

Turning away from the window, Celeste hoped that he was right. She wondered if Jack had made any progress with her locket or with that strange ring. She wondered how he was occupying his time. She could not imagine him shopping, or drinking in taverns or going to the theatre. Were there parks in London where he could walk? Was there a lake where he could swim? It was not only for the sake of his injured arm that he swam. His muscular body was testament to his love of exercise.

In an effort to stop herself thinking of that body, Celeste pulled a chair in front of her canvas. The untrimmed topiary had a fantastical look about it. It reminded her of something. She closed her eyes, willing her mind to go blank, a technique she had honed over the last couple of weeks, when memories had begun to pop into her head at the oddest times. Yes, she had it! Another illustration from the storybook her mother used to read to her.

There was no consistency to her memories, save that they were all from before the time she had been sent away to school. A swimming lesson. A description of a gown which made Maman smile at some secret memory. A sampler Celeste had worked on, depicting the English alphabet, which she'd had to hide from Henri. She could no longer deny that her mother had cared for her, but it made her determined efforts to disguise the fact all the more inexplicable. Celeste wondered, not for the first time, what Jack would make of it all. She laughed inwardly, not for the first time, at herself for wanting to tell him. There was, after all, something to be said for being understood, even just a little. It was not something she had reckoned on.

The sound of feet on the stairs outside the room made her heart give a silly little leap. No one ever came up here uninvited. It could not be Jack, because she'd have heard a carriage. Though the driveway was on the other side of the house. She jumped to her feet as the door opened, and her heart jumped again. 'It's you,' she said stupidly.

'In the flesh. May I come in?'

Celeste took a step back before she could throw herself at that very attractive flesh, trying to remind herself of all the very excellent reasons why she should not. Jack's hair was ruffled, his clothes were dusty and he was in need of a shave, but still her pulses fluttered at the sight of him as he crossed the room.

He took her hand in his, made to raise it to his lips, then changed his mind. 'I see you've been hard at work,' he said, nodding at the canvas.

'What do you think of it?' His opinion of her was not relevant to the success or failure of the commission, but it mattered all the same.

'Charlie will be pleased,' Jack said.

'Yes, but Sir Charles is easily pleased.'

Jack laughed. 'You know perfectly well it's good. You don't need me to tell you that.'

'No. But you *do* like it, don't you?'

'I do.'

Celeste smiled. Jack smiled back at her. Their eyes locked. She lifted her hand, as if to reach out for him, just as he did the same. Their fingers brushed. She turned away to sit on the window seat.

Jack leaned his shoulders against the fireplace. 'I have news. Rundell and Bridge, the jewellers, have confirmed that your locket was purchased through them. It was a private commission, and the maker's mark on your necklace belongs to a former senior goldsmith who has unfortunately retired to the country. However, they have written to him, enclosing a sketch of the item, and have promised to inform me as soon as they hear back from him. What they could tell me was that the stones were of the first quality. It's an extremely valuable piece.'

'*Mon Dieu*, then it is true what you said. Maman must have come from a wealthy family?'

'It seems highly likely.'

'Would it have been a terrible scandal then that she was *enceinte* and not married?' Celeste asked. 'Shameful enough for her family to disown her? I don't know, you see, not really. I mean of course, in

France it is not any more acceptable than in England for any young woman to have a child without a husband, though it is naturally perfectly acceptable for a man to have a child without a wife.'

'Acceptable to some men, but we're not all the same.'

'You're right. I beg your pardon. I think you must have seen much of it though? Many women have a weakness for a man in uniform, and a man in a uniform who has been away from home for a long time— *bien*.'

'*Bien*, indeed,' Jack said wryly. 'I— Good Lord, why did I not think of that!' He had pulled a velvet pouch from his pocket. Now he reached inside and took out the signet ring with the military crest on it, and stared down at it as if he had never seen it before. 'I had a very interesting conversation with my friend Finlay Urquhart regarding this ring. It was most enlightening.'

By the time he had finished recounting his tale, Celeste's eyes were wide with wonder. 'So you think it's possible that this Arthur Derwent might be my real father? Can it be true?'

'It would explain why your mother was in possession of his ring. It's certainly plausible, though at this stage, nothing more.'

'So now we wait once more, on a letter,' Celeste said.

'Actually, there's something else we need to do first.'

He sounded odd. Nervous? He was staring down at his boots. Definitely nervous. 'There is?' Celeste asked.

Jack gave her a reassuring smile. 'Nothing terrible,' he said. 'At least—more tedious, really.'

'Yes? And what is this not-terrible, tedious thing that is making you so interested in your boots?'

Jack laughed, and joined her on the window seat. 'There's one man who can grant me access to information regarding Arthur Derwent,' he said, 'and by coincidence, he's hosting a dinner party at a house not fifty miles from here, on Saturday.'

'Oh. So you plan to call on him there?'

'I plan to attend the dinner party.'

'But you— But the last time you attended a dinner...'

'I almost fainted, I almost spilled my accounts, then the next day I blew up at my brother and his wife and fled to London,' Jack said drily. 'I haven't forgotten.'

But he had managed to mention it without either anger or embarrassment, Celeste noted.

'It was horrible bad luck,' Jack continued, 'the combination of the vegetable stew and the venison at Charlie's table. I was coping. And when I was in London I decided that I wanted to see just how well I could cope.'

'So it is another test?' Celeste pressed his hand. 'I think that is very brave. And a good thing. And I am very, very grateful too, but I don't want you to do this for me, if you think...'

'I'm doing it as much for myself as for you, Celeste. And for Finlay too. My army friend, the Scotsman I told you about. He has other business to attend to, and was eager to find someone to replace him.'

Celeste frowned. 'So there will be— Will there be other soldiers there?' Jack nodded. She eyed him suspiciously. 'This person you have to speak to about the secret file, he must be very important?' Another nod. It couldn't be! 'Jack, please, please don't tell me that you are going to dinner with the Duke of Wellington.'

He grinned. 'I'm not.'

'Thank God,' Celeste said, 'I could not…'

'I'm not,' Jack said, 'but we are.'

Celeste jumped to her feet. *'Non!'* She lapsed into a stream of incoherent French. 'No, Jack. You cannot mean it. Wellington! And this dinner— Will all the guests be soldiers?'

'Officers and their wives.'

'Jack, these soldiers—officers—will they be men who fought with you at Waterloo? The very battle which caused your—your…'

'My condition, for want of a better word,' Jack said shortly. 'My condition,' he repeated firmly. 'It wasn't at Waterloo that I— It has nothing to do with Waterloo.'

Celeste's jaw dropped. 'But I thought— Your wounds, your arm…'

'Those injuries have nothing to do with it. The event which—the circumstances which—that happened two years ago.'

'Two years ago. But how could you— You were still in the army—how did you cope?'

'With difficulty. I kept it under control because I had no choice.'

His eyes were troubled, but he looked at her unwaveringly. Though he had referred obliquely to what he called his condition, he had never before admitted to it so frankly.

'Whatever is wrong with me,' Jack said, pushing back his hair and squaring his shoulders, 'I've decided it's not going to rule my life. I must confront it, and the first step is this dinner which,' he said with a small smile, 'will also further your cause, I hope.'

Celeste felt for his hand. 'You are pretending it's not an enormous challenge, but I can't imagine...'

'Then don't. There's no point in going into battle thinking you'll die or that you'll lose—even when the odds suggest that you might,' Jack said. 'I don't want my aide-de-camp standing at my side like a frightened rabbit trying to decide which bullet to dodge, I want her watching my back. Do you understand?'

Celeste swallowed as the implications of what he was proposing began to sink in. 'Jack, I have never in my life attended such a grand function. I don't even know how to curtsy properly. I am base-born, my father apparently was some sort of spy, I'm French, and I'm an artist. I have no connections, no breeding...'

'Celeste, I don't care a damn about your connections or your parentage or your blood line. You're not a horse, dammit! I don't care who your mother was, or your father, and I don't give a damn about whether you were born on the right side of the blanket or not. You could be from Timbuktu for all I care.'

'But those other people…'

'Will see you for what you are, if you let them. A beautiful, clever, talented woman who deserves their respect and admiration for making her own way in life without compromise. I am willing to bet you'll be the only one of them at the table, what's more. What have I said to upset you?'

'Nothing.' Celeste sniffed. 'I don't know where Timbuktu is.'

'Africa.' Jack wiped a tear from her lashes with his thumb. 'Will you come with me?'

She twined her fingers in his. 'Yes. I won't let you down, Jack.'

'I know you won't.'

His kiss was the merest whisper, the lightest brush of his lips on hers, but it released a torrent of pent-up longing inside her. Celeste sighed. His fingers cupped her jaw. For an unbearable moment, she thought he would pull away. She knew it was what she ought to wish for, but she had only the will to wait, not turn away, because already her body was thrumming with anticipation. And then Jack sighed too.

They kissed deeply, the kiss of a passion too long pent up. Their lips clung, their hands pulled their bodies tight together, as if space, any space between them was too much. Their unbridled kisses made her head spin with delight, made her realise how much restraint they had shown until now. She clutched at him, her desire rocketing, trading kisses with kisses, her breathing ragged, her hands wandering wildly over his body.

'I want you,' Jack said hoarsely, kissing her mouth, her throat, her mouth again. 'I want you so much. I have never, ever wanted—not this much. Never this much.' His kisses grew deeper. She tilted her head back to deepen them further. Her hands wandered over his back under his coat, to the tight clench of his buttocks. He groaned.

They slid from the window seat on to the floor. 'You are so lovely,' Jack said, his hand tightening on her breast, drawing a deep moan from her. 'So lovely.' He sucked hard on her nipple through the layers of her gown, her undergarments. His hand cupped her other breast, his thumb stroking her other nipple.

'Yes,' Celeste said. 'Yes.' She stroked his back, his buttocks, she stroked the firm length of him through his breeches.

'Yes,' Jack said. 'Yes.' He slid his hand under her gown, past the knot of her garter. He reached the slit in her pantaloons and slid his finger into her. Instantly, she tightened around him. He stroked her, his eyes fixed on hers as he did. She flattened her hand on his shaft. He kissed her. Slid his finger farther inside her. Then slowly, tantalisingly, drew it out.

She undid enough of his buttons to slip her hand inside his breeches, and curled her fingers around the silky thickness of his shaft. He moaned. His breathing became ragged like hers. Slide and thrust, inside her. She was teetering on the edge already. Slide and thrust. She tightened in response. Jack was so hard in her hand. She tried to stroke him, but was constrained by the tightness of his breeches.

'Wait. Just—just hold me,' he said.

Slide and stroke. Slide and stroke. His gaze holding hers. She had never been so tight. And then he kissed her, and the thrust of his tongue and the stroke of his fingers was too much. She cried out, jerking underneath him, yanked into a hard, fast climax, shuddering as it took her, wave after wave, clinging to Jack, as if he would save her, her hand clutching at his shoulder, her fingers curled around his shaft.

Panting. And tears. Tears? He kissed her again, hard. She closed her eyes. Her lashes were wet. Tears? Her lips clung to his. She wriggled under him, trying to shift sufficiently to free him from his breeches. To give him what he had given her.

Jack shifted, gently removing her hand. 'Celeste, it's not—it's not that I don't want you.' His voice was harsh. The effort it took him to stop her was obvious. 'It's quite apparent that I do. More than I have ever— ever. But I can't. No, not can't. Dare not.'

He sat up, adjusting himself, fastening his buttons, helping her to her feet, taking her hands, sitting down beside her on the window seat, stroking her hair back from her face. Then kissing her, so deeply and with such regret, she could not doubt the depth of his feeling. 'Dare not?'

Jack stared down at his hands. 'I haven't wanted to. Not since— Not for a long time. I told you that, I think. I thought that aspect of my life was over. And then I saw you.' He kissed her again. 'This, the way we are together, it is so much more than anything I've ever felt before. I'm afraid that I would want so much more from you than I've ever wanted from any woman before and I know...' He kissed her again to stop her speaking. 'I know you've made it very clear that your independence means everything to you, so I'm not presuming—'

He broke off, staring out the window, his jaw working. 'Even if you did,' he said finally, turning back to her, his face stricken, 'it wouldn't be possible. What happened two years ago makes it impossible for me to even contemplate— I don't deserve you, Celeste, and I'm afraid that if I gave in, if I allowed myself to—to make love to you, I would find it almost impossible to walk away, whether you wanted me or not. I have enough on my conscience without that.'

His smile was a grimace. His eyes were darkly troubled. 'There, I had not meant to say as much. You will think me presumptuous...'

'Jack, I think—I don't know what to think. It is the same for me—this, between us. You must know that. It frightens me. It makes me think—want—I don't know what.' She touched his cheek with her fingers. 'You seem changed. You seem— I can see a little of the soldier in you, I think,' she said with a lopsided smile, 'ready to go into battle.'

'It's what I'm doing, I suppose.'

'Won't you tell me what happened, Jack?'

He pulled his hands free, his expression set. 'No,' he said, 'absolutely not. No one knows, and I intend to keep it that way.'

She contemplated pressing him, but his tone made it clear it would be pointless, and she couldn't bear to be at odds with him again after this. He had changed. He was still vulnerable, and he was still in torment but he was, as he said, fighting back, though the cause of his torment remained buried, a festering sore. She shuddered at this stark imagery. She was learning herself that such sores needed to excised.

'I almost forgot.' Jack pulled her locket from the velvet pouch. 'Here. I had the jewellers clean it.'

The stones sparkled. 'I can't believe I ever thought it mere trumpery.' Jack fastened it around her neck. Her fingers closed over it. 'I have missed it.'

He kissed the nape of her neck. 'Celeste?'

'I do understand. I do.' She got to her feet, blushing. 'I don't know what I think, but I understand. And I am—I am very honoured that you have confided in me this much. It must have taken a great deal— We neither of us are very good at it.'

'We're both of us getting better, though.' Jack took her hand again, and kissed the palm. 'Don't mention anything about the dinner. I'm going to spring it on Charlie at breakfast so he'll have no option but to agree. Do you have a gown? I never thought to ask.'

Celeste smiled saucily. 'I am a Frenchwoman. Of course I have a gown.'

Jack laughed. 'I missed you,' he said, then turned away before she could answer. 'I'll see you at breakfast.'

'And I missed you too,' Celeste said as the door closed behind him.

* * *

'So the invite is from the Great Man himself? I thought Wellington was holed up in Paris.' Charlie pushed his empty breakfast plate to one side. His brother, as Jack had anticipated, looked suitably awe-struck.

'He is only in England on a brief visit.'

'Ah. Did you hear that, Eleanor?' Charlie said, turning to his wife. 'Wellington himself has invited Jack to a dinner.'

'Jack and a partner,' Eleanor said, pouring herself a cup of tea. 'It is exceeding short notice to receive such an invitation.'

She was no fool. He forgot that sometimes. Jack buttered some bread and took a contemplative bite. 'The cards were issued a few weeks ago. My friend Finlay Urquhart has been holding on to this one for me,' he said. One of the principles of deception, always stick to as near the truth as possible. 'You remember Finlay, Charlie?'

His brother laughed. 'The Jock Upstart, isn't that what Wellington calls him? Indeed, I recall…'

'So who do you intend to take to this dinner with you?' Eleanor persisted.

'I rather thought I'd take Mademoiselle Marmion.'

Eleanor's breakfast cup clattered into her saucer. 'A painter. A *French* painter, moreover. To dinner with Wellington! Jack, you cannot possibly… Oh. Good morning, *Mademoiselle*. I trust you slept— There is no coffee. They have forgotten to bring— I will just ring the bell.'

'I'll do it.' Jack got to his feet, tugging the cord at the fireplace before holding Celeste's chair out for her. *'Mademoiselle,'* he said, resuming his seat opposite her, 'we were just talking about you.'

'Jack, you cannot— There must be someone more—'

'Eleanor.' It was the voice he used to cut through the excuses of a trooper who had failed to carry out his orders to the letter. Shouting, Jack had learned to appreciate, was not nearly so effective as this quiet, utterly implacable tone. Eleanor's jaw dropped. Jack bit back the urge to laugh. 'I have received a very flattering invitation to a dinner which the Duke of Wellington is hosting,' he said, turning to Celeste. 'I would be honoured if you would accompany me.'

Her eyes widened not from wonder, but from the effort she was making not to laugh. *'Moi?'* She turned to Eleanor, to Charlie, and then back to him with a very creditable attempt at surprised delight. He hadn't briefed her, and he hadn't needed to. Jack bit back his own smile. 'To dinner with the great Duke of Wellington. *Moi?* It is an honour that I surely do not deserve.'

'Actually—' Charlie surprised them all by intervening '—I think it's a capital idea,' he said, casting his wife an apologetic look. 'We all know that the Duke has an eye for the ladies, and *Mademoiselle*, here, is an exceptionally beautiful gal. Come now, Eleanor, you cannot deny it.'

Jack mentally cursed his brother's ineptness. To ask one woman to praise another's looks was to dice with disaster at the best of times. To ask one's wife to do so was to ensure that one slept alone for at least the next week. 'The Duke of Wellington is still, as far as I am aware, infatuated with Lady Wedderburn-Webster.'

Eleanor's eyes widened at the mention of the notorious and by all accounts, fatally attractive lady. 'Is it true, Jack, that the child she bore is his? I believe that she was actually back in the ballroom only days after the birth. I was confined for six weeks after Robert, and a month after Donal.'

'As to that, I'm afraid I have no idea.'

'They say that she has not a single thought worth uttering in that flighty head of hers,' Lady Eleanor said. 'One would have thought that a man of Wellington's calibre would have chosen a more fitting and intelligent...' She stuttered to a halt, flushing, seeming to recall only at the last minute that she was talking about Wellington's mistress, and not his wife.

'Mademoiselle Marmion, you may recall, lives in Paris,' Jack said, bringing the conversation back around to the salient point. 'I thought Wellington would appreciate discussing his adopted city with one of its natives.'

'Excellent idea,' Charlie said, rubbing his hands together. 'The point is, my dear Eleanor, Jack must go to this dinner. There is no doubt that Wellington will be a man of huge influence when he returns to politics, as he surely must. And Jack, you know, must look to his future. He cannot afford to be turning such an invitation down, and it is too short notice to invite another lady to accompany him. Mademoiselle Marmion offers the perfect solution to the problem. It is settled then.'

Charlie beamed. Eleanor smiled frigidly. Celeste looked down at her plate of bread and butter, biting her lip. Mission accomplished! Picking up his fork, Jack cut into an egg and took a bite. It was cold, but surprisingly good. He cut another piece.

Celeste made an excellent accomplice. He'd spent much of the night imagining how it would have been if he had not somehow plucked the willpower to stop yesterday. He almost wished he hadn't been so strong-minded. When he woke up, his morning swim had been a necessity for a very different reason than on any other day. Jack set down his fork. It hadn't been *that* dream. He had not had *that* dream for—he frowned—more than a week?

'Is something wrong, Jack?'

He turned to Eleanor, who had posed the question. 'Not at all. I was merely contemplating having another egg,' he said.

'Then let me fetch it for you,' she said.

She got hurriedly to her feet to do so, rather than summon a servant or allow him to help himself, obviously keen to encourage his returning appetite. Her concern touched him. It struck him that before he went to London, it would merely have irked him. He wondered guiltily how many other such small acts of kindness he'd misconstrued. 'Thank you,' he said with a smile as she handed him the plate.

Eleanor blushed. 'You are most welcome, Jack,' she said.

He made a point of taking a bite of egg and nodding his appreciation. 'By the way, I brought Robert back a present from London.'

'A present? That is exceedingly thoughtful of you. May I ask what it is?'

Eleanor's face lit up, and Jack felt another twinge of guilt. He couldn't remember the last time she'd smiled at him like that. 'It's a box of soldiers,' he said. 'Actually, rather a large box. Models of the armies who fought at Waterloo. I thought he could invite his little friend from the village round later, and I'd set it out for him, just as it was. Explain how the battle unfolded, that sort of thing.'

'Jack!' Eleanor clapped her hands together in delight. 'Jack, that is most—most— I must say, I am quite flabbergasted.' She turned to Charlie. 'Did you hear that, my love? Robert will be delighted.'

'I am sure he will be, but—are you sure about this, Jack? I mean, you've been rather keen to avoid the subject, and...'

'And now I see that it was wrong of me,' Jack said smoothly. 'Robert ought to understand both sides of the story. To read some of the accounts in the press, you'd think that we— Wellington had an easy triumph. In fact the victory meant all the more for our— his having such a worthy adversary in Napoleon.'

'Well then, provided that Wellington still triumphs,' Charlie said with a rumble of laugher. 'Indeed, Jack, that is most— You won't mind if I sit in? I'd be fascinated to hear your thoughts for myself.'

'Not at all.'

'I must go and tell Robert at once,' Eleanor said. 'Will two o'clock suit you? He will be—Charles, my love, come with me. We should both be there when he hears the exciting news. You will excuse us.'

Jack finished his egg. Celeste poured herself another cup of coffee. 'Mission accomplished?' she asked with a quirk of her eyebrow.

He laughed at her choosing his own words. 'I think so.'

'And these toy soldiers, would they happen to be another test?'

Jack pushed his chair back. 'Sometimes the trouble with a beautiful, clever and talented woman is that she is rather too perceptive. I must go, I have a battleground to prepare.'

Chapter Ten

Four days later, Celeste gazed out of the window of her guest bedchamber at Hunter's Reach, the country estate in neighbouring Surrey where Wellington was hosting his dinner—although in actual fact it was Lord and Lady Elmsford, the owners of the house, who were the nominal hosts.

The house had been constructed during the reign of Queen Elizabeth, built in the classic 'E' shape which was a common tribute to the Virgin Queen. Celeste's room was on the third floor on the north wing of the house, facing towards a long sweep of carriageway. Jack had been clearly on edge when they arrived a few hours ago, as much on her behalf as his, but she had managed to reassure him that she was more than capable of playing her part. Though as Celeste watched the stream of carriages arriving, she felt less certain with every passing minute.

Moving restlessly to the mirror, she studied her reflection critically. Her evening dress was of white silk, the overdress gauze woven with sky-blue leaves of flossed silk, trimmed with net and satin. She had had it made in Paris on a whim a month after her mother died, a fruitless attempt to console herself with something utterly frivolous which she would never have the opportunity to wear. She had no idea what impulse had made her bring it with her to England, but she was vastly relieved that she had. Her long evening gloves were also new, as were the sky-blue slippers which matched her gown. Her fingers went automatically to the locket, glittering at her throat. 'I wish I had you here to advise me, Maman,' she whispered. 'You would know all the protocols regarding how deep I should curtsy to each rank of attendee.'

She had refused her host's offer of a lady's maid, never having had one, and kept her *coiffure* simple, in a topknot held by a ribbon to match her gown, with a few artful curls. Now, peering nervously at the result, Celeste worried that it was overly simple for such a grand occasion. She had no shawl, and could only hope that the throng of guests would warm the cavernous rooms downstairs. Another thing she could not understand about the English, the way they made a virtue of the cold. Staring at the empty grate in her bedchamber, she wondered if there was some unwritten rule that fires were not to be lit until the first snowfall.

A discreet tap on the door startled her. 'Jack. Thank goodness. I was not sure if I was expected to make my way down myself. *Sacré bleu!*'

He was wearing the tight red military dress uniform with its high, gold-braided collar. His jaw was clean-shaven, tanned against the gleaming white of his starched shirt and neatly tied cravat, just visible beneath the coat. His hair was swept back from his brow. The gold braid ran in a broad line down the front of his uniform, which fitted snuggly at his waist, where a heavy gold sash was tied. More gold braid on his cuffs, and more on the short tails of the coat, made him look quite magnificent. White gloves, white, very tight breeches, and boots polished so highly that they could have acted as a mirror. 'You look exactly like your portrait!'

'I seem to remember you thought I looked like a pompous ass.'

'You said that. I said you looked like a Greek god, peering down on us mere mortals.' Her smile faded a little as she studied his face. 'I know as your aide-de-camp I am to be all stiff upper lip, but am I permitted to ask how you feel in uniform?'

'Damned uncomfortable.' Jack coloured. 'Fine. Odd. I feel like an imposter. But fine. This is my dress uniform. I never— The only bad memories it has are of dinners such as this one, with too many egos recounting their own particular tales of bravery, and far too many toasts.' He bowed low over her hand, brushing his lips to her glove. 'I have been remiss. Mademoiselle Marmion, may I say that you look utterly radiant.'

'Lieutenant-Colonel Trestain, may I say in return that you look exceedingly dashing.'

He smiled faintly, tucking her hand into his arm and making for the stairs. 'Are *you* nervous?'

'Not at all.' Jack raised his brow. 'Only a little. Mostly of Wellington. Will he look down that famous nose at me because I am French? Then there is your English politics. I can't tell the difference between a Tory and a Wig.'

'Whig. Frankly, neither can they,' Jack said drily. He led her to a first-floor balcony which overlooked the Great Hall. 'You have nothing to worry about, you know. They are just people.'

Celeste gripped the wooden banister, peering down at the glittering crowd through the huge iron light-fitting, shaped like a carriage wheel, which was suspended from the ceiling. 'People with titles, dripping in jewels, who talk as if they own the land.'

Jack laughed. 'That's because many of them do. Where is your Revolutionary spirit?'

'Beheaded,' Celeste said, her eyes fixed on the crowd. Most of the men were in red, a positive battalion of senior British military personnel. If it was daunting for her it would be even more so for Jack, who was doing this for her. She waved her hand at the swarm of Redcoats beneath. 'Do you know all of these officers?'

'Most of them.'

She studied his face anxiously, torn between awed admiration at his courage, and concern lest he fail this challenge he had set himself. Was he really prepared for this? No matter, this was not the time for doubts or questions. Jack wanted his aide-de-camp to watch his back, not cower like a frightened rabbit. She stiffened her shoulders, preparing to do battle. *'Allons, mon colonel,'* she said, tucking her hand into his arm. 'I won't let you down. And if I do make some terrible gaffe, you can blame it on the fact that I am French, since I am sure that is what everyone will be thinking in any case.'

The Duke of Wellington was receiving his guests at the foot of the stairs. He had the aloof carriage and expression of a man who at the same time disdained and expected reverence. He was immaculately dressed, his scarlet coat giving the appearance of having been moulded to his fine shoulders. The famous nose was not nearly so hooked as the caricatures portrayed, Celeste noted, though his eyes were every bit as hooded. And every bit as observant. The mouth was unexpectedly sensual. As he treated the woman in the queue in front of them to a charming smile, Celeste understood why his Grace had his pick of the ladies.

'Trestain. You are looking well. Regimentals suit you.'

Jack, Celeste noticed, instinctively straightened his shoulders as if he were being inspected which, she supposed, he was. 'Your Grace. May I introduce Mademoiselle Marmion.'

'A pleasure, *Mademoiselle*,' the great man said, bowing over her hand. 'I understand that you are an artist. If your paintings are as pretty as you then I am sure you are much in demand.'

Flustered, Celeste nodded, casting an enquiring look at Jack, but he looked just as surprised as she.

'You must not think that because I no longer have you in my service, that I am entirely bereft of spies to gather the latest intelligence on you, despite the exceedingly short notice the Scots Upstart provided me with,' Wellington said to Jack with a diffident smile. 'I confess, I was surprised to hear that you had been tempted out of hibernation. It gives me some hope that we may yet tempt you back into harness.'

Wellington turned to Lord and Lady Elmsford. 'You will know Lieutenant-Colonel Trestain as my code-breaker,' he said.

'It is an honour, sir,' his lordship said, 'I believe your work has been invaluable to his Grace. He tells me you are much missed.'

Jack's smile was tight. 'No one is irreplaceable,' he said. 'His Grace excepted, naturally.'

The Duke of Wellington smiled thinly at this sally, though Celeste suspected he was of the opinion that it was true. The man had an ego the size of France. He was also, she reminded herself, a master strategist, and he clearly wanted Jack to return to his service. It hadn't occurred to her until now that the Duke, if he did grant Jack access to Arthur Derwent's file, would expect to be paid in kind. Surely Jack was not contemplating a return to the army?

'A code-breaker! I am very fond of acrostics myself,' Lady Elmsford was saying to Jack, 'though no doubt you find such puzzles embarrassingly simple.'

'You would be surprised to know how many codes

are based on similar principles,' he replied. 'Unless you wish his Grace to try to recruit you too, I would keep that talent under your hat.'

Jack had not expected quite so many of his fellow officers to be here. He ought to have checked the guest list with Finlay, but then, if he had, there was a chance it would have discouraged him. Now, smiling and exchanging pleasantries with familiar faces, he was not precisely glad he was here, but he would be when it was over.

Celeste's grip on his arm was like a vice. His aide-de-camp was much more nervous than she was letting on. In this rather daunting gathering, she was no seasoned trouper, but more akin to a young ensign bravely carrying the colours. He smiled down at her reassuringly, feeling his own spirits rise. He had not had his nightmare since returning from London. He had worked his way through the entire battle of Waterloo, skirmish by skirmish, in the presence of two small boys and his brother, without faltering once. Now here he was, in his regimentals, engaging in reminiscent chat on that same subject, and his palms were not even sweating.

One of the late Lieutenant-General Picton's men was recounting, for Celeste's benefit, the legend of the Frenchman, dressed as a English Hussar officer, who descended on a British-occupied village, pretending to be on an information-gathering mission from Lord Uxbridge. She was hanging on his every word, her eyes wide, like a child being told a fairy story. Jack had heard these stories so often, they had ceased to mean anything to him, but now he listened afresh, it really was amusing, for the French spy had been so convincing, he'd actually managed to order the British soldiers about, though he disappeared in jig time when their commanding officer turned up.

Waterloo made its appearance as he had expected, in several more conversations, but each time Jack tensed a little less. Not even four months ago, the battle had taken place, but it seemed a great deal more distant. Listening to the men who had been his friends and comrades for so many years, he felt a detachment he had not expected. Their world was no longer his.

A wave of sadness for what he had lost threatened to envelop him. He reminded himself that it was not lost but voluntarily surrendered. A sharp nip on his arm made him look down at Celeste. The eloquent look she drew him made it obvious that she was in dire need of rescue. The lascivious look on the face of the guards captain entertaining her with tales of his own heroism made it clear what she needed rescuing from. He was not the first to seem smitten with her. Jack hadn't exactly forgotten how beautiful she was, but he'd forgotten the impact she made when first encountered. Until now, Celeste herself had seemed oblivious of the admiring glances, raised quizzing glasses and downright leers. Or perhaps she was accustomed to it? Jack slipped his hand around her waist and drew her in to his side. She smiled up at him and slipped her hand back through his arm.

* * *

The dining room at Hunter's Reach was like a very much larger version of the one in Trestain Manor, with exposed oak timbers and extensive panelling. To Celeste's relief, Jack was seated next to her at dinner. Aside from that one moment when she'd had to pinch him, he seemed to be handling the occasion effortlessly. It had been strange, seeing him mingle with those other soldiers. There was no doubting that he was one of them. She had learned more in the last two hours about his life in the army than he had told her in— Was it really less than six weeks since they had first met? The respect and admiration he drew from his fellow officers did not surprise her, but the awe in which a number of them held him did. They spoke of him as if he were a magician, recounted some of his successes as if they were achieved by a form of sorcery. She had thought Sir Charles's claim that Jack was famous had been born from brotherly affection, but it seemed even Sir Charles had no idea of the extent of Jack's abilities.

It struck her afresh how much he had given up when he resigned his commission. Perhaps he was thinking the same thing? The test, as he called it, began to make more sense now. Despite having insisted that his soldiering days were over, perhaps he was still hankering for them after all. He had sounded completely convincing, but that could be because he was trying very hard to persuade himself.

In the company of these senior militia men gathered round the huge table, Jack was a changed character. More intimidating, in a way. She looked at him, chatting smilingly with the overly forward and overly endowed woman on his right. He certainly looked relaxed and in control but she couldn't help remembering what he'd said about putting on a front to go into battle.

As the first course was carried in by a small battalion of footmen, Celeste dragged her eyes and her thoughts away from Jack to the man seated on her left, one of the few in the room not wearing a red tunic. He needed little encouragement to talk about himself and the pivotal role he had played in the introduction of something called the Corn Laws which seemed, confusingly, to have very little to do with bread. When Celeste finally managed to complete a sentence without interruption, the man declared he hadn't realised she was a Frenchie, and embarked upon a description of his recent pilgrimage to the Devon coast to view HMS *Bellerophon*, in which Napoleon was being conveyed to exile on Elba. He seemed to think that Celeste was personally acquainted with the Emperor, and consequently was inclined to take umbrage on behalf of the entire English nation.

The arrival of the next course was the signal for all heads to turn almost as one. Celeste bit back a smile. All heads save one, that was. The woman on Jack's right was still talking. She could not see his face, but the woman was quite unmistakably casting lures. That she was beautiful could not be denied, with blue-black hair almost the colour of Jack's own, huge blue eyes, and an expanse of creamy skin on display. Her eyelashes fluttered. Her hands also. The pink tip of her tongue kept touching the plump indentation in the centre of her upper lip in a brazen gesture of seduction. Even as Celeste watched, she managed to lean over, display her bounteous cleavage, whisper something in Jack's ear and drop her napkin on to his lap at the same time.

Celeste committed the cardinal sin of leaning across Jack's arm. 'You will excuse me, Madam, but I have something most particular to say to Monsieur Trestain.'

'That was rude,' Jack said, though he was smiling.

'No doubt you thought her very beautiful.'

'No doubt that is what you think I thought.'

Celeste narrowed her eyes. 'I think her gown is vulgar. The décolleté is indecent.'

'Only a woman would say so. There is no such thing as a décolleté that is too low, as far as we men are concerned.'

'Nor a bosom that is too full,' Celeste replied tartly.

Jack burst out laughing. 'I cannot believe you said that.'

'I meant only to think it.'

He grinned. 'You know, despite the fact that you are not parading your quite delightful bosom about like a—a houri in a sultan's harem, you must be perfectly well aware that you, Mademoiselle Marmion, have turned every male head in this room.'

'Though not yours,' Celeste said before she could stop herself.

'Oh, mine was turned the moment I first saw you on the banks of the lake.'

He meant it teasingly, but she remembered him then, as she had first seen him, naked, scything at that awkward angle through the water, and heat flooded her. 'I could not take my eyes off you,' she said.

'That,' Jack said, 'is a feeling which is entirely mutual.'

His eyes darkened as he leaned towards her, and she moved too, as if drawn by some invisible force, only the clatter of a spoon on a glass making them leap apart, as his Grace the Duke of Wellington got to his feet and announced a toast: To England, Home and Beauty.

Jack watched impatiently as the port made a slow circuit of the table for the second time. Without Celeste by his side, he was distracted, worrying how she would fare in the company of the ladies. He had always found the endless toasts in the officers' mess tedious, always found the need to disguise the fact he wasn't actually emptying his glass each time tiresome, and tonight was no different, although at least when they were toasting the ladies and the king and their host and hostess and this patron and that patron, there was no opportunity for any other topic of conversation.

A final raising of glasses to the king, and to Jack's intense relief Wellington pushed back his chair. He had managed, in the few moments between the ladies departing and the port arriving, to make his request to be granted access to Alfred Derwent's file. Wellington had raised his eyebrows, looked as if he was going to ask the nature of Jack's interest and then thought better of it, before consenting somewhat grudgingly to have it sent to Trestain Manor. He made it clear that the file contained highly confidential information and it was most irregular for Jack to have sight of it. The Duke then reminded him, in no uncertain terms, that having granted such a great favour, he would require Jack to repay it at a time of his choosing. What that might entail, Jack would worry about when it happened, which of a certainty it would, for the Duke always got his pound of flesh.

Celeste was not, as he had feared, sitting alone and neglected when the gentlemen left the dining room, but at the centre of a huddle of the younger wives. He stood on the periphery, listening with some amusement, for she was confiding in these most fashionable well-heeled ladies, where to shop for the best bargains in Paris. All of the places she mentioned were in unfashionable areas with which none of her listeners would be familiar. The ladies were, however, enthralled. One of them was actually writing notes down on the back of a visiting card. 'And as to undergarments, Mademoiselle Marmion?' a petite blonde whispered, and Jack decided it would be politic to make himself scarce.

He was standing next to a suit of armour, thinking that men in mediaeval times must have been considerably shorter than they were today, when Celeste rejoined him. 'How you ladies do love a bargain,' he said.

'You were listening!'

'I left before you shared the secrets of your under-garments.' Jack looked sheepish. 'That didn't sound quite how I intended.'

Celeste blushed. 'You should not have mentioned it at all. A lady's undergarments are not a fit topic for a gentleman to discuss at a military dinner.'

'Actually,' he retorted, 'you would be surprised at how often the subject comes up.'

'Jack!'

'Celeste.' He raised her hand to his lips. 'You have performed magnificently tonight. Thank you.'

'It is I who should be thanking you.'

'As to that, I have spoken to Wellington. He has agreed to send me Arthur Derwent's file.'

'Knowing his reputation, and what you have told me of the Duke, I'm sure there was a forfeit to be paid.'

'Have I told you that you are very astute as well as beautiful?'

'Yes. Jack, I'm being entirely serious. I would not have you compromise yourself or your principles for me. Are you contemplating going back into the army?'

'No, but there's no harm in letting Wellington think I am.'

'You lied to the Duke of Wellington?'

'Certainly not! I merely withheld the body of truth. Celeste…'

'Lieutenant-Colonel Trestain! Well, I'll be damned. Didn't expect to see you here. Your name wasn't on the guest list that I saw.'

Jack's blood ran cold as the man grabbed his hand

and pumped it vigorously. 'How do you do, Carruthers. I am here in Major Urquhart's place.'

'Ah, Urquhart, the Jock Upstart. I do remember seeing his name. I completely missed dinner. Carriage threw a wheel on the way here, but I thought I'd best show face, keep on his Grace's good side.'

Jack turned to Celeste. 'May I introduce Colonel John Carruthers,' he said. 'Mademoiselle Marmion is— She is an artist. Painting some landscapes of my brother Charlie's estate.'

'Delighted,' Carruthers said, looking at Celeste with indifference, the first man all evening to do so. He had never been much of a ladies' man, Jack remembered. A bluff, old-school but highly respected soldier, he was the type of man who called women fillies, and no doubt rode them as hard and selfishly as he did his horses. It made him unpopular with some of the men, Jack recalled now, his callous attitude to his mounts—the equine kind, that is. Callous treatment of women now, that was deemed, ironically, to be a less heinous crime by a number of officers. One of the many things Finlay found repugnant about the mess. One of the many things Jack and Finlay agreed on.

'...don't you think?'

Jack started. Carruthers was looking at him expectantly.

'Indeed, Monsieur Trestain was saying to me before dinner that he would not be surprised if the Duke became your Prime Minister,' Celeste said, drawing him a meaningful look. 'He will be a Tory, no? And not a Wig? I mean Whig.'

'I heard you'd resigned,' Carruthers said to Jack. 'I must admit, I was surprised. Even in peace time there's a need for a chap with your skills. Trestain here was a bit of a legend, Mademoiselle Marmion, as I expect you've heard a hundred times tonight.'

Sweat broke out on Jack's back like a squall of summer rain. His hands were clammy. '*Mademoiselle* has had a surfeit of our stories this evening,' he said. 'More than enough.'

Carruthers nodded. 'I'm sure. Difficult to believe though, after all these years, that we're really at peace. Do you think it will last?'

'Oh, I think so. Yes.' Jack nodded furiously, relieved that Carruthers had been diverted. Now if he could just close the whole conversation down and escape. He wiped his brow surreptitiously. The room had become stiflingly hot.

'You know, it was a bad business, that fiasco in the north of Spain.' Carruthers's voice broke into Jack's thoughts, his tone sombre. 'I haven't seen you since that day, but I think of it often. Don't talk about it of course. Had to be hushed up, as you know only too well.'

Jack's heart began to race. 'I don't think…'

'A rotten trick, using women and children in that way, like some sort of shield. Not the sort of tactic I could ever imagine an English army indulging in.' Carruthers shook his head gravely.

He could see them. The huddle of women. The children clinging to their skirts. The silence. The smell. Dear God, the smell. Jack took a deep breath.

Another. Another. All he had to do was get away from Carruthers. Or shut him up. 'I don't think this is a fit subject for Mademoiselle Marmion's ears,' he said. His voice seemed to boom, but either he was mistaken, or Carruthers didn't notice.

'No, no, you're quite right.'

'Good.' More deep breaths. He wiped his brow surreptitiously. He caught Celeste eyeing him with concern, and straightened his shoulders. She pinned a smile to her face and turned her attention back to Carruthers, though she also slipped her hand on to Jack's arm. 'I think, if you'll excuse us…' Jack said.

'You know, I've always wondered,' Carruthers burst out, 'where the devil did the enemy forces go? Your intelligence seemed so watertight. And yet they seemed to melt into the landscape. It preys on my mind, keeps me awake at night sometimes, that we didn't capture them.'

Jack's jaw dropped, shock abruptly dispersing the fog in his head. 'That's what keeps you awake at night? Our failure to capture those men? Not the slaughter of innocents?'

'Casualties of war, Trestain, that's what they were. Of course, I wish it hadn't happened but—as an officer, the fact the mission failed is what pains me most.'

Jack began to tremble violently, not because he was in danger of fainting, but because he wanted to smash his fist into Carruthers's face. He was icy cold with fury. Sweat trickled down his back. He could still see them, those huddled casualties of war, struck dumb with fear. 'Innocents,' he said in a low growl.

'Oh, I doubt that very much,' Carruthers said. His brows snapped together. 'Dammit, Trestain, that is the kind of loose talk that the British army will not tolerate. That is the very reason why that whole episode was—well, I should not have brought it up. I see that now.'

Jack's fists clenched. With immense difficulty, he uncurled them. Lights danced before his eyes. He wanted to wipe that pompous, callous look off his senior officer's face. It took him every inch of willpower to hold out his hand. 'You will wish to talk to his Grace. He is over there, holding court. Don't let us detain you.'

Carruthers hesitated only briefly, before giving his hand a brief shake. 'Your servant, *Mademoiselle*,' he said and departed.

Jack stood rooted to the spot. His eyes were glazed. Sweat glistened on his brow. Here, Celeste had no doubt, was the story at the root of his condition. He was glowering at Colonel Carruthers, as if he wanted to run him through with his sword. Though he was not wearing one, his hand was hovering over where, she presumed, the hilt would lie.

'Jack.' He stared at her as if he didn't recognise her. 'Jack!' She yanked hard on his arm. 'We should leave. Now. I am no expert on etiquette but I am sure it is poor form to attack a man—a superior officer— in the middle of a regimental dinner.'

He blinked, but her words seemed to penetrate. Celeste began to walk, keeping a firm hold on his arm, towards the first door she could find, slamming it closed behind her. Jack slumped against the wall. She gave him a shake. His eyes were blank again. 'Jack!' Another shake, to no avail. Muttering an apology, terrified that at any moment someone would open the door, Celeste gave Jack a hard slap across the cheek.

'What the hell?'

'Walk. Now.' Celeste grabbed his face between her hands, forcing him to look at her. 'We have to get you to your room. Do you understand?'

He blinked. He nodded. Then he began to walk, heading down the long corridor at a pace so fast she had to run to keep up with him. Up a set of stairs. Along another corridor, another set of stairs. She had no idea where they were going, but Jack seemed certain. Panting, she followed him until the next set of stairs opened on to a familiar corridor. His bedchamber was directly across from hers.

He threw open the door and dropped on to the bed, his head in his hands. He was shivering violently. Celeste pulled the feather quilt from the bed and wrapped it around him. 'You had better go. Thank you, but you—you should go.'

'Don't be ridiculous, I cannot leave you like this.'

He clutched the quilt around him. 'I will be much restored directly—the worst is— I will be fine.'

She touched his brow. It was soaking with sweat and icy cold. She cursed the resolutely empty fire grate. There was a box beside it. Perhaps that contained coals. She opened the box, but it was empty save for a tinderbox, which she used to light the candles on the night table.

His shivering grew more violent. The front of his shirt was soaking with sweat. 'You need to take your coat off, Jack.'

He stared at her, his expression unnervingly calm while his body shook. 'I can't believe it. How can he think like that? Those women and children. So callous. Casualties of war, he called them. As if they were killed on a battlefield. Innocents! I can't believe it.'

Celeste knelt at his feet to take off his boots and stockings.

'I wanted to smash his face.'

'That was very obvious.' Celeste uncurled his fingers from the quilt and tugged him to his feet, easing him with some difficulty out of his coat with its complex fastenings. He stood motionless, neither helping nor hindering her, racked with sporadic, violent shivers. She quickly undid his cravat. His shirt was soaking with sweat. She struggled, for the fabric clung to his skin, but eventually managed to pull it over his head. Deciding against removing his breeches, she pulled back the bedcovers and ushered him into bed. He lay flat on his back, his eyes wide open, staring up at the ceiling.

'The irony is, Carruthers is in the right of it. Casualties of war, that's how the army sees them. That's what will be written in the file that no one will ever be permitted to look at. Carruthers is right. What mattered is not the slaughter of innocent civilians, but the failure of the mission.' He turned his face towards her, his expression pleading. 'I was a soldier for thirteen years. You'd think it would be easy for me. I've told myself it was my duty to see it their way, Celeste, that I'm letting them down, that I'm not the man I thought I was, for failing in that duty, but it makes no difference. I can't. I can't. And if Carruthers knew the full story—but he doesn't. No one does. No one except me.'

He struggled to sit up. Celeste pushed him back, holding him down, his torment racking her with guilt and compassion. She spoke soothingly, as one would to a child. 'You must rest, Jack. You must try not to torment yourself like this.'

'God knows, I've tried, but it refuses to go away. I dream. And I see them. Like ghosts. Living in my head.' His fingers closed like a vice around her wrist. 'It was my fault. The village. The women and children. I didn't double-check my information. I didn't validate it, cross-reference it as I always did. But they said they couldn't wait, there was no time and because Wellington's code-breaker was infallible they acted. Except I'm not. It was my fault, Celeste. My fault. Oh, God, all mine.' His grip on her wrist loosened. She thought she had never seen a man look so haunted as he turned away, and a racking sob escaped him.

Overcome with pity, feeling utterly helpless, Celeste sank on to the bed beside him and curled into his back, wrapping her arms around him. His shoulders heaved. She could feel his muscles clenched tight in his efforts to control himself. She wanted to tell him it would be all right, but how on earth could she? She could not imagine what horrific images he had in his head, but the ones that Carruthers and Jack had between them managed to instil in hers were bad enough. Here was the dark secret which had scarred Jack for life. Here, laid bare for the first time were the results of that pain, the silent agonies he had kept hidden from everyone. She pressed herself closer against him, wrapped her arms more tightly around him, as if she could somehow stop him from shattering into a thousand pieces.

She pressed her mouth against the nape of his neck. His skin was burning now, where it had been icy only a few moments before. The sobs were quieting now. He was no longer shaking. She kissed him again, closing her eyes, wishing that she could give him something, anything, to ease his suffering.

He pushed the quilt back, putting his arm over hers. The muscles in his back rippled when he moved. His skin was still hot, but dry. She pressed her cheek to his shoulder.

'I'm sorry.' Jack's voice was muffled, but it was Jack's voice.

'Don't be. Please, don't be.' Relief brought tears to her eyes. Stupid. She had nothing to cry about. Her heart ached for him.

He pressed his lips to her fingers. 'You saved me.'

'No. You saved yourself.' She gave him a little shake. 'You were lost for a moment, Jack, but then you saved yourself. You were angry.'

'I wanted to kill him.'

'But you didn't run away. You were not sick. You were in no danger of fainting. I didn't save you, Jack, you saved yourself.'

'But you were there. My aide-de-camp. You didn't let me down.'

'No, but if it were not for me, you would not have been here, Jack.'

'I would have. I told you. For me, as well as for you. Don't you feel guilty about that. We've already enough guilt between us to sink a ship.' He kissed her fingers again. His mouth was warm. Soft. 'Thank you.'

'It was nothing. Please don't. Oh, Jack, I was so— and you did it. You did it. You passed your test. Such a test. I had no idea. None. I can't imagine— I was so worried about you—and I didn't know what to do.'

'You watched my back, just as I asked you to. You got me out of there in one piece. Thank you,' he said, stroking her hair.

'You're welcome,' she said as he tilted her chin up. She said absolutely nothing as his mouth descended hungrily on to hers.

Chapter Eleven

Jack closed his eyes, drinking in the sweetness of her lips, the lushness of her mouth, savouring the soft, pliant contours of her body as Celeste wrapped her arms around him. 'You got me out unscathed,' he said again.

'You saved yourself.'

He had. His anger had saved him. It was not his condition that had sent him into a tailspin, but his railing against it. He had saved himself, and Celeste had been there at his side to rescue him. He had only a hazy memory of the journey from the Great Hall to his bedchamber, but he knew he wouldn't be here without her help. He ached with longing for her. He wanted her so much. He needed her so much. He had not the strength or the will to resist her any more. He kissed her deeply. He trailed kisses over her eyes. He licked the tears from her salty cheeks. He pushed a damp tendril of hair back from her brow, and kissed the flutter of pulse at her temple.

She pushed at the bedcovers, which were tangled

between them. He kicked them away. Her eyes were like gold in the candlelight. Her hair was pale as milk. He kissed her again. Such heady kisses she gave him back, filling him with a longing that seemed to come from deep within him.

He kissed her neck. He kissed the swell of her breasts. He cupped them through her gown. She shuddered. She flattened her palms over his chest. Skin against skin. Naked skin. He wanted to meld himself to her. He wanted to drown in her, and damn the consequences. He ached to have her wrapped around him, to dive into her and to lose himself there for ever. Safe. Lost. The kind of oblivion he was no longer capable of resisting.

He kissed her again, his tongue tracing the shape of her mouth, his hands tracing the shape of her breasts. He was ready, more than ready, but he wanted more. He did not want it to end. He wanted to show her how much she mattered to him, how much he wanted her, how very much.

He kissed her mouth lingeringly, then eased himself from her, putting his finger to her lips when she protested. He moved down her body, pressing kisses all the way before parting her legs to kneel between them, raising her skirts.

He kissed the skin between her stocking and her undergarments, undoing her garters. He kissed her slim calf, her ankle, before taking her stocking off. He could see the rise and fall of her breasts. He could hear her shallow breath. He took off her other stocking. He leaned over her to kiss her mouth again. Then slipped his hands under the delightful curve of her rear, and eased off her pantaloons.

When he covered her sex with his mouth, she cried out. He stilled her, laying a hand on her stomach to ease her back on to the bed. Then he licked into the hot, wet sweetness of her, and the cry she gave this time was guttural.

He took his time. Tasting. Licking. Sucking. Stroking. Kissing. He took his time because he wanted to show her how very much he wanted her. Her breathing was ragged, like his own. The taste of her, the scent of her, the softness of her, made him so hard. He felt her tighten, sensed the change in her breathing, fastened his mouth on her as she swelled, and held on to her as she came, her fingers clutching at his shoulders, her heels digging into the mattress, saying his name over and over.

Celeste lay shattered by a climax so intense she thought she might faint, and at the same time, she thought she might fragment into a thousand pieces. She could hear herself moaning, panting, pleading, and she could do nothing, wanted to do nothing, save yield. She was utterly sated, and yet at the same time, even as the pulsing eased, her body was already demanding a different, more primal satisfaction.

Instinctively she pulled at Jack's shoulders, her back arching under him. He covered her body, rolling her on top of him and kissing her. He tasted of her. The solid ridge of his erection nudged between her legs. His hands tugged at the strings of her corsets. When they were loose enough, she flung them off. With a sigh of satisfaction, he pushed down the top of her shift to reveal her breasts, rolling her on to her back again to kiss them, lick them, taking her nipples into his mouth, sucking, nibbling, sucking.

She could barely think. She was aflame, burning with the need to have him inside her, wantonly, shamelessly egging him on with her hips and her hands and her mouth. The muscles of his back rippled under the flat of her palms. She slid her hands down, inside the waistband of his breeches. His buttocks tautened. He let her go only to rip the fastenings of his breeches open and cast them off. He sat astride her naked body, only for the second time, and for the first time—gloriously naked and thickly erect. She reached out to touch his silky hardness, forgetting all her doubts and all his too, in the need which consumed them.

His kiss changed. Deeper. Slower. He touched her slowly too, his hands on her shoulders, her back, feathering down her spine, then back to her breasts, cupping, stroking, slowly but surely making her tense, tighten, throb, on the brink of another climax, and also, rather curiously, on the brink of tears. She touched him. The hollow in his shoulder where the musket ball had hit him. The hard wall of his chest. His nipples. The curve of his rib cage. The dip of his belly. She curled her fingers around his shaft. One slow stroke. He inhaled sharply. Another.

His hand covered hers. He shook his head. 'Need to— Not that. Too much.' He kissed her again, and rolled her under him, masking her body with his. 'Sure?' he asked.

For answer she wrapped her legs around him and kissed him hard. 'You will be careful, Jack?'

'Of course. I promise. Of course.'

The first thrust was tentative, parting her carefully. The next was surer. She clenched around him, clinging on to her self-control, not wanting to let go yet, though it was already building. Jack's breathing was laboured. The sinews on his arms stood out like ropes. He thrust again, more confidently, higher, deeper. A harsh groan escaped him. She clung to him as he lifted himself, then cried out as he thrust again, and she met him this time.

She sensed his straining for control. She clung desperately to hers. Not yet, not yet, not yet. But their bodies found a rhythm of their own that could not be resisted, thrusting and arching, harder and faster, higher, tighter. He slid his hands under her bottom, tilting her up, and she cried out as she opened up, as he pushed inside her, feeling the waves of her climax take her, digging her heels into his buttocks, her fingers into his back, saying his name urgently over and over as she surrendered, sensing him thicken as she came, another thrust, another that she met wildly, before he withdrew at the last second and his own climax took him, dragging a guttural cry from him as he shuddered, pulsed, shuddered.

The tears might have been sweat on his cheeks. She kissed them away. He wrapped his arms around her, pulling her tight against him. Their skin clung, heat and sweat, rough and smooth. Her own tears tracked unnoticed. She was in another world, floating with bliss, mindless, and at the same time, every nerve was on fire.

But as the final waves of her climax ebbed, the fear was already making its insidious way to the front of her mind. *Dare not*, Jack had said, because he was afraid he would find it difficult to walk away. He had not considered that she might have the same difficulty, but she was already fairly certain that she would.

She had never been in love. She had always thought herself indifferent to love, or even incapable. But then, she'd thought herself indifferent to so many things that had subsequently proved not to be the case. She could see it, sense it, waiting to pounce on her. If she turned her back it would creep up on her. She felt as if she were standing on the top of one of Cassis's white limestone *calanques* and looking down at the turquoise sparkle of the sea. Tempting. Glittering. Lethal.

The urge to flee was very strong. Whatever it was that propelled her to such dizzying heights would also be the end of her if she let it. She would be powerless in its sway. She would be incapable of doing other than its bidding. It might make her wildly happy, but she was pretty certain it would also eventually make her deeply miserable.

Celeste began to ease herself free of Jack's embrace. His arms tightened around her. He opened his eyes. He smiled at her, a sated, satisfied smile that squeezed her heart and destroyed all her resolution. She smiled back. Then his smile faded. He let her go gently, but he let her go.

Jack sat up, pushing his hair back from his forehead. Ought he to feel guilty? He looked at the woman lying on the bed beside him, and felt nothing save this fierce need to hold her, keep her, always. She touched him to the core. The strength of his feelings almost overwhelmed him, but it was the sheer force of them that made him realise he had to make sure that it ended here. In another life, if he was another man, he could allow himself to care. In another life, she would love him back. In another life, he would deserve that love. But he had only this life, and he must endure its vagaries. He could never be happy, while Celeste deserved every happiness. He had to make sure that she understood now, before it was too late, how hopeless it was. He had to save them both from the pain of dashed hope, and there was one sure-fire way of doing that.

'Celeste, there is something we must discuss.'

Her hair trailed over her shoulders, pale against the warmth of her skin. 'There is no need,' she said dully. 'You were right. We should not have— It was a mistake.'

'A mistake we can't repeat,' he said. 'Must not. I need to explain why.'

But even though he knew he had to speak, he found it almost impossible. Nothing to do with the embargo which the army had placed on the subject, everything to do with what he was about to destroy. Jack closed his eyes, leaning his head back against the headboard. 'It was my fault,' he said. 'That's the most important point to understand.' He opened his eyes. 'It was my fault, and nothing I can do will ever change that.'

He sat up, pushing a pillow behind his back. Celeste curled her legs around her, angling herself in the bed to face him. She looked as grim as he felt. 'You heard the gist of it from Carruthers.' He frowned, forcing himself to think back, though he had gone over it so many times, there was really no need. 'We were marching north, aiming for Burgos in Castile. Wellington—he was Wellesley then—wanted to move our supply base from Lisbon to Santander. I got wind that a band of elite French soldiers were hiding out in a small hilltop village. We had been monitoring them for a while. They were responsible for all sorts of surprise attacks on our flanks, a real thorn in our side. We suspected a leak from one of our own informants. There were a hundred very good reasons for us wanting to rid ourselves of them, and I was under a great deal of pressure—but that is no excuse.'

Jack pushed his hair back from his brow again. He was damp with sweat. 'I shouldn't have let on. I should have kept it to myself until it was verified, but I didn't and once it was out, action followed quickly. They were like ghosts in the night. We'd lost them a few times. It was deemed too risky to wait. I should have protested more forcefully. I should have demanded that we wait so that I could check, cross-check, as I always did.'

'Jack, you did protest though?'

'Not enough. No one listened.'

'But you did...'

'Celeste, it doesn't matter what I tried to do, what matters is what happened. We sent our men into that village thinking it was a fortress, based on information I provided. Carruthers was the commanding officer. He took no chances. He went in hard, all guns blazing.' He was cold now. He clenched his teeth together to stop himself shivering, clenched every muscle in his body to stop himself shaking.

'Jack, this is too painful for you. Please stop.' Concern was etched on Celeste's face.

He managed a weak smile. 'Not so long ago, you'd have been prodding me in the chest and demanding that I go on.'

She took his hand. 'I couldn't imagine then what ailed you. I didn't know then quite how much pain you were in.'

'My pain is nothing. I need to tell you. I need you to know what no one else does. I owe you that much.'

I owe you that much. And then it would be over, whether she wanted it or not—and she was a good deal more ambivalent about that than she'd realised. But what she felt didn't matter at the moment. What mattered was Jack. She was terrified of what he would tell her, and terrified of what his telling her would do to him, but she knew, with utter certainty, that he had to get it off his chest. Celeste felt for his hand. Her own was icy. 'Very well. Go on.'

He gave a little nod. 'I knew in my gut that something wasn't quite right. That was why I insisted on being allowed to accompany Carruthers. I wasn't part of the attack, but I went into the village immediately afterwards.' He faced her determinedly. 'Women and children, Celeste. Spanish women and children, whose men fought on the same side as us. But there were no men. Not a sign of the French. Not a trace that they'd been there. We will never know if they were forced to co-operate, to keep silent, or whether we were entirely mistaken. They were dumb with fear, the few that had survived the onslaught. Carruthers's men had attacked the village with all the firepower at their disposal. It took them a while to realise their fire wasn't being returned.'

Goose bumps rose on Celeste's skin. She could see it in her mind's eye. The village. The women. The children. The dead.

'It's what I dream,' Jack continued. 'It's so vivid. My boots crunching on the track. The sun burning the back of my neck. I lost my hat. There was a chicken. It ran right in front of me. I nearly tripped over it. I could hear Carruthers shouting orders, I could hear his men sifting through the carnage, but it was as if I was walking alone through a montage. So quiet. So still. There really is such a thing as deathly silence.'

He was still looking at her, but his eyes were blank. It filled her with horror, and a pity that was gut-wrenching, the more so because she knew she could do nothing to help him.

'After a battle, what you smell is smoke and gunpowder. There was a pall of it so thick on the battlefield of Waterloo, that you could hardly see a yard in front of you. In the village, I know it must have been the same, but I remember it as clear blue skies. The smell—the smell—' Jack broke off, dropping his head on to his hands, pinching the bridge of his nose hard. 'I was ravenous, I hadn't eaten properly for days. There was a stew cooking on a fire. Peasant stuff. Broth. *Herbes de Provence*. It made my mouth water. And then I—then I—that's when I became aware of the smell of the blood and the—the charred flesh. That's when I was sick. And that's when—when—when I—that's when I saw her.'

Jack's shoulders shook again. He dropped his head on to his hands again and scrubbed viciously at his eyes. Celeste could hear him taking huge, ragged breaths, counting them in a low, muttering, monotonous tone. She wanted to hold him, comfort him, but he was rigid with his own efforts to regain self-control. She felt helpless again, and more desperate than ever to help him. She scrabbled in her mind, through the morass of horror that he'd told her, trying to think of something, anything that would help, but her brain was frozen with the shock of it, unable to conceive of what it must have been like for Jack—what it must still be like.

She tugged his hands away from his face. 'I can't

imagine,' she said pathetically, 'I can't even begin to imagine.'

'I don't want you to. I wouldn't wish what is in my head on anyone.'

'The smell. The venison, that broth, that was what happened at dinner that night at Trestain Manor?'

'Yes.' Jack gave a ragged sigh.

'But there is more, is there not?' Celeste forced herself to ask. 'You said that Colonel Carruthers did not know the worst.'

'He doesn't.' Jack began to shake again. 'I've never spoken of it. I don't know if I— No, I can. I can. I can do it.' His knuckles gleamed white. A pulse beat in his throat. 'There was a girl,' he said. 'A young girl. I don't know, twenty, no more. She was standing over me—when I was being sick— I don't know, I didn't hear her, but when I looked up, she was there. Dear God.' Sweat beaded his brow. He mopped it with the sheet. 'She had a pistol in one hand. She was pointing it straight at my head. There was a bundle in her other. Clutched to her chest. A bundle. I thought—I thought it was rags. I don't know what I thought. I was— It was— I was— It was her eyes. Blank and empty. Staring at me. Through me. I was sure she was going to shoot me. I had no doubt she was going to shoot me. She had that look—of having absolutely nothing left to lose. I didn't move. I didn't speak. I felt this—this strange calm. It wasn't that I didn't care. I didn't feel anything except, this is it. This is it. And I waited.' Jack turned to her, his eyes wet with tears. 'I waited. And she turned the pistol to her own head, and she pulled the trigger. And it happened so slowly, so very, very slowly, and I did nothing, until I heard the crack, and I saw her crumple, and the bundle of rags fell, and it was her dead child.' Jack dropped his head on to his hands. 'Dead. Both of them, And it should have been me. It should have been me.'

Sobs racked his body. Celeste held him, rocking him, her own eyes dry, too shocked for tears, numb with horror, wordless with pity. She held him until his sobs stopped, until he pushed himself free and turned his back on her to throw water over his face from the bowl, pull a dressing gown over his damp body. He sat down in the chair at the window. 'So you see,' he said slowly, 'I know all about the torment of futile questions. What if I had kept the information to myself? What if I had checked it more thoroughly? What if I had not insisted on going along? What if I had remained with Carruthers? What if I'd not been sick? What if I'd tried to take the gun from her? What if I'd tried to reason with her? I know what it's like, Celeste, to have the possibilities tear at you until you can't sleep and you can't eat. But the difference between us is that my guilt is entirely justified. That poor, bereft young girl took her own life and it's my fault. Tonight, with your help, I've proved I can manage the symptoms. But I can never be rid of the guilt. And that's the price I will pay for ever. You see, don't you?'

What he said felt quite wrong. She saw a man torturing himself, determined to go on torturing himself because he thought he deserved no better. She saw a brave man, fighting to control his demons, while at the same time determined to carry that burden with him. She could see what he was trying to spare her, but she couldn't see that their cases were so very different. What if this? What if that? Why was he so set on relieving her of guilt, and so determined to cling on to his own?

Celeste stared at him helplessly. One thing was clear. Whether she wanted it or not, there was no future for her and Jack because he would not allow it. That was what he was telling her. Let me go, and spare us both the pain. She could do that. Jack had more than enough to bear already, and she— No, she could not allow herself to want a man who would not permit himself to want her. Not even Jack. Sadly, exhausted, defeated, she nodded, and began to pick up her clothing.

'Celeste,' Jack said as she made for the door. 'Celeste, I need you to know that tonight— I can imagine ever wanting...'

'Do not say that.' She turned on him, suddenly angry. 'Don't tell me how wonderful it has been, and how unique, and perfect and—and—do not tell me. You think I want to be always thinking of that, in the future, when you are not there and I am taking comfort in some other man's body?' She couldn't imagine it, but she forced herself to say it, because what did he expect! 'I am sorry,' she said gruffly. 'I know how much it cost you to tell me that. I can't begin to imagine what you are going through. I am sorry if it is selfish of me to be thinking—and I wish I could

help you as you have helped me—are helping me—
but I can't. I can't tell you what was going through
that poor girl's mind, any more than you can tell me
what was going on in my mother's. But you are set
on absolving me, Jack.'

He made no answer. She supposed it was because
there was no point. Outside, the night was giving way
to a grey dawn. Celeste let herself quietly out into the
corridor.

It was over. He had made certain it was over. Jack
sat in the post-chaise beside Celeste the next day, subdued and silent, trying to persuade himself that he'd
done the right thing. His confession, so long held at
bay, had wrung him dry, but instead of making his
guilt more raw, it seemed to have simply numbed him.
The pain came from looking at the woman seated next
to him, and seeing the dullness in her eyes, and knowing he was the cause. The pain came from knowing
that he had wilfully destroyed something precious.
The pain came from knowing that every day brought
him closer to the day that would be the last day of
their acquaintance. The only way he could manage it
was to vow to himself that he would find her answers
before that day arrived. That should be enough. He'd
make it enough.

As soon as the carriage drew up at the front door,
Celeste gathered up her reticule, picked her hat from
the seat where she had discarded it in a futile attempt
to pass the journey by sleeping, and made her way

into the house, no doubt eager for the privacy of her bedchamber.

Wearily, wishing he could do the same but knowing his brother would be agog to hear all about the dinner, Jack was not surprised to be told that he was expected in the morning room at his convenience. It was the least he could do, and it was churlish of him to resent it, he told himself. Dresses and uniforms, toasts and a few choice anecdotes would do it. He'd managed to fool every one of the dinner guests into believing that Lieutenant-Colonel Trestain was alive and kicking, and none of them meant as much to him as Charlie. Charlie, his brother, his own flesh and blood, who had taken him in without question, and who had put up with Jack's moods and his silences and his absences.

And Eleanor too, his long-suffering sister-in-law. She would appreciate a course-by-course account of the meal, if he could only remember what it had consisted of. Opening the door and summoning what he hoped was a cheerful smile, Jack decided he'd just have to make it up as he went along.

Three days later, Celeste was in her studio, putting the final touches to her painting of the lake. The next painting, a view from the hill of the manor and the village, was already sketched out. She had been working long hours since returning from Hunter's Reach, partly in an effort to stay out of Jack's way, and partly in an attempt to stop thinking about that night. There was no doubt now in her mind that she would be a fool to wish for the impossible, but there were times, moments of weakness, when that was exactly what she did.

Jack's distinctive tap on the door made her jump. One look at his expression made her heart plummet. 'What is wrong?'

He put the tray he'd been carrying down and poured two glasses of cognac. 'Sit down.'

'Jack, what is it?'

He pulled a letter from his coat pocket and handed it to her. 'This arrived in the post this morning. It's from Rundell and Bridge. I'm so terribly sorry, Celeste, but it seems one part of the trail has gone completely cold.'

Her fingers shaking, she pulled out the contents and scanned it quickly. It was only after a second, more painstaking reading that the full import of the words sank in. She picked up the glass of cognac and took a large sip, coughing as the fiery spirit hit the back of her throat. 'And so you are proved correct,' she said to Jack, who was watching her anxiously. 'Maman was indeed a gently bred English lady. "Blythe Elizabeth Wilmslow, only and much beloved child of the late…"' Her lip trembled. She took another, more cautious sip of the cognac and picked up the letter again. '"The late Lord and Lady Wilmslow." So my mother's parents are both dead.' Her fingers went to the locket, which had, according to the letter, been commissioned by them for her mother's twenty-first birthday.

'I'm very sorry.'

Celeste took another sip of brandy. A hot tear trickled down her cheek. She wiped it away. 'I can't think why I am— It's not as if I knew them, these Wilmslow people.'

'They were your maternal grandparents.'

'No, they would never have acknowledged me—because I am illegitimate.' She sniffed hard. 'I always knew that. I don't know why it's harder to accept now that I have the names of these— My mother's parents. Wilmslow. It is a very English name.' Another tear trickled down her cheek. She scrubbed it with the edge of her painting smock. 'It is stupid to feel sad for the death of people you don't know. Especially since, unlike Maman, they did not die prematurely.' She consulted the letter. 'Only three years ago, my mother's father passed away, and then two years ago, her mother. Yet not once did she mention them. Even though they were still alive and living here in England until very recently.' She sniffed again. 'Perhaps there is a family trait that encourages estrangement.'

'Celeste, you know that's not true.' Jack took her glass from her and lifted her hand to the locket. 'Your mother was "the only and much beloved child" it says in the letter. This extremely expensive piece of jewellery is proof of how much her parents loved her. And you must surely see that what is inside is proof of how much your own mother loved you.'

'Despite all evidence to the contrary?'

Jack nodded. 'Despite that.'

He put his arm around her shoulder. Celeste closed

her eyes, enjoying the solid feel of him, letting her tears trickle through her closed lids. The cognac fumes were clouding her brain but something in the letter was nagging away at her. She jerked upright and scrabbled for it again. 'It says here that the Wilmslows' estate was inherited by a third cousin because Blythe Wilmslow died without issue. But when her parents died Maman was still alive. I can understand that they would not know about me, but why would they believe Maman dead?' She jumped to her feet. '*Alors*, why can nothing be simple! Why cannot a question lead to an answer instead of more questions?'

She gazed at her completed painting of the lake. She was pleased with it. The light was just right. Late afternoon, the shadows playing on the water. And here, on the edge, was the hawthorn bush where she had hidden to watch Jack swimming that very first morning.

She turned back round. There he was, sprawled as usual, his long legs stretched out before him, no coat, no cravat, his hair rumpled. He looked tired. Only a few nights ago, she had lain in his arms. Only a few weeks, and she would be finished her commission and return to Paris. Without answers. Without Jack.

'And so it ends,' Celeste said, trying not to let her voice quiver. 'As you said, the trail has run cold.'

'There is another trail.'

'The file? Why did you not say it had arrived?'

'I was worried it would be too much.' Jack rolled his eyes. 'I know I have no right or need to manage you, but it's a habit that's rather engrained into officers, this managing. Are you ready?'

'That sounds ominous.' Celeste sat back down beside him and poured herself another inch of cognac. Jack had not touched his. She lifted the glass and took a sip. 'I'm ready.'

'Right. Well, in 1794 Arthur Derwent was sent on a secret mission to France to rescue a number of well-to-do Englishmen and women from the Terror, including one Blythe Wilmslow. Three out of the four people on his list returned safely but Blythe did not, and nor did Arthur. According to the file, they both died in Paris that same year, 1794.'

Celeste's mouth fell open. She set her cognac glass down untouched. 'You must be making this up. It is too fantastical. A spy despatched to carry out a daring rescue of my mother. It is like something from a lurid novel.'

'I assure you, it's in the file in black and white. France was an extremely risky place to be for a member of the English aristocracy at that time. The dangers were all too real.'

'Maman's parents, this Lord and Lady Wilmslow, they must have been besides themselves with worry. I don't understand, Jack—if France was so dangerous for Maman then why did she stay?'

Jack shook his head. 'You're right, it doesn't make sense, but there's nothing more in the file. We can, however, deduce one rather important fact.'

'Jack, I am an artist, not a code-breaker. What is this important fact?'

'For good or bad, Arthur Derwent could not possibly have been your father. He went to France in 1794. You were already four years old.'

Celeste clutched at her brow. 'You must think I am an idiot.'

'On the contrary. You have an enormous amount to take in, that's all.'

'But then why did my mother have this man's signet ring? Did he really die or did he too disappear, like Maman seems to have done? And when did Henri come into the picture?'

Jack shrugged. 'I don't know the answer to any of those questions, but I know where we should start looking. It's just a hunch. No, it's more than that. Call it an educated guess.'

'What is?'

'That the answer lies in France. In your mother's house in Cassis.'

Chapter Twelve

South of France—October 1815,
one month later

Celeste stood on the deck of the small blue-and-white fishing boat as they made their way into Cassis harbour after the short sea journey along the coast from Marseilles. A weak morning sun glinted off the familiar white cliffs. The sea was the same colour as the central stone in her locket. The sun dappling the water, the tang of salt, and of this morning's catch, mingled with that herby scent she could not define but was the essence of the south, combined to fill her senses.

It was strange to be speaking her own language again, more strange to hear the rough dialect of Provence. She had forgotten how very beautiful it was here, and how much she loved the sea. Dread had been her primary emotion on every visit she could recall as an adult, and there had been blessed few of them. The last time, it had been to bury her mother.

Today, she thought to herself with a sad smile, she was here to try to finally bury the past along with her.

The fishing boat bumped against the harbour wall. The fisherman jumped on to the jetty and tied up. Jack lifted their few bits of luggage out of the boat before helping Celeste out.

As he paid the man, talking easily in his excellent French, Celeste stood on the jetty, looking up at the village which ran along the edge of the shore. It had never felt like home, but today there was a sense of homecoming. She was excited to be here. She was a little daunted. She was afraid that despite Jack's assurance that there was always something which had been overlooked, that they would reach another dead end.

He was still talking to the fisherman. His face was tanned from their days at sea, for he had spent much of their journey to Marseilles up on deck. He had explained their trip to Sir Charles as army business in such a way that his brother immediately assumed it was also cloak-and-dagger business. With the advantage of Celeste having met Wellington, he mendaciously informed his brother that the Duke himself insisted that she accompany him on this mysterious mission as part of his cover. Sir Charles was entirely unconvinced, but refrained from saying so, content to indulge Jack in the hope that whatever the purpose of his trip, it would aid his recuperation.

The arrangements for their travel had been made and executed so efficiently that Celeste could almost have been persuaded that Jack really was taking her on a secret mission. He had been, for the most part, the rather intimidating commanding officer she had witnessed at Wellington's dinner. It effectively created a distance between them, which Celeste knew was the point. That night at Hunter's Reach had been their beginning and their end. She could only surmise that his determination to expedite her quest was rooted in his desire to put an end to their time together. She tried very hard to persuade herself that he was acting in her interests as well as his own. She tried, with considerably less enthusiasm than she once would have, to persuade herself that she was as set upon remaining the one and only architect of her own future.

'Ready?'

Celeste grimaced. 'As I will ever be, I suppose. Jack, do you really think you will find something?'

He nodded. 'I told you, there is always something to be found if you know where to look.'

She wandered over to the edge of the pier and gazed out to sea. 'Such a—a tangle of revelations have brought us here. I still find it difficult to make sense of any of it. My mother was so reticent. She was like a mouse, scuttling about, hoping no one would see her. You know, I'd even forgotten how beautiful she was until I looked at the miniature in my locket. She always covered her hair with caps, and her clothes…' Celeste wrinkled her nose. 'Black, black, brown and black.' Her face fell. 'Why did I never notice that, do you think?'

'Because she didn't want you to?'

'You are right. How she hated questions, Maman. Almost as much as she hated being noticed.'

'I would imagine that you would have caused a great deal of notice when you were growing up. Even as a child, if the picture in the locket is true to life, you were ridiculously lovely.'

Celeste flushed. 'It is just a trick of nature that makes my face appear beautiful you know. Symmetry…'

'I don't much care what it is. You have the kind of face and figure that turns heads wherever you go, as that dinner of Wellington's proved.' Jack touched her hair. 'This alone must have got you noticed here in the south. The people here are generally very dark.'

'I don't remember.'

'Yes, but you were sent off to school when you were ten, weren't you?' Jack said, looking much struck. 'And to Paris, where you would not exactly blend in with the crowd, but nor would you be quite so distinctive.'

'What do you mean?'

'Your mother patently came here to disappear. A daughter who would have every lad in the village setting his cap at her would hardly be conducive to anonymity.'

'That's ridiculous, Jack.' Celeste rolled her eyes. 'Though no more ridiculous than the idea of Maman being forced to go into hiding in the first place. And I suppose it is a little bit more palatable a story to swallow than that she wanted to be rid of me.'

'I thought you had accepted by now that that simply wasn't true.'

'Oh, I think she loved me in her own way, but her own way was to make sure she didn't show it. I don't understand why.' She brushed a tear away angrily. 'Now you will think me a pathetic creature.'

'I think you many things, but pathetic is not on the list.' Jack dabbed at her cheeks with his kerchief. 'The wind and the salt air are the very devil for making one's eyes run.'

Celeste managed a watery smile.

'I'm sorry,' Jack said. 'I have been so set on getting us here, that I have not thought about what an ordeal it will be for you.'

'Not an ordeal. It's just a house.'

'Stuffed full of painful memories. Perhaps it would be best if you went to an inn, if there is such a thing here, and I can search the house.'

'Jack, I am not precisely looking forward to going back to the house, but I do need to go. I'm sure if there's anything to be found that you will find it, but you can't lay my ghosts for me.'

'When we first met, you were adamant that there were no ghosts to lay.'

'When we first met, I was very sure about a good many things, and I have been quite wrong about almost every one. English cooking. English weather. Englishmen.'

Surrendering to the urge to touch him, she flattened her palm over the roughness of his cheek. He caught her hand, pulling her tight up against him.

'Celeste.' His lips clung to hers for a long, tantalising moment, then he dragged his mouth away. 'If you knew how much I have to struggle not to— If you knew.'

The feelings she had been working so hard to control made her snap. 'If it is such a struggle, Jack, then perhaps we are wrong to deny it.'

'We know we're not.'

'*You* know we are not,' she said sadly, turning away. Out at sea, the sky was darkening. A wind had blown up. The tide was on the turn. The fisherman who had brought them here was already on his way, the boat scudding along the white-crested waves, heading back to Vallons des Auffes. Celeste pulled her cloak around her. 'We should go,' she said to Jack brusquely, picking up a portmanteau and striding ahead of him, along the jetty and into the village.

The house stood apart at the far end of the meandering street, at the opposite end of which stood the village church. The key was where it had always been kept, under a large plant pot to the side of the door. Celeste struggled to turn it in the lock. The salt water made everything rusty here. Jack edged her aside and pushed open the door. She steeled herself, but the only smell was of dust. She took a tentative step into the hallway. 'It's cold,' she said, turning to Jack.

He put down their bags and closed the door behind him. It creaked, just as it had always done. She'd forgotten. No, obviously she had not forgotten. She had rolled the carpets up when she was here the last time. Her feet echoed on the boards as she made her way to the sitting room. Her stomach was churning. As she opened the door, she realised she was half-expecting her mother to be there, sitting at the table by the window, making the best of the morning light, painting or embroidering or drawing.

'Always doing something,' she said to Jack. 'My mother. Her hands were never still.'

The furniture was covered in cloths, as she had left it. The grate was empty. The spaces on the walls where her mother's paintings had hung were clearly marked. As she stepped into the room, her nose twitched. The dusty smell of watercolours assailed her, mingling with the dried lavender her mother kept in a bowl on the hearth. The bowl was empty. The watercolours were in Celeste's Paris studio.

She went over to the window. The surface of the table was covered in tiny droplets of paint. She could make out every colour. She ran her fingers over a bump of muddy brown, her failed attempt to mix red, she remembered. 'Henri was furious,' she said to Jack, 'though Maman made more of a mess than I ever did.'

His chair was over there in the corner. Maman's faced it. She had had a stool. It wasn't here now. She'd never been back long enough to merit anything more comfortable. A few weeks ago, she would have sworn that this was because she was not welcomed. Now she recalled many times when she sought any excuse not to come.

'You should start on your search while the light

is still good,' she said to Jack. 'Let me show you the rest of the house.' She led him quickly through the dining room to Henri's study where the glass-fronted bookcases covered the walls. 'I was never permitted in here,' she told Jack. She led him down to the kitchen and scullery. Then back up to the top floor. The fifth stair creaked as it always had.

'Henri's bedchamber.' Celeste threw the door open. 'Maman's bedchamber.' Another door thrown wide. The bed was stripped, the mattress rolled. Her feet fixed themselves automatically on the very edge of the threshold, as if the invisible barrier was there still, even though her mother was no longer here to forbid her to enter. Celeste stepped boldly in and threw open the cupboard. Maman's few remaining clothes were here. Thick woollen skirts and jackets. Her heavy black boots.

She could not have described that very particular smell that was her mother. Wool, powder, roses, but there was something else. She closed her eyes. It was still there. Faint, but there. 'Essence of Maman,' she said softly to herself. A fleeting image of herself howling in pain, of two hands swooping down on her, and then that smell as she buried her face in her mother's neck and was comforted.

She blinked. Jack was watching her carefully. 'Memories,' she said, closing the cupboard. 'Don't look so concerned. They are not all of them bad.'

But some of them were. The last room was her childhood bedchamber. Thinking only that this had been her sanctuary, Celeste opened the door almost without thinking. It swung wide, the panel slamming into the coffer which was positioned behind it. Positioned in that precise place to obscure the corner of the room, where a small girl could crouch down, hidden from the open doorway, and where that small girl could cry inconsolably because there was no one to care that she cried, or why.

In a daze, Celeste entered the room, curling herself into the tiny space, wrapping her arms around her waist. 'They never beat me. They never touched me. Neither cruelty nor love, but indifference is what they gave me, and forced me to give them in return. That was what was so hard.'

Jack lit the fire in the kitchen because it was the one room where there were no bad memories. They set out the picnic they'd brought with them from Marseilles. He had little appetite, though Celeste ate with her usual enthusiasm. The wine was rough and young. He drank only a little, contenting himself with watching her. She seemed different. Despite the tears she had shed, she seemed happier. He remembered the first time she'd broken down in front of him, how appalled and embarrassed she had been. She still hated to cry, but she no longer fought quite so hard not to. This afternoon, when she'd been curled up like a child in the corner of her bedchamber remembering God knows what misery, she hadn't been embarrassed by his presence. She had shared her ghosts with him as she led him through this loveless place, not hidden them.

An odd melancholy gripped him as he watched her carefully spreading tapenade on a piece of bread. As she always did, she studied the morsel carefully, as if she was thinking of painting it, before popping it into her mouth. She wiped her mouth with a napkin before taking a sip from her wine glass, something else he had observed was an ingrained habit.

'You're not hungry?' she said, looking up from preparing another morsel. She inspected it carefully, gave a satisfied nod and smiled at him. 'Try this.'

The olives were rich and salty with anchovy. The bread was heavy with a thick crust. Jack nodded, smiled, because she was looking at him so anxiously. 'Delicious,' he said.

'Tomorrow I will go to the church and put flowers on the graves,' Celeste said. 'Maman is buried beside Henri. They think she drowned, the people here. They don't know that she— No one else knows about the letter.' She handed him a thin slice of the blood sausage topped with a small square of hard goat's cheese. 'Try this.'

He ate obediently, aware that she was feeding him as if he were a child or an invalid, but happy to indulge her for the sake of watching her. There would not be many opportunities to watch her in the future. A few more days. A few more weeks. Too many to endure, and not nearly enough. He had already decided he wouldn't be going back to Trestain Manor while she finished Charlie's commission. Seeing her like this, conquering her ghosts, he had the strangest feeling, as if she was walking away from him, disappearing into the distance while he stood rooted to the spot, watching her, unable to follow.

Jack shook his head, mocking his own flight of fancy. Celeste handed him a neat quarter cut from a tart of roasted tomatoes and artichoke hearts. 'I'm sorry I was so—so emotional today,' she said. 'It must have been embarrassing for you.'

He pressed her hand abruptly, perilously close to breaking down. 'It was— I am honoured that you allowed me to— I was just thinking how horrified you would have been, only a few weeks ago, by my witnessing— I am honoured.'

'You look so sad, Jack.'

'No.' He cleared his throat, took a sip of wine, coughed. 'I did not like seeing you so sad, that is all.'

'I was sad here, when I was little. I had forgotten how much I cried. I thought I never cried. But I'm not sad now. Today I remembered that it was not all so very bad.' Celeste gave one of her very French shrugs. 'Not so very good, but not always so very bad. Thank you for making me come here.'

'I had no idea, Celeste, that this house held so many terrible memories. I was fortunate enough to have had a very happy childhood.'

'Though you were deprived of Hector the horse?' she teased. 'Don't feel sorry for me, I've done enough of that myself over the years, and you know, I think I have been a little bit self-indulgent. I was never hungry or cold. I have never been in want of a roof over my head. I was never beaten, and I've never been reduced to selling myself for money. Selling my artistic soul a few times,' Celeste said with a chuckle, 'but nothing else.' Her smile faded. 'In Paris, you would not believe the poverty which is taken for granted. Sometimes, I wonder what on earth our so-famous Revolution was for. These people don't see much evidence of *égalité*.'

'These are the people that armies rely on in times of war, sad to say,' Jack said. 'I doubt France is much different from England. Or Scotland,' he added with a nod to Finlay. 'Napoleon said an army marches on its stomach. I reckon more than half our enlisted men signed up to fill their bellies. Skin and bone, some of them are when they join, and riddled with— Well, what you'd expect from men who have spent their lives in rookeries where they sleep ten to a room, and you have to haul water from a pump fifteen minutes' walk away.'

'You seem to know a deal about it.'

'When you eat, sleep, march and fight with the same men for months on end, you tend to learn a lot about them,' Jack said. 'Besides the fact that I helped write hundreds of their letters, and paid the occasional visit to the families of some of the men who died in battle.' He grimaced. 'Once, to check on a man—a very good man—who had lost both legs.' Jack pursed his lips. 'I remember at the time he said it would have been better for his family if he had died. I told him he was wrong, that they would rather have him alive at any cost. I had no idea how patronising that was of me, until I saw— Well, I've not forgotten it.'

'Since Waterloo, the streets of Paris have been

filled with men who fought with Napoleon. I don't know what will become of them.'

'London is no different.' Jack took a sip of wine. 'Victors or vanquished, the soldier's fate is often the same. That is the true price of peace. Something ought to be done.'

'I will paint them, and you will have engravings made of my work, and you will use them to show all the people with money and influence—your Parliament, your brother, the Duke of Wellington—and they cannot fail to see that something must be done.'

'It's a good idea, though I doubt Wellington will wish to have anything to do with it. Too embarrassing for him to be faced with the evidence. I know,' Jack said, amused by the indignant expression on Celeste's face, 'they were his army. Without them he would not have had his great victory.'

'Nor his great ego,' she interjected.

Jack laughed. 'You have his measure very well. It has to be said though, it was his great ego that won us the battle. He never once faltered in his belief that we would triumph, and there were times, believe me, when many other of his officers did.'

'Not you?'

'No, not me. The man is a pompous, conceited, philandering egotist, but as a soldier, as a commanding officer, he is second to none. Not even Napoleon.'

Celeste's brows shot up. 'You admire the man you spent all those years at war with?'

'As a soldier.'

Jack looked down at his plate and discovered he'd

eaten the tomato tart. His glass was empty. Celeste had folded her napkin neatly on her own empty plate. He got to his feet and moved the shabby settle closer to the fire, stoking the embers with more of the wood which he'd found neatly stacked in one of the small outbuildings. They sat together, watching the flames and sipping the last of the wine. 'I don't think I'd make a very good politician,' Jack said. 'I am a man of action. Or I used to be.'

Celeste's hand found his. 'You still are. If it were not for you, I would still have been trying to work up the courage to enlist the help of one of those Bow Street running men. You have solved the mystery of Maman's locket and discovered the names of her parents. You have traced this Arthur Derwent, and you persuaded the great Duke of Wellington to tell you top-secret information that I would never have known existed, never mind obtained permission to read. Which puts me in mind of something I have been meaning to ask. Has he called in his favour and asked you to return to his service? Could you do so without returning to the army?'

'Half of his staff have done so in diplomatic roles. The embassy in Paris is full of my former comrades. This most likely sounds paradoxical, given my former role, but I never practised or approved of deception. I may be wrong, but my impression is that deception, flattery and downright lies are at the heart of the diplomatic service.'

Celeste laughed softly. 'In that case, I can think of no one less suited.'

'I wish that were true, but you know it's not.'

'Jack, you could not be more wrong. It is the fact that you are honest, and that you have a conscience, and that you will not accept the lies of the army and of Wellington that makes you different from that Colonel Carruthers and all the others.' Celeste turned sideways on, gently forcing him to look at her. 'You are the one who is right, not them. What you saw, regardless of how it happened, it was a terrible thing, and it will always be with you. As it should be. But that is a very different thing from taking on the burden of blame.'

'It was my fault, Celeste. I thought I'd made it plain.'

'It may have been. It may not have been. I might have saved my mother from drowning herself if I'd listened to her. I may not have. You are so very set on proving that I could not have, so very set on sparing me the guilt that you are so very determined to keep to yourself. Are the cases really so very different?'

'Yes,' he replied automatically, 'of course they are. You know they are.'

'I know you think they are. Just as I know you think this—us—is hopeless.'

'Don't. Please don't. I can't bear it.'

'Jack.' She touched his cheek. 'Jack, you don't have to.'

'I do.'

'Then I must bear it too.'

Only then did he realise that she had hoped. Only then did he realise that it was already too late. He loved her. There was nothing that could be said, and so without access to words Jack did the only thing he could do to tell her, just this once, how he felt. He kissed her.

Celeste melted into his kiss without a thought of denying him, her lips clinging to his, her arms twining around his neck. It had been there for days, weeks, ever since that night they had made love, that knowledge. It had been growing more insistent throughout this day. This house and its ghosts had stripped her of the last of her armour, leaving her defenceless. Tonight, in the domestic intimacy of the one room not populated by ghosts, by the flickering light of the fire as they ate and talked, it had taken hold of her. She loved him. She was in love with him. She was in love with Jack Trestain.

She kissed him to stop the words babbling out. She was in love. 'Jack,' she said, because it was all she could trust herself to say. 'Jack.' She loved him. She kissed his eyelids. She loved him. 'Jack.' She loved him.

'Celeste.' He kissed her again. 'Celeste.' His voice was ragged. 'Oh, God, Celeste, I want you so much.'

He caught her face between his hands and kissed her passionately. Then he groaned. 'We shouldn't.'

Panicking, she kissed him again. 'We can. We must.'

He hesitated for only a second before his mouth claimed hers once more. His kiss was hot and hard and all she had craved since the last kiss, and all she would crave when this became the last kiss. She closed her mind to this and concentrated on remembering. She loved him. The silkiness of his hair. The way he let it grow too long over his collar. She loved him. The hollow in his throat. The peculiar gouge in his shoulder where the musket ball had been cut out.

She pushed him gently back and got to her feet. She loved him. She turned to allow him to unfasten her gown and her corsets. She slid both to the ground, standing before him in her shift and her stockings. She loved him. She slipped her shift from her shoulders. She loved the way his skin tightened when he was aroused. She loved the feel of his hands, gentle on her breasts, and that circling thing he did, and the soft pluck of his lips on her nipples that made her blood tingle.

She undid his waistcoat. She pulled his shirt over his head. She knelt at his feet and took off his boots. She loved him. She leaned over him to kiss him again, grazing her nipples on the rough smattering of hair on his chest.

She loved the way he looked at her. She loved the way his hands were always drawn to cup her bottom the way he did. She undid the fastenings of his breeches and helped him to kick them away. The firelight danced on their skin. She loved him. She kissed him. He tried to pull her on top of him, but she shook her head. She loved him. She knelt between his legs, licking and kissing her way down his chest, his belly. She felt the sharp inhale of his chest as she brushed the tip of his shaft with her mouth.

She looked up, willing all that she felt to be there in her eyes, and then she began to make love to him with her mouth and her tongue and her hands, trusting her instincts to teach her what she had never done before, nor desired to do.

She loved him. His hands were on her shoulders. In her hair. He was saying her name urgently. His chest was heaving. She licked and she kissed and she stroked. Satin skin sheathing hard muscle. He jerked against her. Swore. 'Not yet,' he said, 'not that, Celeste. Delightful—dear God, delightful as it is. Please.'

Please. She let him pull her to her feet. He spread the blanket from the settle on the hearth, pulling her down with him. He kissed her. Firelight danced on her skin. Heat pooled between her legs. He rolled under her, lifting her on to him, and she sank down on to the thick length of him.

She was slick. She was tight. She tilted her body to take him in higher. Jack moaned, his hands on either side of her waist. She circled her hips, pulling him deeper. He shuddered. He cursed. His fingers curled around her breasts. She loved him. Celeste tilted back her head, and began a slow lift and slide, lift and slide, lift and slide, until she could hold back no longer, crying out as her climax shook her, the pulsing of her muscles triggering the same pulsing in his as he lifted her free. 'Jack,' Celeste said with a sigh, 'oh, Jack.'

Afterwards, they lay entwined in front of the fire, watching the flames turn to embers, the embers to ashes. Celeste dozed fitfully. As dawn broke, she rose, carefully, reluctantly, with aching sadness, disentangling herself from the man she had given her heart to. He was sleeping. She stood for a moment, looking down at his beloved face, his tousled hair, in the grey light of dawn, before quietly gathering up her clothes and creeping up the stairs to her childhood bedchamber to ready herself for a visit to Maman's and Henri's graves.

The sky was overcast, the sea a froth of white. Clutching her cloak around her, the hood pulled over her face, Celeste made her way down the main street of the village to the churchyard. She sat by the graves for a long time, closing her eyes and allowing the memories, good and bad, to wash over her. There were still many more painful than pleasant, but she made no attempt to filter them. They were all hers, every one of them. She allowed herself to cry for the first time for the simple loss of her mother. Looking at Henri's stark grave, she felt no sorrow, only pity for the very unhappy man she saw now he had been, and anger too that he had taken whatever ailed him out on the innocent child she had been.

'As you did too, Maman,' she said, kneeling down and spreading her fingers wide on the stone. 'I love you,' she whispered. 'I can tell you that now that you are not here to prevent me. I love you and I wish—I am still angry, a little, with you for not allowing me to. So I do want very much to be able to understand, because I do want, very, very much to be able to forgive you. And myself.'

* * *

Leaving the churchyard an hour later, Celeste found herself reluctant to return to the house. Stopping at the café for a breakfast of *café au lait* and freshly baked rustic bread, she watched the last of the fishing boats set sail, and the sky, in the way it did at this time of year, change from grey to pale blue. As she approached the house, her footsteps began to drag. She did not want Jack to tell her that he'd been unable to find any clue as to her mother's connection with Arthur Derwent. This was her last chance to find her answers, and she needed them more than ever. She didn't want to have to live with thinking so badly of Maman.

More selfishly, she did not want to have to learn to live with the not knowing, and the guilt which nagged and niggled at her every time she thought of her mother's last visit to Paris. She remembered all those weeks ago—goodness, a lifetime ago— asking Jack how the families of the men who had taken their own lives coped without answers. She furrowed her brow, trying to recall what he had replied, and realised that he had not. He had spared her the truth, that in most cases there were no answers. He would never know for certain why the girl chose to kill herself. He would never know if his being there made any difference. He would never know how close he had come that day to his own death. The girl had spared him. If only Jack would spare himself.

Celeste walked on past the house to the end of the village and the coastal path. The series of lime-

stone cliffs known locally as *calanques* embraced
the vivid blue of the Mediterranean like welcoming
arms. Some were deep-water bays, some more gently shelving sandy coves. Here was the one where
the deep fissures formed a cave she had once been
taken to on a boat trip. It had been summer. She remembered diving from the boat and swimming into
the dark, dank cavern. She closed her eyes, trying to
picture herself. Twelve? Thirteen? So she had been
home from school for the summer. Another memory
she had suppressed.

The gentle breeze whipped her hair across her
face. She had not bothered putting it into her usual
chignon, but had tied it back with a ribbon. In the
summer, the heat made walking along the *calanques*
unbearable. Scrub fires were common. Surrendering
to impulse, Celeste found the narrow footpath that
zigzagged down the cliff to the sandy bay beneath.
Sitting on the white sand, watching the waves lap at
the steeply shelving beach, she finally allowed her
mind to turn to last night.

She was in love with Jack. A smile played on her
lips, thinking of the wonder of their lovemaking, only
for it to fade into sadness as she faced the sheer wall
of hopelessness. Her own journey into her past had
peeled from her the years of hard-earned indifference, exposing her to the storm of emotions she'd
weathered since first reading her mother's letter. This
new Celeste could be hurt. She cried far too much.
She felt guilt and anger, but she also felt love for the
first time in her life. That too would cause her pain,

because the man she loved could not come to terms with the horrors lurking in his own past.

Thinking back to that night when Jack had told her about the massacre in the village, the horror of it struck her afresh, but she could not, as she had done until now, quite equate Jack's story with Jack's determination to make himself miserable. '*Mon Dieu*, that is exactly what he is doing, just exactly like Maman!'

She picked up a handful of the soft sand and watched as it trickled through her fingers. Guilt. An emotion with which she had become very familiar, thanks in a way to Jack himself. He had known from the beginning how inextricably mixed were suicide and guilt. His desire to save her from that guilt was, she saw now, her thoughts racing, one of the reasons he had been so eager to help her from the first. But why must Jack's guilt be any different from hers?

And then there was the problem of Maman and the guilt which drove her to spurn her daughter's love, and to reject her parents. Lord and Lady Wilmslow thought their daughter was dead. Who had told them this? Could it have been Maman? Ridiculous. Yet Jack had seemed certain only yesterday that Maman was hiding here in Cassis.

Questions and more questions and yet more, whirling around her head like a sandstorm. But there, at the centre, like the sun, was her love for Jack. Only an hour or so ago, she'd knelt at her mother's grave and told her that she loved her. All those years she had been forced to suppress her feelings.

'Not again,' Celeste said decidedly. 'Never again. Even if it is hopeless. Even if this terrible, dark secret of his stops him ever accepting it. I'm going to tell him before he leaves me for ever. After we come to the end of this other dark secret of Maman's—however that might end. Then I will tell him.

'I will tell you, Jack Trestain, that I love you, whether you want to hear it or not,' Celeste shouted at the now cloudless sky. Throwing off her clothes, and plunging into the bay, gasping as the water stung her Parisian-pale skin, she struck out strongly into the waves.

He retched violently, spilling his guts like a raw recruit, in a nearby ditch. Spasm after spasm shook him until he had to clutch at the scorched trunk of a splintered tree to support himself. Shivering, shaking, he had no idea how long the young girl had been looming over him. She raised her hand and pointed the pistol at his head. In her other hand, clutched to her chest, was a bundle of rags. Her eyes were vacant. Jack waited, certain that this was his last moment. The girl turned the gun. So slowly, yet he did not comprehend what she was doing until he heard the sharp crack.

Jack sat up, gazing dazedly around him, the sweat cooling quickly on his naked skin. The room was freezing. The blanket in which they had slept was knotted around his legs. There was no sign of Celeste. In the scullery, he cranked the pump of the huge sink. Only then, as he ducked his head under the icy water, did he realise what he'd dreamt. The girl. The gun. Her face. His feeling of utter inertia. Just as he'd described it to Celeste, but never before had he dreamt it.

Pulling on his crumpled clothes, he checked his watch and was astonished to discover it was past ten. Outside, the sun was making an attempt to part the clouds. He lit the fire, filled the kettle with water and set it on the hook which hung from the chimney, having decided, after one look at the complicated stove, that it was beyond him. There were coffee beans in a box in the larder. They smelled dusty, but he ground them anyway. Still no sign of Celeste, but her cloak was gone from the hook at the front door. He remembered now that she had been intent on visiting her mother's grave.

He could not decide whether it was progress or not, this extension to his dream. A direct result of his conversation with Celeste last night, that was certain. *You are so very set on sparing me the guilt that you are so very determined to keep to yourself. Are the cases really so very different?* Were they?

The coffee tasted as dusty as it had smelled, but he drank two cups and ate some of last night's stale bread. He had always assumed himself at fault. He had never once questioned that. Yet he had from the beginning seen Celeste's case in completely the opposite way. Was he wrong?

'Wishful thinking,' he muttered, 'and you know bloody well why, Trestain.'

He put his empty coffee cup carefully down. Love.

He closed his eyes, but it didn't go away. He loved her. Last night, he had made love to her. He was a bloody fool. He loved her. Jack swore. Then he frowned. That didn't change the fact he had no right to love her, and he was not fit to love her. But, dear heavens, how he loved her.

Jack pushed his chair back, making it screech on the flagstones. 'To work,' he muttered. 'Answers are what she needs, she told me so last night. And since I can't provide her with anything else, the very least I can do is make sure that she has those.'

He was in Henri Marmion's study when Celeste arrived back several hours later. Her hair was wet. Her skin was flushed. Her eyes sparkled. Jack's heart gave the most curious little flip. *Here she is*, a voice in his head whispered insidiously. *Yours.*

He was already halfway across the room when he caught himself and came to a sudden halt, feeling decidedly foolish and a little bit sheepish and rather angry with himself. 'Has it been raining?' he asked gruffly.

'I've been swimming.' She smiled at him. 'And thinking.'

'Right.' Did she want him to ask what she'd been thinking? 'You look—different.'

Her smile widened. 'Yes? That is because my hair is sticky with salt and my clothes are full of sand and my skin is red with the sun. And because I have made some very important decisions.'

'What decisions?'

'I will tell you, but not yet.' She hesitated, then put her hands on his shoulder and kissed his cheek. 'That is for last night. And because I know you don't want to talk about it, then I won't, but I want you to know that I will always, always remember.'

His arms went round her waist of their own accord. 'Celeste…'

Her expression became serious. 'Do not tell me you regret it, Jack.'

'Never,' he said fervently.

'Bien.' She slipped from his embrace and looked around the room, taking in the open doors of the bookcases, the stacks of books on the desk. 'What on earth?'

'I thought yesterday that this little library must have cost a small fortune to amass. Look at these,' Jack said, pointing to a row of thick volumes bound in tooled leather. 'A full set of the *encyclopédies*, no less.'

'I feel so stupid,' Celeste said, running her hand along the shelves. 'I was never permitted into this room, but even when I was here in January, I didn't think— It is like the school fees, no? Where on earth did the money come from?'

Jack grinned, producing the letter with a flourish. 'At last,' he said, 'I think I might be able to answer one of your questions. I found this hidden away inside a copy of the *Odyssey*.'

Celeste gave a little squeak. 'Jack! What is it?'

'A letter from a Madame Juliette Rosser of Boulevard de Courcelles, Paris. *Madame* encloses a draft

for the usual amount,' Jack said, 'and expects a receipt by return of post.'

'And that is it?'

'It is enough.'

'But—what shall we do?'

'Isn't it obvious? We go to Paris.'

Chapter Thirteen

Paris—one week later

As the carriage came to a stop, Celeste smoothed a wrinkle out of her gloves. Her jade-green walking dress was simple but very well cut, the matching, short pelisse with long, narrow sleeves fitted to perfection. Her brown boots matched her gloves. The ribbon on her hat matched the strings of her reticule. Even in the rarefied surroundings of the exclusive Boulevard de Courcelles, which overlooked the elegant Parc Monceau, she hoped she would pass muster.

Jack too was dressed elegantly, in knitted pantaloons and Hessian boots, his tailcoat fitting tightly over his shoulders. Unlike her, he did not seem nervous. No uniform, but today he was Lieutenant-Colonel Trestain. Rather than intimidating, for once Celeste found it reassuring.

'Have you been able to find out anything about this Madame Juliette Rosser?' she asked.

'The Rossers are a very old family. *Madame* is related somehow to the Comte de Beynac, whose main estates are in the south-west near Cahors, where you thought Henri originated—which may or may not be a coincidence. This is the Comte's hotel, though I gather Madame Rosser has been in residence for many years, through most of the Terror, unusually. She is one of those grandes dames of Parisian society whom everyone fears and few are permitted to actually visit.' Jack smiled ironically. 'It seems we are most honoured. Or rather you are, since we must assume it is the Marmion name which gained us this audience.'

'I don't know why, but I thought that a woman named Juliette would be young.'

'Just because the most famous one of all died young doesn't mean that none of her fellow Juliettes survived past twenty.' Jack covered her hand with his. 'You are nervous, and no wonder, but remember, this might prove to be another dead end.'

'You don't believe that, do you? You have one of your famous code-breaker hunches, don't you?' His smile was non-committal. Most certainly, he was the Lieutenant-Colonel today, Celeste thought. Caution personified.

The door of the carriage was opened. She stepped out, and the butterflies in her stomach multiplied a hundredfold as she eyed the ornate portico of the Hotel Beynac. Behind these huge double doors might very well lie the answers to her questions. Which would mean the end of her journey. Which would mean, more than likely, and most importantly, the end of her time with Jack, for she could not imagine him returning to Trestain Manor.

So be it. Celeste's heart would be broken, but she would at least tell Jack that she had a heart and that it belonged to him and always would. He would not love her, but she would not let him deprive her of her love for him. She would not be miserable. Well, for a time perhaps, but misery was better than indifference, and she was done with indifference. She would find a way of being happy. She absolutely would!

The door swung noiselessly open. Jack took her arm, smiling down at her reassuringly. Her heart turned over. Celeste gritted her teeth and walked passed the liveried footman, her head held high.

Madame Juliette Rosser was exceedingly tall, exceedingly thin and exceedingly old. Her white hair was piled high on top of her head. She had the kind of cheekbones on which, Jack thought, a knife could be sharpened, and the kind of long, thin nose that could cut paper. She was dressed in the height of fashion, in a black-silk afternoon gown with an overdress of grey—and very expensive—lace.

The Hotel Beynac was also dressed in the height of fashion—also very expensively, though it had the kind of elegance which could only be achieved by a combination of money and power. The furnishings were new, but the tapestries were old, and the array of objets d'art which adorned every surface looked worthy of the Palace at Versailles. Which might well indeed have been where some of them had originated.

As he made his bow low over Madame Rosser's liver-spotted hand, Jack was aware that her gaze was fixed on Celeste. She nodded absently at him, but when Celeste made a deep curtsy showing, Jack thought proudly, not a trace of her considerable nerves, Madame Rosser raised the eyeglass which hung from her neck on a gold chain and slowly inspected her from head to foot.

Celeste tilted her chin at the woman. 'I trust I pass muster.'

Jack bit back a smile. Madame Rosser, to his surprise, gave a crack of laughter. 'Yes, there can be no doubt about it,' she said.

'Excuse me, *Madame*, but no doubt about what?'

The woman raised her thin brows haughtily. 'Why, that you are Georges' daughter. I assumed that was why you were here.'

Celeste's hand went to her breast. 'Georges?'

'My nephew. Georges Rosser, the Comte de Beynac.' The thin eyebrows were raised even farther as Celeste's jaw dropped. '*Sacré bleu*, I don't believe it. The little English milksop actually kept her mouth shut all these years. You had better sit down,' Madame Rosser snapped, 'and you too, Mr Trestain,' she added in English.

'I can speak French passably well,' Jack said, helping Celeste on to a gilded sofa covered in wheat-straw satin.

The old woman ignored him and picked up a hand

bell, which was answered so quickly Jack suspected the butler must have been standing outside the door of the huge first-floor drawing room. 'Cognac,' she snapped, 'and then you may go, Philippe. We are not to be disturbed.'

'I am not going to faint,' Celeste said, though Jack thought she looked as if she might very well. 'I don't need a cognac.'

Madame Rosser sat down on the chair opposite. 'Perhaps not,' she said, 'but I most certainly do.'

'They were betrothed in 1788, Georges and your mother,' Madame Rosser began. 'Blythe Wilmslow was not the match my family wished for such a prestigious title as the Comte de Beynac, but my nephew was one of those fellows who had read that dreadful man Rousseau's *la nouvelle Héloïse*. Foolish boy, perhaps if he'd claimed a better acquaintance with Rousseau, he could have persuaded that madman Robespierre he was on his side. Rousseau, you know, was much admired by Robespierre and Saint-Just,' Madame Rosser said. She took a sip of cognac and sighed heavily. 'Perhaps you don't know. You are so young. You can have no idea of what Paris was like then, during the Terror. Every knock on the door sent one's blood running cold. There was no rhyme or reason, by then, for many of the arrests. A slighted neighbour. An old score being settled. Mourning too openly for a guillotined husband. Anything.'

She slumped back in her chair, closing her eyes and rubbing her temples. Celeste looked helplessly at Jack. 'If this is too much for you, *Madame*...' she said tentatively.

The old woman's eyes snapped open. 'No. I do not like talking of those times, but it must be done. You have a right to know what blood flows in your veins, though you have no entitlement to claim it, or aught else. I sincerely hope your motive for coming here is not based on avarice. If it is you will be sorely disappointed.'

'All I require from you, *Madame*, is the truth, nothing more,' Celeste said firmly.

The old woman took another sip of brandy, visibly bracing herself. 'Then you will have it. Your mother and my nephew were betrothed. Blythe Wilmslow was in France on the Quatorze Juillet, when the Revolution began. Her parents wished her to return to England, but...' Madame Rosser shrugged. 'We all thought at the time that the Revolution would come to nothing.

'They were here with me in Paris when Georges' arrest put an end to any hope of a marriage. I told Blythe that she should go back to England, but of course,' Madame Rosser said sarcastically, 'the little English miss was too much in love and too foolish to leave Paris without Georges.' *Madame* took another sip of brandy. 'And too much in love and far, far too foolish to refrain from surrendering to her grand passion. You, Mademoiselle Marmion, were conceived in the *conciergerie* where my nephew awaited trial.'

'I think, if you don't mind, I would welcome some of that cognac now,' Celeste said faintly.

Jack jumped to his feet to pour her some, holding

the glass while she drank, for her hands were shaking. 'You might have employed a little more tact in imparting such shocking news,' he said angrily.

Madame Rosser eyed him disdainfully. 'I am not aware that it is any of your business, Mr Trestain. What exactly is your role in all this?'

Celeste raised her brows haughtily. 'I am not aware that it is any of your business, Madame Rosser.'

Jack laughed. *Madame* pursed her lips. 'You are the image of your mother, save for the eyes, which you have from our side of the family, and where also, I think, you get that…' She shrugged. 'Insouciance. All very well in a Rosser of Beynac, *Mademoiselle*, but not so acceptable in one conceived in a prison and born on the wrong side of the blanket.'

'How dare…?'

Celeste grabbed Jack's wrist, shaking her head. 'I would be obliged if you would finish your story, *Madame*, in plain speaking, and I will remove my tainted blood from your presence. For good, before you ask.'

Madame Rosser nodded. 'In plain speaking, then, *Mademoiselle*, your mother was trapped in Paris, for by then the borders were closed. I could not have her here in her condition, but I made sure she was safe, and I paid for the doctor to attend her lying-in. Of this, her parents knew nothing. Then out of the blue, an Englishman turned up looking for her.'

'Arthur Derwent.'

'Yes. That is him. How did you know?'

'Maman had his signet ring.'

'He was sent here covertly to take your mother and

three other prominent Englishmen home. She stubbornly refused to go. She wept and wailed and batted those big eyes of hers at the poor man, and said she would be compromised if she returned with a child and no husband. He was young, and an honourable man too. But he was also one of those rash young men rather too fond of glory. He agreed to attempt to rescue my nephew from imprisonment. It had been done. It was not the impossible he attempted, but it was ill-fated. He was shot dead by one of the guards. A few days later, my unfortunate nephew was sent to the guillotine. Whether that was a result of the botched escape attempt we do not know. I expect Derwent gave your mother that ring for safekeeping. I would imagine it would have been awkward for the English if his identity were to be discovered. He never returned to reclaim it.'

Madame Rosser sighed wearily. 'With Georges dead, your mother was something of an embarrassment, but I too have a sense of honour. Henri Marmion's family have served the Rossers for centuries. It was fortunate that he was in Paris at the time. Your mother was like you, a very beautiful woman, and one who had that...' She snapped her fingers, then looked pointedly at Jack. 'As I suspect Mr Trestain can vouch. *Bien*, it took only the lure of being able to call such a beauty his wife and the promise of an annuity small enough to be insignificant to me, large enough to be very significant to Henri. Blythe took a little more persuading, but she had no other option in the end, save to do as I bid.

She was not married to Georges, but she was English, and she had borne his child. There was a great chance she would be arrested. And so—that was it.'

Madame Rosser got to her feet and pulled the gold cord which hung from the ceiling by the fireplace. 'I trust I have answered all the questions you wished to ask? You will accept my condolences for the loss of your mother,' she added coldly without giving them a chance to answer. 'When my last bank draft was returned, I made enquiries and discovered she had died. Drowning, I think.'

'Suicide,' Celeste said calmly, getting to her feet. 'Unlike you, Madame Rosser, it seems my mother had a conscience.'

'I may not have a conscience, but I do have a sense of duty, *Mademoiselle*.'

'You may rest assured that your duty is now done. I require nothing further from you. I thank you for your time, *Madame*, and I bid you good day.' Celeste dropped a shallow curtsy.

'The allowance, *Mademoiselle*, my nephew would have wished me to—'

'You cannot buy my silence. I have adequate means of my own. Good day, *Madame*.'

Celeste walked from the room without looking back. As the door to the salon closed, Jack caught her arm. 'You were magnificent,' he said.

Jack, torn between fury at the callous treatment Madame Rosser had meted out and admiration at the way Celeste had dealt with it, bid the driver take them back to her studio post-haste. She shook her head when he tried to talk to her, and when he made to escort her through the courtyard door, she told him that she needed time to think, and asked him to call on her later in the evening.

When he arrived back at the apartment a few hours later, she looked relatively calm. 'Go in,' she said, 'I will be only a moment.'

The door to her studio stood wide open. A huge room with tall windows opening out on to the roof, and even at this time of year and at this time in the evening, the impression of light. Canvases were stacked against the walls. There were three easels, a huge cupboard, a long trestle table and a number of crates which he supposed must contain her mother's work.

The windows of her main living room also opened out on to the roof. Two large comfortable sofas faced each other across the hearth, draped in a multitude of coloured shawls and cushions. A small table contained a bottle of wine and two glasses. A larger table and chairs sat in front of one of the windows. A dresser stood against one wall, but the rest of the room was painted in the palest of green, the only decoration being the canvases on the walls.

Faces. Lots and lots of faces. Not a single landscape in sight. There were children playing on the banks of the Seine. There were studies of old women and washerwomen. There were men playing boules. Old men smoking pipes. An organ grinder. A soldier in a ragged uniform with only one leg. A woman in a café with a glass of what he presumed was absinthe.

'They are not very good, but they are mine. Not that anyone would commission this kind of thing, even if I wanted them to.'

Celeste was wearing a long, flowing garment of scarlet silk embroidered with flowers, tied with a sash around her waist. 'How are you?' Jack asked. 'After this afternoon, I'm surprised you're still in one piece.'

'I was not when I arrived back here, which is why I wanted you to come back later,' she said ruefully. 'I didn't think I had any tears left to cry but I surprised myself once again.'

He smiled, because she wanted him too, but he was not convinced. 'You handled it perfectly. I wanted to grab her by the throat, but you looked down your nose at her in exactly the way she looked down that nose of hers, and it was a much more effective put-down.'

'For two whole minutes. That woman is impermeable. Like stone. Would you like a glass of wine?'

Without waiting for an answer, she poured them both a glass, setting them down on a small table by the fire. She sat down on the sofa, tucking her legs under her. Jack sat at the other end. She took a sip of wine. It reminded him of Madame Rosser, the way she sipped. Steadying herself. Bracing herself. For what? She seemed on edge. And no wonder, considering what she had just been through, Jack told himself. But she was watching him—oddly.

'When I went for my walk on the *calanques* that morning in Cassis, I realised that you and Maman had a great deal in common,' Celeste said.

'I don't see how—'

'For example, there is your sense of duty,' she interrupted. 'My mother promised that horrible woman never to tell anyone the story of my origins. After the Revolution was over, there was no possible threat to her life or to mine, yet she said nothing. She was by then, as far as the world was concerned, a respectably married woman. She could have gone back to England, but she allowed that woman—presumably it was she, that scheming, Machiavellian *salope* who will not claim me for her grand-niece, I presume it was she who informed my mother's parents that she was dead,' Celeste said bitterly.

Jack, who had in fact come to pretty much the same conclusions himself, wished now that he had given vent to some of the many pithy things he'd wished to say to Madame Rosser. 'I'm so sorry this has turned out so badly,' he said.

Celeste looked surprised. 'But no. I cannot doubt now that Maman loved me, for she went to such pains to keep me. I am sure if she'd wished it, Madame Rosser could have arranged for me to be given away. Maman must have loved my father a great deal to risk so much for him. And he—as she said in her letter, he would most likely have loved me too, because he obviously loved Maman. You are wondering that I am not more upset? I told you...'

'I'm wondering what it is you're really thinking,

because I get the distinct feeling you're not saying it,' Jack said frankly.

Celeste smiled. 'You are right, but I will. Only I— It is difficult.' She took a sip of her wine. 'It is complicated. I am sad, of course, but I understand Maman so much more now. I will never know for certain if I could have made a difference that day, when she came to me here, but I do know now the source of the guilt which made her life unbearable, and I know I could never have changed that. It was her decision, her life. I think— I hope that I will learn to accept that in the future.'

'So you have your answers finally?' Jack asked.

'I have my answers—or all the answers I'm ever going to get,' Celeste agreed. 'You have done what you promised, and I am very grateful because without you—I don't know.' Her voice quivered. She closed her eyes, her fingers clenched tight on the cushion she was holding against her. 'Jack, I have things I need to say before you go.' She tilted her head and met his gaze determinedly. 'I know you will go, I know that. But I need to— You need to— I need you to listen before you do, because I love you.'

And so after all her careful rehearsing, she had blurted it out! Celeste held her breath. Jack simply gazed at her as if she had shot him. Had she expected him to throw his arms around her and tell her he loved her too? Angrily, Celeste was forced to admit that she might indeed have hoped this. 'Don't look so surprised,' she snapped, 'you must have guessed.'

'I did not dare.'

'Well, I do,' Celeste said, crossing her arms over the cushion. 'I love you, and I'm telling you because I decided in Cassis that I won't let you do what my mother did to me.'

'Your mother?'

'Yes, you know I too am a little tired of talking about her, but she is— You and she have so much in common, Jack. She wouldn't let me love her either.'

He flinched. 'Celeste, don't say that.'

'I love you, Jack, and you can't stop me.'

'Celeste, I…'

'No.' She shook her head stubbornly. 'You have to listen first. I have thought it all through, so you have to listen. Only now I forget what I was saying.'

'Duty,' Jack said.

'Yes, yes. There is Maman doing her duty by Henri and Madame Rosser, even though she has to hurt me. And I can understand that now a little, but why, I ask myself, was she so determined to continue with the situation when it was making her miserable? Now I know the answer to that too. She felt guilty. She had been the architect of the death of one man, and she no doubt blamed herself for having failed to rescue the man she loved, and every day she could look at me, and see the evidence of what she had lost, and— so you see, guilt. She didn't feel she deserved to love me. She certainly didn't feel entitled to be happy, and so she chose to be miserable.'

'Chose?'

Celeste nodded firmly. 'Chose. I think it was her penance.'

'And you think that is what I am doing?'

She flinched at the cold note of anger in his voice. 'I don't think you choose to be miserable, but you don't try to be happy either. And I do think that you see your life as a penance, as Maman did.'

'You don't know what you're talking about.'

'But I do. I know perfectly, because no matter how many times you say it is not, our cases are the same.' Celeste tried desperately not to panic. Jack looked as if he was on the verge of leaving. What had seemed so clear was now becoming jumbled in her mind. 'I love you,' she said, resorting to the one thing that had not changed. 'Jack, I love you so much. You've done so much to help me, why won't you let me help you?'

'Because you can't. Because nobody can.'

'Because you won't let them!' Frustrated with herself for making such a hash of things, and with Jack for refusing to listen, Celeste spoke without thinking. 'You told me right from the start that it was a mistake, digging up Maman's past. You told me that it would hurt me. I didn't believe you. I was wrong. It has hurt me so much, but you must have seen, Jack, did I not tell you in Cassis, how much it has helped me too? I am not the person I was, and I'm glad. I'm not the Celeste who built this great big wall around herself and pretended that she was happy there was no one inside her castle with her. Now I laugh and I cry and I love, Jack. I am in love with you and I'm not going to pretend otherwise.'

'Celeste, I can't—'

'Jack, you can. Listen to me,' she said urgently. 'Listen. The thing my mother felt most guilty about was being alive, when my father and Arthur Derwent were dead. She didn't kill them, but she felt responsible. And she paid with her misery. You did not kill that girl, but you act as if you did. You are giving up your own life in payment, Jack, can't you see that, just as Maman did. You did not kill that girl. She took her own life, Jack, when she could have taken yours. She spared you.'

'Spared me?' He stared at her, incredulous.

'Yes, spared you. You thought it was your last moment. You thought she was going to kill you. You accepted it. You did nothing. If you had, perhaps she would have pulled the trigger on you. Perhaps she was testing you. Perhaps your lack of resistance proved to her that you regretted what had happened, that you accepted her right to kill you. I don't know.'

'I will never know.'

'No, you won't. Like me, you will never know exactly why. Like me, you will never know if you could have stopped her. But if I can learn to live with that, why cannot you? She spared you, Jack, and you are acting as if you wish she had not.'

He jumped to his feet. 'You're wrong.'

'No, I'm not.' Celeste grabbed his arm. 'If our cases were reversed, if I told you I couldn't let myself love you, that I had to spend the rest of my life atoning by being unhappy, even though you were desperately in love with me, what would you do?'

'I do love you.' Jack turned blindly for the door. 'I do love you. It's the only thing I'm sure of.'

'Jack!' He was out of the apartment before she could catch him. She heard the pounding of his feet on the stairs and ran after him as fast as she could. The door to the courtyard was swinging open. Celeste stepped out into the Paris street in her bare feet, darting uselessly in one direction and then the other, but he had vanished into the night.

He ran blindly at first, as fast as he could, careless of where his feet took him. Curses followed him as he collided with another man, but he ran on, oblivious, with Celeste's words pounding in his head.

I love you.

You can't stop me.

I love you.

I won't let you do what my mother did to me.

I love you.

If I can learn to live with that, why cannot you?

I love you.

Jack turned a corner too tightly and staggered into a wall. The pain that shot through his injured shoulder brought him to his senses. He was in a dark alleyway strewn with rotting vegetables. A market, he surmised. Looking around at the dark holes of he gaping doorways, he felt that he was being watched. His senses on full alert, he walked casually towards the pinprick of light which he hoped would prove to be a main thoroughfare.

It was a barge passing on the river. The alleyway

led directly down to the Seine. Across on the other bank, he could hear singing, but here, all was quiet. He walked, keeping one eye out for trouble, until he reached a well-lit street. And then he walked until he reached an area he recognised. And then he walked on and found himself back at the apartment he had fled from several hours before.

He was sick of running. Celeste loved him. And he loved her. Jack leaned against the courtyard wall, staring up at the starless sky. Celeste loved him, and she was determined to keep loving him, no matter what. She deserved to be happy.

While he deserved only misery? Was he actually wallowing in his guilt, as she had suggested? Was he choosing unhappiness as atonement, as Blythe Marmion had done? No, there was no comparison between them. None.

And even if there were—which there was not— the cases were still different. Celeste's mother had been unhappy, but she had been perfectly normal. Her guilt did not manifest itself in nightmares and temper flashes and forgetting where she was and—all the things he was learning to control. All the things Celeste had helped him to understand. He had passed the tests he had set for himself. It was not a canker, as he'd imagined it for so long, a parasite which fed on his guilt—it was part of him, his condition. Another battle scar, and like the hole in his shoulder, he was learning to live with it.

Which brought him back to guilt. *If our cases were reversed, if I told you I couldn't let myself love you even though you were desperately in love with me, what would you do?*

He would still love her. He would tell her he loved her, and he would keep telling her until she believed him and until she accepted that she had no reason at all not to love him back. He wouldn't walk away. Even though that was what he was expecting Celeste to do? To sit back, and accept his decision and to live with it? Was that arrogance or was he back to wallowing in his guilt?

Guilt stopped Blythe Marmion loving Celeste. Jack did love Celeste. But Jack could never make Celeste happy because Jack didn't deserve to be happy. Because it should have been Jack who died, and not the girl.

But the girl had spared him.

Celeste had all her answers now, and not many of them were pleasant, yet tonight she'd seemed surprised when he suggested it had turned out badly. He remembered what she'd said in Cassis, about laying ghosts. He remembered wishing he could do the same. He remembered concluding, as he always concluded, that it was impossible. But if Celeste could do it, why couldn't he?

What if he was wallowing? What would the girl say to that? He had always assumed that she was torturing him with her suicide. He had always believed it was revenge for her child's death, for all the deaths. *Remember this, soldier. Never forget this, soldier.* What if she simply couldn't bear to go on?

What if she was sparing him?

What if he allowed himself to love Celeste?

The idea filled him with such happiness, he felt light-headed. It felt—it felt right.

What if he lost her? What if he walked away, and she stopped loving him and she found someone else? He couldn't contemplate it. He couldn't imagine it. He had, he realised with horror, assumed that she would always be there, waiting for some indeterminate point in the future when he might feel entitled to claim her. He cursed himself under his breath. Arrogant, stupid, fool. What was he waiting for? The future could be now, if he was willing to take a chance. If she was still willing to take a chance.

Jack looked up at the apartment building. 'Dammit, there's only one way to find out.'

'Oh, Jack!' Celeste fell on him, wrapping her arms around his neck. 'Oh, Jack, I have been so worried. I am so sorry. I should not have said— I only meant to help you.'

'You did.' He pulled her tightly against her, holding her so close she could hardly breathe. 'You did.'

She leaned back to look at his face. 'What has happened?'

He laughed. 'You,' he said and kissed her. He tasted of the Paris night. He kissed her hungrily. 'I love you so much,' he said. 'I don't know if I can forgive myself for what happened in the village that day, but I do know I'd never forgive myself for losing you. I can't believe how close I came to that, Celeste. Oh, God, Celeste, I love you so much.'

He kissed her again, more wildly, and the heaviness in her heart shifted. He loved her. She framed his face with her hands. 'Is it true? You really love me?'

'I really do love you, more than anything. That's the easy bit,' Jack said, kissing her again. 'I love you, and I don't want to waste another moment of my life without you. You were right. About the guilt. About atoning. About all of it. I was spared. I don't know why, but I was spared, and it's time I claimed my life back. I don't know how I'll do it, Celeste, but I want to try. I love you, and I'd be a bloody fool to pass up the chance of happiness with you.'

'And you are not a bloody fool.' She beamed at him. She didn't think she had a smile wide enough for him, so she kissed him. 'I love you.'

'And I love you. I don't know what that means for us, Celeste. I have no idea what our future will be, but I can promise to love you always, and to try.'

'Jack, *mon coeur*, that is all I want.'

There would be a time for explanations, but it was not now. Celeste led him into her living room, where the fire burned and the uncurtained windows showed them the night-time Paris sky. They kissed, the deepest, thirstiest of kisses, as they shed their clothing, claiming each other with their mouths and their hands. They kissed, and they touched, and they sank on to the rug in front of the fire and they made love. There would be a time to discuss the future, but what mattered now was that they had a future, and it started here.

Epilogue

Trestain Manor—two years later

' "It was with some interest that we attended the exhibition of paintings which is currently being displayed at the town house of a certain celebrated member of the ton."' Sir Charles looked over the newspaper at his wife. 'Well, we all know who that is a reference to. I wonder how Jack managed to persuade him?'

Lady Eleanor finished pouring the tea. 'My love, when I think of the amount of money Jack has persuaded the great and the good to part with for this enterprise of his, convincing his lordship to hang Celeste's pictures in his salon would have been an simple matter.'

Sir Charles laughed indulgently. 'Very true. Though I confess, they are not the sort of pictures I'd want hanging in my salon. I much prefer those landscapes she used to paint. Very pretty, they were,' he said.

'Yes, one could think of many words to describe her recent works, but pretty would not be one which springs to mind,' Eleanor said with a shudder. 'Those portraits which she made of the Waterloo veterans, for example. Why must she choose the— Well, frankly, Charles, the shabbiest and the most pathetic of men. As I recall, one had no legs, and another— His face. I could not get the image of that poor man's face out of my mind for days.'

'Which was rather the point, don't you think?' her husband said drily. 'That particular set of paintings was, I gather from Jack, almost solely responsible for raising the funding needed to establish the hospital in Manchester.'

'Jack would say that. I have never seen a man so besottedly in love. Or so proud of his—his wife.' Lady Eleanor put down her tea cup. 'You know, it is such a relief to finally be able to address Celeste as Mrs Trestain. I don't know why it took them so long to get married.'

'There was the small matter of her origins, though I believe that dear Celeste was rather more concerned about that than Jack.'

'She is the daughter of an English lady and a French count. *Such* a romantic story. It is a pity they were not married, but look at the FitzClarences. Being base-born never did them any harm.'

Sir Charles patted his wife's hand. 'Would that everyone saw it your way, my dear, but Celeste's French family will not even acknowledge her.'

'Well, her English family are very happy to own

her. Now that she is finally Jack's wife, of course. Do read me the rest of that piece, my dear.'

Sir Charles cleared his throat. '"The portraits are painted by Mademoiselle Celeste Marmion, who has, we understand, lately taken on the name of Mr Jack Trestain, formerly Lieutenant-Colonel Trestain, known to many of us as the Duke of Wellington's renowned code-breaker." Wellington will not like that. He has made it very publicly known what he thinks of Jack's fund-raising.'

'To his detriment. I never thought I would say this of the man who saved England, but I think his attitude towards those poor men who fought for him, indeed laid down their lives for him, is shameful.'

'Absolutely. It is enough to make one consider turning Whig,' Sir Charles said. He waited for his wife to laugh at his joke and, slightly unnerved when she didn't oblige, once more returned to the newspaper. '"Contrary to what we have come to expect of Mademoiselle Marmion's work, this latest selection of paintings is bucolic, a mixture of landscapes and portraits, all of which were made in the north of Spain. The funds which Mr Trestain hopes to raise from the sale of the paintings are to be directed towards one village, in recognition of the support which the Spanish peasants gave the British army in the latter years of our war with France."'

'It is rather an odd thing to do, is it not?' Lady Eleanor asked, frowning. 'Why this particular village?'

'I am sure it is merely a case of it being representative,' Sir Charles replied, folding up the newspaper.

'Symbolic, don't you know. Shall we take a trip up to town next week? We can take a look at Celeste's latest exhibition, and we can have dinner with the pair of them. Jack is in fine form and excellent company these days. He is quite restored.'

'I like to think that we played some small part in his recuperation.'

'I rather think Celeste must take the lion's share of the credit for that. And Jack himself. I must say I'm immensely proud of what he's achieved, even if it is considered beyond the pale by some of my acquaintances.'

'One can only hope that marriage has moderated their billing and cooing. I was positively embarrassed, the last time we met.'

'My love.' Sir Charles got up from his seat and kissed the nape of his wife's neck. 'Nurse has taken Robert and Donal and the baby out for a picnic. I was rather hoping that we could indulge in some billing and cooing ourselves.'

'Charles!' Lady Eleanor exclaimed, looking shocked.

He pulled her to her feet and kissed her.

'Oh, Charles,' Lady Eleanor said in a very different voice as she allowed him to take her hand and lead her out of the breakfast room.

* * * * *

Historical Note

The first thing to say is there's a fair bit of history in this book. Thank you so much to the other Harlequin Historical authors who shared research recommendations and helped me out with references to what we now refer to as post-traumatic stress disorder. In particular, thanks to Louise Allen for sharing her amazing research catalogue and for the insights from Dr Martin Howard's book, *Wellington's Doctors*.

Four books in particular were of immense help in the gestation of this story—and all four are now looking as dog-eared and exhausted as I feel, having written it!

Christopher Hibbert's *The French Revolution* is an excellent all-encompassing account of the Revolution from its early days right through the Terror until Napoleon stepped in. It gives a real sense of what it must have been like in the last days of the Terror, when Celeste's mother was hiding in Paris and, as Madame Rosser attests, arrests became quite indiscriminate.

The case she mentions of a woman guillotined for grieving too openly for her husband is a true one.

Richard Holmes's *Redcoat* tells the story of the British army from an ordinary soldier's point of view. It's stuffed full of fantastic anecdotes, including stories about interminable mess dinners and endless toasts, which mirror the dinner Jack and Celeste attend. Finlay, of whom we shall see much more in the next book in this miniseries, came to life as a direct result of my reading in *Redcoat* that almost no enlisted men made it up through the ranks of Wellington's army. Who could resist a man who beats the odds—and the ingrained snobbery too?

If you only read one book about Waterloo I'd highly recommend choosing Nick Foulkes's *Dancing into Battle*. This is not a blow-by-blow account of the battle itself, but of the men who fought it, their wives and children, and the gossipmongers who watched from the sidelines. It's irreverent, funny and, unlike many historical tomes, a very easy read.

Lady Richmond's famous ball, which is mentioned in this book, gets the full treatment here, as does the Duke of Wellington's relationship with the fatally attractive though apparently quite empty-headed Lady Wedderburn Webster, which so enthrals my Lady Eleanor.

The story of the French spy who passed himself off as one of Lord Uxbridge's men also originates from here.

And then there's my favourite example of the British stiff upper lip: when Lord Uxbridge was wounded, he said to Wellington, 'By God, sir, I've lost my leg.'

'By God, sir, so you have,' the Duke replied.

George Scovell, an engraver's apprentice, was Wellington's real code-breaker, and if you want to know more about him try Mark Urban's book *The Man Who Broke Napoleon's Codes*. As to Jack's dark secret—though the setting and timing, near Burgos in 1813, is historically accurate, the event itself is an invention wholly of my own. In fact it owes rather more to the Vietnam War than the Peninsular one, when the Vietcong used innocent villagers as shields, as may or may not have happened, in Jack's story.

A lot of reading and research, but luckily I have another book to write on the same subject. Finlay's story is next. Though how that will turn out at this moment in time I have absolutely no idea!

THE SOLDIER'S
REBEL LOVER

Chapter One

Basque Country, Spain—July 1813

Major Finlay Urquhart of the Ninety-Second Regiment of Foot scanned the rough terrain through the eyepiece of his field telescope, his senses on full alert. 'Got ye!' he whispered to himself with grim satisfaction.

The French arms dump was partially concealed, set in the lee of a nearby hillock. It was obviously a large cache and therefore a strategically important discovery, especially if it could be destroyed before Wellington began his siege of the nearby fortress at San Sebastian. There were no guards present that he could discern, but they could not be far away, and might return at any time. The French army was severely stretched in the aftermath of the Battle of Vitoria, where they had sustained heavy losses, but even against their presumably depleted defences, any planned assault on the arms cache would carry significant risk, since it was located some distance behind enemy lines.

As was he, Finlay reminded himself. The light was fading fast, and with it any chance of making it back to base tonight, for his journey would take him through some treacherous and hostile terrain. It would be much more prudent to hole up for the night under cover in the small, heavily wooded copse a couple of miles distant where he'd tethered his horse.

'Aye, and Prudence is my middle name, right enough,' Finlay muttered to himself. Despite the perilous nature of his situation, he couldn't help grinning at his own joke. With any luck, he could be back in camp and feasting on a hot breakfast not long after sunrise.

He could not have said what it was that put him on his guard. A change in the quality of the silence, perhaps. Maybe the fact that the hairs on the back of his neck were standing up. A sense, acute and undeniable, that he was not alone. Definitely. Finlay's hand moved automatically to the holster that held his pistol, but the failing light, and fear of the sound it would make when he primed it, made him hesitate and reach instead for his dirk, the lethal Scottish dagger he carried in his belt.

His ears pricked, Finlay listened intently. A faint scrabbling was coming from the ditch on the other side of the rough track. A rat? No, it sounded like something much larger. He waited on high alert, crouched in his own ditch, and was rewarded by the faint outline of a man's head peering cautiously out. No cap, but it could only be a French sentry, for who else would be concealed here, so close to the arms cache? He could wait it out and pray he was not discovered, but sixteen years in the army had taught Finlay the value of the pre-emptive strike. Taking the *sgian-dubh*, the other, shorter dagger he carried tucked into his hose, in his other hand, he launched himself at the enemy.

The Frenchman was in the act of aiming his pistol as Finlay threw himself at him, knocking his arm high and sending the gun spiralling harmlessly into the air. The man fought like a dervish despite his slight physique, but Finlay had experience and his own considerable brawn on his side. Within moments, he had the man subdued, wrists yanked painfully together behind his back, the glittering blade of the dirk only a hair's breadth from the French soldier's throat.

'Make one sound and, by all that is holy, I promise you it will be your last,' Finlay growled in guttural French.

His captive strained in Finlay's iron grasp. He tightened his grip on the man's wrists, noting with surprise how slender and delicate they were. Now that he was close up, Finlay could see he was not, in fact, wearing a French uniform. What was more, as he struggled frantically to free himself, it became clear that there was something much more profoundly incongruous about his captive.

'What the devil,' Finlay exclaimed, so surprised that he spoke the words in his native Gaelic. 'What the hell do you think you're playing at, woman,' he added, lowering his voice and switching to Castilian Spanish as he turned the female round to face him, 'creeping about in the dead of night in man's garb? Don't you realise I could have killed you?'

The woman threw back her head and glared at him. 'I might ask you the same question. What the hell do you think you are doing, creeping about in the night in woman's clothing? I could just as easily have killed you.'

The sheer audacity of her remark rendered him speechless for a moment, and then Finlay laughed. 'This, *señorita*, is a kilt, not a skirt, and you did not for a moment come close to killing me, though I don't doubt that you'd have tried if I'd given you half a chance. Why did you point a gun at me? Could you not see that I am wearing a British and not a French uniform? We are supposed to be on the same side.'

'If you could tell that my tunic was not a French uniform, why did you come leaping out of the darkness brandishing two blades like some savage?' she countered.

'Aye, well, fair enough,' Finlay said grudgingly, 'but that doesn't explain what you're doing out here dressed as a man. Are you alone?'

'I am here for the same purpose as you, I expect. To locate the position of this arms store. And yes, I am alone. You can let me go now, I won't shoot you, I...'

'Wheesht!'

Finlay pulled them both back down into the ditch as the sound of horses' hooves grew louder. Three riders, and this time undoubtedly French. He turned to warn the woman at his side not to move a muscle, but there was no need; she was stock-still, as silent and tense as he. She was a plucky wee thing, that much was certain.

The horses drew closer and then stopped almost

directly in front of them. One man dismounted, and Finlay slowly slid his pistol from its holster. Before he could stop her, the woman had wriggled a few feet away to pick up her own discarded weapon, careful to make no sound. Not just plucky, but cool-headed, then. Under cover of the ditch, he could barely see her, only sense the slim, coiled figure readying herself to attack. He shook his head imperceptibly, and to his relief she nodded her understanding. There were times when patience was a virtue. No point alerting the French to the fact that the arms cache had been discovered. It would only make any future assault on it more fraught with danger, as they would doubtless reinforce their defences.

After a few tense seconds, Finlay heard an unmistakable tinkling sound that was accompanied by tuneless whistling. This was followed by a long groan of satisfaction as a small cloud of steam rose into the night air. *'Zut alors!'* he heard a disembodied, and quite literally relieved voice say, and had to bite his lip not to laugh out loud. This whole bizarre episode was going to make a fine tale for the lads in the mess. Provided he made it safely back, that was. He himself was therefore equally relieved to see the soldier remount his horse before the trio set off in the direction of the arms cache, where presumably they would set up camp.

'We must move now, for they will almost certainly send out a patrol once they are settled.' The woman spoke in English. Her accent had a slight lisping quality that was undeniably charming.

One look at the sky, where a full moon was making its presence felt from behind the scudding clouds, made his mind up for him. Finlay nodded his agreement. 'My horse is hidden in a copse just over that ridge.'

'I know it. Let me lead the way, I know this terrain like the back of my hand.'

It went against the grain for him, but his instincts told him to trust her. They made their way along the ditch, inch by painfully silent inch, for half an hour as the moon rose higher and higher and the stars above them hung like lanterns suspended in the sky. Finlay was struck, as he was on every single clear night like this in Spain, by how much brighter and closer to earth they seemed compared to the tiny twinkling lights in the Argyll sky, back home in Scotland.

Ahead of him, the woman stopped and looked cautiously out of the ditch before standing up. 'We can follow this track here. It will take us over the ridge. Now that you have located the arms dump I presume the English army will destroy it?'

'It's a British army, with Scots and Irish and Welsh soldiers as well as English.'

'And you, I think, with that skirt, are Scottish?'

'Kilt. *Plaid* if you like, but not a skirt. Skirts are for women.'

He saw the glint of her teeth as she smiled at him. 'And you, soldier, are decidedly not a woman.'

Finlay surveyed her for the first time, in the fluorescent glow of the moon, and wondered how he could ever have thought *her* anything else. She was young, no more than twenty-three or four, he reckoned. Her rough woollen breeches were tucked into sturdy brown boots. Over her heavy tunic, the leather belts worn cross-wise held gunpowder, a pistol and a knife. The uniform of a partisan, a rebel fighter. But the long legs inside the breeches were shapely. The belt cinched a waist that even underneath the bulk of the tunic was slim. The hair pulled back from the face had been silky soft against his unshaven chin. And her face... The large, almond-shaped eyes under finely arched brows, the strong nose, the full lips—there could be no mistaking that for anything other than a woman, and a very attractive one, at that. 'We have established the reason for my presence. But what, may I ask, are you doing out here?' he asked.

Her smile faded. 'I told you, the same thing you are doing. Locating the French armaments.'

'But alone. And you are...'

'Female.' She stood straight, tossing her head and glaring at him. 'You think a woman is any less observant than a man?'

'Quite the contrary, but I do think sending a woman on her own on such a mission was a bloody stupid thing to do. These French soldiers would not necessarily have killed you straight away, lass,' Finlay said gently, 'if they had captured you.'

'I would not let them capture me. Under any circumstances,' she added darkly.

'You should not have been sent—assuming that whatever guerrilla group you belong to did actually authorise your foolhardy mission?'

She glowered at him again, opened her mouth to

speak, then obviously thought better of it. 'We should not be standing here debating in the open. It is not safe.'

She had a point. She also clearly did not trust him, despite his uniform. And why should she, Finlay thought wryly as he allowed her to lead the way along the narrow track he'd followed earlier. The problem was, he needed her to trust him enough to tell him what her fellow partisans' plans were. If they meant to liberate the French weaponry and use it against them, it would save his men a job—and he could ill spare his men for such a mission, no matter how vital. Vitoria had knocked seven colours of shite out of them, and now Wellington was champing at the bit to attack the fortress towns of Pamplona and San Sebastian, despite the fact that desertion, sickness and sheer bloody exhaustion, to say nothing of the unseasonal and relentless rain, were having a serious impact on morale. If he could spare his men even one sortie...

Finlay frowned. He could not see how it was to be done. He knew no more about this woman than she knew about him. If he could at least find out who she took her orders from, for he was pretty certain he knew all the local guerrilla groups, and those he did not know his friend Jack, Wellington's master codebreaker, of a certainty would. If only he could get her to talk.

They were climbing steeply now, pebbles from the narrow rocky path skittering down behind them. The moon was high enough in the sky to cast ghostly shadows. The woman moved lithely, her long legs in their tight boots seemingly tireless as she set a pace that would have left some of Finlay's men gasping for breath. Raised in the Highlands, a childhood spent roaming the narrow sheep tracks on lower but equally rugged terrain, Finlay followed, his kilt swinging out behind him, his eyes alternating between his booted feet and the beguiling curve of his companion's shapely behind. There was a lot to be said for women in trousers.

There was a lot to be said for men wearing kilts, too. As an officer, he'd the right to trews, but Finlay had always preferred the freedom of his plaid. Other officers from other regiments, especially those up-their-own-arse cavalry, saw Finlay's loyalty to the kilt as one more piece of evidence of his barbarity. The Jock Upstart, Wellington had christened him when he had first, against all the odds and much against the duke's inclination, clambered out of the ranks. Finlay, smiling through very gritted teeth, had sworn to be true to this moniker forever. His plaid was just one of the many ways he maintained his rebellious streak. Sometimes subtly and subversively. Frequently, less so.

He wondered what this woman's family thought of her wandering about the countryside armed to the teeth. Perhaps they didn't know. Perhaps she was married to a rebel warrior herself. It struck him, as it had often recently, how very different it was for the Spanish who fought alongside them, or who fought as this woman did, in their own underground guerrilla groups. Finlay was a soldier, doing the job he'd been trained to do, had been doing, man and boy. His cause was whatever his country and his commanding officer decreed it to be, his enemy whomever they nominated his enemy to be, and for the past few years it had been the French. He loathed the barbarities they had been responsible for, but he equally loathed the atrocities his own side, drunk on bloodlust and wine, had committed in the aftermath of Ciudad Rodrigo. But he did not hate the French indiscriminately. He admired their soldiers—they were worthy adversaries—and he would be a fool to do anything other than respect Napoleon's military genius.

Napoleon, however, had not invaded Finlay's homeland. The French army were not living off Finlay's family's croft, eating their oats and butchering their cattle. This woman, still striding out tirelessly as they crested the hill, was fighting for her country, her family, her village. And he, Finlay, might not be the enemy, but his men were still laying waste to the countryside in battle, laying siege to their ancient fortress towns and eating their hard-earned grain, even if they were paying a fair price for it. No wonder she had taken up arms. He'd bet his own sisters would do the same.

'What do you find amusing?'

They had come to a halt on the ridge. The copse where Finlay's horse was tethered was in the valley, about a hundred feet below. He hadn't realised he was smiling. 'I was trying to imagine my mother's reaction if she caught my sisters playing the soldier, as you are.'

The woman bristled. 'This is no game. Our sovereignty, our very existence is at stake.'

'I did not mean to trivialise the actions of you and your comrades, lass—*señorita*. In fact, I was thinking just then how much I admire what you are doing. And thinking my sisters would likely do the same, if our lands were invaded as yours have been.'

'You have many sisters?'

Finlay laughed. 'It feels like it at times, though there's only three of them.'

'And brothers?'

'Just the one. What about you?'

'Just the one,' she said, with a twisted smile. 'He is with our army, fighting alongside you English— British. I don't know where he is exactly.'

'You must worry about his safety.'

She shrugged. 'Of course, though if he was close at hand I would not have the opportunity to be so—' she indicated her tunic, her gun '—involved. And so it is perhaps for the best, since we can both fight for our country in our own way.'

'Your family don't object to your active participation?'

'My mother is dead. My father is—he is sympathetic. He turns the closed eye, I think that is what you say?'

'Blind eye. Your English is a lot better than my Spanish.'

Another shrug greeted this remark. 'I have been fortunate in my education. Papa—my father—is not one of those men who thinks that girls should learn only to cook and sew. Unlike my brother. Without Papa's support and encouragement I would not be here, and we would not have known about that cache of arms.'

'So your partisan group do intend to do something about it?'

The question was out before he could stop it. The result, he could have predicted if he'd given himself a chance to think. She folded her arms and turned away. 'As a soldier yourself, you cannot expect me to disclose sensitive military information like that to a complete stranger. I will accompany you to the copse down there, and then we must go our separate ways.'

Cursing under his breath in Gaelic, Finlay followed her, determined more than ever, now that he'd made it even harder for himself, to find a way of making her trust him. If he was to do so, he'd need to stop her leaving. Which meant abandoning his plans to be back at camp by dawn, bidding farewell to the prospect of anything more appetising than the hard biscuits he had in his knapsack. On the other hand, it was not as if a few hours in the company of such a bonny and intriguing lass would be any great hardship. Even if their situation was fraught with danger. Maybe precisely *because* their situation was fraught with danger.

Isabella watched the Scottish soldier stride over to his horse, which was tethered to a tree on a rope long enough to let the animal reach the stream burbling along the valley floor. She watched him as he quickly checked that the beast was content before hauling a large bundle that must be the saddle from where it had been concealed under a bush.

He was a big man, solid muscle and brawn, with a fine pair of powerful legs revealed by that shocking garment he wore, and a broad pair of shoulders evident under his red coat. She knew enough to tell that it was an officer's coat, though she had no idea what rank. He did not have the haughty manners of a typical Spanish officer. There was none of their pompousness and vainglorious pride in his demeanour. Perhaps it was different in the English army? British—she must remember to call them British.

His hair was the colour of autumn leaves. It glinted in the moonlight, and the stubble on his face seemed tinged with flecks of gold. His eyes… She could not tell the colour of his eyes, but she could see well enough that his face was a very attractive one. Not exactly handsome, but nonetheless, the kind of face that would always draw a second look. And a third. The smile he gave her now, as he walked back towards her, was the kind of smile that would ensure its recipient smiled back. She bit down firmly on her own lip, and equally firmly ignored the stir of response in her belly.

'Major Finlay Urquhart of the Ninety-Second Foot,' he said. 'I know it's a bit late in the day for introductions, but there you are. I am delighted to meet you, *señorita*…?'

'I—Isabella. You may call me Isabella.'

To her surprise he took her hand, bowing over it with a graceful flourish, brushing her fingertips with his lips. 'Isabella. A pleasure to make your acquaintance,' he said, as his smile darkened and took a decidedly wicked form.

'Major Urk…Urk…'

'Urquhart. It's pronounced Urk-hart. It might be easier if you called me Finlay.'

'Finlay,' Isabella repeated slowly, smiling. 'Yes, that

is better. Well, Finlay, it has been very nice to meet you,
but I must…'

'Don't go just yet.'

Truthfully, she did not want to, though truthfully,
she did not want to admit that to herself. It was not
the journey home that bothered her; she could do that
blindfold. It was him. She ought—indeed, she had a
duty—to discover what the British plans were with
regard to the French arms dump. Reassured, she gave
a little nod. 'I will stay for a moment,' Isabella conceded, 'and rest a little.'

'You don't sound in the least as if you need a rest.'

'I don't,' she said, instantly defensive, almost as instantly realising that she had contradicted herself. 'But
I would welcome some water. I am parched.'

'Sit down. I'll bring you some.'

'I am perfectly able…'

'I'm sure you are, but I have a cup in my knapsack—
it's a mite easier to use than your hands. Sit down there,
I won't be a minute.'

Though she was loath to do as he bid her, loath to be
waited on as if she was a mere woman, Isabella sat. The
water was cool and most welcome. She drank deeply,
and consented to have more brought for the sake of pla-
cating the soldier, and for no other reason. *'Gracias.'*

'De nada.'

He sat down beside her, leaning back against the tree
trunk. His eyes, she could see now, were a startlingly
deep blue under heavy brows, which were drawn together in a faint frown. Despite the fiery glints in his

hair, his skin was neither fair nor burned by the sun, but tanned deep brown.

'Well, now, Isabella, it seems to me that it would be daft for us both—my men and yours—to consider launching a sortie against this French arms dump, would it not? No point treading on each other's toes unnecessarily.'

His accent was strange, lilting, soft, and some of the words he spoke she could not translate, but she understand him only too well. He was going about it more subtly this time, but he was still interested in one thing only from her: what were the partisans' intentions with regard to the French arms cache? Fine and well, for that was also the only reason she was interested in him. The thought made Isabella smile, and her smile made the soldier look at her quizzically, an eyebrow raised, his own sensual mouth quirking up on one side.

'I'd give a lot to know what is going on in that bonny head of yours, *señorita*. I mean,' he said, when she looked confused, 'I'd like to know what you are thinking.'

'I wager you would, soldier, but I'm not going to tell you.'

'Finlay. It's Finlay.'

'Finlay,' she repeated.

'Aye, that's it, you have it. There's not many use my name these days, apart from at home, that is. But it's been nigh on seven years since I've been there.'

'And where is home?' Isabella asked.

'A village in Argyll, not far from Oban. That's in the Highlands of Scotland. My family live in a wee cottage not unlike the ones you see in the villages hereabouts, and they farm, too, just like the villagers here, though they grow oats not wheat, and it's far too cold and wet for grapes, so there's no wine. Mind you, my father makes a fine whisky. He has a boat, too, for the fishing.'

Isabella stared at him in surprise. 'So your family are peasant stock? But you are an officer. I thought that all English officers were from grand English families. The Duke of Wellington, he is famous—'

'For saying that an officer must also be a gentleman,' Finlay interrupted her, making no attempt to hide his contempt. 'I'm the exception that proves the rule—an officer who is definitely not a gentleman,' he clarified. 'And I'll remind you, for the last time, that I'm not English. I'm Scottish.'

'I'm sorry. I think it is like calling a Basque person Spanish, no? I did not mean to insult you.'

'I've been called much worse, believe me. Are you from the area, then? I hope I've not insulted you by speaking Spanish. I'm afraid the only words I have in Basque I would not utter in front of a lady.'

The word was like a touchpaper to her. 'I am not a lady. I am a soldier. I may not wear a military uniform like my brother, but I, too, am fighting for the freedom of my country, Major Urka—Urko—Major Finlay.'

'By heavens, you've some temper on you. I've clearly touched a raw nerve there.'

'You have not, I am merely pointing out...'

He picked up one of her hands, which was curled into a very tight fist, and forced it open. She tried to resist but it was a pointless exercise; his big calloused hand had the strength of ten of hers. It was only when he let her go that she realised he could easily have hurt her, and had taken good care not to. Was he being chivalrous? Patronising? Was he showing her, tacitly, that a man was better, stronger than a woman? Why was it always so complicated? And why, despite his show of strength—or muted show of strength—did she feel no fear? She was alone in the dark of night with a complete stranger. A man who could overpower her and force himself on her if he wanted to. Her hand slid to her holster, though it was rather because she knew she ought to do so than because she thought she needed to.

'I won't harm you.' He was looking pointedly at her hand. 'You have my word. I have never in my life forced myself on a woman.'

He would have no need. And even though she knew, as everyone knew after being so long at war, what many soldiers did to women in the aftermath of battle, she could not imagine that this man would. There had been a grimness in his voice when he'd warned her about the French soldiers; it spoke of experiences he would rather forget. But then everyone involved in this struggle, including her, shared those.

Isabella gave herself a shake. 'I believe you,' she said, realising that Finlay was still waiting on an answer.

'Good.'

His tone was curt, though he should be grateful for her trust. And she did trust him, which was extremely surprising and, little did he know it, very flattering. She glanced at him, as he sat, eyes closed, head thrown back, resting on his elbows. He did not look like the poor son of a farmer. He did not look like a peacock officer, either, and while he certainly didn't have the hands of a gentleman, he had the manners of one. No, that was not fair. He had not treated her as a fragile flower with no mind. He had treated her with respect, and she liked that. He would be a popular officer, she was willing to bet, and those were few and far between, if her brother was to be believed. She tried to imagine her brother wearing that skirt—kilt. He would look like a girl, while this man—no, there was nothing at all feminine about this man.

'Once again, lass, I'd give a lot to know what's going on in that head of yours.'

Caught staring, Isabella looked hurriedly away. 'I was thinking that you must be a very good soldier, to have become a major.'

Finlay laughed. 'That is a matter of opinion. Being a good soldier and a good officer don't necessarily go hand in hand. It's taken me a great deal more time and effort than most to get to where I am. As you said yourself, Wellington is not at all keen on the idea of commoners rising through the ranks.'

'In that, I think the Spanish and the English— British armies are the same,' Isabella said. 'Before the war, most of the officers were more concerned with the shine of their boots than the fact that some of their men had no boots at all. Things will be different when we have won our country back from the French.'

'You speak with conviction. It is not over yet.'

'No, but when it is…'

'Oh, when it is we can but hope that the world will turn in a different direction,' Finlay replied. 'Maybe they'll even allow women soldiers,' he added with a wry smile. 'Though if you asked me to tell the truth, I'd say that right now, the army is no fit life for anyone, man or woman. We've been fighting too hard for too long, and all we want is for it to be over.'

'That is all my people desire, too.'

'Aye, you're in the right of it. You must be desperate to see the back of all of us.'

'If you mean that we want you to go home...'

'To have your country back.'

'Yes.'

'And your life.'

'Yes,' Isabella said again, though with less certainty.

'Provided that it doesn't go back to exactly how it was before, eh?' Finlay said, as if he had read her mind. 'Now that you've had a wee—a small taste of freedom?'

'Yes.' Isabella smiled. 'A wee taste of freedom,' she repeated carefully. 'And you, too, you will be able to go back to your father's farm in Scotland, and see all your loved ones. You will like that?'

'I will look forward to it,' he said, after a moment, sounding, to her surprise, as hesitant as she had.

'You do not wish to see your family?'

'Oh, aye, only I don't—ach, no point in talking about that. The war's not over yet. Once we've kicked the French out of Spain, we'll like as not have to chase them across France for a while. Which leads me back to that cache of arms.' He sat up, pushing his hair back from his forehead. 'Look, you don't know me and I don't know you, but these are unusual circumstances we find ourselves in. We can't allow the French to turn those guns on either of us, and I can make sure that they don't. Have I your assurance that the local rebel forces won't interfere and queer the pitch?'

'I don't know what that means, but regardless, I think it would be much better to leave it in our hands,' Isabella said firmly. 'We will put the arms to good use, and—and it would be excellent for morale and quite a coup if we were successful.'

Finlay pressed his fingertips together, frowning down at his hands. 'I'll be frank with you. I would quite happily agree to what you suggest if I could only be sure that the mission would be successfully accomplished. You understand, much as I'd like to, I can't just simply take your word for it.'

She bit back her instinctive retort, frowning now herself. 'If I told you that the information I have gathered tonight would go direct to El Fantasma, would that be enough to convince you?'

'You *know* El Fantasma?'

Isabella nodded.

Finlay looked unconvinced. 'He is like his name, a ghost. Everyone has heard of him, nobody knows him.'

'I do,' she said firmly. 'At least, I know how to get in touch with him.'

'Can you prove it?'

'I cannot. I can only give you my word.' She spoke proudly, held his gaze without blinking and was rewarded, finally, with a small nod of affirmation.

'You have three days to act. If I don't receive word that you have been successful by then, I'll send my own men in to finish the job.'

'Thank you. You can be sure that word will be sent to you before the three days are up.'

He took the hand she held out, enveloping it in his own. 'You don't ask *where* to send word.'

With a smile of satisfaction, she told him exactly where his men were encamped. 'One of our men will find you.'

'I'm beginning to think they will.' He still had her hand in hers, but instead of shaking it as she had seen Englishmen do, he once again bent his head and brushed her fingertips with his lips. 'We have an agreement, then,' he said.

Once again, the touch of his lips on her skin gave her shivers. Isabella snatched her hand away. 'We have indeed,' she said quickly.

She had what she wanted; she was free to leave. Reluctantly, she made to get to her feet, but the Scotsman's hand on her arm stopped her. 'Stay until it's light, won't you? It's not safe for me to leave before then. Unlike you, I don't know the terrain. Also, it's been a while since I've had the company of a woman. It would be good to talk of something other than guns and field positions.'

'You think I cannot?'

'Why in the name of Hades are you so prickly? I'm not one of those men who think women have no mind of their own. If you met my mother, you'd know why.' He turned to look at her, his gaze disconcertingly direct. 'As to you women being the weaker sex—if ever I thought that, just seeing what the wives following the drum have to endure would change my mind. They have to be every bit as tough as their menfolk. Tougher, in some cases, when they have bairns with them. Though I'd be lying, mind, if I said I thought it was an appropriate life for them.'

He broke off, giving himself a little shake. 'Ach, I'm sorry, I didn't mean to rant at you. If you want to talk guns and tactics, then that's what we'll talk. Only indulge me with a few hours of your company, and grant me the pleasure of looking on your bonny face, for it will be a while, I reckon, until I get the chance to do either again.'

His smile was beguiling. The look he gave her neither contrite nor beseeching, but—charming? He was not a man accustomed to being refused. On principle, she should refuse, but she was rather sick of principles, and what, after all, was the harm in allowing herself to be charmed for such a very short while?

Isabella permitted herself to smile back. 'I do not think a man like you has any trouble at all in finding female company.'

He laughed again, showing her a set of very white teeth, shifting on the ground, giving her a brief, shockingly tantalising glance of a muscled thigh as he did so. 'The trouble is, I'm a bit fussy about the female company I choose,' he said. 'I prefer to get to know a woman before I—before— What I mean is, I've a taste for conversation that I've not recently been able to indulge. Now, that makes me sound like I'm right up my own ar— I mean, like a right fop, and I'm not that.'

Isabella chuckled. 'I am not exactly sure what this fop is, but I am very sure it is not a label that fits you.'

'What I mean is, I like the company of women for their own sake.'

'And I think that women like the company of Major Urk—of Finlay.'

'Right now there's only one woman's company I'm interested in. Will you stay a few hours, Isabella?'

Why not? Her father would cover for her absence if necessary, but likely she'd be back in her bed before anyone noticed it had not been slept in. What harm could it do to indulge this man with a few hours' conversation? The fact that he had a beguiling smile and a handsome face and a very fine pair of legs had nothing to do with it. 'Why not?'

He smiled. 'Tell me a bit about yourself, then. Are you from these parts?'

'Hermoso Romero. It's not far from here. We have— My family has some land.'

'So they're farmers, peasant stock as you call it, just like mine?'

'They live off the land, yes.'

'And it's just you and your parents you say, for your brother's in the army?'

'Just me and my father. My mother is dead.'

'Oh, yes, you mentioned that. I'm sorry.'

'Thank you, but I never knew her. She died when I was very young.'

'Then, I'm very sorry for you indeed. A lassie needs her mother, especially if she's not got a sister.'

'I cannot miss what I have not had,' Isabella said stiffly.

Finlay opened his mouth to say something, thought the better of it, and shrugged, reaching over to pull his saddlebag towards him. 'Would you like something to eat? I'm hungry enough to eat a scabby-headed wean.'

'A— What did you say?'

'I said I'm very hungry. This is all I have, I'm afraid,' he said, passing her a handful of dry biscuits. 'It tastes better washed down with this, though,' he added, holding out a small silver flask. 'Whisky, from my father's own still. Try it.'

She sipped, then coughed as the fiery spirit caught the back of her throat. 'Thank you,' she said, returning the flask and wrinkling her nose, 'I think I will stick to water.'

'It is an acquired taste, right enough,' Finlay said, putting the cap back on after taking, she noticed, only a very small sip himself. 'Tell me a bit more about yourself. For example, how does it happen that such a bonny lass is not married?'

'How does it happen that such a—bonny?—man is not married?'

Finlay laughed. 'No, no, you don't describe a man as bonny, unless you wish to impugn him. I'm not married because I'm a soldier, and being a soldier's wife is no life worth having. Since I am a career soldier, my single status is assured. Now I have explained myself. What about you?'

Isabella shrugged. 'While my country is at war and under occupation, I cannot think of anything else.'

'Aye, I can understand that. It's hard to imagine what peace will look like after all this time.' Finlay pulled a blanket from his saddle and offered it to her. 'Here, it's getting mighty cold.'

'I do not need...'

'For the love of— Come here, will you, and we'll share it, then.' Taking her by surprise, he pulled her towards him, throwing the blanket around them. He grabbed her arm as she tried to struggle free, and slid his own across her shoulders. 'I'd do the same for one of my own men if I had to,' he said.

'I don't believe you.'

'It's a sacrifice I'd be prepared to make—I hope. Luckily I've never had to put myself to the test.'

She felt the rumble of his laugher, and the warm puff of his breath on her hair. She had not noticed how cold it had become until he put the blanket around her. It would be churlish to push him away now, and a little silly, for then she would have to walk in the morning with stiff, cold limbs. She did not relax, but she no longer struggled, and allowed herself to lean back against the tree trunk. 'Tell me more about Scotland,' she said. 'Is it very different from Spain?'

'Very. For a start, there's the rain. The sky and the sea are more often grey than blue. Mind, all that rain makes for a green landscape. I think that's what I miss the most, the lush greenery that carpets the valleys and hills.'

'We have a lot of rain here in the north, in the winter.'

'Aye, but in Scotland, on the west coast, it rains most days in the summer, too. Are you sleepy? Should I stop babbling?'

Isabella smothered a yawn. 'No, if you mean should you stop talking. Tell me what other countries you have visited as a soldier.'

'Many campaigns. Egypt. Portugal. France. Ireland. America.'

'You are so lucky, I have never been out of Spain.'

'I'm not sure that you see the best of a country when you go there to fight.'

'No, but—tell me please. Describe what America is like. Is it the wild, untamed wilderness that I have heard tell of?'

'Once you leave the east coast, yes. And vast. A man could lose himself there.'

'Or find himself?'

Finlay was still musing on that thought when Isabella wriggled around under the blanket to look up at him. He tensed, willing his body not to respond to the supple curves of her. Her hair tickled his chin. He was inordinately grateful for the thick layers of clothing between them, and tried discreetly to shift his thigh away from hers. Concentrating his mind on answering her questions, he found she drew him out, that his desire, while it remained a constant background tingle, was subdued by his interest in her, by hers in him.

Eventually, as the moon sank and true darkness fell, they grew silent. He thought she slept, though he could not be sure. He thought he remained awake, though he could not be certain of that, either. They moved neither closer nor farther apart, and that, Finlay told himself, was as it should be.

In the morning he was glad of it. She stirred before sunrise, and he lay with his eyes closed, affording her some privacy. Only when she stood over him did he pretend to wake, getting to his feet, trying not to notice the way the water she had splashed on her face had dampened her hair, making a long tress of it cling to her cheek.

'You will find your way back to your own lines?' she asked.

He nodded. 'It'll be easier in daylight, provided I keep a weather eye out for French patrols.'

'I will send word when we have—when it is done, I promise.'

'I believe you.'

He took the hand she offered him. In the dawn light, her eyes seemed more golden than brown. He wanted to kiss that nervously smiling mouth of hers. He wanted, quite fervently, to have her body pressed against his, her arms around his neck. He took a step towards her. For a moment he felt it, the tug of desire between them, that unmistakable feeling, like the twisting of a very sharp knife in his guts. It was because he wanted to kiss her so much that he stopped himself, bent over her hand, clicking his heels together, then let her go. '*Adiós*, Isabella. Good luck. Please be careful. Stay safe.'

'Goodbye, Finlay. May God protect you and keep you from harm.'

She turned and slowly walked away, following the path of the stream as it meandered along the floor of the valley. Finlay watched her until she disappeared from sight behind a large outcrop of rock. Then he picked up his saddle, and within a few moments, just as the sun streaked the sky with pink-and-orange fingers, he, too, was on his way, heading in the opposite direction.

Chapter Two

England—autumn 1815

'So, Jack, are you going to spill the beans on why you had me hotfoot it down here? I'm intrigued. But then knowing you, you old fox, that was precisely your intention when you composed the enigmatic message I received.'

They were strolling in the grounds of Jack's brother's home, Trestain Manor, where he was currently residing, Finlay having arrived post-haste in answer to an urgent summons. Now he eyed his friend grimly. 'You're looking a bit rough around the edges, if you don't mind my saying so. Is this anything to do with the information I dug up for you regarding your wee painter lassie?'

'Her name is Celeste, and she is not, as I told you in London, *my* wee painter lassie,' Jack snapped. 'Sorry. I'm just— What you told me helped me a lot, and I'm hoping to solve the rest of the puzzle now that I have permission from Wellington to delve into those secret files.'

'But things concerning the lassie herself don't look so hopeful?' Finlay asked carefully.

Jack shrugged. 'Let's just say I'm advancing on some fronts but have sustained some collateral damage on others.' The words were light-hearted but the tone of his friend's voice told Finlay the subject was not open for further discussion. 'The reason I asked you here is nothing to do with that, although indirectly it brought it about.'

Finlay rolled his eyes. 'Would you get to the point and stop talking in code, man!'

Jack smiled faintly. 'A habit that's difficult to break. It's a delicate matter, though, Finlay, and obviously everything I tell you is in the strictest confidence. I don't mean to insult your utter trustworthiness, but Wellington made me promise…'

'Wellington!'

'When I accosted him at that dinner I attended on your behalf with my little problem of those secret files, he told me about a little problem of his own.' Jack's expression darkened. 'Save that it's not only the duke's problem, Finlay. I see it as very much mine. When we were in Spain, do you recall talk of a partisan commander called El Fantasma?'

'The Ghost! I'd have had to be deaf and dumb not to. He was a legend in the north during the Peninsular Campaign.'

'Yes, he was. The partisans in that area were incredibly effective in targeting the French supply lines thanks to him, and in intercepting mail. He was one of my most reliable and effective spies. The information he provided saved a great many lives.' Jack plucked a long piece of grass, and began to twine it around his finger. 'The thing is, Finlay, this El Fantasma knows some pretty compromising stuff, politically, that is. Some of the things that were done in the name of war—they wouldn't stand up to much scrutiny in the press.'

'Jack, none of the reality of war would sit well with the peacetime press.'

'You're right about that. To be honest, I think it would be a good thing if some of it did come into the public domain. Since Waterloo, no one wants to know about the suffering of those who fought, the pittance they have to live on, the fact that the army has cast them aside, having no further need for them.' Jack broke off, fists clenched. 'Sorry, I know I'm preaching to the converted in you, and I've strayed from the point again. The problem, as far as the duke is concerned, is that, were El Fantasma to fall into the wrong hands, it could be extremely embarrassing, not to say damaging to his political career.'

'The wrong hands being…?'

'The Spanish government. Since Ferdinand was restored to the throne, the ruling elite has been cracking down on the former partisans and guerrillas who continue to speak out against them. Many of the more vocal liberals, the ones with influence, have been exiled, a significant number of them executed. El Fantasma, however, is still a thorn in their side. Rather more than a thorn, actually. You know that the freedom of the press in Spain is one of the many liberties that's been curtailed? Here, take a look at this.'

Jack handed Finlay what looked like a political pamphlet. It was written in a mixture of Spanish and Basque, from what he could determine, and the printed signature at the end was quite clearly that of El Fantasma, the small image of a spectre on the front page providing confirmation.

'This edition calls for the Constitution of 1812 to be restored, among many other things. Advocating that alone could get him hanged. I imagine the other editions espouse equally revolutionary views.' Jack was now frowning deeply. 'Wellington has been tipped off through one of his various diplomatic connections that the Spanish government are determined to flush El Fantasma out. He is a dangerous focal point and voice of anti-government rhetoric, and they intend to silence him once and for all. You can guess what that means.'

'It means I wouldn't like to be in his boots if they snare him.'

'And they will, Finlay. It's only a matter of time.'

'Which is what has put the wind up Wellington, I presume?'

Jack nodded. 'He says it is a matter of state security. It goes without saying that his concerns are partly driven by self-interest, but you know as well as I do how wide that man's sphere of influence is.'

'If the duke says it's a matter of state security, then undoubtedly it is. So he wants to get to El Fantasma before the Spanish do, I take it, and he's thinking that you are the man for the job, since a great deal of your information came from that very source?'

'El Fantasma did an enormous amount for us, and

risked his life every day to do so. We owe it to him—*I* owe it to him personally, to make sure no harm comes to him. Which is where you come in.'

Finlay stared at his friend, his head reeling. 'Wellington wants me to go to Spain?'

'*I* want you to go to Spain. Wellington agreed to leave the matter in my hands. Since I'm the only person he could think of with the first clue of where to start, he had little option. I have his permission to act as I see fit and to use whatever resources I require. It's official business in that sense, though if anything goes wrong, of course, he'll deny all knowledge. In war and politics, there are always shades of grey, aren't there? Well, this is one instance. The Spanish want to silence our partisan. Our government, being afraid of what he might reveal in order to save his neck, also wants to silence him, Finlay. Do you see?'

'I do. And what, I'm wondering, is it you really want me to do for you?'

'Get El Fantasma out of Spain and the government's clutches by any means possible. Forcibly, if need be. It's for his own good. That will be difficult enough, but then there is the small matter of keeping him out of Wellington's clutches thereafter,' Jack said with a chilling smile. 'Here's how I think it can be achieved.'

Finlay listened in silence as Jack explained his plan and then let out a low whistle. 'You certainly haven't lost your touch, laddie. You do realise if the powers that be find out, it could be interpreted as a treasonable act,' he said, eyeing his friend with something akin to awe. 'It's a bold and possibly reckless strategy.'

'Precisely why I thought of you,' Jack quipped, though his face was serious. 'I know it's asking an enormous amount, but I can't think of anyone else I'd trust with the task. I would go myself, only I can't. I am not—not in the best of health, and there are things I am embroiled in here... If it could wait a few weeks, but I am not sure that it can, and so...'

'Jack, there's no need to explain yourself. Whatever is going on between you and your wee painter lassie is your business. I just hope the outcome is a good one,' Finlay said. 'Besides,' he continued hurriedly, for his friend was looking painfully embarrassed, 'can you not see that I'm bored out of my mind? Is this not the kind of scrape that you know fine and well I love beyond anything?'

He was rewarded with an awkward smile. 'I did think that you might be tempted, but...'

'Let me tell you something. When I got your note, I confess I was relieved. I'm not used to having all this free time. It doesn't suit me one whit. You know I've never been comfortable with mess life, and it's even worse now there's no battles to be fought, and the talk is all of dancing and parties and who is the fairest toast in the town and what particular shade of brown this Season's coats should be. I'm a man who needs to be doing something.'

Jack smiled, but his expression remained troubled. 'I thought the plan was for you to spend some time back in the Highlands.'

'I did go back, briefly,' Finlay replied, 'but—ach, I don't know. My brother has the croft well in hand,

and I don't want to be standing on his toes, and...'
He shook his head. 'It all seemed so tame and so very
quiet.'

'I know what you mean,' Jack said wryly. 'Trestain
Manor is hardly a cauldron of excitement, though it
would be churlish of me to complain. My brother, Charlie, and his wife, Eleanor, have been good enough to
take me in since I resigned my commission.' The two
men sat down on the bank of a stream. 'What about
you? Will you stay in the army, do you think, now that
it looks like lasting peace has finally been achieved?'

Finlay shrugged. 'Soldiering is all I know. Anyway,
no point thinking about the future when there's work
to be done,' he said brusquely. 'It's agreed. I'll go to
Spain and smuggle this El Fantasma out of the country, by hook or by crook. Just tell me what he looks
like and where I might find him.'

Jack grimaced. 'That, I am afraid, is the first of
many hurdles to be overcome. I have no idea what he
looks like, never having met the man. The partisans
operated in small, isolated groups to preserve anonymity. I dealt only with third parties—contacts of contacts, so to speak. Even assuming they have survived,
which is by no means certain, many of them went into
exile at the end of the war. It will be like looking for
a needle in a haystack.' Jack ran his fingers through
his hair. 'What you need is a starting point, and we
don't have one.'

'Actually, I think we might have,' Finlay said slowly.
'Do you remember my tale of the occasion I attacked
what I thought was a French guard, and it was...'

'A female Spanish partisan.'

Finlay smiled. 'Isabella, her name was. I've often wondered what became of her.'

Jack laughed. 'I'm sure her charms, as you described them to me, were grossly exaggerated. Moonlight and a dearth of females to compare her to will most certainly have coloured your view.'

'Not at all, she was a right bonny wee thing, and a brave one, too, but that's not what's important.'

'Now you're the one talking in riddles.'

'She claimed to know how to get in touch with El Fantasma. Now, I know virtually nothing about her. I don't even know for certain if she was telling the truth. It'd be clutching at straws. A very long shot, indeed. But in the absence of any other lead...'

'It is at least a potential starting point, although as a partisan, there's a good chance she may not have survived the war.'

Finlay grimaced. 'She didn't even tell me her full name. All I know is that she came from a place not far from where I found the arms cache. Roma? Roman? Romero? Aye, something Romero, I think that was it, but to be honest I can't be sure. If I could take a look at a map I reckon I could pinpoint it.'

'Don't go leaping into action just yet,' Jack cautioned. 'You'll need a cover story, papers, funds. I have contacts in London who will arrange everything you need, including passage on whatever naval ship is heading for Spanish waters. You may have to leave at very short notice.'

'If it means not having to take part in another mess

discussion about the best way to tie a cravat, I'll go today.'

'I am very much in your debt. You will send me word, won't you, as soon as you are back safe in England?'

Finlay clasped his hand firmly. 'I will return, never fear. Where would Wellington be without his Jock Upstart?'

North of Spain—one month later

Finlay had endured a long journey, and since arriving in Spain, one increasingly redolent with memories of the campaign there, some of them very unpleasant indeed. Though more than two years had passed, the legacy of the war was evident in the ruined fortress port of San Sebastian where he had made landfall, and in the surrounding countryside as he travelled south through Pamplona, thankfully avoiding the site of that last bloody battle at Vitoria.

Here, in the wine-growing countryside of the La Rioja region, was his final destination. Hermoso Romero. He was still not absolutely certain he was heading for the right place, but it was the only one on the map that had anything approaching the name he thought the Spanish partisan had mentioned. It was not, as he had imagined, a small hamlet where her family had a farm, but as the Foreign Office research had revealed, a very large winery where presumably the partisan's family were employed to work on the estate, which was the largest in the region.

Finlay dismounted from his horse and shaded his eyes to gaze down into the valley. Hermoso Romero was a beautiful place, the pale yellow stone walls and the terracotta roofs mellowed by the late-autumn sunshine. The grapes had been harvested from the regimented lines of vines that fanned out on three sides from the house, while cypress trees formed a long windbreak on the fourth. The main house was a large building three storeys high, the middle section of which was graced with arched windows. What must be the working part of the estate was located to one side, built around a central courtyard, while at the back of the main block he could see what looked like a chapel, and some elegant private gardens contained by a low wall constructed of the same yellow stone.

Jack's mysterious contacts at the Foreign Office in London had done an impressively thorough job in providing Finlay with a cover story. The owner of the winery, Señor Xavier Romero, was by all accounts an extremely ambitious man, with a very high opinion of his Rioja wine. So when Señor Romero had been informed through a 'reliable' diplomatic source that an influential English wine merchant wished to pay him a visit to discuss a potential export deal, an invitation was immediately extended.

'He's likely to push the boat out a bit,' the man at the Foreign Office had warned Finlay. 'Be prepared to be courted. It would be advisable to crib up a little on the wine-production process if you can find the time.'

But time had been in very short supply. 'It is to be hoped that Señor Romero is more interested in allowing me to taste the wine than grilling me on my knowledge of grape varieties and vintages,' Finlay muttered, patting his pockets to reassure himself that his forged papers and letters of introduction were still in place. Though maintaining his alias was really the least of his problems. The scale of his task, the lack of information, the lack of any certainty at all, meant the odds of success were heavily stacked against him.

'So we are going down there,' he said, addressing his completely indifferent horse, 'filled with hope rather than expectation. Let's face it, laddie, there's a hundred reasons why this could be a wild goose chase. Would you like to hear some of them?'

The horse pawed at the ground, and Finlay chose to take this for assent. 'Let's see. First, there's the fact that though I think my partisan lass came from Hermoso Romero, I could be misremembering the name completely. Two years and a lot of water under the bridge since, it's likely is it not?'

He received no answer, and so continued, 'Then there's the lass herself. A woman who, if she did not actually fight with the guerrillas, most certainly was one of them. What are the chances of her having survived? And if she has, what are the chances of her remaining here, if indeed here is where she lived? And if she is alive, and she is here, how am I to know I can trust her? It's a dangerous thing, to espouse the liberal cause in Spain these days. My lass may well side with the royalists now—or at the very least, she'll simply keep her mouth shut and her nose clean and herself well clear of associating with the likes of El Fantasma, won't she?'

Receiving no answer once more, Finlay nodded to himself. 'And if by a miracle she is still alive *and* still a liberal, why in the name of Hades would she trust me enough to lead me to the great man? For all she knows, I could be out to snare him myself. And in a way, she'd be in the right of it, too. The Ghost. I have to find him, for I most certainly don't intend to let him haunt me for the rest of my life. So there you have it, what do you think of my chances now, lad?'

To this question, his horse did reply with a toss of his head. Finlay laughed. 'As low as that, eh? You're in the right of it, most likely, but devil take it if I don't try to prove you wrong all the same. I've never been a death-or-glory man, but I've always been a man who gives his all.'

Mounting his trusty steed and turning towards the wide, new-built road that wound down towards the winery, Finlay felt as he did surveying the field before a battle: excited, nervous, with every sense on high alert, dreading the start and at the same time wishing it could come more quickly. It was one of the worst feelings in the world, and one of the best. He felt, for the first time since Waterloo, truly alive with a sense of purpose. He had missed it greatly, he realised.

'Mr Urkerty. It is an immense pleasure to meet you. Welcome to Hermoso Romero.'

'Urquhart. Urk-hart.'

'Ah, yes, forgive me.' Xavier Romero, a good-looking man of about Finlay's own age, decided against a second attempt at the unfamiliar pronunciation, and instead shook his hand firmly. 'If you are not too tired after your long journey, I would very much like to take you on a short tour of my winery. I am anxious that you see the quality of what we produce here.'

'And I am just as anxious to sample it, *señor.*' Finlay had no sooner nodded his consent than he was escorted by his host back out of the front door, along the sweeping gravel walk and through another door that led into the courtyard he had spied from the top of the hill.

'Of course, the harvest is over for the year. It is a pity you could not have been here just a few weeks earlier. The soil here, as you will see when we go out into the vineyards tomorrow, is very heavy, mostly clay with some chalk. This gives the wine...'

Xavier Romero's English was extremely good. He seemed to require nothing from Finlay but nods and smiles, which was just as well, for he was clearly a man with a passion for the wine he made and all the technicalities of the process. From the briefing he had received, Finlay knew that Romero had served as a lieutenant in the Spanish army, fighting alongside several British regiments in the last two years of what the Spanish called the War of Independence, while their British allies referred to it as the Peninsular Campaign. Señor Romero's fellow British officers, two of whom Finlay had tracked down, had little to say of him other than that he seemed like a sound fellow, which Finlay took to mean that he was innocuous enough, and unlike the Jock Upstart, had the prerequisite amount of blue blood in his veins to fit in to the officers' cadre.

'We use oak barrels as they do in Bordeaux, but our grape varieties are very different. The main one is Tempranillo, as you will know, but...'

Señor Romero said nothing about his estate workers, a subject that interested Finlay much more than grape varieties, given the real nature of his business here. There was a small hamlet about a mile away, a cluster of cottages and farmland, planted with what looked like olive groves. Was it possible that the woman he had so fleetingly encountered lived in one of those cottages? He seemed to remember she said her family had some land.

Señor Romero was still pontificating. 'Of course, the estate is quiet at the moment while we wait for the first fermentation, but you should have seen it in September and October,' he said proudly, 'a veritable hive of activity. Grape picking is seasonal work. Once the harvest is in we have a big fiesta, which goes on for days. If only you had timed your visit better—but there, it cannot be helped.' His host pulled out a gold timepiece from his pocket and consulted it, a frown clouding his haughty visage. 'I apologise, Mr Urker, I got quite carried away. We must leave the rest of our tour until tomorrow, when I will do my best to answer the many questions I am sure you must have. I hope you do not mind, but tonight I have taken the liberty of arranging a small gathering in your honour. A few friends, only the best families in the area, you understand. Some of them produce Rioja, too. They will try to tell you it is superior to mine.' Señor Romero laughed gently. 'They are misguided.'

'I am sure that I will prefer your Rioja to anyone else's,' Finlay said.

He would make certain he did, even though he suspected he'd taste not a blind bit of difference between them.

As he wallowed in the luxury of a deep bath situated behind a screen in a luxurious bedchamber with a view out over the vineyards, Finlay was in fact starting to feel a wee bit guilty for raising his host's expectations, knowing that nothing would come of them. He hoped that two or three days at most would be sufficient for him to establish contact with the female partisan or to establish that she was not contactable, one way or another. The thought that she might be truly beyond any earthy communication was not one he wished to contemplate.

A glance at the elaborate clock on the mantel informed him that he had no time for contemplating anything other than getting himself dressed. He had refused the offer of a valet, but the evening clothes that he had, thankfully, packed at the last moment, had been pressed and laid out on the bed for him. Finlay dressed quickly. A brief assessment in the mirror assured him that he was neat as a pin and that his unruly hair was behaving itself for once. He would pass muster.

He gave his reflection a mocking bow and braced himself. Señor Romero had gone to a lot of trouble, but the idea of an evening spent making polite talk to the man's family and blue-blooded friends filled Finlay with guilty dread.

* * *

'Ah, Mr Urkery, here you are. Welcome, welcome.' Xavier Romero broke away from the small cluster of guests as Finlay entered the large vaulted room.

The collection of friends and family was significantly larger than Finlay had anticipated. This gathering reminded him of the glittering balls he had attended in Wellington's wake in Madrid. The scale of the room took his breath away. It was the full height of all three storeys of the building, with a vaulted ceiling, making it resemble the interior of a cathedral. The tall, arched windows were above head height and facing west, so that the fading evening sun cast golden rays over the assembled company of, Finlay reckoned, about a hundred if not more. The ladies' gowns in vivid colours of silk were high waisted and low-cut with puff sleeves as was the fashion in England, though their heads were dressed with the traditional mantilla of lace held in place with jewelled combs. The gentlemen, in contrast, seemed to be as Finlay was, dressed in black with pristine white shirts and starched cravats.

It was stifling in the room. Fans were fluttered, handkerchiefs used to mop brows. Jewels glinted; conversation buzzed. It was everything he hated. He had a very strong urge to turn tail and leave, but Xavier Romero was handing him a glass of sherry and telling him that he must before all else introduce his guest to his family.

As they made their way around the room, Finlay was the centre of attention. Women peeped at him over the tops of their fans. The men stared at him openly. He was probably the only outsider present. A small orchestra was tuning up. The acoustics of the place were impressive. That pretty woman over there in the red dress was making it very clear she would not be averse to an invitation to dance. She had a mischievous look that appealed to him. He would ask his host to introduce them later.

'Ah, at last. Allow me the honour of introducing you to my wife. Consuela, my dear, this is Mr Urkery, the wine merchant from England who is our guest of honour. I am afraid my wife speaks very little English.'

'No matter, I speak some, admittedly very bad, Spanish,' Finlay said, switching to that language as he made his bow. 'Finlay Urquhart—that is Urk-hart—at your service, Señora Romero. It is an honour.' The woman who gave him her hand was young and very beautiful, with night-black hair, soft, pretty features and a plump, voluptuous figure. 'And a pleasure,' Finlay said, smiling. 'Your husband is a very lucky man, if I may be so bold as to say so.'

Beside him, Xavier Romero managed to look both flattered and discomfited. 'Mr Urkerty is going to introduce our Rioja to the English, my love,' he said, edging closer to his wife. 'I am pleased to say that he believes, as I do, that they should drink wine from the vineyards of their allies, not Bordeaux from the vineyards of their former enemies. It is long past time that they did so, do you not agree, Mr Urkyhart? They have been happy to import as much port as your Portuguese friends in Oporto can supply. Now you and I, we will make sure that Rioja, too, takes its rightful place in the cellars of England, no?'

'The cellars of Scotland being too full of whisky, I suppose you're thinking,' Finlay said with an ironic little smile.

Fortunately, Romero simply looked confused by this barb. 'I must introduce you to—' He broke off, frowning, and scanning the room. 'You will excuse me for just a second while I fetch my sister. She has obviously forgotten that I specifically told her...'

He spoke sharply, clearly irked by his sister's non-compliance. Finlay had already taken a dislike to his host. Despite his attempt at obsequiousness, he had an air of entitlement that grated. Señor Xavier Romero considered himself as superior as his wine, his wife and sister mere chattels in his service. Finlay felt a twinge of sympathy for the tall woman about ten feet away whose shoulder Romero was gently prodding.

She wore a white lace mantilla. From the back, it obscured her hair and shoulders completely. Her gown was white silk embroidered with green leaves and trimmed with gold thread. Her figure was slim rather than curvaceous. She turned around, the lace of her mantilla floating out from the jewelled comb that kept it in place, and Finlay, not a man often at a loss for words, felt his jaw drop as their eyes met.

Dark chestnut hair. Almond-shaped, golden eyes. A full sensuous mouth. A beautiful face. A shockingly familiar face. Merciful heavens, but the person he had come on a wild goose chase to attempt to track down had, astonishingly, landed in his lap. The gods were indeed smiling on him.

Finlay's fleeting elation quickly faded as two thoughts struck him forcibly. First, she might very publicly blow his cover wide open. And second, she was clearly not who she had said she was. Extreme caution was required. Resisting the urge to storm across the room and cover her mouth with his hand before she could betray him, he forced himself to wait and watch.

That she recognised him was beyond a doubt in those first seconds. The shock he felt was mirrored in her own expression. Her mouth opened; her eyes widened. For an appalling moment he thought she was going to cry out in horror, then she flicked open her fan and hid behind it. Relief flooded him. She no more wanted him to acknowledge her than he wanted her to acknowledge him. He was safe. For the time being.

'May I present my sister? Isabella, this is Mr Urky-hart.'

'Urk-hart,' Finlay corrected wearily. 'Señorita Romero. It is a pleasure.'

'Mr Urquhart.' Isabella made her shaky curtsy. Her heart was pounding, her mouth quite dry. It was undoubtedly him. The English wine merchant bowing over her hand was the Scottish major she had encountered in a ditch more than two years ago. The man she had spent the night with. *Dios mio*, what was he doing here?

She gazed beseechingly at him. She had forgotten how very blue his eyes were. He was clean-shaven, his auburn hair brushed neatly back from his forehead. He was not wearing his kilt. If only she had mastered the Spanish art of communicating with her fan, she could beg him not to betray her secret partisan past. He had said nothing yet. She had to find a way of ensuring he kept silent about their previous encounter.

She slanted a glance at her brother. Xavier had made such a song and dance about this visit, seeing it as his chance to finally have his Rioja recognised as the great wine he believed it to be. Grudgingly—very grudgingly—Isabella admitted that her brother knew what he was talking about, but still, she had very much resented his command that they do all they could to make the man's visit memorable. If Xavier only asked rather than ordered it might be different. When she was feeling generous, Isabella put his tendency to command rather than request down to his years in the army. But she, too, had given orders during the war, and she had not returned to play the dictator.

Her brother drew her one of his looks. 'The first dance is about to start. I believe Gabriel wishes...'

Isabella threw the wine merchant another beseeching glance. Fortunately, he seemed to be able to read this look easily. 'If you would do me the honour, Señorita Romero, I would very much like to dance with you.'

'*Gracias.*' In a daze, she took his arm, propelling him towards the dance floor before Xavier could protest or stake Gabriel's prior claim.

'This,' the Scotsman said to her *sotto voce* as they

joined the set, 'is rather a turn up for the books. A very unexpected surprise, to put it mildly.'

The vague, ludicrous hope that he had not recognised her, or that he would ignore their previous meeting completely, fled. Isabella felt quite sick. The first chords of the dance were struck, forcing them to separate. She cast an anxious glance around her. They had spoken in whispers, but even if Xavier was not watching, that cold little mouse of his wife would be.

As the dance began, fortunately one that required only simple steps as they progressed up the line, she tried desperately to regain her equilibrium. The shock of seeing the Scottish soldier again, and in such incongruous circumstances, had fractured her usually immaculate composure. There was too much at stake. She had to pull herself together.

He was alive. In the shock of the meeting, this salient fact had escaped her. She had occasionally wondered what had become of him as the conflict in Spain had drawn to a close and the British and French had taken their battles into the Pyrenees. He had clearly survived that false end to the war. He must have left the army then and established himself in business. He had obviously done very well indeed for himself, though that was not really surprising. He had struck her as a very, very determined and resourceful man.

He had also struck her as a very attractive man. That had been no trick of the moonlight, and judging by the way every other woman in the room was slanting him glances, she was not the only one to think so. She was drawn to him just as she had been before, despite the fact that he could turn her world upside down. When he had brushed a kiss to her fingertips, the memory of his lips on her skin all that time ago had come rushing back with unexpected force. Isabella had no idea whether it was this, or the reality of his touch now, or the underlying terror of exposure that made her shiver. Whichever, it had taken her by surprise, for she had not thought of him in a long time.

He cut as fine a figure in his evening clothes as he had in his Scottish plaid. The tight breeches clung to his muscled legs; the coat made the most of his broad shoulders. She couldn't help comparing him to Gabriel, the man whom Xavier was eager for her to marry. There was no doubt her brother's friend was more handsome, but Gabriel's was the kind of beauty that reminded Isabella of a work of art. She could admire it, she could see he was aesthetically pleasing, but there was none of the almost feral pull that she felt towards this mysterious Scotsman.

Finally, the dance brought them together. 'May I compliment you on your *toilette*,' he said with a devilish smile. 'So very different from the outfit you wore the last time we met, though I must confess, your gown does not do justice as your trousers did to your delightful derrière.'

Colour flamed in her face. She ought to be outraged, but Isabella was briefly, shockingly inclined to laugh. 'A gentleman does not remark on a lady's derrière.'

'I seem to recall telling you when last we met that I am not a gentleman, *señorita*. And now I come to think of it, I recall also that you took umbrage at being called a lady.'

She had forgotten what that particular smile of his did to her, and how very difficult it was to resist smiling back as the dance parted them once more. He was dangerous, dangerous, dangerous.

'I never got the chance to thank you,' he said when they next crossed the set. 'I'm told your guerrillas did a very thorough job.'

They circled, hands brushing lightly. 'Of course we did,' Isabella replied in a whisper. 'Did you think I would not keep my word?'

He could not answer, for they were once again on opposite sides of the floor, but he shook his head and silently mouthed the word *no*.

The set moved up. They were separated by ten or twelve feet of dance floor, but she was aware of him watching her. She tried to keep her eyes demurely lowered, but could not resist glancing over at him every now and then. She was merely doing what every other woman in the room was doing. He was the only stranger at the ball, but it was not that that made the female guests flutter their lashes and their fans. Hadn't she recognised that night they had met, that he was a man who would attract a second and a third glance? Here was the proof of it, and there, in that sensual smile and those sea-blue eyes, was the warning she ought to heed. *Dangerous, dangerous, dangerous*, Isabella repeated to herself.

She had to make sure he did not talk. She had to! This thought plummeted her back to earth. When next the dance brought them together she rushed into speech. 'I must ask you to keep our previous acquaintance a secret.' There was no mistaking the urgency in her voice, but this was not a time for subtlety. 'Please,' she said. 'It is very important.'

'Why is that?'

The music was coming to an end. Isabella's heart was pounding. 'I will explain, I promise you, but not here.'

She made her curtsy, and the Scotsman made his bow. 'Where?'

'Promise me you will say nothing,' Isabella hissed, 'until we talk.'

He frowned, seemingly quite unaware of the urgency. She wanted to scream. She wanted to grab at his coat sleeve and shake him. Instead, she forced herself to wait what seemed like an eternity for him to consider, though it must have been mere seconds before he finally asked her where, and when.

Consuela was beckoning. Gabriel was by her side. Isabella began to panic. 'Tomorrow morning. Meet me in the courtyard behind the chapel at eight. Promise me…'

He nodded, his expression still quite unreadable. 'Until tomorrow.'

He had not promised, and now it was too late. 'Isabella.' Consuela arrived with Gabriel in tow. 'I have assured Señor Torres that you will give him your hand for this next dance.'

Gabriel's smile would have most other ladies swooning. Isabella, who had become adept at mimicking other ladies' responses, was tonight incapable of producing more than a forced smile.

'Indeed, I hope that you will,' Gabriel said, 'else I will think you prefer the company of an Englishman to a true Spaniard, and that will break my heart.'

Isabella stared at him blankly. 'Mr Urquhart is Scottish, not English.'

'A minor distinction.'

'Indeed, it is not.'

The Scotsman spoke the same words as she did at the same time. A small, embarrassed silence ensued. 'Mr Urquhart was just explaining the difference to me while we danced. To call a Scottish man English is like calling a Basque man Spanish.'

Another silence met this well-intentioned remark. Isabella resorted to her fan. Gabriel stared off into the distance. The visitor made a flourishing bow. 'Señora Romero, would it offend your husband if I asked for the hand of his beautiful wife for the next dance?'

Consuela coloured and gave the faintest of nods. 'If you will excuse us.' Gabriel made a very small bow as the orchestra struck up the introductory chords.

The Scotsman made no effort to return Gabriel's bow, Isabella noticed, and felt, in the way his hand tightened on her arm, that Gabriel had noticed, too. He swept her onto the dance floor. Looking over her shoulder, Isabella saw Consuela smile and blush coquettishly in response to some remark made by Mr Urquhart.

'You are looking very lovely tonight. There is no other woman in the room who can hold a candle to you.'

Gabriel's compliments, like his smile, were practised and meaningless. He was rich, he was well born and he was handsome. He had no cause to doubt that he was an excellent catch, and enjoyed enthusiastic encouragement of his suit from Xavier. Isabella was nearly twenty-six. Too old, in the eyes of most of her acquaintance, to hope for such an excellent match. To be wooed by Gabriel Torres was flattering indeed. Looking at him now, as he executed one of the more complex dance steps with precision, Isabella could nonetheless summon nothing stronger than indifference.

Chapter Three

Finlay threw open the doors that led out from his bedchamber onto the balcony and sucked in the cold night air. It had been a very long evening. He was fair knackered, to use one of his Glaswegian sergeant's phrases, but his mind was alert, his thoughts racing, just like in the old days. He stared up at the stars that hung like huge silver disks, struck anew by how much brighter they seemed to shine in the sky than at home.

Home. It had not felt at all like home when he'd gone back. Ach, his ma and da had been the same. And his sisters, and his brother, too. None of them had changed. Their lives, the landscape had not altered, but he had, and there was no point pretending otherwise. He hated himself for it, but he couldn't help but see the croft and the village and his family and their friends as his fellow officers would view them. No, he didn't share their contempt for them, and yes, he still loved his family, but if he had to spend the rest of his life there he'd go stark staring mad. He would rail against the provincial predictability and cosy safety of it, the very things that he had thought he'd crave after the bedlam of war.

'I'm just a big ungrateful tumshie,' he muttered, 'with ideas well above my station.' But no matter how guilty he felt, he knew that if he left the army and returned to Oban, he'd make his family every bit as miserable as he.

He had never been anything other than a soldier. He had surrendered his real family long ago, and had no idea what he would do without the one he had adopted in the army. If he did choose to leave, that was. And what would he do with himself, if he did?

Sighing, Finlay leaned on the stone balustrade and gazed out over the formal gardens of Hermoso Romero. The future would have to take care of itself. Fortunately, he had plenty other things to occupy his mind. Such as rethinking his strategy in the light of this evening's extraordinary turn of events.

Calm and clarity of mind returned. A light breeze had picked up, making the tall cypress trees bend and sway gracefully in the moonlight like flamenco dancers. Finlay shivered in his shirtsleeves and, returning to his chamber, stretched out on top of the bed. It had been a major shock to see Señorita Romero at the dance tonight, but it had been a much, much bigger shock for her. The lass had been scared out of her wits that he'd betray her, and that was all for the good, making it highly unlikely she'd betray him first. Even if she did, he had a plausible cover story to explain his presence here. He just had to stick to it.

He pondered this course of action, staring up at the

shadow from his candle dancing on the corniced ceiling, and decided that there was a great deal of merit in it. Gradually, the miracle of having found his partisan right here, in plain view, began to supersede his concerns for his own safety. He only had to bide his time and see how the land lay with her. Not all ex-guerrillas and partisans were liberals. If she espoused her brother's politics, then she represented everything El Fantasma railed against in his illegal pamphlets.

Finlay frowned at this. She'd seemed a feisty thing during those few hours they'd shared together under the stars. He'd admired her, the way she stood up for herself. Tonight, he'd seen a glimpse of that fire when they were dancing, but for the rest of the evening she'd behaved like a shy, retiring wee mouse with little to say for herself.

'In other words, Finlay, just exactly like an unmarried high-born Spanish lady. Which is exactly what she is, now that the war is over.'

Though two years ago she had implied she was a farmer's daughter. Why? Like as not, it had simply been a ruse to hide her identity. One thing, her being a female partisan with a gun he'd encountered in a ditch. Quite another, if that partisan was a lady, the sister of the biggest local landowner. He smiled to himself. That would cause quite a stir were it discovered. Though now he came to think of it, there had been mention of a father. She had seemed right fond of him, too, but he obviously wasn't around, presumably dead. Poor lass. Whatever her politics, if she had any, it must be tough trying to fit back into this privileged and class-conscious world. He could sympathise with that, and then some.

Watch and wait, that was what he needed to do. Spend a bit of time in her company, find out if he could trust her, and encourage her to trust him. It would be no hardship. She was every bit as bonny as he remembered. Jack had been wrong about that one. Finlay rolled off the bed and undressed quickly before snuffing the candle and clambering between the sheets. He was looking forward to his early-morning encounter with Señorita Romero.

Isabella was at the assignation point early. She wore one of her favourite gowns—dark blue merino with long sleeves that covered her knuckles, the bodice, cuffs and hem trimmed simply with cream embroidery. She had eschewed a shawl or pelisse, the woollen dress offering sufficient protection from the early-morning chill. The colour and the simple style suited her, she knew. Dressing for a man was not something that sat well with her, but this man held the sword of Damocles over her head, and if it helped to look well, then she would make every effort to do so.

She was nervous, though a long night's reflection had helped her regain most of her habitual composure. It had also revealed to her some fundamental issues to be addressed. Her reaction had been too extreme. Her fear must have been obvious. She reassured herself once more that the Scotsman's having said nothing so far made it less likely that he would say anything at all. As she watched his tall figure striding across the grass towards her, Isabella tried very hard to convince herself of this.

'*Buenos días.* You're looking bonny this fine morning, Señorita Romero.'

'Thank you. I trust you slept well?'

'Like a baby. Shall we get away from the main house? There's that many windows looking out on us, I'm sure you'd rather we were not observed.'

'I'm sure the feeling is mutual, Mr Urquhart.'

He smiled enigmatically, either oblivious to her implied threat, or indifferent. 'I'm glad you've finally mastered my name, but I seem to recall you calling me Finlay before.'

'As I recall, you were a major in the British army at the time.' Isabella headed for the walkway flanked by two rows of cypress trees where they would not be observed. 'Your life has taken a very different turn since then. It seems rather remarkable for a soldier to transform himself into a prosperous wine merchant.'

'No more remarkable than for a partisan to transform herself into a lady.'

'I am not *transformed*,' Isabella said sharply. 'I am merely *returned*.'

'Returned.' He eyed her speculatively. 'I wonder, *señorita*, if anyone knows that you were ever away. I suspect not. It would certainly explain why my appearance last night terrified you out of your wits.'

He spoke softly, but his tone was all the more menacing for that. 'I was taken aback, that is all,' Isabella replied.

'No. *I* was taken aback. You looked like an ensign confronted with a bayonet for the first time.'

'If you are implying that I would run away from facing the enemy...'

He laughed. 'Are you implying that I am the enemy?'

'Are you? If so, I fail to see how my coming here quite alone could be construed as running away.'

The conversation was not progressing as she had planned, mostly because she had signally failed to play her part. It was his fault. This Scotsman, he made her speak without thinking. She had to regroup her thoughts, stick to what she had rehearsed. She had to remember there was no shame in it, that the means justified the end. 'You are right,' Isabella said with what she knew to be a forlorn little smile. 'I was afraid.'

'Because that brother of yours has no idea that you fought with the guerrillas?'

'My brother is a very influential man, Mr Urquhart, and his estate is the largest in La Rioja. It would be most embarrassing to him if it was discovered that his sister was...that she acted in an—an unladylike manner.' *To say the least!*

'Unladylike. That is one way of putting it.'

'You have another way?' she asked sharply.

He smiled at her. 'You were fighting for your country, just as he was. I'd say what you did was brave and honourable. If you were my sister, I'd be proud of you.'

His praise, so unexpected and so very rare, made her flush with pleasure. 'Thank you.'

'I meant it.' He caught her hand, bringing them both to a halt. '*Señorita*, I have been remiss. Your father, I take it he passed away? Please accept my condolences. You gave me the impression that you were very fond of him.'

'Yes. We were very close.' A lump rose in her throat. Papa had always preferred his daughter to his son, yet it was to Xavier that all of the condolences had been given when Papa died, just as it had been Xavier who had received all the gratitude and admiration for fighting for his country. 'It happened just after the end of the war. At least Papa lived to see peace return to his beloved Spain.'

'And now you have had peace for two years. Is it what you imagined or hoped? Does the world turn in a different direction?'

'I think it was you who expressed that hope, actually.' Isabella shrugged, pulling her hands free before turning away. 'As far as my brother is concerned, the world turns in exactly the same manner as it did before the war. He has a very modern approach to wine, but in every other respect Xavier, like our king, prefers the old ways.'

Despite herself, she had been unable to keep the edge of bitterness out of her voice and the Scotsman noticed. 'I take it that you do not share your brother's views?'

'Mr Urquhart, I am a woman, and in the eyes of the law I am my brother's property now that I am no longer my father's, and will remain so until I am my husband's.'

'You have changed a great deal in two years, if what you're telling me is that you don't have any views at all.'

The temptation to contradict him almost overwhelmed her, but the dangers of doing so restrained her. Isabella forced a brittle smile. 'We have both changed a great deal, I think. Neither of us are soldiers now. You are a businessman. I am a lady. I would therefore very much appreciate it if you kept what you know of my past to yourself. To expose me would cause my brother a great deal of embarrassment.'

'I'd say embarrassment was putting it mildly.'

'What do you mean?'

'If it was discovered that your brother was nourishing a liberal viper in his midst...'

'I am not a viper!'

His sea-blue eyes sparkled with amusement. 'I note you do not deny being a liberal.'

Too late yet again, she realised she had betrayed herself. 'Mr Urquhart, you are here to do business with my brother. Lucrative business for you, I believe, for there is substance to his boasts. You will not find a better Rioja than ours. Surely you cannot be thinking of putting such a deal in jeopardy? Please,' she urged when he made no reply, swallowing the last remnants of her pride, 'whatever you think of me, whatever you know of my past, you understand that it can only hurt Xavier.'

He frowned, pushing his hair back from his brow, though it was cut considerably shorter than before, and there was no need. 'Very well, Señorita Romero, you have my word that I will keep quiet about your patriotic past. After all, we Scots have a well-earned reputation for being canny and shrewd businessmen with an eye for a profit,' he concluded wryly.

'Thank you. I— Thank you.' Her relief was apparent in her voice, but so it should be. 'It is better, I think, for the past to remain in the past now the war is over.' They were Xavier's words, and often uttered. Isabella rolled her eyes metaphorically as she spoke them.

The Scotsman, however, looked—sad? 'You think so?' he asked. 'You really want to forget it happened?' He leaned back against the trunk of a tree, head back, looking up at the pale expanse of sky visible through the foliage. 'All that sacrifice, all those lives lost. Now that Boney is stuck on an island in the middle of the Atlantic, at least we are done with wars for a while.'

'And there is no more requirement for soldiers to fight them,' Isabella said softly, as understanding dawned. And empathy.

'No, there's not.' He stood up, rolling his shoulders. 'So now I buy and sell wine, and you sit at home embroidering or knitting or whatever it is fine Spanish ladies do.'

She couldn't help but laugh. 'Oh, if you want an example of the perfect Spanish lady, you must look to my sister-in-law. Consuela can set a perfect stitch, sing a perfect song, bear a perfect child, and all the while smiling a perfect smile. She is a bloodless creature.'

'I think she is simply very young and very shy and very overwhelmed by all this,' Finlay said, nodding back at the house. 'She misses her sisters.'

'She told you all that while you were dancing? It is more than she has ever seen fit to tell me.' Isabella shook her head incredulously. 'You must have misunderstood. Her family would be welcome to visit any time. She only has to issue an invitation.' She waited for him to answer her implied question, but he said nothing. 'What is it, what did she say to you?'

'I never break a confidence. You'll have to ask her yourself.'

'A confidence! You only met her last night, and she is confiding in you.'

'I'm sorry, I didn't mean to offend you.'

The Scotsman touched her cheek. Isabella jerked away. 'Why should I be offended? Consuela is very beautiful, and you are very charming, and if she chose to speak to you of matters that—well, that is none of my business.'

'She is indeed beautiful, but in the manner of a painting, you know. You can admire her, and you are happy to look at her, but as to anything else...'

'But that is exactly what I was thinking about Gabriel only last night.'

'The Adonis who looked down his nose at me? What is he to you?'

It was none of his business, but it was so refreshing to talk to a man who actually spoke what was on his mind and expected her to return the favour. 'He is my brother's best friend. They were in the army together. My brother hopes to make a match between us. It would be a very good match for me.'

'But it would also be—what was your phrase—bloodless.'

'What do you mean?'

'I mean you don't find the idea of kissing him appealing. You see, that's the difference between you and your brother's wife. While I'm more than happy to look at her, I don't feel the slightest inclination to kiss her.'

Isabella's mouth went dry, and her pulses fluttered. The Scotsman's fingers circled her wrist loosely. She could easily free herself. His other hand rested on her shoulder. She seemed to be standing very close to him. 'I am very glad,' she said, 'because I think Xavier's hospitality has limits.'

He laughed softly. 'You know that I would very much like to kiss you, don't you?'

'I think you wanted to, two years ago.'

'It's something I've often regretted, that I did not.'

Her heart was pounding wildly. She was playing with fire, but she was enjoying it far too much to stop. She was so rarely afforded the freedom to be herself. It was exhilarating. 'It is something I, too, have regretted, that you did not,' Isabella said daringly.

She had surprised him. She could see from the way his eyes darkened that she had also aroused him, and that knowledge heightened her own awareness of him. 'There is nothing worse than regret,' he said.

'Nothing,' she agreed.

He made no move for a long moment, and despite the longing twisting inside her, she had reached the limits of her boldness. If he did not kiss her now, he never would. If he did not kiss her now, she would always wonder. If he did not kiss her…

He kissed her. His lips touched hers with the softness of a whisper. She closed her eyes and stepped forward into his embrace. A hand slid around her waist, another cupped her cheek. His kiss was so gentle, she hardly dared move lest he break it. His mouth was warm on hers. It felt odd, different, in the nicest way possible. She angled her head. She slid her arm around him. He gave a tiny sigh and pulled her closer and kissed her again. Not so gently, but still carefully.

She had never been kissed like this before. She let him coax her mouth open. It didn't cross her mind that her ignorance would betray her or make her seem foolish; she thought only that she wanted to kiss him back, and so she did. His fingers curled into her hair. Her fingers curled into his coat. She could feel the hardness of his body against hers. He was so much bigger than her, but it didn't make her feel weak. He felt so warm; she felt so secure against the solid bulk of him. He was making her feel very hot. His tongue touched hers, and she leaped back in astonishment.

He cursed. At least it sounded like a curse, though the language was foreign to her. 'I'm sorry,' he said, raking his hand through his hair again. 'I didn't realise...'

Isabella flushed with mortification. He would think her a child. 'Please,' she said, turning away, 'let us forget about it.'

Any other man would be happy to do exactly what she asked, to spare himself the embarrassment of an apology if nothing else. This man, she ought to have remembered, was not like any other man. He caught her arm, pulling her back to face him. 'I am truly sorry. I went too far, and mistook your experience.'

Isabella was too proud to look at the ground, and she

could not bear pity. 'No, you mistook my enjoyment,' she said, giving him a haughty look. 'I think it is not always true that good things come to those who wait.'

For a split second, he looked as if she had slapped him and then, to her astonishment, he burst out laughing. 'That's me told, then. I must be more out of practice than I realised.'

'I do not think a man like you lacks women to—to practise on.'

'Now that, *señorita*, was quite uncalled for. I remember quite clearly that one of the things I told you that night was that I'm not the kind of man who has a taste for kissing any and every available woman. Not that it's any of your business, but in the two years since last we met, there has been only one woman in my life, and that fleeting *affaire* ended in Brussels nearly four months ago.'

There was not a trace of humour in his voice now. He released her, taking several paces back. The look he gave her would be quite intimidating if she was the kind of woman to allow herself to be intimidated. The kind of woman she pretended to be. But Isabella was beyond playing such a part for now. 'Your women— or your lack of women—are none of my business,' she said, anxious more than anything to close the subject.

But the Scotsman seemed determined to prolong it. 'No, they are not, save that I wouldn't have kissed you if there had been any woman in my life, and I would sure as hell have *stopped* kissing you if you'd given me the least bit of an idea that you didn't want me to. I told you—*another* thing I remember telling you very clearly—that I never, ever force myself on a woman.'

He was angry, though he was trying very hard not to show it. She had to acknowledge that he had a right. 'I'm sorry.' Isabella closed her eyes. 'You were right. I have not... I lack—I lack the experience you attributed to me. I'm sorry. It was my fault, not yours.'

She was blushing. It had cost her dear, that admission, and she shouldn't have been forced to make it. His anger dissipated like melting snow. Finlay touched her cheek gently. Her eyes fluttered open. 'No, you are too generous. It was my fault. I got carried away, and forgot that you are not the woman I spent the night with two years ago, but a lady whose innocence I quite forgot to take account of. Will you forgive me?'

'There is nothing to forgive.'

'I took advantage. Your brother...'

Her big almond-shaped eyes flashed at him. 'Do not bring Xavier into this. Who I choose to kiss or not to kiss has nothing to do with my brother.'

Finlay was pretty sure that Xavier held a very different opinion on the subject. And he was, on reflection, pretty certain that an innocent like Isabella should not be choosing to kiss any man until she was betrothed. That she was an innocent, after that kiss there could be no doubt, but he was struggling to reconcile the lady who claimed to be feart of offending her brother with the one who crept about behind enemy lines brandishing a gun.

They came to the end of the cypress walk. 'I will

leave you here,' Isabella said. 'I hope that we have an understanding between us now?'

'I believe we do,' Finlay said with a smile he hoped was reassuring. He believed quite the contrary, but what to do about it, he needed to consider. He watched her go, standing in the shadow of one of the tall trees. She walked with the long, graceful stride he remembered until she came within sight of the house, when she stopped abruptly, looking up at one of the windows. When she resumed, her walk had that slow, floating grace that made her look as if she was gliding. He could tell from the line of her neck that her gaze was demurely lowered.

Was she playing the part of a lady for whoever was watching, or had she played the part of the feisty partisan to keep Finlay sweet—and quiet? Had she kissed him for the same reason? Had he initiated the kiss or she? He could remember only that he had wanted to kiss her more than he'd wanted to kiss any woman for quite some time. Had she pretended to enjoy it as much as he had?

He cursed in Gaelic under his breath. 'Kisses are not the point here,' he told himself. 'Forget the kisses and concentrate on what you came here for. You need to get her to give you the information you need, or decide she's not going to, in which case you will need to rethink your strategy.'

Consulting his pocket watch, he cursed again. Señor Romero would be waiting to take him on the promised tour of the vineyards, a prospect Finlay was far from relishing, not least for fear of betraying his own ignorance. It was such a waste of time, too, and he had no idea how much time he had if he was to beat the Spanish to El Fantasma. It would be much more constructive to spend the time with Isabella. Much more constructive, and considerably more appealing, Finlay thought, shuddering as he anticipated long hours of Xavier's obsequious condescension. He had to find a way of swapping the brother for the sister after today. It would be a challenge, but Finlay relished a challenge.

Isabella sat in the shade of a tree while her horse drank from a small stream. Taking advantage of the fact that Xavier was too engrossed in showing the Scotsman around the estate to wonder what his sister was doing, she had ridden out without an escort. She was hot and tired, but the tension she had hoped to work off was, if anything, aggravated.

She had to clear her head. She had to try to think straight. Take a step back. Gain perspective. Something. Isabella got to her feet and pulled off the long boots and stockings she wore under her riding habit. Picking up her skirts, she scrabbled down the banks into the stream, gasping as the icy water that tumbled down from the mountains caressed her skin.

It was painful and exhilarating at the same time. It struck her as pathetic that she was reduced to obtaining pleasure from paddling in a mountain stream. When Finlay Urquhart had kissed her this morning, it had been just like this, only more. Who would have thought that a man's lips could have such an effect?

She had felt wild, locked in his embrace. She had felt strangely free.

But what a stupid mess she had made of it afterwards. Isabella waded over to a large boulder in the middle of the burbling water and sat down, tilting her face up to the sun. Gabriel had never attempted to kiss her. Was it because it would be improper until they were betrothed, or because he did not want to? She tried to imagine kissing Gabriel, but instead of his dark good looks, she could picture only the Scotsman's fascinating blue eyes, his wicked smile, the glint of his auburn hair. There was a recklessness about him that had appealed to her that night they had spent together two years ago. It still appealed.

Xavier would be utterly furious if he knew that his sister had been kissing a mere wine merchant. Isabella laughed, but her smile faded almost immediately. She had behaved shockingly. She had spoken much too freely. But, oh, it had been so good to do so. For long moments, she had been herself with the Scotsman. It had been a relief not to pretend that the Isabella he'd met before had never existed. It had felt so good. She longed to be that woman again, just for a little while. She would like to spend more time in his company, to cross conversational swords with him. He spoke to her as if she had a mind of her own. It made her realise, sadly, that almost no other man of her acquaintance did, save those she knew from the war, and they were now in a minority of one.

Had she been rash? He had given her his word not to betray her. He had given her his word once before, and kept it. Major Finlay Urquhart had been an honourable man. Was there such a thing as an honourable wine merchant? The incongruity of his choice of profession struck her anew. He was a man of action. A man who had taken on the task of surveillance himself when he could surely have sent one of his men. Just as she had. A man who liked to make his own decisions. Just as she did. Not a man who would relish haggling over the price of a hogshead of wine, caught in the middle between supplier and buyer, she would have thought. The man she had met that fateful night and the man he appeared to be now seemed almost incompatible. There was something about Mr Finlay Urquhart, wine merchant to the gentry, that did not quite ring true.

Sliding down from the boulder, Isabella picked her way over the slippery stones back to the shore, pulling her stockings and boots on over her numbed feet. She ought not to be wasting time thinking about a man who would be walking out of her life for good in a few days. She ought to be considering her own future.

Could she really contemplate becoming Señora Gabriel Torres? She tried to imagine spending her days engaged in domestic pursuits. It was not the housekeeping or the children that she rebelled against; it was not even surrendering herself to the care of a man, for in the eyes of the law, she was Xavier's property until he gave her up. What appalled her the most was the surrender of her mind. She would not be expected to think beyond what to put on the table for dinner. Her opinions would not be consulted. She would not be permitted to discuss politics or business.

What was it the Scotsman had said this morning? Embroidery and knitting. Isabella had always taken perverse pride in being very bad at both. She was not about to learn now.

Yet she must marry, for Xavier was set on it, and he could make her continued presence in his house unpleasant. Gabriel was rich, he was handsome, he was popular, she reminded herself. He was an excellent match.

'And at my great age, I cannot expect to do better, according to my brother,' she said to herself as she prepared to mount her horse. 'Loath as I am to admit it, Xavier is right. If I do not accept Gabriel soon, he will find someone else, and then where will I be? Better the devil you know, perhaps?'

She settled her skirts around her, thinking as she always did, how much she missed the freedom of riding astride in breeches. As the wife of Gabriel Torres, there would be no question of her ever doing that again. Exasperated, she dismissed the question of her future. Right now, she had a contradictory, disconcertingly attractive Scotsman to deal with. Really, for Xavier's sake she needed to ensure that he was what he claimed to be, and if that meant spending more time in his company, so be it. Having happily reconciled her inclination with her duty, Isabella tapped her heels lightly against her horse's flank and headed in the direction of home.

It had been, as Finlay had predicted it would be, a long and tedious day. He had not thought anyone could discourse at such length on the subject of viticulture, but Xavier Romero seemed to be tireless. His passion for all things Rioja led him to expound at length on soil types, grape varieties, vine diseases, pest control, pruning methods, harvesting methods and the weather, from frost, to hail, to sun and humidity. Fortunately, his enthusiasm was second only to his love of his own voice. Finlay had contributed very little to the conversation, if such it could be called. His head, however, was throbbing as if they had drunk six bottles of Rioja when in fact the only thing they hadn't done was sample the blasted stuff.

They were quitting the stables when Señorita Romero arrived. Alone, and on horseback, when she saw her brother, she could not disguise her dismay. 'Xavier, I thought you would still be out with Mr Urquhart.'

'Where is your groom?'

'He was busy elsewhere. I am quite capable of saddling a horse and going for a ride.'

Her tone was mild, though Finlay thought he saw a flash of anger in her eyes. She dismounted with a rustle of her skirts, and a tantalising glimpse of leather riding boots. How long were they? he wondered, momentarily distracted. Did they stretch to her knee, or higher still?

Xavier clicked his fingers to summon a stable hand. Isabella handed over her reins to the boy with a friendly smile. Her brother however, was not happy. 'I have told you several times that it is most improper for a sister of mine to ride about the countryside without an escort.'

'I have been riding about this countryside all my

life. Everyone knows me, I know everyone. Papa never insisted I take a groom.'

'Our father was far too lenient with you. Besides, it is I who is now custodian of Hermoso Romero,' her brother replied stiffly. 'Your reputation is a reflection on me. It will be said that I cannot take care of my own sister, if you are seen out alone. It will be said that I do not treat her with respect.'

'Then, you can reply that you trust me to be on my own. That is treating me with respect. That is what Papa would say.'

Romero seemed with difficulty to control his temper. For some reason, Finlay noticed with interest, the subject was a sore point with him. 'Our father is dead,' he said, speaking sharply to his sister. 'It is clear to me that you have been completely overindulged. I do not envy Gabriel the schooling of you.'

There was no mistaking the flash in the *señorita*'s golden eyes at this remark, though she clasped her hands tightly round her riding crop and did not rise to the bait. Finlay however, who had been standing quietly to one side, could not resist. 'She is not a child, Romero.'

'She is a woman. It is almost the same thing,' the other man snapped. 'Excuse me, but this is none of your concern, Mr Urkarty.'

'I beg your pardon, *señor*.' Finlay spoke through clenched teeth, although his smile was conciliatory—he hoped. 'Señorita Romero strikes me as a most competent horsewoman.'

'Naturally. It is in her blood.'

The arrogance of the man! 'And she has, I understand, been accustomed to riding out alone while your father was alive, without damaging her reputation?'

'That is not the point, Mr Urkarty.'

'No, Señor Romero, you are quite right, it is not. The point is to choose your battles more carefully. I have three sisters of my own, and so speak from experience. A little leeway in small matters will buy you a great deal of credit when it comes to the larger ones.'

Romero's temper hung in the balance for a few moments. The man was not accustomed to being contradicted, that was for certain. Finlay shot a warning glance at the object of their conversation, but her eyes were fixed firmly on her boots. Unlike her brother, she knew when to keep her mouth shut.

Finally, Romero spoke. 'Three sisters,' he said with a smile every bit as forced as Finlay's. 'I confess, I don't envy you that. Perhaps it is because I have only the one that I am overprotective. Very well, I will take your advice, Mr Urkety. Provided she confines herself to our estate, I do not see why—you see Isabella, how magnanimous I can be.'

'I— Thank you, Xavier.'

Her brother, however, was distracted by the return of his stable hand carrying a note. Señorita Romero turned to Finlay. 'I must thank you, too, Mr Urquhart,' she said softly. 'Every time I am permitted to slip my leash a little, I will think of you.'

Her smile was demure, but her eyes were stormy. 'If it was in my power I would cut your leash completely,' Finlay replied. 'You know, I…'

An exclamation from Romero made them both turn

around. 'It is Estebe, who is in charge of the winery. The man has fallen from a tree, would you believe.'

'Oh, no, Xavier, is he badly injured?'

Romero frowned. 'A broken leg. It is very inconvenient, for I had intended he take Mr Urkety on a tour of the cellars tomorrow. I have urgent business elsewhere, which I am loath to cancel, but...'

'Cannot Señorita Romero escort me instead?' Finlay asked.

'Oh, yes, please allow me to take Estebe's place,' Isabella urged. 'While you were at war, while Papa's health was failing, I helped Estebe a great deal. Of course I know that compared to you and Estebe, I am a mere novice, but I do know the history of our home and of the wine, and I am sure that is something Mr Urquhart will wish to be able to impart to his customers.'

Romero pursed his lips. 'It would be most irregular.'

'Aye, but your sister speaks the truth,' Finlay corroborated, masking his surprise. 'My customers like to know a bit about the background and provenance of the wines they are being asked to pay a pretty penny for. And I would hate to deflect you from important business.'

'Very well. Yes, when you put it that way.' Romero smiled thinly at his sister. 'Another favour granted, Isabella. I hope you are keeping count. You may supervise some tastings, brief Mr Urkety on the history, perhaps even compile some notes for him. She writes a fair enough hand, Mr Urkety, I will grant her that. And now, if you will excuse me, I must return to the house. I will see you both at dinner.'

Señorita Romero watched him go before turning to Finlay. 'If I was not cursed with the brain of a mere woman, I would suspect you of very manipulative behaviour, Mr Urquhart.'

'Ach, now, I wouldn't put it quite as strongly as that.'

She narrowed her eyes at him. 'How would you put it?'

'Now, there, you see, you've put me on the spot, for if I was to confess that your brother's company is not nearly as appealing to me as yours, you would likely accuse me of being condescending rather than manipulative. But don't, I beg you, try to pull the wool over my eyes.'

'What do you mean, Mr Urquhart?'

'It's Finlay.' Glancing over his shoulder, he caught her hand and pulled her into the shelter of the stable door, out of sight of prying eyes. 'I can understand why you don't want your brother to know anything about your past. I have promised to keep that between us, and I keep my promises. But what I don't understand, my fair former partisan, is why you're so determined to hide your true self behind a demure facade. What are you trying to conceal?'

If he had not been watching her so closely he would have missed the flicker of fear in her eyes. It was quickly masked. 'I don't know what you're talking about, Mr Urquhart.'

'Finlay.'

She closed the distance between them to whisper in his ear, 'I am not concealing anything, Finlay. I assure you.'

'No?' Her hair tickled his cheek. Her smile was beguiling. Her eyes gleamed. Not a trace of the demure lady now; this woman made his blood heat. She made him lose his train of thought, distracting him with the proximity of that mouth, the memory of that kiss this morning.

But this was business, life-and-death business, not pleasure. He stepped away from temptation. 'As my friend Jack is wont to say, "I'll believe you, thousands wouldn't."'

Chapter Four

Isabella peeled an orange and carefully separated it into segments. Xavier had breakfasted hours ago, setting off on his business trip to Pamplona before the sun had risen. Across the large, ornately laid table in the breakfast room, Finlay had finished his substantial selection of ham, cheese and bread, and was taking a second cup of coffee. He was chatting to Consuela about the latest French fashions. Isabella knew nothing about such things, and so could not tell if he was extremely knowledgeable or merely extremely plausible. Her sister-in-law was more animated than Isabella had ever seen her. Several times she had broken into a ripple of girlish laughter. Now, she was reading him a mock lecture, wagging her pretty beringed finger at him and fluttering her long lashes. Consuela never teased Xavier like this, but then Xavier, though handsome, had not a fraction of Finlay's charm and even less interest than Isabella in women's fripperies.

She ate a piece of her orange. The fruit was at its

best at this time of year, succulently sweet, rather like Consuela. And that, Isabella reprimanded herself, was a shrewish remark quite unworthy of her.

She slanted a look at Finlay. He caught her eye and flashed her a smile. She looked down at her plate. It had seemed complicit, that smile. As if they had a secret. As if they knew something Consuela did not. A flutter of nerves sent her back to her coffee cup. She took a reviving sip, reminding herself that Finlay had no grounds for whatever suspicions he was nurturing. If he challenged her again about playing the demure lady, she would invoke the need to behave as her brother expected her to while under his roof. And in the meantime, she would pursue her own suspicions regarding him.

'Xavier tells me that you are taking Mr Urquhart on a tour of the wine cellars,' Consuela said, getting to her feet. 'That was generous of you. They are horrible, Mr Urquhart, cold and I am sure swarming with rats. It is no wonder my husband is reluctant to go down there. I only wonder that Isabella is so fond of them. Now you will excuse me, if you please. I must go and tend to my son.'

'So your brother is uncomfortable in his own wine cellars,' Finlay said, closing the door behind Consuela. 'That explains why he was so easily persuaded to allow his sister to spend time in the company of a mere wine merchant.'

'It is not the dark or the rats Xavier fears, it is the fact that the cellars are so far underground. He has never liked them.'

'And yet you, according to the lovely Señora Romero, are very fond of them.'

'I don't share my brother's temperament. I have been wondering, Mr Urquhart—Finlay—what it was that made you turn to the trading of wine, when you left the army?'

'It is a lucrative business. As a canny Scot, that was reason enough.'

'With the right contacts I am sure that it is indeed lucrative. I wonder, you see, since you told me that you had not been home to England—I beg your pardon, Scotland—for so many years, I wonder how you have managed to establish sufficient customers so quickly.'

Isabella took a sip of coffee, but kept her eyes on Finlay. Did his eyes flicker? Did his fingers tighten on his cup? She could not be sure.

'I'm wondering,' he replied, 'if it is any of your business. Are you worried that I'll sell your brother's wine to someone who has not the palate to tell the difference between your fine Rioja and the stuff they drink from the barrel in the village bodegas? Are you thinking I should test the colour of a man's blood before I sell to him? Blue—yes, you can have as much as you like. Red—no, sorry, laddie, not good enough.'

He was still sitting, seemingly relaxed, at the table, but there was an edge to his voice that should have warned her to drop the subject. Isabella popped another segment of orange into her mouth. 'It is not a question of blood, Mr—Finlay. It is a question of money.'

'They all too often go hand in hand, I find, *señorita.*

One begets the other. Lack of one tends to mean lack of the other.'

'But you are the son of a farmer, and yet you became a major in Wellington's army, and now you are a wealthy merchant. You are, as I seem to remember you telling me before, the— I forget the English phrase.'

'The exception that proves the rule.'

Isabella nodded. 'That was it.'

'The Jock Upstart, is what Wellington calls—called me. A man who does not know his allotted place in the scheme of things.'

'The Jock Upstart,' Isabella repeated slowly. 'Ah, I see, because it rhymes with Urquhart. That is clever. Though also condescending.'

'Add in licentious, ruthless and charming, and you have encapsulated the essence of the Duke of Wellington, taking the fact that he is on the whole a brilliant strategist as given.'

Isabella raised her brows. 'You don't like him very much.'

'No, but then he does not like me very much, either. It doesn't stop him thinking me useful.'

'You use the present tense, I think?' Isabella asked sharply. 'But you have left the army...'

This time she was sure she saw a flicker of unease in his eyes, though he smiled blandly. 'Useful in terms of supplying him with the best wine in Spain. If your brother will sell it to me.'

Isabella could not argue with the sense of this, though still, she was sure he was not telling the whole truth. 'You know, for a man who is so successful, you

are very—I don't know, contradictory? You look down
your nose at the Duke of Wellington and at my brother,
and at me, too, I think, and you say to yourself, you
are our equal, if not our superior. But you don't really
believe it.'

'What precisely do you mean by that?'

She had no idea what she had meant, save to rile
him into betraying himself. He was sitting perfectly
still, but his expression was forbidding. She ought to
back down, but she was exceeding tired of biting her
tongue and eating her words and quelling her so unladylike thoughts. 'You don't realise how lucky you are,'
Isabella said. 'You are a man.'

'I'm lucky because I'm a man? You'll have to explain yourself a bit more, if you please.'

On the contrary, what she ought to do was keep
her mouth closed. Isabella pushed her plate away with
some force. 'It is obvious. When you walk into a room,
people do not think, there is that—what was it?—Jock
Upstart? They don't think about your family tree or
your bloodlines or any of those things. They think,
there is a man who knows who he is. A confident man.
A man who commands respect as well as admiration.
Do you think my brother would be taking such pains
to cultivate you if he thought anything else?'

'I'm still not getting your point, lass.'

Exasperated, she jumped to her feet and threw back
the curtains that kept the sunlight Consuela dreaded
from the room. 'You are a man! Do you not understand, that is the most salient point! You can do what
you want with your life, make of it what you want. I

am a mere woman. All I have is my bloodline and my family tree. When I walk into a room, people think, there is Señorita Romero, sister of Xavier Romero, whose dowry would make an excellent addition to our family coffers.'

'That's not what I think when you walk into a room, I can tell you, and I'd be very surprised indeed if it was the first thing any man thought.'

'If you are going to mention my derrière again…'

His low chuckle made her turn away from the window. The wicked look was back in his eyes. 'There, that's the problem, you see. When you walk into a room, you do not make a man want to treat you like a lady. Well, not this man, at any event. And that was a compliment, incidentally, just in case you weren't sure.'

Isabella folded her arms. 'You make it very difficult to argue with you.'

'I wasn't aware that we've been arguing.'

'I think that behind the bravado, you have a very low opinion of yourself, Major Finlay Urquhart.'

'No, Señorita Romero, I leave that to other people.'

'You don't. That is what we were arguing about.' Smiling triumphantly, Isabella got to her feet. 'You see, contrary to popular opinion, I am not just a pretty face,' she said, patting Finlay lightly on the cheek. 'I will meet you at the winery in half an hour, Mr Urquhart, and you shall have your tour of the cellars. Although I am sure an acknowledged expert such as yourself should be giving me the tour.'

She left that remark hanging in the air as she swept from the room.

* * *

The entrance to the wine cellars was through a huge trapdoor set in the floor of the main pressing room. The heavy oak and iron hinges were lifted by means of a pulley that Isabella attached to the ringed handle. Finlay found it turned very easily, revealing a steep set of stone steps disappearing into the gloom below.

'This is the original entrance. There is another, much wider one, cut when oak casks were introduced to the process, but I thought you would like to see this,' Isabella said.

She was wearing a long cloak over her cotton gown. The thick walls of the winery's working buildings kept the rooms cool. The air coming up from the cellar entrance was chilly. Finlay was glad of his coat. Isabella lit two lamps and handed him one. 'Be careful—the steps are very worn in places.'

His instinct was to insist on going first, but he managed to restrain himself and follow in her wake, just as he had done on the hillside track two years previously. The staircase was narrow enough for him to touch the rock on either side. In places as they descended, the arched roof was no more than a few inches from the top of his head. Isabella moved sure-footedly, swiftly enough for her cloak to flutter out behind her. Señora Romero was in the right of it; Isabella was obviously no stranger to this place.

As they stopped at the bottom of the steps and Finlay lifted his lamp high, he whistled. 'What a place for a wean to play.'

'Wane?'

'Wean, bairn, child,' he clarified.

'Ah, yes. When I was a little girl I loved to come here.'

'I'll bet you did. It's absolutely cavernous.'

'Oh, this is just the beginning. Wait till you see.'

The passageway led off in both directions. They turned to the right through an arched entranceway into a wider corridor, one side of which was stacked high with oak barrels. The individual cellars themselves led off the passage, each with vaulted ceilings cut directly out of the limestone. Dusty bottles, some shrouded with cobwebs, lay in wooden racks, stacked along every wall and set in islands on the stone floors.

'Each cellar is devoted to a different vintage,' Isabella told him, pointing to the marked boards. 'Farther along there are some very old vintages, indeed. This year's wine is still maturing in the casks, which are stored on the other side of the cellars.'

The lamps made shadows on the pale limestone. As they made their way farther into the cellars the rooms became smaller, the ceilings lower. 'So you and your brother played here as children, then,' Finlay said, looking round one of the smallest rooms, where the bottles were encrusted by a thick film of dust.

'I told you, Xavier has a fear of very small spaces, he rarely comes down here if he can help it.'

'And you—you are not afraid of the rats, *señorita*? I'd imagine there are plenty down here.'

'They are more afraid of me than I of them.'

There seemed to be another archway at the end of the room, smaller than the rest, and the gap covered by one of the tall wine racks. 'What's through here?' Finlay asked.

'Nothing. It is blocked off.' Isabella put her lamp down on a small table in the centre of the room, and after a few moments' pondering in front of one of the racks, selected a bottle. Blowing the dust off the neck, she produced a corkscrew from a cupboard built into the table and expertly opened the bottle, sniffing the cork delicately. 'It is far too cold, of course, and it should be allowed to breathe, but this is one of our better wines, I think you'll find.'

Two glasses were produced from the same cupboard. They sat down on the stools by the table, and Isabella poured the wine. *'Salud!'*

'Salud!' The wine was soft and fruity, to Finlay's untutored palate. 'It's very nice,' he said, taking a second appreciative sip.

Isabella laughed. 'I hope you manage to be a little more enthusiastic with Xavier.'

'It's extremely nice?' he suggested, grinning.

Isabella picked up her glass. 'You must first talk to him about the nose,' she said, swirling the wine around before sniffing. 'So this one, it is sweet, like cherry, do you smell it?'

Finlay nodded, mimicking her actions, though his eyes were on Isabella. She was explaining the layers of taste now, swirling the wine around in her mouth. There was a cobweb clinging to her hair. Her eyes really were golden, like a tiger's. And her mouth— He had an absurd wish to be the wine swirling around in her mouth. Her lips would taste of it. What had she said, cherries? Yes, her lips would taste of cherries, and…

'You are not tasting, Mr—Finlay.'

He took a sip of wine. 'Cherries,' he said.

'And?'

'Strawberries,' he answered, looking at her mouth.

'Really? I do not…'

Finlay leaned over to touch his lips to hers. 'Strawberries,' he said. 'Definitely.' He tucked back a silky strand of hair from her face and pressed his mouth to the pulse behind her ear. 'Lavender?'

'My soap.'

Her voice was low, breathy. Her fingers touched his hair. He pressed fluttering kisses down the column of her neck, then placed his lips on the pulse at her throat. 'Lavender.'

'Yes,' she agreed.

He lifted his head. She was looking at him, her lips slightly parted, tense, waiting for what he would do next. Nothing, was what he ought to do. He bent his head and kissed her again. Her lips clung to his. Her fingers curled into the sleeve of his coat. He was trying to muster the courage to stop when her tongue touched his.

Finlay slid his arms around her, under her cloak. Isabella swayed towards him on her stool, her mouth pressed to his. She tasted so sweet. Wine and strawberries and a sizzling heat that sent the blood surging to his groin. Their kisses became wilder, deeper. Her fingers tangled in his hair, fluttered over his cheek, curled into his shoulders. He flattened his hands over the narrow span of her back. He could feel her shoulder blades through the cotton of her gown, the complicated strings and boning of her corsets. He licked along her plump lower lip, kissing each corner of her mouth.

'You taste delightful,' he said. 'Delicious. Like vintage wine.'

She kissed him deeply, her tongue tangling with his. Fast learner. Very fast. He could not keep up with her. 'Vintage kisses,' Finlay said. 'If only they could be bottled, you would have an elixir beyond price.'

He kissed her eyelids. He kissed her nose. He kissed her mouth again. And again. And again. Their knees bumped as they tried to get closer. He was hard. It would not do at all to get any closer. It was all he wanted. He kissed her again. She gave a tiny whimper that sent his pulses racing.

Slowly, he lifted his head and let her go. Her mouth was dark pink. Her eyes were wide, dark. He could feel the flush of passion on his cheeks, and lower down— Finlay shifted uncomfortably on the stool. 'I don't expect you'll believe me if I tell you I'd resolved not to do that,' he said.

'We could blame it on the wine.'

'We've not even finished one glass yet.'

Isabella picked hers up and swallowed the contents in a single gulp. 'That was sacrilege,' she said, wiping her lips.

'Then, we must not waste a drop.' Finlay licked the wine from the back of her hand. She shuddered. He didn't mean to, but somehow his lips found hers again, and somehow they were kissing again, and this time they were very different kisses. Dark and hot, tongues stroking, touching, thrusting. The kind of kisses that demanded more. The stools clattered to the stone floor as they stood, pressing their bodies hard against each other, still kissing, and kissing and kissing, until Finlay knocked against the table, and the wine bottle fell over and the precious wine began to spill out over the wood and drip onto the stone floor.

He grabbed it and set it upright. There was less than a third left.

'Now, that really is sacrilege,' Isabella said.

'Or a warning. I should not have— I did not mean— Have you any idea how ravishing you look?' Finlay groaned. 'What am I thinking!'

'I sincerely hope that it is not leading to an apology.'

He laughed drily. 'I'm not sorry, though I should be.'

'Good, because neither am I.' Isabella was tidying her hair, concentrating on adjusting the fastenings of her cloak, pouring the last of the wine. Finally, she met his eyes. 'I wanted you to kiss me. I wanted—after the last time, I wanted to get it right.'

'You got it a trifle too right.'

'Did I?'

'I'd have thought, from the way I couldn't keep my hands off you, that it was obvious.' Finlay brushed the cobweb from her hair. 'But I should not have taken advantage.'

She flinched away from him, the light dying from her eyes. 'You think I kissed you because you wanted me to, and not because I wanted to?'

'No, I don't. You really are a prickly—but you probably have cause. Look at me. Please.' He touched her cheek gently. 'The fact is that I've a deal of experience in these things and you have none. To put it bluntly, I am not a seducer of virgins.'

She coloured, but held his gaze. 'It was just a few kisses, Finlay.'

He laughed softly. 'There, you see, your innocence is showing if that's what you think. Those were the kind of kisses to keep a man awake at night, wanting more. Now, shall we drink this excellent wine and get on with the rest of the tour?'

She took him back through the wine vaults to the barrel vaults, and began to explain the process of ageing. The cellars were so familiar to her that Isabella could lead the way without a lamp if necessary. The questions Finlay was asking were intelligent enough. Some wine merchants knew more, true, but not all. Their field of expertise was in the tasting. Had Finlay been teasing her when he had pretended to know nothing of the nose? Or flirting? Back up the stairs to the main winery, she took him through to the coopering shed. Here he surprised her, clearly knowing a great deal more than she of the process.

'From my father,' he told her when she asked. 'He learned from his father, who most likely learned from his. There has always been a still in our family for the whisky.'

Isabella perched on the top of a finished barrel to watch as he ran his hands over the staves waiting to be formed into another barrel. 'Will you take it over from your father, then—the farm, making the whisky?'

Finlay turned his attention to one of the finished barrels. 'I used to joke about it in the mess, my wee Highland hame.' He picked up a coopering hammer. 'Some of them—the other officers, I mean—to hear them talk, you'd think I was born in a sheep pen. They think everyone north of Glasgow lives off porridge and neeps—that's turnip, which I know you have here.' He grinned. 'I used to come up with some fine tall tales for them.'

'Tell me what it is really like,' Isabella said. 'Your family farm, and the place where they live—it is by the sea, yes? You said before that your father has a fishing boat.'

'He does. Nothing fancy, just a single sail. They are built wide and shallow where I come from, not like the Spanish fishing boats, and they catch very different fish.'

'And the farm?'

'We call it a croft. Our farmers are crofters, which means they do a bit of everything. The croft sits up on the hill above the village. The house is long and low, with a thatched roof. Half of it forms the barn for the beasts. We have harsh winters, and it rains a lot. Warm rain in the summer, freezing in the winter. I don't miss that at all.'

'And your sisters, do they live in the farm—croft? I think you said you had four?'

'Three. It can feel like five or six mind, when they are all in the same room. Mhairi, Sheena and Jean.

They are all married now, with their own crofts, and have a gaggle of bairns between them.'

He talked of them all with obvious affection. As she listened, Isabella couldn't help comparing his childhood with her own. It had been harsh, there was no doubt about it, though he did not dwell on it, but they were obviously a loving family.

'You have been back then, since the war?' she asked. 'I think you told me it had been many years since you had been home.'

Finlay's smile faded. 'Aye, I've been back.'

'After such a long time away, you must have found it very changed.'

He looked troubled. 'No, it was almost exactly the same.'

'And your family, they were all well?'

'Aye.' He put the hammer down with a sigh. 'They were all very well, and very pleased to see me, and I— ach, it doesn't matter.'

'It obviously does.'

'What I meant was, I don't want to talk about it.'

'I can see that from the way you are scowling at me.'

'I don't scowl.'

She wrinkled her face into a fair imitation of his expression. 'What is that, then?'

Finlay was forced to laugh. 'What it means is, when I say I don't want to talk about something, I don't want to talk about it.'

'After the war,' Isabella said, picking her words carefully, 'I found it very difficult to go back to being Señorita Romero again. I felt as if I was acting a part.'

'You look to me as if you're still acting. Not now, but with other people, your brother—'

'Who thinks it's high time I was married,' Isabella interrupted hurriedly. He *was* suspicious. It was imprudent of her to have embarked upon this comparison between them, but she had never been able to discuss how she felt before, and most likely would never be able to discuss it again. 'Xavier is right,' she continued. 'I am much older than most Spanish brides, but I—I don't know.' She shrugged. 'I am afraid Gabriel will be disappointed in his side of the bargain. He is a nice man. He is a perfect husband for me. Everyone thinks so. Perfect. Only I am not sure that I could be such a perfect wife. Or—or want to be. Do you understand what I mean?'

Finlay shrugged, picking up the hammer again, turning it over in his hand.

Deflated, Isabella slid down from the barrel. 'Never mind.'

He caught her arm as she passed him. 'I do understand.' His smile was crooked. 'I do. It's what I thought I wanted, what I used to think about on the nights before a battle, when it seemed morning would never come. Going back to the croft. Taking over from my father. Settling down. It's what I always thought I'd do, when peace came. Thing is, I never really thought peace would come, and now it's here...'

'You are not so sure anymore?'

He flinched. 'That's the problem,' he said sadly. 'It's one thing I'm very sure of. I'm not cut out to be a crofter.'

'So that is why you became a wine merchant?' She waited, but he merely shrugged. 'Do you miss the war, Finlay?'

'Not exactly. Certainly not the bloodshed and the suffering.'

'But the excitement of it. Knowing you made a difference, that your contribution was vital. Knowing that so many men relied on you. The responsibility.' Isabella smiled. 'And the danger.'

'Aye. All of that. People don't understand it, but the army has been my life.'

'It was my life, too, for a time, during the occupation. I miss it, too, just as you do.'

'Do you? Aye, I can see that you might, though it's not the same.'

The empathy she was feeling trickled away. 'Why not? Why is it not the same? Because I am a...'

'For the love of— It has nothing to do with your being a woman, if that's what you were about to say. What a chip on your shoulder you have,' Finlay exclaimed. 'It is not the same because I have spent my entire adult life in the army. I know nothing else, whereas you had a life before, and a life to come back to. The war here has been over two years. You must be accustomed to peacetime life by now.'

She clenched her fists and was about to retort angrily, when the incongruity of his remark struck her. 'Your entire adult life has been in the military? You told me you left the army when Napoleon was sent to Elba, which was nearly two years ago, and since then you have been assiduously building up your wine business.'

Finlay waved his hand dismissively. 'What I meant is that the army has dominated my life so much that it feels as if I have always been a soldier. And speaking of my new career,' he said, looking at his watch, 'it is high time we were getting back to change for dinner. It wouldn't enhance my negotiating position with your brother if I were to insult him by having the bad manners to keep his wife waiting.'

In his room, taking a quick bath before dinner, Finlay cursed himself for a fool. What an eejit he'd been, to get caught out so easily. Luckily it had not been too costly a faux pas but he would have to be much more careful in future.

'Aye, for example, please refrain from mentioning over dinner that you fought at Waterloo a matter of months ago, Finlay, there's a good chap!'

The fair Isabella was as sharp as a tack, and he had once again allowed himself to be sidetracked by those big eyes of hers, and those luscious lips. He poured another jug of hot water over his head. He wasn't doing her justice. Her kisses were delightful, sure enough, but it was her, Isabella herself, who intrigued him. She was an enigmatic mixture, and a fascinating creature. 'And a gie clever one, you'd do well to remember, Finlay Urquhart.'

He'd recovered the situation, but only temporarily. Her suspicions had been aroused, which meant he had to be a step ahead of her by the morning.

He'd think of something. He always did. In the meantime, there were other, more delightful things to think of. Such as the fact that Isabella's chamber was only a few doors down the corridor. Most likely she was taking a bath, too. Her hair would be all damp curls, clinging to her back. Her face would be flushed from the heat of the water. She'd be lying back as he was, her eyes closed, as his were. The water would be lapping at her breasts. There would be tantalising glimpses of her nipples through the suds. Her soapy body would be slippery to the touch, and when the bubbles burst as the water cooled, so much more would be revealed…

Chapter Five

Consuela placed the letter she had received on the breakfast table and poured herself a cup of chocolate. 'It is a brief note from Xavier. Unfortunately he will be detained in Pamplona for a further few days. Isabella, he asks that you ensure Mr Urquhart is given a comprehensive tour of all aspects of the work of the estate. To that end, you are to take him to visit Estebe, the head winemaker, and—but here, you may as well read it for yourself.' Consuela pushed the letter across the table.

Isabella took the letter, raising her brows at the list of tasks her brother had compiled for her. Necessity and greed had forced Xavier into trusting her with an important task. Though not enough to actually write to her himself.

'Mr Urquhart is tardy this morning,' Consuela said, eyeing the clock.

Isabella, who had been anxiously thinking the same thing, began to rearrange the bread on her plate. 'You like our foreign guest, don't you?'

Consuela bristled slightly. 'I hope you are not imply-ing that my behaviour has been improper in any way?'

'Not at all. Only that he is very handsome and ex-tremely charming. All women like him, I think. Even I do.' *Though I am fairly certain he is a fraud and not who he purports to be.* The butterflies in her tummy started beating their wings again. She wished that there was another conclusion, but once again decided there was not.

'Isabella, you know that it would not be appropri-ate, or wise, to grow to like this man too much? He *is* charming, but he is a wine merchant. You think I am empty-headed. I know you do, because you never discuss anything of any import with me save my son, and...'

'Consuela, I...'

'No, let me speak for once. You think that because I say nothing I don't see what's happening under my nose, but I do. The way you look at Mr Urquhart... You have never looked at Gabriel like that.'

'Gabriel has never looked at me the way Mr Urqu-hart does.'

Consuela, to her surprise, giggled. 'Mr Urquhart looks at you as if he would like to have you for his din-ner. I think that it would be very nice, to be Mr Urqu-hart's dinner, to be devoured by him.'

'What on earth can you mean by that?'

Her sister-in-law gave her a coy look. 'You must trust me on that, and you must wait to find out for yourself when you are married. You *are* going to marry Gabriel, aren't you?'

'Everyone seems to expect it, but my feelings for him are tepid at best, since we are being frank.'

Consuela rolled her eyes. 'I forget you have no mother to guide you. I will tell you, then, what my mother told me. Love blossoms after marriage, not before. It is perfectly natural, when you think about it. Until a woman truly knows her husband, as his wife, she can have no reason to love him any more than she loves any other suitor.'

'Do you love Xavier?'

Consuela looked surprised. 'But of course. He is my husband. It happened just as my mother predicted. She is never wrong. It will happen to you, too, when you marry Gabriel.'

Love was not a subject to which Isabella had given much consideration, and it was not one that much interested her, either. Consuela's persistence, though, made one thing clear that had not occurred to Isabella before. 'It would suit you for me to be married off and gone from Hermoso Romero, wouldn't it? I am sorry. I have endeavoured not to interfere in the running of your household since you arrived as Xavier's bride two years ago. I have been at pains to give you your place, but you must appreciate that I have been de facto mistress of Hermoso Romero for many years.'

'I do understand that, and I assure you, it is not a big problem for me. I don't dislike you. I don't see you as a threat, Isabella, though I know you think I do. Xavier thinks that because you are his sister and I am his wife, that you should also be my sister. But you're not,' Consuela said simply. 'The truth is I would love my real sister to come here to live, but while you are here Xavier will not countenance it. So for that reason, you understand, your presence is—inconvenient.'

'Oh.' Isabella felt like a fool. She also felt—rejected. 'I had no idea.'

'You have never asked. I am very relieved that you have broached the subject now.'

Mortified, she remembered that Finlay had hinted she do so. What a fool she had been. 'Yes. I see.' Isabella smiled weakly. 'I am sorry.'

'It is easily remedied. Gabriel Torres is waiting only for a sign from you and he will propose. I am glad we have cleared the air. And now here is Mr Urquhart at last.' Consuela rose from the table. 'I have had a letter from my husband. Isabella will explain. You must excuse me. I promised to take my son for a drive in the carriage today.'

The door closed on a swish of silken skirts. 'My sister-in-law has just informed me that I am to marry Gabriel in order to allow *her* sister to come and live here in my place,' Isabella said dully. 'But you knew that, didn't you?'

'I did, yes. I'm sorry.'

'There is no need. At least now I understand my position.'

'It's a damned unfair one. This has been your home much longer that it's been hers.'

Her own thoughts exactly. Hearing them expressed aloud made Isabella feel marginally better. Finlay had poured himself a cup of coffee, though he had not sat down. He had a tiny nick on his chin, a cut from shaving. There was a rebellious kink of hair standing up like a question mark at his hairline. It was oddly endearing. He was wearing buckskin breeches and top boots. She wondered if his legs had lost their tan. Looking up, she caught his eye. 'Do you miss wearing your kilt?' she asked.

'In London, it caused more bother than it was worth. Ladies either found it indecent or intriguing. A fair few found it to be both. I was never quite sure whether it was indecently intriguing or intriguingly indecent! Do you miss wearing your breeches?'

'Yes, I do.' Isabella smiled faintly. 'In Spain, we pretend that ladies do not have legs, you know.'

Finlay laughed. 'It is no different for ladies in England.'

'You seem to know a lot about English ladies and fashion, unless you were inventing it for Consuela's benefit.'

'I've been to my fair share of balls and formal dinners.'

'Do you know the steps to this new dance, the waltz? Xavier thinks it is too shocking to be danced in polite society.'

'I reckon I could teach you. Do you want to be shocked, Isabella?'

She began to rearrange the untouched bread on her plate again. 'Your turning up here is quite shocking enough. Since you left the army, though, you will have had little time for balls and parties, I would imagine, while building your business. All work and no play, as the saying goes.'

Silence fell. Finlay poured another cup of coffee, but still did not sit down. He was waiting for her to speak. A knot formed in her stomach. 'I have something…' Isabella cleared her throat. 'We need to talk,' she said.

'I agree, we do.'

'Finlay, I do not profess to know why you are here, but it is of a certainty not to purchase wine.'

'No, I'm not.' He finished his coffee in one gulp. 'Take a walk with me, and I'll tell you the real reason I am here.'

Isabella had pulled a fringed shawl around her shoulders. Her gown was simple but elegant, the plain white material relieved by a bold pattern of what looked to be strawberries running around the hem and diagonally across the skirt. The high waist suited her tall, slim figure. Her feet were clad not in the delicate slippers favoured by her sister-in-law, but in much more sturdy and practical boots. She kept pace easily at his side as they walked, despite her narrow skirts. There were gold highlights in her hair, sparked to life by the weak winter sunshine. The cold morning air caught in his lungs, their breath visible as they continued on their way.

On balance, Finlay had come to the conclusion overnight that Isabella would not betray him. He had pondered the possibility of inventing another story to fob her off for a few more days, but quickly abandoned that idea. Though he disliked Xavier Romero, Finlay disliked the lies he was obliged to tell the man even more, the false expectations he was raising.

But lying to Isabella… That was a whole different kettle of fish. There had existed, from the very first time they had met, an unmistakable spark between them that he, for one, had never experienced before. It went against the grain with him not to be straight with her, though he was fairly certain she was doing a fair bit of dissembling herself. If she was, as he hoped, merely protecting his quarry, he could not blame her for that. In fact, it was a rather admirable display of loyalty.

He led the way past the chapel, along the cypress tree walk and out onto a path that climbed between the serried ranks of vines to an ancient wooden bench with a panoramic view out over the estate. Isabella did not speak as they snaked their way up the hillside. He sensed her tension as they sat down, saw it in the rigid way she held herself, her hands clasped together under her shawl.

'Right, then,' Finlay said. 'I'll speak first and save you the trouble of asking. I'm not a wine merchant. In fact, I'm still a soldier, same as I've always been.'

Isabella jumped to her feet. 'So everything you have told me has been a lie?'

'No! Not all. My family, the croft, all that is true.'

'But you did not leave the army when Napoleon was sent to Elba? You presumably fought at Waterloo, then?'

'Aye.' He grabbed her wrist and pulled her back onto the bench. 'Who I fought and when are beside the point. Listen to me now, because it's vitally important. Lives are at stake here, including my own if things go badly. I had no option but to lie to you until

I knew whether or not I could trust you. It's been two years since we met after all, and a lot can change in two years. When I arrived here, I wasn't even certain that I'd be able to find you.'

'Find me? You mean you came here looking for me?'

Finlay grinned. 'I came looking for a wee peasant lassie, and there you were in that fine white lace mantilla and that silk gown, not only a lady, but the sister of the estate owner. I couldn't believe it. I damn near panicked, I can tell you.'

'You hid it very well,' Isabella responded tartly. 'Unlike me.'

'Aye, that was one of the things that set me off wondering about you from the first, but then when you explained about your brother, and I could see for myself he was no friend of the liberal cause, I thought that was the cause of your panic. But the real Isabella kept popping through the lady's demure facade that you have clearly donned since the end of the war. I am hoping I'm not the only one who is not what he appears. In fact, I am staking quite a lot on it.'

'Why?' she asked baldly.

'You told me once that you knew how to get in touch with a partisan known as El Fantasma, in order to convince me that the partisans be allowed to attack a French arms cache. The fact that they succeeded proves to me that your claim was genuine. El Fantasma is clearly known to you.' He felt her flinch at the name, and though she said nothing, it was enough. 'Isabella, the man is in deep trouble. I think you know where he might be found. I think you might still be involved in some way with his cause. I need you to take me to him.'

'Take you to him?' she repeated blankly.

'To El Fantasma. His life is at risk.'

'For El Fantasma there are always risks.' Isabella waved her hand dismissively. 'You think he cares about that?'

'Frankly, he'd be a fool not to care. There's bravery and then there's sheer recklessness.'

She narrowed her eyes. 'Perhaps he thinks that the cause he fights for is more important than anything else.'

'More important even than his life?' Finlay snapped. 'Isabella, the British government believe that your Spanish government are determined to track him down, and the net is closing around him. I'm here to prevent that happening.'

'What!' she exclaimed incredulously. 'You cannot mean—are you saying that you have been sent here to *rescue* El Fantasma?'

'That's the gist of it.'

'You don't think that's incredibly presumptuous? I am very sure he neither wants nor needs to be rescued.'

He shook his head, taken aback by her vehemence. 'How can you be so certain?'

Isabella bit her lip, eyeing him speculatively, then gave a little shrug, followed by an enigmatic smile. 'Because,' she said, 'I am El Fantasma.'

It took Finlay a full minute to unscramble his reeling senses before he could muster a response. '*You*

are The Ghost? *You* are El Fantasma? By all that is—
I can't believe it.'

'No,' she said, drawing him an arch look, 'you did
not for a moment consider it could be me, did you?'

'Not for a single second,' he admitted frankly. She
was beaming at him now, her golden eyes shining with
a mixture of pride and glee. Finlay burst into laughter.
It was ridiculous, outrageous, fantastical, though in a
way it made an awful lot of sense. 'Good Lord, does
that brother of yours know?' he asked.

Isabella tossed her head. 'Of course not. No one
knows, save for my deputy, Estebe.'

'Estebe! By all that is…' Finlay cursed under his
breath.

'Estebe himself has four deputies, though they do
not know each other, of course, and below that—but
you know how partisan groups are structured to protect anonymity and preserve security, I think. Estebe
helps me with the printing press we use to publish our
propaganda pamphlets. It is…'

'Hidden in the winery cellars.' Finlay finished for
her as the pieces began to tumble into place.

Isabella's smile faded. 'How did you know?'

'I didn't, but it's obvious now that I—' He broke off,
shaking his head. 'Have you any idea how dangerous
a game you're playing?'

'It is not a game, and I am not stupid. Of course I
know it is dangerous, but what does that matter, when
we have so much at stake?'

'Aye, such as the lives of your family. Your brother.

For God's sake, Isabella, that printing press in his cellar— If it was discovered...'

'It will not be.' Her voice hardened. 'You do not understand, Finlay. We are fighting for our future.'

'I think it's you who doesn't understand. What I'm trying to tell you is that if you carry on, you'll have no future.'

Her eyes blazed. 'If we stop, if we give up, the future will not be worth having! We sacrificed so much during the war—has it to be for nothing? We must fight on, if not with guns, then with words. Those in power do not want to hear what we have to say, but we will continue to say it until they listen.'

She spoke with such conviction, such passion, that he was momentarily disarmed. He could not doubt her claim to be the infamous partisan, but however inspiring she was, it was her very idealism that worried him, for it made her quite reckless and completely, misguidedly without fear. He'd seen far too many brave men slaughtered. A dose of healthy fear was essential to survival, in his book—not that he'd admit to it himself, mind.

'I'm not doubting your sincerity, or indeed your cause,' Finlay said, choosing his words carefully, eager not to estrange her further.

'I am glad to hear that.'

'Aye, but this government of yours, the men in Madrid who wield the power here in Spain, to put it bluntly, the louder you shout, the more determined they will be to shut you up.'

Isabella tossed her head again. 'Do you not see,

the very fact that they wish to do so is evidence of El Fantasma's success? As the voice of protest grows, so, too, does our power to change things. We will force them to listen, Finlay. We will force them to act.' She caught at his jacket sleeve, giving his arm a shake to emphasise her point. 'Yes, it is dangerous because we say what they do not want to hear, but how much more dangerous would it be to remain silent?'

Silent was what she would be, as the grave, if she was not careful, but she looked so magnificent standing there, a fervent light in her eyes, a flush on her cheeks, a proud smile on her delightful lips, that Finlay found himself quite torn. She was so sure she was right, and he was equally certain she was wrong, but he could not bring himself to destroy her illusions. Not yet.

'You're a very brave lass. I still can't quite believe that you are The Ghost,' he said. Here he'd been, thinking the hard part of his mission was going to be tracking El Fantasma down, but the really tricky thing was going to be persuading her to come away with him. The irony of it, the sheer unlikelihood of it, made him shake his hand, marvelling at this twist of fate. Isabella was still clutching at his jacket. Finlay took her hand between his, fascinated by the slenderness of it, how delicate it looked in his own rough paw. 'I'm still struggling to take it in,' he said ruefully.

She chuckled. 'We are neither of us what we appear to be, it seems.'

'That's for certain.'

'And now we can stop pretending.'

'That is very true,' he said, much struck by this. He smiled, revelling in the simple pleasure of looking at her for the first time without any barricades or withheld secrets between them. 'You do know,' he said, 'that I haven't been pretending all the time. I did not pretend to enjoy your company. I did not pretend to enjoy your conversation.'

'Since we are in the business of confessions,' she said, 'I will admit that I, too, have very much enjoyed our conversations. Being alone with you, I have not had to pretend to be the dutiful, and frankly boring, Lady Isabella.'

Did she know how bewitching her smile was? Did she realise what it did to him, that smile? And the way she looked at him with those big eyes of hers... Did she know she was playing with fire? Almost without meaning to—almost—he pulled her closer. 'Above all, you do know that I did not pretend to enjoy kissing you, don't you?'

'No? Why, then, did you kiss me, Major Urquhart?'

He tried to remind himself that she was an innocent, but the demure Spanish lady she purported to be was nowhere to be seen in this feisty, bold, brave, beautiful woman smiling seductively up at him. 'I kissed you,' Finlay said roughly, 'for the very simple reason that you are irresistible.'

'I think that is what is known as serendipity,' Isabella replied, 'for it's the very same reason I kissed you back.'

'Serendipity,' Finlay said, sliding his arm around her waist. 'I've always wondered what it tasted like.'

'Strawberries, and lavender, and vintage wine, I believe is how you described it.'

'No,' he said decidedly. 'It tastes of nothing other than essence of you. The most intoxicating and delicious taste imaginable.'

There was a different quality to Finlay's smile that excited Isabella. There was something different in the way he looked at her, too, a gleam in his sea-blue eyes, as if he could not quite believe what he was seeing. There was a very different quality to their kiss, too. This time it was he who was tentative, she who was daring. He kissed her as if he was not sure who he was kissing. She kissed him back with the boldness, the wild elation she felt at finally being able to reveal her true self.

Her response ensured he was not tentative for long. The pressure of his lips increased as she opened her mouth. The touch of his tongue on hers set her aflame. His hands slid down to cup her bottom, pulling her hard up against him. She slid her hands under his coat, flattening her palms against the smooth silk of his waistcoat, feeling the rippling of his muscles as she touched him, up the length of his spine, back down, to the waistband of his breeches.

His mouth was hot on hers. She closed her eyes, the sunlight dappling crimson inside her lids, and slid her hands over the smooth leather of his breeches to the taut muscles of his buttocks. He moaned, plunging his tongue into her mouth. She could feel the unmistakable ridge of his arousal pressing between her thighs.

Heat trickled through her. She felt potent, wild, that intense, fierce focus from the old days. The pinpoint of danger, though this time the threat was not of capture but surrender.

Still they kissed. His jacket fell to the ground. They were on the bench now, and she was splayed on top of him, her skirts rucked high, his erection pressing against her. She flattened her palms over his shoulders. His breath was ragged. His kisses grew wilder and more passionate. Her own lips pressed against his, as if they would meld. His hand on her breast made her gasp. Her nipple hardened sweetly, painfully beneath her corset. She wanted to moan with frustration for the layers that lay between them, his skin, her nipple. She dug her fingers into his hair, clutching the soft silkiness, tilting her hips to rub herself against him, panting as his mouth devoured hers, as his hand tightened on her breast, as something inside her tightened like a knot, too.

She tensed her thighs against his. More kisses. Behind her closed lids, crimson, blood red. Her blood hot. Danger. She remembered then, seeing him that first night at the ball. Dangerous. He was dangerous. He was so delightfully dangerous. And she was so unafraid.

Finlay muttered something soft in what she assumed must be Gaelic, and dragged his mouth from hers. Gently, he began to disentangle himself from her. 'I'm sorry. I don't know what I— I didn't mean to— And here, of all places. What the devil was I thinking!'

His eyes were dark, his pupils dilated. His hair was in wild disarray. The pins had come out of hers. Isa-

bella knew she ought to be shocked at her own behaviour, but all she could think about was the tension
inside her, the urgent need for release, the feeling of
hanging on a precipice, desperate to let go, the slow
realisation that she would instead have to clamber back
down to reality. 'I don't believe either of us was thinking,' she said, trying to herd her errant thoughts into
some sort of coherency.

'No, I don't suppose we were.' Finlay stooped to
gather some of her hairpins from the ground, handing them to her with a rueful smile. 'You are the most
distracting lass I've ever come across. I look at you,
and my head says one thing and my body something
else entirely.'

'My body is not in the least bit interested in what
my head is saying at this moment.'

Finlay's eyes darkened. 'Dear heavens, nor is mine.'
He reached for her, then pulled his hand away as if
he had been burned. 'We need to talk. We need to
decide—you are El Fantasma. I still can't get my head
around that one.' He gave himself a little shake. 'Aye.
Right. El Fantasma. We need to think about what we
do next. I had already taken the precaution of making
some prior arrangements on the assumption I would
track him—you—down, but...'

His words brought Isabella tumbling firmly back
to earth. 'I am not interested in your arrangements.
There's nothing to think about, nothing to discuss,' she
said sharply. 'Now you know the truth, you can return
to England forthwith and tell the Duke of Wellington

that El Fantasma thanks him for his concern but has no desire for, or need of rescue.'

He stared at her for a long moment. She could not read his thoughts. In truth, she did not really wish to contemplate his leaving here, not just yet. It would be a huge relief to be able to be herself for a little while longer, in this beguiling man's company.

'Isabella, can you not see…'

'Finlay, can you not see!' She grabbed his arm. 'I know what I am doing. You have no right to interfere.'

'I'm trying to save your life.'

'And I am trying to save many, many other lives,' she declared hotly. 'I wish I had not told you.'

He paused in the act of putting his coat on. 'Why did you?'

'I don't know. I've never told anyone else. I suppose I hoped you would understand.' She began to stick pins randomly into her hair. 'I thought that you would see we were similar. You were wrong when you told me I don't know what it is to be a soldier, don't you see? I *am* a soldier, just like you. You cannot expect me to do anything other than stay and fight this battle, when it is exactly what you would do if the roles were reversed.'

He was silent for a long time, his brow furrowed. When he spoke again, it was with a deliberate detachment. 'There's little to be gained by us arguing from implacably opposed viewpoints. We both have a lot to digest and reflect on. I'm going for a wee walk. I'll see you at dinner.'

He turned and began to make his way up the track,

leaving Isabella to stare at his retreating back, fighting the urge to call him back to convince him of the validity of her case and the equally strong urge to call him back and demand that he finish what he had started.

Finlay strode off up the hill towards the tree line. *Is fheàrr teicheadh math na droch fhuireach.* Better a good retreat than a bad stand. He was not running away, but though it went against the grain with him to leave Isabella alone after all that had happened, he knew if he stayed it would be a strategic miscalculation.

'You need to start thinking with your head, and stop letting yourself be driven by your other body parts, my lad,' he muttered under his breath. He could feel Isabella's eyes on him as he climbed the steep path. He quickened his pace, forcing himself to ignore the urge to look back. Upward, onward, away he marched, just short of a run, enjoying the way the exercise made his heart beat faster, the way the fresh air stabbed at his lungs. And finally, as he cleared the tree line and emerged on the next ridge and his calf muscles began to protest, finally, his head began to clear itself of the fog of confusion triggered by this latest bewildering turn of events.

He stopped, taking deep, recuperative breaths, and looked at the landscape spread out below him. Ochre soil, the warm yellow stone of Hermoso Romero, the regimented row of pruned vines, the soft green foliage of cypress trees, the pale winter blue of the sky and the silvery lemon of the winter sun. It was a beautiful place, no doubt about it. If he lived here, he'd be loath to leave. But it wasn't all this beauty that made Isabella determined to remain here—it was all the things you couldn't see. The poverty. The injustice. The constraints of the old ways. The same feudal culture that made her brother the region's biggest landowner and one of its most influential men. It was ironic that Xavier Romero represented all the things Isabella wanted to change.

'And I can't blame her for fighting for change, since by and large I share her views,' Finlay said, smiling to himself as he recalled the fire in Isabella's eyes as she had spoken of El Fantasma's cause. He squatted down on his heels, wiping the sweat from his forehead. The death of the old ways, a new beginning, a new world. Hadn't he been fighting for the same things himself?

His face hardened. Waterloo, the battle that had finally defeated Napoleon, the battle that had brought peace to Europe, had taken place five months ago. He sat back heavily, causing a limestone rock to clatter down the path. Peace was a fine thing and to be welcomed. No more death. No more bloodshed. He had not lied when he'd told Isabella he didn't miss that. Peace would bring prosperity, the press said.

'To the likes of Wellington, to those who had always been prosperous, aye, that it would, but what about the rest of us?' Finlay muttered. London was already full of ex-soldiers, cast out of the military once their usefulness had expired, reduced to begging on the streets. Back home, in the Highlands, things were just the same as ever, the crofters just as poor as ever. And it was as Jack had said—no one wanted to know.

Nothing had really changed, despite all the sacrifice. Was this what he'd fought for?

Here in Spain, it was worse. Here in Spain, they'd taken a few more steps backwards. But Isabella had not given up. Isabella was still fighting, though it was, in Finlay's opinion, a very lost cause, indeed. Did that make her wrong? Was her deluded optimism better or worse than his pragmatism?

An unanswerable question. But one thing he did know, Isabella's deluded optimism was clouding her judgement. She thought herself a hardened soldier, she thought her cause more important than her life, but she had no idea. It was all very well to wave away a theoretical threat, but the reality was something else entirely. Finlay, all too easily able to imagine what would happen if she was caught, shuddered at the horrors Isabella would be forced to endure. Indeed, not only Isabella, but her brother and his wife, too, like as not. Yet she seemed quite unable to grasp this fact. Or mayhap she simply didn't want to acknowledge it? Aye, that was more likely.

He picked up a rock and threw it so forcefully down the mountainside that the limestone split into a cloud of powder. Reluctant as he was to spell it out to her, that was what he had to do. Better to fill her head with horrors than to have to face the reality of them, surely? He picked up another small rock, rolling it over in his palm. The idea was extremely unpalatable. Isabella's idealism was her Achilles' heel but it was also her shield. What right had he to tell her to stop fighting her battles? What right had he to destroy her illusions? None, and what was more, he did not want to.

Yet what he wanted was quite beside the point. The case was simple. Isabella's life was in mortal danger. Finlay had been sent here to get El Fantasma out of Spain. He was here under Wellington's, albeit indirect, orders. More important, he was here to keep a solemn promise made to Jack. More important still, if he could not get Isabella to see sense, she might very easily be taken, tortured or executed before he spirited her away.

Still, the thought of acting against her very decided wishes and taking matters into his own hands gave him pause. Finlay got to his feet and hurled the rock down the mountainside. One more chance. He'd give her one more chance to see sense. There was time yet for that.

Chapter Six

Isabella pushed her papers aside with a sigh of frustration. El Fantasma's next pamphlet was due to be printed this week, but Estebe was still confined to bed, and though she could set the type and do all the preparation, she could not work the printing press alone. She scanned the piece she was working on, making a few changes before casting it aside once more. There was nothing wrong with it, but nor did it contain anything fresh. The demand for the pamphlets was increasing, but when would talk turn to action?

Would it ever take that definitive step? Pulling back the long voile curtains, Isabella threw a soft cashmere shawl over her nightdress, opened the window and stepped out onto her balcony. The night air was invigorating. It had a sharpness to it that told her winter was not too far away. There would be snow on the mountains soon, perhaps within a few weeks. And before that, perhaps within as little as a few days, Finlay would be gone.

It was for the best, she told herself, gazing up at the

stars with the usual pang of regret that she could no longer look at them through the telescope with Papa. Another thing Xavier had appropriated. Star gazing, it seemed, was not a pastime fit for females, though neither was it a pastime her brother had shown any inclination to take up. She wished that she could love Xavier as she ought. She wished that she could trust him with her secret. She wished that he could see her for who she truly was. She sighed, irked with herself. There were more important things to wish for.

Her brother was no fool, and Finlay knew as much about wine as she did about Paris fashions. The moment Xavier stopped boasting and pontificating about his precious Rioja and started asking searching questions, Finlay's cover would be blown. How did he plan to extricate himself? He would not go to the lengths of placing an order, she was fairly certain. 'No, of that I am absolutely certain,' Isabella said aloud. 'Lies, they do not sit well with Finlay Urquhart.'

Leaning on the balustrade, she looked out along the side of the house. She could see the adjacent balcony that served as Finlay's bedchamber. The room was dark, the window to his balcony closed. Was he sleeping? She pictured him sprawled on his back, one arm above his head. His nightshirt would be open at the neck. Though perhaps he did not wear one? Would his chest be smooth? No, a smattering of hair. Dark auburn, it would be. She closed her eyes, recalling his contours under her hand. He was solid, not slim like Gabriel. Yes, that was it. Solid.

Today, on the hillside, he had given her a taste of

what Consuela had hinted at. Remembering the way he had touched her, kissed her, the feel of his lips on hers, his tongue, his hands—she wanted more. The urgent tension he had left her with, that tightly furled feeling inside her had given her just a flavour of what could exist between a man and a woman. How much more was there to experience?

She shivered. What had Consuela meant when she said that she would like to be devoured? Isabella didn't like to think of Finlay devouring any other woman, though he had doubtless savoured many. She tried to imagine kissing Gabriel as she had kissed Finlay, but it was no use. Gabriel would be shocked to the core. A good Spanish woman went to her wedding bed innocent of such things. Isabella turned away from the stars and headed back inside. How she very much did not want to be a good Spanish woman!

It was late. The warming pan was cold on her feet. She pulled it out from under the blankets and set it on the hearth before getting back into bed. The very few who had known her in the past as El Fantasma treated her as an honorary man. They had respected her. Some had feared her. All had obeyed her orders unquestioningly. Finlay had been excited by her revelation. He had not seen her as a threat, but a challenge. To him, she was no honorary man. Not an equal precisely, but— Was there such a thing as equal and different? He made her feel less masculine and wholly feminine. It was very strange. And really, not the point at all.

She plumped her pillow and turned onto her other side. There was a point, but she couldn't remember—

Ah, yes, now she did. Lies. Finlay did not like to tell lies. His deceit made him extremely uncomfortable, which meant there must be a very, very important reason for him to resort to it.

Isabella sat up in bed and began to unravel her long plait. What if the net truly was closing in on El Fantasma? Certainly, the more vociferous liberals were now being persecuted. El Fantasma stood for all that the government wished to repress. He was subversive, but was he really dangerous enough for the state to pursue him?

The idea was much more thrilling than frightening. If it was true, it meant they really were starting to make a difference. Isabella ran her fingers through her hair and began to divide it up and plait it again. There were times when it felt as if the country she had fought for had gone backwards since the end of the war. It was not just the withdrawal of the constitution or the persecution of its supporters, it was the return of the Inquisition, the loss of freedom of the press. All that bloodshed, all that sacrifice, to go back to how things were before. She had put her life on the line for her country, for change. No politician in Madrid was going to stop her speaking out! None! She would not allow it. Absolutely, she would not!

And as to danger? For a moment, recalling just how vociferous Finlay had been, Isabella felt a little bit sick. She hadn't ever considered the risk to Xavier of the printing press being found in his cellars. 'But who would find it!' She tied her plait tightly. The sickness faded. 'This to danger,' she said, snapping her fingers. 'We cannot stop now. The fight must go on.'

The problem, she mused, was that Finlay did not understand. If she could make him see how important their cause was then he would leave, explain to the great Duke of Wellington that El Fantasma was in no need of rescue. Tomorrow, she would show him, quite literally. Smiling, Isabella snuggled back down under her sheets. Tomorrow, Finlay would start to see things her way.

'I should have guessed.' The small wine cellar looked just as it had when Isabella had brought him here a few days ago, though the bottle and the glasses had gone from the table. 'It's behind here, then?' Finlay studied the wall that she had claimed to be blocked. 'How does one gain access?'

Isabella pulled a wine bottle out and slipped her hand in behind the rack covering the lower part of the wall, and he heard a small click. 'Will you help me? You need to push that way.'

He did as she indicated, and the rack slid with ease along the wall to reveal a small wooden door. Isabella stood back to allow him through as soon as she had turned her key in the lock. He had to stoop. Holding the lamp high, he was surprised to find that this secret cellar was nearly twice the size of the one they had come through.

The bulky wooden printing press stood on three sets of trestles. It took up most of the floor space and would, when the frame holding the paper was extended, make the place very cramped indeed. A long table covered most of one wall, stacked with paper, trays of type, bottles of ink and all the other accoutrements necessary to the production of El Fantasma's pamphlets. The press was about seven feet long and the same height in the middle, Finlay reckoned. 'I take it you brought it in here in pieces and then assembled it,' he said, eyeing the small doorway.

'Estebe assisted me. It took us three nights to bring all the parts down through the cellars.'

'It's as well that brother of yours has his phobia,' Finlay said. 'Does anyone else know of this place?'

'Not now that Papa…' Isabella turned away, busying herself with lighting another lamp. 'Only Estebe and I know, now that Papa is no longer with us. During the war, we stored arms here.'

'We? You mean your father knew?'

'Not about the printing press, that was after he— After.' Isabella turned around, smiling sadly. 'But the arms—yes, it was his idea to use this place. It was he who had the new door fitted.'

'Aye, but what I meant was, did he know what you were up to?'

'Oh, yes,' she said, with a whimsical smile. 'My father was a very influential man, Finlay, and a very enlightened one. He had access to a great deal of privileged information, you know. How do you think El Fantasma came to be so well informed?'

'Your father knew you were El Fantasma, the partisan! Hell's bells, how many more of these revelations are you going to hit me with!'

Isabella laughed at his astonishment. 'Only one more. My father was actually the original El Fantasma.

All I did was act as his liaison between certain trusted guerrillas at first, and then gradually, as he became sick and as I became more…adept?—then I took over. You see, you could describe it as the family business.'

'I doubt your brother would see it that way,' Finlay responded drily.

Isabella's expression hardened. 'I told you, my father was a very enlightened man. As his son, Xavier was destined to take on the legacy of Hermoso Romero, and Papa made sure that he was fit for that purpose. Expensive schooling. The army. The management of the estate. The production of the wine. Xavier will do the same for his son. To me, Papa bequeathed El Fantasma. I do not interfere with my brother's management of his legacy. My own legacy is none of Xavier's concern.'

It was not so much the words as the tone in which she spoke that made Finlay's heart sink. She sounded as he did, when giving orders. Cool, calm and utterly implacable. He wasn't simply dealing with a woman on a mission to bring about change. Isabella's dreams were also her father's. How the devil was he to convince her that she had to give them up forever?

'You will not,' she said. 'Persuade me to give El Fantasma up,' she clarified, 'if that is what you were thinking?'

'So you're a mind reader now, are you?'

She shrugged. 'I know that you are not a man who countenances failure. I made it very clear yesterday that I would reject any offer of rescue, but your orders are nonetheless to rescue me, and Major Finlay Urquhart is a soldier who, I suspect, never fails to obey an order.'

'You're quite wrong there, lass,' he said harshly. 'If I hadn't been quite so capable of insubordination, I'd be Colonel Urquhart by now, at the very least.'

Isabella spread a sheaf of pages out on the table in front of her. 'Instead, you are the Jock Upstart—have I that right?'

'You do.'

'Then, they will not be so very surprised, your superiors, when you disobey this particular order,' she said, glancing over her shoulder. 'Once you have seen for yourself how important El Fantasma's work is, I am hoping you will agree that they were quite misguided when they sent you here.'

So she was laying down the gauntlet. He was not surprised. Though it would have made his life a damned sight easier if she'd turned around and agreed with him, he'd have been disappointed. And maybe a wee bit sceptical, too. Isabella was not the type to simply roll over. 'I'm afraid it is you who are misguided, lass,' Finlay said, shaking his head.

'No,' Isabella said firmly. 'No, you will not ever persuade me to that way of thinking, so instead I must persuade you to think differently. Come, see for yourself.'

Why not? he thought, joining her at the table. She deserved a fair hearing, even if the outcome was already, in his mind, decided.

Joining her at the table, he saw she had a large rectangular frame set in front of her. 'This will be the front page of our next pamphlet.' Isabella began to select tiny blocks of characters to place into it. 'You see, all the letters have to be inserted in reverse. I used to practise with a mirror. Even after two years, I am still very slow.'

She didn't look slow. Finlay watched her reaching for the individual characters with only a cursory glance, the columns of the page forming at an impressive speed. 'This is called a forme,' she said, indicating the frame. 'When it is finished, it sits on the coffin, that flat bed on the press there, and you can apply the ink if you wish. We may as well take advantage of your presence and do some printing. It requires two people to operate the press, and with Estebe out of commission I have been unable to print anything. Unless assisting El Fantasma counts as insubordination?'

Treason, more like. Finlay sighed to himself. This pamphlet was never going to see the light of day if he had anything to do with it. Not that his so-called superiors gave a damn about El Fantasma's pamphlets or, frankly, his cause.

'This is El Fantasma's symbol.' Isabella held up the small woodcut on which was embossed the inverted shape of the phantom.

'Aye, I saw that on one of your pamphlets back in England.'

'Really?' Isabella exclaimed. 'I had not realised our message had spread so far and wide.'

She looked so pleased, he could not bring himself to burst her bubble. 'What symbol would you use for me, then?' Finlay asked instead.

Continuing to set characters into the frame at speed,

she pursed her lips. 'A man in a kilt? Though I think that would be too difficult to cut.'

'And it might be mistaken for a woman in a skirt.'

She turned to him, her eyes dancing. 'No one would mistake you in a plaid for a woman in a skirt.'

'Any more than anyone would mistake you in a pair of breeches for a man.'

'Yet I fooled you, did I not?'

'For a few moments, in the dark. The minute I held you in my arms, I knew unmistakably what you were.'

Isabella's heart did that funny skipping lurch it seemed to have developed since Finlay's arrival in Spain. 'You make it sound as if we were dancing,' she said, trying to ignore it. 'In fact, we were rolling around in a ditch.'

'I've rolled around in a few ditches in my time,' he replied, with one of his devilish smiles, 'but I reckon that was the most memorable. And the most enjoyable.'

'You are easily amused,' she told him, trying and failing to suppress her own smile.

'On the contrary. You undersell yourself, lass.'

Lass. It meant *girl.* Young woman. The way he said it, in that lilting accent of his, it felt more like a caress than a word. That smile of his was fascinating. How could a man smile in one way and seem merely amused, another and seem so—so tempting? Isabella dragged her eyes away. Now was not the time to be tempted to do anything other than finish the pamphlet.

'And you, I think, overrate yourself, Finlay Urquhart,' she said firmly. 'I am not going to be charmed into kissing you.'

'Not now, or not ever?'

'Oh,' Isabella said, smiling in what she hoped was a saucy way as she turned back to her work, 'I never say never. Now, are you going to help me or not?'

Without waiting for a reply, she picked up the completed forme and slotted it carefully into position on the stone coffin bed of the press. Next, she measured ink onto the wool-stuffed pads and handed one to Finlay. 'It must be applied very evenly. Watch, I will show you.' She did so, then handed him the second pad. 'Good. Careful now. Excellent.'

He had a deft touch, she noted. Trying to keep her mind firmly on the work in hand, Isabella turned her attention to dampening the paper. She had brought Finlay here this morning to persuade him that his mission was pointless. El Fantasma did not need to be rescued. El Fantasma was needed here. Yet here they were, printing El Fantasma's latest pamphlet together, and all Isabella could think of was kissing!

And Finlay wasn't helping, with that smile of his, and that tempting mouth of his, and those sea-blue eyes. Why did he have to be so—so distracting? Why could not the Duke of Wellington have sent a much older man with liver spots on his bald pate, or a man who did not like to wash or clean his teeth, or a man with those spindly legs and knobbly knees she hated, or—or any man, other than Finlay Urquhart!

Finlay Urquhart, who looked at her as if he would like her for dinner. Yes, she would like to be Finlay's dinner, whatever that meant, though she should not be thinking of dinner or kisses or any of these things at the moment, Isabella scolded herself. The paper. The ink. The setting of type. Those were the things she ought to be thinking about.

She put the first piece of paper into position, frowning hard. 'The first press will soak up any excess of ink,' she said, refusing to look at Finlay. 'Now it is a case of turning this handle, and we will see.'

He turned the handle and the press rolled into motion. Isabella checked the results. 'Almost perfect,' she said, keeping her eyes on the page. 'Now, if you will turn, I will set. We require at least two hundred copies.'

'As well I'm a big brawny Highlander, then,' Finlay said.

Without thinking, she lifted her eyes. He had flexed his arms. His smile was mocking, teasing. Why did he have to smile at all? She wished he would not. 'Browny?'

'Brawny. It means…'

'Strong.' Before she could stop herself, she touched his flexed muscle. 'I thought so yesterday when—' Isabella broke off, blushing foolishly and busied herself with the paper.

Finlay turned the press. Another sheet was spread out to dry. Another sheet inserted. He turned the press. They worked well together, their actions dovetailing seamlessly. He said nothing, though she was aware of him slanting her covert glances. He understood the power of silence. He had given her more than enough to think about. Too much. She couldn't think. She didn't want to think. She inserted another piece of paper. He checked the ink without her having to ask. The press turned and turned and turned.

It was hot work. Finlay took off his coat and waistcoat. They each drank a glass of the cool water that came from the well under the cellars. The press turned with metronomic regularity. Finlay removed his cravat. Isabella undid the top button at her throat. His shirt clung to his chest. She could see a smattering of hair, just as she had imagined. She could see the dark circles of his nipples. Her own tightened in response. A bead of sweat trickled down her back. Only twenty more sheets. Only ten.

'Done.'

Finlay drew a fresh bucket from the well. They drank thirstily. He dipped his handkerchief into the icy water and ran it over his brow, his neck, his throat. Watching him, Isabella's own throat constricted. He caught her looking, and heat of a different kind flared between them.

He dipped the handkerchief into the bucket again. He touched the cool linen to her brow. To her temples. To her cheeks. 'Hot,' she said.

'Hot,' he repeated.

Another dip. A trickle of water on the back of her neck. Then round over her collarbone to the damp skin at the base of her throat. Her heart was pounding. He must be able to feel it. Was his the same? She raised her hand to touch him, felt the damp of his shirt, heard the sharp intake of his breath, then he caught her wrist.

'Wait,' he said.

'Wait?' Isabella blinked at him stupidly. *What was she doing?*

'This,' Finlay said, 'between us, I don't want it misconstrued. I will not have you thinking I seduced you in order to persuade you to come away with me.'

'I told you I had no intention of kissing you. You will never persuade me to come away with you.'

'Never say never, is what you said.'

'Do you think I would kiss you in order to persuade you to leave me alone?'

'I'd like to think not. I'd be sore offended if I thought you were playing me like a fish on a line.'

Was he teasing her? She didn't think so. 'I wonder how a man who turns every head in a room can think such a thing possible,' Isabella said. 'Every lass would want to kiss you, I think. Even my very proper sister-in-law says that she would like to be your dinner. I asked her what she meant, but she wouldn't tell me.'

Finlay still held her hand, but when she flattened it over his chest, he made no protest. 'I wouldn't describe you as a mere dinner,' he said. 'You are a feast. A banquet. Dinner doesn't do you justice.'

His words conjured up such images, of his mouth on her breasts, of his tongue on her skin, tasting her, savouring her, relishing her. She imagined herself spread naked for him on a damask cloth, and a wrenching twist of desire made her shudder. 'Consuela cannot have meant—*that*,' Isabella said, shocked at her lurid imagination.

Finlay's laugh was low, his voice husky. 'Well, I'm

not sure exactly what you mean by *that*, but I reckon she did.'

This assertion, Isabella found more shocking than anything. 'She would not!'

He eyed her with some amusement. 'You're surely not thinking that your sister-in-law is one of these women who sees lovemaking as a marital duty without pleasure?'

'Her husband is my brother. I have not thought of it at all.'

'Have you not seen the way the pair of them look at each other?'

Isabella didn't like the way Finlay was looking at her. It made her feel foolish. 'You've heard the way Xavier talks. My brother is interested in Consuela as the mother of his children and nothing more.'

His response was to shake his head, smiling in a way that made her both embarrassed and uncertain. 'Aye, that's what he'd like the world to believe, for it is not the done thing, is it, for a man to admit he's in thrall to his wife? You are not the only one in this household to lead a double life.'

Was he right? Certainly, Consuela had said that she loved Xavier, but Isabella had assumed she meant in a—a wifely way. A dutiful way. She had assumed that Consuela was as bloodless as—well, as bloodless as Isabella assumed a dutiful Spanish wife would be. She had assumed that there was nothing more to Consuela than the blank, cold, demure facade she presented, until Finlay suggested she look again.

'You must think me very arrogant,' she said, turning

away from him, feeling very small. 'It is no wonder that Consuela wishes to replace me with one of her own sisters. I have made no attempt to get to know her. Worse, I have assumed there was nothing worth knowing.'

'Now you're being daft.' Finlay caught her shoulder, turning her back around to face him. 'Look at all this,' he said, waving at the stack of drying pamphlets. 'You've been carrying the burden of El Fantasma for two years all alone, fighting for more years than that for your country. You'd be more than entitled to boast about what you've achieved, instead of which, what you're concerned about is not having done enough.'

'That is no excuse. Consuela is family.'

'That's true. She's your brother's wife, which makes her, in the way of things, above you in the hierarchy. Has she made any attempt to understand you? Has she confided in you?'

'No, but...'

'You were here first. That's not Consuela's fault, but your brother must have known you had the running of the place while he was off at the war. Has he tried to understand your feelings?'

'He has tried to marry me off to his best friend. In Xavier's eyes, that is taking care of me, I suppose, though I doubt very much if Gabriel would be so eager to offer for me if he knew his new bride was El Fantasma.'

She meant it as a poor attempt at a joke, but Finlay did not smile. 'Is that what you're thinking? To give it up and marry Torres?'

'No.' Her denial took her aback, for her tone was

quite decisive. Was it only a few days ago, she had been contemplating quite the opposite?

'Why not?' Finlay spoke sharply.

Isabella shook her head in confusion. 'I can't,' she said, again with absolute certainly. 'If I told him the truth he would not wish to marry me, and if I married him I could not tell him the truth.'

It was a perfectly logical, perfectly reasonable, perfectly honourable response. Finlay looked unconvinced. 'If you loved him…'

'That has nothing to do with it. Consuela assures me that I would, after we were married but—you know this is none of your business, Finlay.'

'Far be it for me to contradict your sister-in-law,' he continued, ignoring her. 'It may be true that love follows the wedding vows, but I reckon there has to be something there first of all.'

'What something?'

'A wee spark. Do you think of kissing him? Do you imagine making love to him?'

'No!' A lie. More accurately, she had tried and failed. She prayed that her flush of embarrassment could be attributed to the heat from the press. 'It is not possible to imagine what one has not experienced. As you have pointed out on several occasions, I am a virgin,' she said baldly.

'It didn't stop your imagination a wee minute ago.'

'What…?'

'When I said you were not a dinner, but a banquet.' Finlay's eyes were alight with devilment once more. 'What was it that you imagined?'

'Nothing. I have no idea what you meant by it.'

'One of the problems I have with you is that I look at you and I have far too many ideas.'

Her skin was tingling. The tingling was spreading. 'What kind of ideas?'

'Indecent ones. Ideas I couldn't possibly put into words.'

Finlay's upper lip was beaded with sweat. It took Isabella's every ounce of self-restraint not to lick it. His cheeks were high with colour. She could see his chest moving under his sweat-damped shirt. Was his heart beating as fast as hers? Did he ache, as she did, for the touch of his skin on hers? She would not make the first move. She could not bear it if he did not. 'If not words, what about actions?' Isabella asked. 'An appetiser, perhaps?'

'This sort of thing, do you mean?' He kissed her. A fleeting, soft and utterly delicious kiss, his tongue licking into the corner of her mouth, his hand resting lightly on her breast, and then she was free.

'I believe it is customary to serve more than one appetiser at a banquet.' Surrendering to temptation, Isabella licked the sweat from his upper lip, allowing her breasts to brush fleetingly against his chest.

Finlay moaned and kissed her ardently. 'That's the problem with an appetiser,' he said, gently easing her away.

Isabella looked at him blankly.

'It leaves one wanting more. A great deal more.' He checked his pocket watch and picked up his waistcoat. 'Talking of appetites, I think it would be prudent if we both cleaned off all this rather incriminating ink before joining Consuela for dinner.'

'Yes, of course. Dinner,' Isabella said. But her thoughts were not of food.

Chapter Seven

'I thought I might show you a little more of our beautiful countryside today,' Isabella said, 'since I think it would be unwise for me to take you to visit Estebe as Xavier requested. Your knowledge of wine is so sparse, he would be suspicious of you within a few minutes. If Xavier asks, we will need to concoct a story to explain why we—'

'Is your brother due back today?' Finlay interrupted.

'No, but when he does return, we need to have a plausible explanation for not visiting Estebe. Xavier will be most displeased that I have disobeyed his direct instructions.'

'I am not planning to be here when your brother returns.' Finlay was not planning to be here beyond tomorrow, and he was not planning to leave alone, either, though it was clear that his plans and Isabella's did not currently coincide.

Her face had fallen momentarily at his terse tone, but she recovered with a determined smile. 'I did not think you would go so far as to place an order for Xavier's precious Rioja that would not be fulfilled, but as he is not likely to be home for a few days yet, you do not have to rush off on his account.'

'Isabella, it's not your brother I'm worried about.'

'No, but—you did not expect to find El Fantasma so quickly, did you? I mean, if you had not found me, or if I could not lead you to him, or if it turned out that I could, but it took some time to arrange—' She broke off, looking flustered. 'What I mean is, you must have anticipated having to spend a considerable amount of time in Spain searching for El Fantasma. Having achieved your objective with relative ease, why not reward yourself with a tiny hiatus from your duties as a soldier while the opportunity presents itself? You must admit, the Hermoso Romero estate is a beguiling place.'

She was blushing. She looked so enchanting, it was all Finlay could do to stop himself from leaning across the breakfast table to kiss her. Of course, he knew she was not indifferent to him, and he was certainly not indifferent to her, but he suspected that their mutual attraction was more to do with the heightened tension of the situation they found themselves in than anything else.

Still, he wished she hadn't dangled further temptation in front of him. He took a sip of coffee and took another, unwanted, slice of cured ham. Señora Romero had not joined them this morning, leaving them to breakfast alone. There was something very appealing in looking at Isabella across the breakfast cups.

She would be even more appealing if they were taking breakfast together in their bedchamber, her hair down, wearing a lacy gown and nothing else. He had always been a man who preferred to contemplate the forthcoming day in solitude, but...

What the devil was he thinking of? 'It is indeed a beguiling place, but not as beguiling as one of its inhabitants. However,' Finlay added quickly, 'I'm here on a mission, not on holiday, and my objective is far from achieved.' Ach! Now Isabella looked as if he'd slapped her. 'I'll tell you what,' he added, softening his tone, 'why don't we ride out, like you suggest? We need to talk, but there's no necessity for us to do it here. A good gallop and some fresh air would be most welcome.'

'I would like that. I know some lovely spots hereabouts. But as for needing to talk, I'm afraid there is nothing to discuss, Finlay. We must agree to differ.' She crossed her arms, looking mulish. 'I am not in need of rescue. I told you...'

'And I listened. Now it's your turn to listen to me. No,' he said, when she opened her mouth to protest again, 'you're not being fair. You've had your say, now it's only right that you let me have mine.'

'The world is not a fair place.'

'Doesn't El Fantasma advocate free speech for all and a fair hearing?'

She laughed, holding up her hands in surrender. 'You use my own rhetoric against me! I call that very unfair, indeed. But all is fair in love and war, that is what you will say, no? I shall go and change. Meet me at the stables in half an hour.'

He caught her arm as she made for the door. 'We're not at war, Isabella.'

'No.'

Their eyes met and held. Her mouth softened into a sensual curve. The urge to touch her, to kiss her, simply to hold her tightly against him was so strong, it almost overpowered him. 'No,' Finlay said, letting her go, 'we are not at war.'

As to the other, he thought, as the door closed behind her, he would be a fool to contemplate it. And Major Finlay Urquhart had never been guilty of being a fool.

A couple of hours later, they were sitting side by side on a blanket, leaning against an overturned tree in a pretty glade at the edge of a forest located some distance from the estate. The sun had obligingly come out, and there were only the slightest, puffiest of clouds in the pale blue winter sky. Isabella opened the top button of her jacket and lifted her face to the warmth. Finlay had taken off his coat, and sat in his waistcoat and shirtsleeves. His leather-clad leg was not touching her skirts, his arm was not brushing hers, but she was so aware of him, it was almost as if they were. She didn't want him to leave. Not yet.

No, not yet. She hadn't realised until he'd turned up out of the blue how lonely she had been. She had her cause but precious little else. She hadn't realised how rarely she was her true self. Not even with Estebe could she talk as she did with Finlay, and she had never, ever thought of kissing Estebe. Now she seemed to do nothing else but think of kissing Finlay.

He shifted against the tree and she opened her eyes to find him studying her intently. 'What is it? Have I dust on my nose?' She brushed her face roughly, not for fear of dust but to conceal the effect his gaze had on her. She felt flustered and flattered in equal measure. She wrinkled her nose. 'Has it gone?'

Finlay grimaced. 'Stop being so endearing. For pity's sake, it's difficult enough having to say what I have to say, without...'

'Then, don't say it, Finlay.'

'I have no choice.'

'Not yet.' She knew, absolutely, that what he had to say would signal the end, and she so desperately didn't want it to end. 'Not yet,' she said again, smoothing her hand over his hair, his cheek.

He turned his face, his lips brushing a kiss on her palm, then, taking her by the wrist, he kissed each of her fingers. 'Why did it have to be you?' he murmured. 'Why do you have to be so irresistible?'

'Then, do not resist.' She caught his hand and did as he had done, brushing her lips over his palm, her tongue over each of his fingertips. His eyes flickered shut as he inhaled sharply. She pushed the cuff of his sleeve back, kissing the pulse on his wrist. And then his mouth found hers and she forgot everything save for the taste of him and his touch and his drugging, sweet, heady kisses.

He whispered her name as he kissed her. He said her name like no other did, his soft, lilting accent making a caress of it as his hands stroked her cheeks, her neck, unfastening the buttons of her riding coat to slide inside and cup her breasts. She kissed him back hungrily, her own hands roaming over his back, his shoulders. She held him tightly to her, pressed herself against him, for fear he would stop. She could not bear it if he stopped, not this time.

He kissed the tops of her breasts above the gown of her habit. She laced her fingers into his hair. Her corsets felt too tight. She was hot. Her nipples were hard under his caress, aching for more. '*Más,*' she whispered urgently.

Finlay muttered some gentle endearment in his native tongue. His eyes were dark, his cheeks flushed. His neckcloth was undone, his waistcoat open. She could sense him wrestling with his conscience. She did not want his conscience to win. 'Please do not stop,' she said, made shameless with desire.

He groaned. 'Don't look at me like that. How am I to resist you when you look at me like that?'

'Then, don't.' She pulled him back towards her. 'Don't resist,' she said, and kissed him fiercely.

This time he obeyed her command. His kisses were harder, his breath became more ragged, his hands touched her more surely, cupping her breasts, making her arch up with pleasure. He slid his hand under the skirts of her habit, stroking his way up her leg, over her stocking, her garter, to the soft flesh of her thigh. Her body pulsed and throbbed. Her skin tingled. Inside her, the tension, the heat, pooled between her legs. Finlay's skin was hot, too, under the linen of his shirt, his nipple hard against her flattened palm. His eyes, intent on hers, reflected the fire building inside her.

'Are you sure?' he asked.

'*Si.* Yes. Sure,' she answered. Though she was not at all sure what he meant, she was sure she wanted it, and when his hand cupped her sex, when he slid his finger inside her, she was certain, whimpering with delight. 'Yes, yes, yes,' she said as he touched her. 'Yes.'

She surrendered to it, to him, to the exquisite pleasure of the tension his touch was building, lying back on the blanket, his body half-covering hers. She closed her eyes as he kissed her again, lost in the pleasure of his mouth, his tongue, his touch. Stroking. Thrusting. Stroking inside her, moving instinctively with him, clinging on to the knot until she could bear it no longer, and it exploded, forcing a strange, guttural cry from her as she shuddered and pulsed, clinging to his shoulders to anchor her, convinced that if she let go of him she might fly straight up into the pale blue winter sky and burst into flames like a firework.

Isabella lay sprawled on the blanket, half-covered by his body, the embodiment of temptation, the image of sated delight. Her eyes fluttered open, and Finlay could not resist kissing her one last time. His erection throbbed. It took him every ounce of willpower to move away from her. He could not believe he'd allowed himself to go this far.

He sat up abruptly. 'Enough,' he said, aloud this time. Her smile faded. There was hurt in her eyes, and confusion. Steeling himself, Finlay grabbed his jacket and shrugged it on, deliberately putting some distance between them.

Isabella, too, sat up, buttoning her jacket, the glow fading from her cheeks, her expression hardening. 'For the avoidance of doubt, do not even think of apologising. What happened was entirely at my instigation. I did not realise that you were so reluctant. Or indeed that my own—enthusiasm—was so one-sided.'

Finlay cursed. 'It's not that. How can you think that?' he said, reaching for her instinctively. 'If you mattered less to me, this would all be a damned sight easier. I've never wanted a woman so much. Did I not tell you only a few moments ago, I've never met a woman like you?'

'Then, why— I don't understand. Why are you sorry for—for what happened, if I am not?'

She was blushing adorably. He wanted to kiss her. He wanted to hold her. He didn't want to let her go. It was this thought that stopped him in his tracks and forced him to do exactly that. 'Enough,' Finlay said once more. 'The time has come to stop faffing about. I want you to sit down, and I want you to listen to me.'

His tone brooked no argument. He spoke as he would to his men, and he told himself that from now on that was how he had to think of her. She was one of his lieutenants, not to be reasoned with or cajoled, but to be informed of his orders, and instructed to discharge them forthwith. Isabella cast him a resentful look, but she sat down on top of the overturned tree and looked at him expectantly. Good. Fine. Finlay put his hands behind his back and stood a few steps away. 'Right, then. Here's the bald truth of the matter.'

He told her in plain, unvarnished facts what Jack had told him when he had briefed him. 'Two years ago,' he concluded, 'you were a partisan fighting in a legitimate war for your country. That war is over now. Yes, for El Fantasma and his supporters, the fight goes on, but it's no longer legal. El Fantasma, his supporters… They're not soldiers in the eyes of the law, they are traitors. You are the enemy within, Isabella, and if you carry on as you are doing, I doubt very much you'll live to see your next birthday.'

She was pale, but still defiant. 'They will never catch me. No one will ever suspect that El Fantasma is a woman.'

'Estebe knows who you are. His deputies know who he is. Their deputies, in turn, know who they are. For the authorities, it is simply a case of working their way up the chain. That is what they are busily doing right now.'

'Estebe would never betray me.'

'Isabella, the things they would do to him would make Estebe betray his own mother.'

'She is dead. Besides, he would not…'

'Aye, he would,' Finlay said firmly, and proceeded to explain, in graphic detail, exactly how they would set about it.

'You are making it up,' Isabella said faintly, when he was done. 'Or at the very least exaggerating. I may violently disagree with the government but we are Spanish, not barbarians. They would not treat one of their own citizens so inhumanely.'

'You give your government, all governments, come to that, too much credit. They will do what is expedient. The would not hesitate to use torture if necessary. I'm speaking from experience. Not of what I've inflicted, but of what I've witnessed,' he said implacably, refusing to allow himself to take pity on her. Taking pity on her could only harm her. 'What's more, your being a woman would not protect you. Quite the reverse. It would leave you open to other, even more degrading treatment, if you take my meaning.'

'No.' She jumped to her feet, her fists balled. 'No. What would be the point? If they had El Fantasma, if they really did manage to capture me, which I don't believe, why would they— What would be the point of torturing me?'

'For the love of God, woman! You said it yourself—people are listening to what El Fantasma has to say, and what he has to say is treason. It's not a case of simply shutting you up. They will want to make sure that there's no one left to fill your shoes. They will want names from you. Associates, contacts, sympathisers. Information. Such as the location of the printing press. Where the funding comes from. They know about your previous collaboration with the British. They'll want to know everything that went on back then. And when they've got all that—and believe me, you'll tell them everything they want to know, including my highly irregular and diplomatically explosive presence here—then they'll have done with you.'

'No! You are trying to frighten me. I won't listen.'

'Isabella…'

'No!' She turned on him, shaking his hand away from her arm, her face aglow with anger. 'You know, from the very start, I have been thinking, I have been asking myself, why are you really here?'

'What do you mean? I've told you—'

'Yes, that you are here to rescue El Fantasma from the Spanish government,' Isabella interrupted with a sneer. 'But why would you do that, Finlay? You are a soldier, an English—British soldier. You are here, by your own admission, under orders from the Duke of Wellington himself. But the Duke of Wellington does not care a fig about Spain. He stopped caring about Spain the moment he chased Napoleon across the border into France. No, Wellington does not give this,' she said, snapping her fingers, 'for what El Fantasma has to say now that we are no longer at war. He does, however, care very much about what El Fantasma could say about how that war was won here in Spain, yes? A campaign the duke himself had ultimate responsibility for.'

There was no point in pretending to misunderstand her. 'Yes,' Finlay said, 'you're quite correct. Whether as a result of his direct orders, or merely acts carried out in his name, there are many unsavoury aspects of the conduct of the war here that Wellington and his coterie would prefer left unsaid.'

'Especially now that he has hopes of becoming prime minister,' Isabella said, folding her arms across her chest and glaring at him. 'And he would go to some lengths to protect those hopes, I think. To the extent of sending one of his men here to Spain, even. To ensure the—what was your phrase—*diplomatically explosive* information does not fall into Spanish hands.'

'Aye, that he would.'

'Oh.'

His blunt admission took her aback. She had been a deal less certain in her accusations than she'd sounded, Finlay thought, but what the hell, the lass deserved the whole truth. 'You're right,' he said. 'Both our governments have the same aim, albeit for differing reasons. My orders were to get to you before they did and take you back with me. Whether you'd subsequently end up a prisoner in exile under house arrest, or whether you'd simply quietly disappear I don't know, but the net result would be the same. Silence.'

She put her hand to her breast, staggering away from him in horror. 'You knew that, and yet you—you tell me this, and you expect me to consent to—to allow you to—to abduct me? You have been lying to me all along. I don't understand. Why are you telling me all this?'

'To knock some sense into you!' He grabbed her, and when she shrank from him, gave her a tiny shake. 'Don't be so daft, lass. You can't possibly think I would harm a hair on your heid! I'm telling you what my orders were, but that doesn't necessarily mean I'm going to follow them.'

'You're not?'

'The Jock Upstart has a reputation for insubordination to uphold,' he said with a thin smile. 'I've told you the truth from the start. I'm not here to kill you. I'm here to save your life.'

'But how— What…'

'You have to get out of Spain, but there's no way I'm taking you to England. You're bound for America, lass, and safety,' Finlay said gently. 'You asked me why I was sorry for what happened there, between us. That is why. You have no choice but to make a new life for yourself a whole continent away, and I can play no part in that life, even if you wanted me to. The arrangements are already in place.'

He had said far more than he intended, implied far more than he would admit to feeling, made the matter personal when it should not be, but before he could regret it or retract it, Isabella pushed him away.

'America! I am not going to America. I am not going anywhere. Why would you think— No, wait. Something does not make sense. You had already made arrangements, planned to send El Fantasma to America, before you knew he was me—that it was me? That implies that you had always planned to disobey Wellington's orders.'

'I'm not here for Wellington. I'll admit, my orders originate from Wellington, but that's not why I'm here. I'm here because Jack asked me to come.'

'Jack.' Isabella stared at him blankly.

'My friend and comrade. Lieutenant Colonel Jack Trestain. Better known as Wellington's codebreaker. But then you know that because El Fantasma was one of his most trusted partisan contacts, although they never actually met. Jack says you've been responsible for saving literally thousands of lives, and now he feels he owes you yours. I've known him for the better part of a decade. We've been through some tough times together, so when he asked for my help I could not refuse him, despite the risks. Jack came up with the plan to send El Fantasma incognito to America. Wellington will be told El Fantasma perished in the course of the attempted abduction. Problem solved and everybody happy. A simple but elegant plan typical of Jack. But the key point is this. If Jack believes you are in mortal danger, believes it enough to ask me to risk my reputation and possibly my neck, then you surely need no further proof that the threat to your life is real.'

'I don't know. I need time to think about everything you have said.' She put her hand to her eyes, but he saw the sheen of tears lurking there.

He longed to comfort her, to allay her fear and distress, but he could not afford to risk diluting the message he'd hammered so brutally home.

'Isabella, that is a luxury we cannot afford. Time is of the essence.'

'No.' She threw her shoulders back and glared at him. 'This is my life we are talking about, Finlay, not yours. My life, and Estebe's and many others', too. I won't be rushed into a decision. I need time to think. At the end of the week...'

'No. Tomorrow,' Finlay said, hardening his heart. 'You have until tomorrow at the very latest.'

Isabella took another sip of cognac and stared into the fire. She had retired to her bedchamber immediately upon her return, both shaken and shocked by Finlay's words. For some time she sat, completely numb, almost unable to assimilate what he had told her, but as the hours passed and she replayed the conversation over and over, the truth began sink in. It was the manner in which he had spoken, almost as much as the words themselves that had finally convinced her. Finlay had laid out the detailed facts so clearly and concisely. He'd made no attempt to disguise the horrors, but nor had he overdramatised them. He had not been trying to frighten her, but to open her eyes to the stark reality of the situation.

As an upshot she was, nonetheless, extremely frightened. She had never thought of herself as a traitor. Listening to Finlay, she could only guess at the plethora of shocking, horrific experiences that lent credence to his words. Listening to Finlay, Isabella had been forced to concede to herself that she was not, as she had always imagined herself, a soldier fighting a noble fight. At least not a true soldier as he was.

She shuddered. She had thought, in the past few days, that she had come to know him, but it was difficult to reconcile the charming Finlay with the man who had sent her world crashing around her this afternoon. The horrors he must have witnessed. The savagery. The brutality. The bloodshed and suffering. He seemed quite untouched by it, yet she knew he was neither a brute nor a savage. He had come here, all this way, not because of an order but because of a promise he had made to his best friend and comrade. Finlay was an honourable man. Finlay was in many respects a gentleman. Finlay was also the most attractive man she had ever met. Her face flamed as she recalled her wanton behaviour this afternoon, but her unrepentant body began to thrum at the memory. He *had* wanted her—of that she had no doubt. But he had resisted the temptation, because he knew her fate was to lead a new life, in safety but in exile, on another continent. A life that he could have no part of, even if either of them wanted it.

Reality intervened once more, like being doused with a bucket of cold mountain water. Isabella threw back the remains of her cognac, coughing as the fiery liquor burned its way down her throat. Whatever her future was, wherever her future lay, it did not involve Finlay. Not only was it pointless to speculate, she had far more important things to think about now than her feelings for him. Whatever they were.

Jumping to her feet, she began to pace the floor, from the long doors that opened onto her balcony, to the door that opened onto the corridor, and back again. She no longer questioned the danger she was exposed to, but the consequences— No, she was not ready to accept those.

She threw open the windows and stepped out onto the balcony. A thin film of cloud covered the night sky, but a luminescent moon shone through it, bathing the vineyards below with a ghostly grey light. This was her home. She had never known another. Her family were here. And her life's work. She could not leave. There must be another solution.

A tap on the door made her jump. Isabella turned

and saw her sister-in-law slip into the room. 'Consuela. What are you doing here so late—is something wrong? Is Ramon...?'

'My son is safe and well in his nursery. I intend to ensure that he remains so. Which is why I am here.' Consuela turned the key in the look and crossed the room, taking one of the chairs by the fireside. 'I would have come earlier, but I have had to spend the past hour with the wife of one of Xavier's tenants. It seems the man has disappeared off the face of the earth.'

'What man?'

Consuela waved her hand dismissively. 'I cannot remember the name. He works for Estebe. He will be off on a drunken spree, I don't doubt. Or run off with another man's wife. Of course, when I hinted at such, the woman became quite furious, claimed her husband never drank and never looked at another woman, but...'

They are working their way up the chain. That was what Finlay had said. No, she was being foolish. It was simply a coincidence. 'How long has he been missing?' Isabella asked.

'Almost a week. I don't know what the woman expects me to do. I told her to come back when Xavier has returned. But I did not come here to discuss missing farm workers. Sit down, Isabella, and pour me a glass of that cognac, if you please. It is time you and I had a little talk.'

'Can it not wait until morning? I am very tired.' The fact that the missing tenant worked for Estebe was a coincidence, nothing more. She was edgy, and no wonder. The last thing she wanted was to listen to another lecture on marriage. 'Really, Consuela, if you have come to further Gabriel's suit, I should tell you that you are wasting your time.'

'That is not why I am here, but that is indeed one of the things I suspected. Sit down, Isabella. I do not care how tired you are, this will not wait.'

There was something in her tone that made her heart sink. Consuela sounded quite implacable. She sounded horribly certain, just as Finlay had done earlier today. Isabella dropped abruptly onto the chair. 'What is it you wish to say?

Consuela took a measured sip of cognac. 'Why is Finlay Urquhart here?'

The question took Isabella utterly by surprise. 'To buy wine. But you already know that.'

'Do not play games with me. There is no time,' her sister-in-law said with an angry sigh. 'He knows even less about wine than I do. Xavier was suspicious from the first day—so much so, that he decided to check Mr Urquhart's credentials. What business did you imagine was keeping him so long in Pamplona?'

'I had no idea what my brother was doing since he rarely takes me into his confidence. Has Xavier proof that Finlay—Mr Urquhart—has he irrefutable proof that he is *not* a wine merchant?'

Consuela shrugged impatiently. 'What is he, Isabella? Who is he? And how is he connected with whatever it is you have secreted in my husband's wine cellars?'

A trickle of sweat running down her spine made Isabella shiver. Fear made knots in her stomach. 'What do you know of that?' she asked, the shock of this revelation on top of the tumultuous events earlier so severe that denial did not even occur to her.

Consuela curled her lip. 'You think you are the only one with eyes?'

'Clearly not.'

'I have watched you sneaking out of the house at night. At first I thought it was to meet a lover, but you had not the look of a woman who had experience of such matters until lately. You have allowed Mr Urquhart to take liberties, I think. That was foolish of you, but not, I think the most foolish thing you have done.'

Her throat was dry. She must not panic. She must—she must— Dear heavens, what was she to do? 'Consuela...'

'What is in the cellar, Isabella?'

Her life was crashing around her ears. She was beyond prevaricating. 'A printing press,' she whispered.

Consuela's hand went to her breast. Her eyes widened in horror. '*Madre de Dios*, are you insane?' She jumped to her feet, clutching at the mantel for support. 'It is illegal to merely own such a thing, far less print anything. If it is discovered, Xavier could be imprisoned. Worse. A printing press! And what is it that you are printing?' She swayed, the blood draining from her face. 'That madman. The spectre. No, that is not right. The Ghost.'

'El Fantasma.'

Consuela swayed. 'You are actually printing that man's material here, at Hermoso Romero? Has that man been here? Isabella, if you have—if they discover—it does not bear thinking about. They would hang Xavier. They would hang us all. What have you been thinking?'

Not thinking. She had not been thinking. Finlay had tried to warn her, but she hadn't listened. Hadn't wanted to listen. Isabella felt sick. She felt faint. Dimly, she was aware that Consuela had not guessed the whole truth. Yet. 'I— It will— I will put an end to it,' she said. 'I am so sorry, I…'

'Sorry!' Consuela turned on her viciously. 'What good is sorry! Sorry will not save us.' She took a sip of cognac. The glass clattered against her teeth. A sob shook her, and the glass fell onto the hearthrug, splattering brandy over her feet. 'What have you done, Isabella? What are we to do?'

'Nothing.' Seeing Consuela so close to hysterics forced Isabella back from the brink of her own. She poured her sister-in-law another glass of cognac and held it out to her. 'You must do nothing. Say nothing. This is my problem. It is for me to resolve.'

'How?'

'The less you know the better, Consuela, but I promise you, you will all be safe.'

'What about that man? Mr Urquhart, what has he to do with all this?'

'It doesn't matter. He, too, will be—attended to, I promise. Now, if you please, go to your bedchamber, and forget we had this conversation, and when Xavier returns, it would be much better if you did not mention any of it.'

'You think I am stupid!' Consuela drained the glass

and got shakily to her feet. 'He will be back in two days, no more. Is that enough time for you to rectify things?'

'It will have to be,' Isabella said with grim determination. 'For all our sakes.'

Chapter Eight

As Finlay eased the chapel door closed behind him, the smoky scent of candle wax and the evocative, cloying aroma of incense caught him unawares, hurtling him back in time to the services he'd attended in his childhood with his mother and sisters. He closed his eyes, remembering the sense of defiance that had preceded each clandestine trip to the ramshackle longhouse that had served as their place of worship, for the Catholic religion was officially proscribed in Scotland. It shamed him now, thinking of all the years in the army when he had neglected his church, but it was crime enough to be the Jock Upstart. To proclaim himself a Catholic to boot—no, that would have been beyond the pale. His faith had never truly left him, but he'd kept it well hidden. It wasn't something he was proud of, looking back on it.

This morning, awaking from a fitful sleep, anxious as to how this pivotal day in his mission might play out, he had been drawn to the silence and sanctuary of the little chapel in the grounds of the estate. Leaning against the door, he drank in the stillness of the space, the hushed serenity he recalled from his youth, and which he had always found notably absent in the ceremonial services in huge churches and cathedrals he'd attended on regimental duty over the years.

This little church, though plain and modest on the outside, was rather ornate and beautiful inside. The nave was tiled with marble and flanked with a number of pillars, painted in bold, bright colours with scenes from the Bible. The vaulted ceiling was dark blue, speckled with stars and bordered with gold. The walls were a paler blue, hung with ornately framed paintings that looked, to his unpractised eye, to be of the Italian Renaissance period. The pews were padded with rich, crimson velvet. The candlesticks on the altar were wrought from solid gold. Above it, the stained glass would speckle the floor with vivid colours later in the day when the sun streamed in. So much wealth and opulence, left quite unattended. Xavier Romero clearly considered his possessions inviolate. One must be very sure of one's position in society to be so complacent. Looking around him, Finlay was forced to reconsider the man's standing. If it was discovered that his sister was El Fantasma— No, the possibility did not bear countenancing.

He did not notice Isabella at first. She was kneeling in the tiny chapel dedicated to St Vincent of Saragossa, the patron saint of winemakers, Finlay guessed, judging from the symbolism of the paintings. Her head was bowed low. Her hair was covered in a mantilla.

There was something so vulnerable about the fall of lace over her head, the slight curve of her shoulders as she prayed. Whether she was aware of him or not, Finlay decided not to disturb her, retreating into the nave to light a candle and to make his own request for divine guidance.

It was not that he lacked the resolution to act. The situation demanded it. His orders demanded it. His word of honour to Jack demanded it. He could all but hear his friend's voice in his ear. *Finlay, you must get El Fantasma out of Spain at any cost.*

It was worth it. By doing so, he would save Isabella's life. In the light of this one salient fact, it was gie pathetic of him to wonder just how different his own life would be if circumstances had been different. Of all the women in the world to fall for, he'd chosen this one. Not that he had fallen heavily yet. No, a man did not fall in love in a matter of days. He had caught himself in time, but he'd be an eejit if he let himself fall any further in thrall to her.

He rubbed his eyes, gazing up at the beautiful stained-glass window in search of inspiration. He had wondered, in the middle of the night, if he dare enlist Romero's help. The estate owner could have the printing press broken up. He could certainly insist on an end to Estebe's participation, and force the winery manager to end all contact with his men. But Romero would most likely have his sister incarcerated in a nunnery as a consequence. Hidden away from the world she'd be safe, she'd be alive, but what kind of existence would that be for her? Finlay couldn't bear to contemplate it.

If Isabella was a man, he would not have to wrestle with his conscience like this, he thought, looking over at her still bowed figure. If she was a man, he'd not be taking any account of those beguiling eyes of hers, or that sensuous mouth, or that delectable body. Or that determined, clever mind of hers, either. He cursed, then raised his eyes to the altar and apologised.

He was going round in circles. A promise was a promise, and he'd given one to Jack weeks before he'd met Isabella. Jack was depending on him. Blast it, when it came down to it, he was under orders, albeit orders that he intended to bend to a more palatable shape. 'So stop dithering, laddie, and let's get on with it,' he muttered.

Isabella chose this point to get to her feet, and Finlay got up from the pew to join her at the font in the atrium. 'You are a Catholic?' she asked in surprise when he dipped his hand in the font to bless himself and genuflect.

'I was raised one,' he replied, stepping outside into the early-morning mist.

'Did you come to church this morning in search of divine inspiration?'

'Is that what you were praying for?'

'No, I was praying for the wisdom to find a successful resolution to this quandary. Consuela came to my room last night.'

Isabella's voice faltered several times as she recounted her sister-in-law's visit. There were shadows under her eyes, which were heavy-lidded. She'd likely had less sleep even than he, poor lass. Finlay's heart went out to her for the weight of the burden she was carrying, but he suspected that sympathy was the last thing she would want from him, and so he forced himself to listen in silence.

'I feel quite—quite appalled, to think of the danger in which I have placed my family. You are right. It is time to put an end to El Fantasma,' Isabella concluded. 'I do not yet know what that means for me, but...'

'It means you will have to quit Spain. You've no option.'

She flinched. 'Of a certainty, it means leaving Hermoso Romero. As to the future—that I will think about later. For the moment, I have other more important matters to attend to.'

He did not like the way she tilted her chin when she spoke this last sentence. He did not like the way the sadness in her big golden eyes turned to something like defiance. 'Such as?' Finlay asked.

'Such as Estebe,' she said, and this time there was no mistaking the stubborn note in her voice. 'It is my duty to warn him, to give him the chance to warn his men, too.'

'Are you mad, woman?'

'It is my duty to warn him,' she repeated. 'I would never forgive myself if I did not.'

Finlay rolled his eyes. It was exactly what he'd have said himself. 'I understand that you feel it's your duty, but it's too much of a risk,' he said. 'No matter what Señora Romero might have promised you in the middle of the night, do you really think she's going to keep something like this from your brother?'

'Xavier will not be home until tomorrow.'

'We can't rely on that. We need to be away from here now.'

She turned on him fiercely. 'I have been successfully running this operation for nearly two years without your advice. I do not require it now. If our situations were reversed, if Estebe was your second-in-command, you would not dream of leaving without alerting him to the danger he is in.'

She really was a feisty wee thing, and what was more she was in the right of it. But unlike Isabella, Estebe was a hardened soldier who knew the real risks. 'No,' Finlay said firmly. 'No, I'm sorry, but from now on you're following my orders. You need to go and pack. Take only what you can carry on horseback. And it might be an idea to bring anything valuable you have. Jack and I, we've made provision for you, but…'

'I do not need your blood money.'

Pick your battles, Finlay told himself firmly. 'Fine, then, have it your own way. I won't force it on you. Now will you go back to the house and pack?'

'What are you going to do?'

'Attend to that blasted printing press.'

'What is the point? Only Estebe and I know about it. Besides, it is far too big. You will never be able to destroy it on your own.'

'At the very least, I can put it beyond use, and get rid of that damned incriminating pamphlet.'

Isabella opened her mouth to protest, then changed

her mind. Obviously she, too, was picking her battles. 'That is likely to take you some time,' she said.

'Aye, well, that's for me to worry about. I will meet you back here at noon, and then we'll take it from there.'

'Very well.' She turned on her heel and walked purposefully back towards the main house.

Finlay watched her go, allowing his gaze to linger only fleetingly on her retreating derrière, before turning away towards the winery. She had, he thought as he lit the lantern and made his way down the stone steps, accepted his orders with reasonably good grace, all considered. Poor lass. In fact she was bearing up remarkably well. She was not at all resigned to her fate, but she was at least finally reconciled to leaving.

He made his way towards the secret cellar with only one wrong turning. Señora Romero, now…she might pose a problem. It was a pity Isabella had let fall so much of the truth—though not the full truth, thank heavens for small mercies. The *señora* had no inkling that her sister-in-law was anything more than a conduit for El Fantasma. He'd have to find a way of keeping it that way. Would the cover story he'd dreamed up be sufficient?

He smiled grimly to himself. An elopement. Romero would be mortified at the idea of his sister and a wine merchant—a man who *claimed* to be a wine merchant. A word in Señora Romero's ear and Finlay was sure that she could be persuaded to drum up a witness or two, a maid perhaps, who might have seen one of their early-morning trysts in the cypress walk. It was a good story, and a far more likely explanation of Isabella's sudden disappearance than any link with El Fantasma. Xavier Romero and his family would be safe from questioning. Estebe…

Finlay paused in the act of moving the wine rack. If Estebe had been his deputy, he *would* have warned him, regardless of the risk. It was a matter of honour, as well as his duty as a commanding officer, just as Isabella had pointed out. And if it was his printing press hidden behind the wall here, he'd want to attend to it himself, too. The press, the pamphlets… Isabella poured her heart into them, yet she had not suggested…

'Ach, bugger it!' Finlay picked up the lantern and began to make his way as fast as he could back the way he had come. By God, he admired her. She was as stubborn as a mule, but her heart was in the right place. Even so, that lass had an awful lot to learn about insubordination. A smile crept over his face. *The Basque Upstart.* Aye, they were a well-matched pair, indeed!

Isabella brought her horse over to the mounting block in the courtyard and buttoned up the skirts of her riding habit before climbing agilely into the saddle. Today would be the last time, perhaps for years, perhaps forever, that she rode out to the village. Today she was leaving Hermoso Romero, leaving her family, leaving Estebe and El Fantasma behind. She couldn't take it in. She felt sick thinking about it. The unknown future loomed like a giant black mountain in front of her. She couldn't do it. She couldn't.

Her horse fidgeted. She gave herself a little shake and urged him into a canter. Best not to think too far ahead. Best to think only of this next step, and after that— No, she would not even think of that. She would instead concentrate on taking in all she could of her homeland, to impress it on her memory for a future when it might be of comfort. But she would not think of that future yet. 'Courage, Isabella. Courage.'

Her horse's ears twitched. They had reached the outskirts of the village now. It was very quiet. Smoke from some of the chimneys floated lazily aloft, for the air was quite still. Isabella dismounted, tethering her horse by one of the many streams that ran through the valley here. She paused to say good day to old Señora Abrantes, who was sitting on a stool in her garden, working on one of the beautiful pieces of lace she crocheted. Her latest grandchild was asleep in a wooden cradle by her side. Matai, Isabella recalled. He had been baptised in the estate chapel just a few weeks previously.

'He looks just like his papa,' she said encouragingly, though in truth all babies, boys and girls, looked to her like little old grumpy men.

'You've come to call on Estebe?' Señora Abrantes asked.

'*Sí.* My brother returns from Pamplona soon. He will be anxious to know how his manager fares.'

'He has been walking a little, with a stick. That doctor your brother sent, he has been here many times. I think that Señor Romero is worried for the health of his wine.'

'And the health of the man in charge of it,' Isabella said. Which was true, she thought as she made her way towards Estebe's house at the far end of the village.

Estebe and Xavier were childhood friends. Xavier believed there was no one more loyal than Estebe. When she had tried to discuss this with him though, concerned at the possibility of Estebe being torn between loyalty to his employer and loyalty to El Fantasma, Estebe had merely shrugged. 'What Xavier does not know cannot harm him,' he had said. 'Xavier has everything, while we fight for those who have nothing. For me, there can be no question of which comes first.' In one sense it was flattering, but as his sister, she couldn't help feeling sorry for Xavier, who not only trusted Estebe completely, but whose affection for the man stemmed back to those childhood days, and—unusually for Xavier—existed regardless of the huge disparity in their stations in life.

The winery manager, standing in the doorway of his cottage, was, as Señora Abrantes had predicted, on his feet, supporting his splinted leg with a stick. In his early thirties, he had the swarthy skin and black hair typical of the Basque, and the laconic temperament also typical of the region. Estebe rarely smiled, but when he did, Isabella was reminded that underneath that slightly surly exterior there was a very handsome man. She had asked him once, in an unguarded moment, why he had never married. He had informed her curtly that he was a soldier, she remembered. Like Finlay, he believed that soldiers should not take wives.

'Is something wrong?' Estebe said guardedly. 'I thought we agreed it would be unwise for us to be seen together in public. It might arouse suspicions as to the nature of our relationship.'

'I am here on official estate business, at my brother's behest. He wants to know how your recovery is progressing, how soon you can return to work,' Isabella replied loudly, for the benefit of anyone who might be listening. 'I made a point of saying so to Señora Abrantes,' she added *sotto voce*.

'The doctor your brother sends says I must wear the splint a few more weeks, but I have told him the wine will not wait a few more weeks. You can tell Xavier I will return to my duties next week. Tell him to do nothing with the vintage until then. Tell him that I said patience is a virtue.'

'Estebe,' Isabella said in an urgent undertone, 'I'm not really here for Xavier. I need to talk to you.'

'You should not have come. People will talk, and we cannot afford any talk. Have you heard that young Zabala has disappeared?'

The man Consuela had mentioned last night. 'He was one of ours?' Isabella asked, dismayed.

Estebe shrugged. 'It could be nothing, but—we will see. Since you are here, I want to talk to you about that man. The Englishman. I don't know why he is here, but is it a coincidence that one of our men disappears shortly after he shows up?'

'Estebe, Mr Urquhart is on our side. He's the reason I'm here, not to ask after your health. If I could just explain…'

Estebe's head jerked up. He pushed her out of the way, shading his eyes to scan the horizon. 'Señorita Romero, you need to get out of here at once.'

'What is it?' She screwed up her eyes in an effort

to see through the dust being raised. It was some sort of carriage. 'I wonder...'

'Isabella!' Estebe grabbed her by the shoulder, dropping his stick. 'You have to leave immediately. Do not let them see you. Do not, whatever happens, show yourself to them. Do you understand?'

It was his use of her name rather than the tone that made her blood run cold. 'Are they— Do you think that they are...?'

'I don't know who they are, but I am certain it does not bode well,' Estebe replied, his voice clipped as he limped over to the wooden dresser, pushing it away from the wall and retrieving a pistol, which he proceeded to load with astonishing speed before aiming it at her. 'Get out. Believe me, if they capture you, you will wish I had put this bullet in your head.'

He meant it. Blood rushed from her head, making her stagger. She took a deep breath, clutching the door frame. The cart was at the other end of the street now. There were two men. Well dressed. She looked around frantically, wondering in terror if she had left it too late.

'The woodshed,' Estebe said, pushing her down the steps. 'And remember, no matter what happens, you must keep silent. Promise me you won't do anything rash.'

Isabella dumbly nodded her reluctant assent and stumbled down into the dusty darkness of the woodshed as Estebe secured the door behind her.

Riding towards the village, Finlay spotted the dust cloud raised by the open, rather ornate carriage. It looked so incongruous in the midst of such modest surroundings of farms and cottages that Finlay's senses immediately went on high alert. Reining his horse back, he followed the carriage at a distance, taking care to keep out of sight, knowing that it could only be headed for the village, all the time hoping against hope that it was not. There were two male occupants. They could be here for any number of reasons, but he knew, with the sixth sense he relied upon when going into battle, that they were not. There was only one likely explanation, and it was an extremely alarming one.

When they turned into the village, Finlay tethered his horse by a ruined outbuilding and followed cautiously on foot. Isabella's horse was pawing the ground by the tethering post, confirmation that he had guessed her intentions correctly—as if he'd needed it confirmed. The carriage was drawing up at the top of the little street. As he made his way stealthily towards it, he could sense the eyes of the villagers peering from their cottages. An old woman holding a piece of lacework beckoned him, but he ignored her.

The two men who descended from the carriage were well dressed. They pounded on the door of the furthest cottage calling Estebe's name. 'Señor Mendi! Señor Mendi!'

The accent was not local. Finlay no longer had any doubts. Madrileños! As the door opened, he braced himself, drawing his *sgian-dubh* from his boot. In the rush to follow Isabella he had not had time to retrieve his pistol, but the vicious little knife, a coming-of-age gift from his father, had served him well enough in the past.

'Señor Mendi?'

Estebe, his leg in a splint, stood leaning on the door. 'Who wants to know?'

Finlay could see no sign of Isabella. Creeping around the other side of the carriage, behind the backs of the strangers, he took a chance, allowing Estebe a brief glimpse of his presence. Either Isabella had briefed him, or Estebe, realising how dire the situation was, saw Finlay as the lesser of two evils. Whichever. The man gave him a tiny shake of his head, the smallest gesture to the side of the house where a lean-to stood.

Waiting for the coast to clear, he missed what the men said next, but it caused Estebe to open the door wider, ushering them into the cottage.

Isabella, her ear pressed to the adjoining wall of the cottage, had her back to the door, foolish lass. Finlay grabbed her from behind, covering her mouth before she could cry out. 'It's me,' he whispered, and her rigid body ceased struggling immediately.

'Government agents,' she whispered, her eyes wide with fear. 'Estebe said—he said that they may have taken one of his men a few days ago. Do you think that is why—how...?'

'Hush. Aye.'

She was shaking piteously. He took no pleasure in being proved correct. The Spanish government were working their way up El Fantasma's chain of command. The question was, would Estebe talk? Finlay pressed his ear up to the wall, but could hear only muffled words. Later, he would tear a strip or two off himself for not taking matters into his own hands much earlier. He could not find it in himself to be angry at Isabella, but he wished with all his heart that she'd been a wee bit less loyal to the man next door, and a bit more careful of her own safety. As he would have been? Aye, right enough.

He shook his head in frustration as the room next door went quiet. 'I can't hear a thing,' he whispered, just as a loud crash made Isabella jump, only his instinctive covering of her mouth once more preventing her from screaming.

It all happened so quickly after that. 'Careful, he has a gun. Put the weapon down, *señor*,' one of the Madrileños cried out, his voice ringing clearly through the connecting wall now. Then followed the sounds of a scuffle, another piece of furniture being upturned.

Isabella strained in Finlay's firm grasp, her eyes above his muffling hand pleading with him to go to the rescue, but he held firm, shaking his head. He could take them on, he might well overpower them, but his remit was to protect El Fantasma at all costs, which meant he could not take the chance in acting rashly, no matter what the collateral damage turned out to be.

The front door of the cottage flew open, and a shot whizzed out into the open air. For a moment, Finlay thought that it would be one of the Madrileños who would pay the price, but then he heard Estebe's voice. 'I am El Fantasma,' he shouted. 'I would rather die than fall into your hands.'

'We have good reason to believe that you are not.

However, you can lead us to him. Put the gun down. Do not shoot. If you cooperate you will not be harmed. You have our word. Put the weapon down. There is no need for this.'

'I tell you, *I* am El Fantasma.'

This time, the sharp crack of the bullet came clearly from inside the cottage, followed by the dull thud of a body falling to the floor This time, it was not Estebe but the Madrileños who cried out, though frustratingly, Finlay could still make out nothing of what they said. Locked tight against him, Isabella was weeping silently. They waited for what seemed like hours, though it was only a few minutes. Finlay, holding his dagger in his right hand, motioned to Isabella to get behind the woodpile, positioning himself behind the door, ready to pounce, but more minutes passed, followed by the sound of the carriage being manoeuvred around in the narrow street.

He crept out, watching as the strangers drove back down through the village. Only when the carriage turned out onto the track heading west did the villagers start to emerge from their cottages. 'Wait here,' Finlay said.

The table in Estebe's cottage was overturned. Estebe lay on the floor, his splinted leg splayed at a very odd angle. A noise in the doorway alerted Finlay. 'Isabella, don't come any closer,' he said, grabbing the tablecloth, but it was too late. Isabella looked at the place where the wine manager's skull should be and screamed. It was a long, piercing, anguished scream that seemed to echo round the narrow village streets for an eternity.

* * *

Isabella sat slumped in her bedchamber, wrapped in a blanket, staring into the fire. She could not stop shaking. Again and again, she replayed the horrific scene in her mind, trying desperately to come up with a scenario in which she could have altered the outcome, trying equally desperately to assure herself there was nothing she could have done.

When the Madrileños had gone, her screams had given way to numb horror, leaving Finlay to deal with the situation. He had taken charge with an authority that was obeyed without question by the villagers. The version of events he presented them with had Estebe shot by the Madrileños as he'd attempted to escape captivity. Thanks to Finlay, Estebe's body now lay in the village church.

But Isabella knew the true story. Estebe was dead by his own hand. Estebe, a man she had come to think of as invincible, had chosen death and purgatory over captivity and torture. Her deputy had died trying to save her, turning his gun on himself rather than risk betraying her. A huge shudder ran through her. Finlay had been right when he'd said those men were ruthless. At least Estebe's suffering had been short-lived. She could not bear to contemplate what he would have endured if the Madrileños had taken him.

They would be back. Without a doubt they would be back. They had not believed Estebe's claim to be El Fantasma. They would be back, and they would not give up until they found her. Fear clutched like icy fingers around her heart. Estebe had died trying to protect her. She could picture him all too vividly, lying there on the ground. The shockingly bright red of the freshly spilled blood. The unnatural angle of his splinted leg. And his poor head...

She shuddered so violently her teeth chattered. It was one thing to defy danger when it was merely an abstract concept, but to be confronted with the stark, terrible reality of it—that was very different matter.

She did not want to die. If they caught her, she was not sure she would be brave enough to take the option Estebe had done. The icy fingers closed tighter around her heart. Fear was a very, very cold creature, but anger, and action, they fired the blood. She could not allow his death to have been in vain. 'No, now is not the time for tears,' she told herself, getting up to pour a large measure of cognac with a shaky hand. 'Now is the time for courage, and resolve.' She swallowed the brandy in one cough-inducing gulp. Fire burned a path down her throat and into her belly. She poured herself another measure, and gulped it down, too.

'Courage, Isabella,' she muttered, pulling a portmanteau from a shelf in her cupboard and setting it on her bed. 'There is much to be done.'

Finlay prowled restlessly around his bedchamber dressed only in his breeches and shirt. Dealing as best he could with Estebe's tragic death had taken up too many precious hours already. Time was of the essence, with Romero due back imminently. Much more important, those Madrileños would be back. If only they had believed Estebe's last, valiant claim to be the man they sought, it would have solved a wheen of problems. But they clearly, very clearly had not. And Finlay had faffed around far too much. He felt sick to the stomach, thinking how close Isabella had come to being captured. A lesson sorely learned, putting his inclinations over his duties. He should have had her out of here and on her way to the boat the moment she'd confessed her identity.

Poor wee soul, she had been distraught at what she'd seen this afternoon, though it had certainly brought home all he'd been saying. She'd barely said a word on the ride home, staring sightlessly ahead, though she'd sat straight enough in the saddle. She'd had the stuffing knocked out of her. It made his heart ache to think that instead of comforting her, he was going to have to wrench her away from her home and her family without even the chance to say goodbye.

He paced restlessly around the room, from window to door, window to door, his mind whirring. The elopement story might just about hold if Señora Romero was prepared to cultivate it after they were gone. It would be better if he could find a way to speak to her, but short of breaking into her bedchamber...

Finlay laughed shortly. No, if he was to break into any bedchamber it would be Isabella's. Struck by this idea, he opened the window and stepped out onto the balcony. Isabella's room was two doors along. The curtains fluttered the window was open. He eyed the gap between the parapets. It was no more than five feet. And the fall was a good thirty, more than enough to break his legs if not to kill him. Anyone would think he'd not had enough high drama for the day. Returning to his bedchamber, Finlay decided he'd try the more conventional route.

'Finlay. I was on the point of coming to find you. Come in.'

Isabella ushered him in, closing the door softly behind her. She was fully dressed, though her hair was not up, but tied in a long plait down her back.

'How are you bearing up?' he asked her.

'I am sorry that I was of so little use to you earlier,' she replied, ignoring his question. 'I am very, very grateful for what you have done. If my brother knew— Xavier is—' she gulped '—was, extremely fond of Estebe. That you have spared him the truth… For that, and for the sake of all of Estebe's friends, I cannot thank you enough, Finlay.'

'It was nothing.'

'No. It was a great deal more than nothing. I deeply regret that I was not of more assistance, but I assure you, I am ready now to do—to do…'

She broke off, screwing her eyes tight shut, but when he tried to take her in his arms, she shook her head. 'Please, do not—I do not deserve to be comforted. If I had listened to you, perhaps Estebe would still be alive. He is dead, and he died to save me. I owe it to him to try to save myself now. And I owe it to my family, too. My remaining here is dangerous for them. You were right. I did not truly understand the consequences of my—of El Fantasma's actions, but I do now. So, I am ready to go with you,' she concluded firmly. 'I am ready to follow whatever arrangements you have made for me.'

'America, I told you. It's the only place you can be safe.'

The very idea terrified her, but she nodded her head stoically. 'Then, I will go to America.'

Finlay bit his lip, eyeing her with some concern. 'Isabella, you could not have saved Estebe. His death is not your fault.'

She had picked up a hairbrush from the dressing table and was now putting it into the half-packed portmanteau lying open on the bed. 'If I had listened to you earlier, I could have warned him.'

'They would still have come for him.' This time, when she tried to shake him off, Finlay resisted, putting an arm around her waist to anchor her to him. 'Even if you had warned him, what difference do you think it would have made. Would Estebe have fled?'

'Of course not, but—Finlay, do you think they will kill them all? If I could warn them—though I know only a few of the names—if I could warn them, give them a chance to escape...' she said, looking up at him pleadingly. 'Do you think...?'

'I think that Estebe's death is warning enough. I think your conscience is clear on that matter, and even if it were not—Isabella, my conscience will not allow you to devote any more time to such matters. I should have gotten you out of here days ago.'

'I would not have agreed to come.'

He smiled sadly. 'I should not have allowed that fact to make any difference.' She looked so vulnerable. His arms ached to embrace her. Catching himself in the act of bestowing a tender kiss on her forehead, Finlay let her go. 'Right, then,' he said brusquely, 'to work. I'm glad to see you've packed. I've been thinking about how best to leave things here. We need a story that will explain our sudden disappearance without linking it in any way to Estebe's death or, obviously, El Fantasma, so what I was thinking was, we could elope. Pretend to elope, that is. If you could write a letter...'

'I have every intention of writing a letter,' Isabella interrupted, 'but it will be the truth.'

He stared at her uncomprehendingly. 'The truth?'

'My confession. Those Madrileños did not believe Estebe when he said he was El Fantasma. They will be back, and they will be looking for a man close to Estebe, only more powerful. Who do you think they will settle on?'

'Xavier,' Finlay said with a sick feeling in the pit of his stomach.

'Xavier,' Isabella repeated. 'I will not allow my brother to pay the price for my actions.'

'Isabella, he's innocent.'

'Finlay,' she retorted with a sad smile, 'innocent or guilty, it makes no difference with those men. You told me so yourself. Once they have him, he will confess to anything. I will not permit that to happen.'

'No, I can see you wouldn't.' And he could see all his carefully laid plans toppling over like so many dominos. He could see the danger she was putting herself in. They'd have to flee north for their lives, for her confession would put those devils on their tails. She had no idea, and he had not the heart to tell her, that she was risking her own life for the sake of protecting her family. She was, however, once again doing exactly what he'd do himself.

Finlay sighed. 'I'd best see what I can do to cover up the evidence, then. I doubt there's much can be done with the press, but we must not leave that pamphlet.'

'I'll come with you. No,' Isabella said, smiling wanly, 'don't try to stop me. Two pairs of hands will be quicker than one, and it's time I started taking some responsibility for my actions. And I have you to thank for teaching that painful, but valuable, lesson.'

Chapter Nine

Four days later

They had ridden hard each day in their desperation to get as far away from Hermoso Romero as quickly as possible, stopping only for a few hours' fitful sleep and to rest and water the horses. The road ahead, the steady gallop of the steeds who carried them, were their only focus. The landscape thereabouts afforded little in the way of cover. The roads were no more than rough dirt tracks in places, meandering through the rolling hills, the lower slopes of which were covered in a patchwork of vines. This was her land, her home territory, but to Isabella it felt disconcertingly alien, almost as if she was the stranger here, not Finlay. Which she was, she supposed, since she had forgone the right to call it home. She forced herself to sit upright in the saddle, concentrating on looking forward, not back. Quite literally.

Pamplona and then north was the obvious and quickest route to the coast and the ship that would take her across the ocean, but Finlay insisted that was too risky, since any pursuers would know that and follow suit. No, better to take a more circuitous route. It might be slower but it would significantly improve their chances of avoiding capture. Isabella did not question him. In truth she did not care where they went. When he opted to follow one of the old pilgrim routes that lead to Santiago de Compostela, she did as he bid her. She had never been to the city. She wished fervently that it truly was their destination. She did not want to think about the country where she was to make a new life. Fear froze her imagination whenever she tried.

She barely spoke as they travelled. She had not cried, not since Estebe—no, she would not think of that. She did not deserve the release of tears. She did not deserve Finlay's sympathy, the comfort of his strong, reassuring embrace. Not that he offered it. The man who rode beside her was unquestionably a soldier. No trace in that steely expression of the sensual Highlander who had charmed her. This man had a duty to perform, and he was clearly set on executing it. Well, she, too, had a duty, to the memory of Estebe. He had died to protect her. She would not allow his sacrifice to have been in vain, so she could do nothing save put as much distance between herself and her family as possible, in order to protect them. There was nothing to be said, nothing to be done save do as Finlay bade her without question: eat what was put in front of her, lie down and close her eyes in whatever shack or shepherd's hut he found each night, feign sleep until he roused her at dawn, continue on in the saddle each morning without complaint. An obedient and uncomplaining trooper, that was what he required, and so that was what she would be.

They were following the River Aragon today, and reached the outskirts of the little town of Sanguesa in the late afternoon. One of the many overnight refuges for weary pilgrims that dotted the Camino Way, the jumble of whitewashed houses was perched on the hill-side looking, from a distance, like a set of steps lead-ing up to the magnificent Romanesque church of Santa Maria la Real. Finlay reined his horse in, casting an anxious look at the sky, which looked as if it augured rain.

'I'm sorry, lass, but we can't risk staying in town,' he said regretfully, 'much as a proper meal and a comfy bed for the night would be a welcome treat.'

'No matter,' Isabella replied, casting an uninterested gaze at the town. 'If we follow the river, we can take shelter in the next valley.'

She had become so accustomed to spending long periods lying wide awake, alternated with fevered nightmares of trying to escape endless dark tun-nels, that it was a surprise when Isabella struggled to open her eyes. She was lying on the wooden shelf that served for a bed in a ramshackle shepherd's hut. She could remember arriving here, remember Finlay lighting a fire, forcing herself to eat, forcing herself to lie down and close her eyes, waiting for the darkness and the guilt and remorse to envelop her. Instead, it had been as if all the bones had been removed from her body. She had slept dreamlessly. And now she felt—different.

She was warm, surprisingly comfortable. The blanket covering her smelled faintly of horse. She turned onto her side. The door of the shelter was ajar, giving her a glimpse of the grey, predawn sky and Finlay a few yards distant, sitting by the horses, on guard as he had been every night. Did he ever sleep? For the first time, she wondered what it was he was watching out for, who it was he expected.

The dull stupor that had enveloped her since leaving Hermoso Romero had gone, and so, too, had the heavy pall of grief and regret, leaving her mind clear. Isabella counted the days since their flight, and was surprised to discover that this must be the fifth. Almost a week since Estebe died, since she left her home and her family, who were more dear to her than she had realised. But they would be better off without her. Consuela could have her sister come to live with her. Xavier would most likely mourn the loss of his winery manager more than his sister.

Isabella gave herself a shake. 'Be honest,' she told herself. 'Xavier will be so shocked at what he reads in that letter you left, he will be thankful you did not wait to say goodbye. "Finally," he will say to himself, "now I understand why my sister was such an unnatural woman. Gabriel has had a lucky escape."' Which was very true, though she doubted very much that Xavier would go so far as to inform his friend of the exact nature of his good fortune.

Isabella sat up abruptly. She had been quite distraught when she had written the letter admitting to being El Fantasma, intent only on sparing her family by accepting sole responsibility. But what, exactly, had she imagined Xavier would do with such a confession? Show it to the government officials when they came calling, as they inevitably would? Why should they believe him? What credence would such a confession truly have, when Xavier was a much more likely candidate to be El Fantasma than his demure little sister?

The letter had made no mention of the printing press. The pamphlets she and Finlay had shredded, El Fantasma's last words, had been forced down the well, the pulpy mess anointed with ink and scattered with metal lettering. As she had pulled the wine rack over the concealed door for the last time, Isabella had wondered if any curious soul would ever discover it. Her nephew, perhaps? A few weeks ago, she would have smiled at the idea of passing on El Fantasma's legacy to an as-yet unborn niece. Now the notion filled her with horror.

The Madrileños would demand proof from Xavier, and when he had none to give them—what would they do to him? Remembering Estebe's determination not to fall into the men's clutches, Isabella shuddered. Consuela might tell them about the printing press, but would that not rather condemn rather than acquit him? Isabella clutched at her head. She had been so proud of the fact that no one would ever believe El Fantasma was a woman. Now—*Madre di Dios*, what a fool she was! No one would believe her confession. Pride truly did come before a fall.

* * *

'Finlay!'

The panic in Isabella's voice was unmistakable. He ran to the bothy just as she jumped out of the make-shift bed and grabbed him by the arm. 'What is it?'

'I have to go back. Xavier—they'll never believe him. I have to go back.'

She was dressed only in her underwear. Her hair was tumbling down her back, free from the long plait she usually wore. Her face, which had been so pale and set for days, was now flushed, her eyes bright. Thank the stars she was back to something like herself. He caught her hands between his. 'Wheesht, now, you know that's not possible.'

'I have to,' she said urgently. 'They will come for him, and even with the letter— Finlay, they won't believe him. They'll take him away. I can't let them take him away. I can't let them— We have to go back, Finlay.'

'We can't. There's no going back. I'm sorry.'

'But…'

'No, Isabella. Listen to me now,' he said, before she could speak again. 'You're in the right of it. That confession of yours won't protect your brother. It's an unlikely story, I'd be the first to admit, that the great El Fantasma is a mere woman. Indeed, I'd have had a great difficulty believing it myself, had I not become acquainted with you in that ditch beside an arms cache during the war.'

He had meant her to smile. Instead, she frowned deeply. 'No one will believe it. If only I had been Xavier's brother, and not his sister, things would have been so very different.'

'Aye, well, I'm not denying that would have made things a mite easier,' Finlay said, unable to suppress his smile, 'but a lot less interesting. I wouldn't have missed meeting you again for the world.'

'I have been a great deal of trouble to you. You told me not to go to Estebe, and…'

'Isabella, you did only what I'd have done myself, in your shoes.'

'You're not angry with me?'

'If I'm angry at anyone it's with myself for faffing about, for not getting you out of there sooner.'

'I made it very difficult for you. I was so stubborn, and I didn't listen, and I thought I knew best, and— Finlay, what will he do? Xavier, I mean. When they come for him, how will he save himself if they do not believe him?'

He had stupidly hoped she would not ask him this question. No doubt about it, the shock had worn off, and her mind was as sharp as ever. He could lie to her, but she'd work it out for herself soon enough, and besides, he would not lie to her. 'Sit down,' Finlay said, steering her onto the bench and taking a seat beside her.

She did as he bid her, but without the docile obedience of the past few days. 'What is it? What do you know?'

'I don't know anything for sure.'

'You think they will discount my confession, don't you?'

'I do, I'm afraid.'

'So they will arrest Xavier? Finlay, I can't allow that.'

'Haud your wheesht a minute. The authorities have been meticulous and thorough in their pursuit of El Fantasma, Isabella, we know that. They might struggle to believe that a wee lassie could be El Fantasma, but they couldn't dismiss it out of hand. They'd be obliged to check it out—to eliminate the possibility. They are not the type to leave any stone unturned.'

'So they will be looking for me.' Isabella paled. 'And Xavier will— Do you think he will— What do you think he will do?'

'You know your brother better than I do, Isabella. What do you think?'

'I don't know!'

'Think about it,' Finlay said with a heavy heart. 'What is most important to him?'

'His son, his wife.'

'No, there is something even more important than that.'

Now she was nodding to herself, clearly beginning to follow his meaning. 'My brother has been raised to believe that he is the custodian of Hermoso Romero. It is his—I don't know what to call it—duty? His heritage? His destiny? If he was shamed, if they took him, accused him of being El Fantasma, he would lose everything.' Another little nod. 'So what you think is— what you think is that he would do anything to avoid that?'

Though she had paled, she looked him straight in the eye. 'Aye,' Finlay said. 'I do.'

'*Sí*. And the only way to avoid it, is to— You do not think he will try to stop them coming after me, do you?'

'I'm right sorry, but I don't see how he can. Even he has not that power, and frankly, it is not in his best interests.'

'I see.' Isabella clasped her hands together tightly. 'So that is why you have been so eager to put so many miles between us and Hermoso Romero. That is why you have been standing guard every night while I slept.'

'Aye,' he said, heart sore at watching it dawn on her just how alone she was.

'If they capture me, Xavier will be safe.'

'I've no intentions of letting anyone capture you, or me for that matter.'

Another faint smile greeted this remark. 'But if they do not, then suspicion will fall on my brother.'

Romero would be in the clear. The plan Jack had hatched would leave neither the British nor the Spanish in any doubt that El Fantasma had been silenced, but Finlay couldn't bring himself to explain this to Isabella just yet. She was only just recovering from one huge shock, only just starting to reassess her future. Time enough to explain just exactly what that future would entail another day. 'Your brother is a powerful man and not without influence. I wouldn't bet against him finding a way of convincing the authorities of his innocence.'

Her lips tightened. 'If that is true, then had there been a way to save me, he could have found it. The fact that you did not even consider giving him the opportunity to do so…'

Finlay managed a wry smile. 'Actually, I did, but I concluded the result would be your spending the rest of your life locked away in a nunnery.'

She stared at him in astonishment. 'You are probably right. I think you know my brother better than I. It would have been the perfect solution for you, too, I think. I could not betray the Duke of Wellington from a nunnery. You would not have been burdened with me. You could have gone back to England, having done your duty. Why did you not…?'

'Would you have *liked* to spend the rest of your life in a nunnery?'

'No, but—I do not *like* being a burden to you.'

'You're not.' He took her hand again, stroking the back of it with his thumb. 'You're not a burden.'

'But I am. My actions have put your life in danger as well as mine. I have been so blindly selfish. I am so very, very sorry.'

'Don't be daft. I was sent to protect you.' He carried on stroking her hand. Her fingers curled into his. 'And I won't be leaving your side until you're safely on that boat to America.'

'Because you promised your friend Jack?'

It was what he ought to say. It was the truth, but looking at her now, at those big golden eyes shadowed with lack of sleep, and the determined set of her shoulders, and thinking of the fearless way she had confronted the most unpalatable of facts, Finlay knew it was only a very small part of the truth. He could not tell her the whole of it, but he could not resist telling her a wee bit. 'Because you're a brave and honourable woman, the finest one I've ever met, and you deserve a future,' he said.

'I'm not feeling very brave right now.'

Her smile was shaky, but it was a smile. 'It's precisely because you're feart, and yet you are still ready to face the truth, that makes you brave,' Finlay said.

She touched his cheek, the pad of her thumb soft against the roughness of his stubble. 'Almost, I believe you, but I think you are just trying to make me feel better.'

'And is my ploy working?'

'Yes.' She brushed his hair back from his brow. She leaned into him, and brushed her lips to his forehead. 'It is working, but I think I have an even more effective ploy,' she said, twining her arms around his neck and pressing her lips to his.

She'd caught him unawares. She tasted so sweet, he could not resist her. His arms slid around her back, pulling her tight up against him. Her tongue touched his, and his shaft sprang immediately to life. He ran his fingers through the long, silken weight of her hair, spanned the slim indent of her waist, slid them up to cup the swell of her breasts, covered only by her chemise. Her nipples were hard buds beneath the soft linen. She moaned, a soft, guttural sound that sent his blood racing.

Their kisses deepened, grew wilder. She lay back on the wooden bench. Tugging his shirt free from the waistband of his breeches, she stroked her fingers up his spine. He shuddered with delight. He kissed her throat. He kissed the mounds of her breasts above her chemise. He took one of her nipples between his lips and sucked. The fabric of her undergarments became damp from his mouth, making the dark pink nub beneath clearly visible. He turned his attention to her other nipple. She moaned again, digging her nails into his back, arching up under him, brushing her belly against the hard, throbbing rod in his breeches.

He had never wanted any woman so much. He ached to slide into her tantalisingly slowly, inch by inch by inch, relishing every single moment of it, until he was as high inside her as he could be, and then he'd tilt her delightful behind up and push deeper. His shaft pulsed in anticipation. As if she could read his mind, Isabella's hands roved down his body, cupping his buttocks, pulling him tighter against her.

'Finlay,' she said, in that hoarse, breathy voice that set his blood on fire. 'Finlay.'

He kissed her again, hard on the lips, and she met his passion with a fire of her own. If he could only have her this once... If they could make love just this once... He'd give almost anything for that.

Almost, but not quite. He tore himself away, too appalled at his lack of control to care how it must look, jumping down from the bench and tucking his shirt back into his breeches, swearing furiously in Gaelic.

Isabella sat up, pushing her hair back from her face. Her eyes were huge, desire giving way to confusion. Confusion! She should take a look inside his head! 'You are under my protection,' Finlay said raggedly.

'A fine way I have of discharging my duty, taking advantage of you like that.'

'I rather think that it was I who took advantage of you. I thought it might make us both feel a little better.'

'I've absolutely no doubt that it would, temporarily,' he said, running his hands through his hair. 'Isabella, I know that I have been—before— I know that I have been very much— Ach, for heaven's sake, you know perfectly well that I find it almost impossible to keep my hands off you. But the fact is we are fleeing for our very lives with half of Spain looking for us, so it's no surprise if neither of us is thinking quite straight. But that is precisely what we need to do. Keep our heads and focus on the task in hand.'

'So what do you propose we do?' Isabella asked.

'I don't know about you,' Finlay said, with as much gravitas as he could muster, 'but I'm going to sort the horses out.'

'Well, that certainly put me in my place,' Isabella muttered to herself as she stared at his retreating back in disbelief. 'Spurned for a horse!' Her body was still throbbing with unsated desire as she padded over to the doorway of the hut. Dawn was just breaking. In the growing light she could see that Finlay was not tending the horses, but standing on the banks of the stream that ran through the valley, less than ten yards away. *Which I suppose is some sort of consolation*, she thought, managing a self-deprecating smile.

She watched as he pulled his shirt over his head. He was close enough for her to see the ripple of his muscles as he stretched. Her breath caught in her throat. His skin was paler than she had imagined. His waist tapered down to the band of his leather breeches, which hung low on his hips. A silvery line of darker, puckered skin ran the full length from his left shoulder down close to the line of his spine. It must have been a horrific wound to leave such a scar. He rarely talked of the army, yet he had been a soldier his entire adult life. *It's not the same*, he'd told her, when she had compared her time as a soldier to his. She had been annoyed, she recalled. Looking at that scar, remembering how she had fallen apart when Estebe had shot himself, she was forced to acknowledge that she had been presumptuous. In fact, she knew very little about Finlay. Always, he turned their conversations away from himself. This man she was watching, this man who shared her biggest secret, whose body she ached for, was in many ways still a stranger. He joked about being called the Jock Upstart, but he was no mere soldier. A major, and promoted rather than commissioned. A hardened campaigner. A man accustomed to command. It was a wonder that he had tolerated her equivocation as long as he had. Not that he had any right to order her about, but…

Isabella sighed. Actually, under the circumstances, he had every right, and yet he had refrained from doing so. He was an honourable man. A very honourable man. An *extremely* honourable man. She had offered herself to him, and he had refused, not for lack of desire, but because she was under his protection. Even if she could persuade him that gratitude had played no role in her kissing him, he would still have torn himself free of her. She couldn't help wishing he was not quite so honourable. But then he would not be Finlay.

He had picked up the leather bag that contained his shaving things, and was heading a few yards upstream now, towards the small cascade that fed the stream. The water would be ice-cold. Isabella looked on, mesmerised, as Finlay undid the buttons of his leather breeches. She should not be watching. She should look away. This was an invasion of privacy. Her mouth went dry as he slid the last item of clothing to the ground. His legs were long and well muscled. There was a tan line that stopped just above the knee. His buttocks were unexpectedly shapely. She really should not be looking. He stepped out of his breeches, kicking them to one side, and she had a brief glimpse of him from the front. Colour rushed to her cheeks as she saw the jutting length of his arousal. Her knowledge of male anatomy came only from art. In the flesh—Isabella put a hand to her fluttering heart as Finlay splashed into the stream and stood under the waterfall—in the flesh, this man at least was quite blood-heatingly delicious.

Not a feast, but a banquet. She recalled Finlay's words in the printing-press room. He had his back to her now, stretching his arms high over his head, letting the freezing water fall in rivulets over his body. He seemed to be relishing the cold, embracing it. It occurred to her, with a shock, that the icy cascade was an antidote to his passion, and she looked with fresh eyes at the waterfall, thinking that she, too, could cool her throbbing body there. What would Finlay say if she joined him? She smiled, allowing herself to picture the scene, but she could not imagine having the nerve to carry it off, and even if she did, Finlay would most likely reject her.

He would be right to do so. Their perilous situation was clouding her judgement, making her foolish and rash, and she was neither. Her smile faded. As he began to lather himself, Isabella turned slowly and returned to the shack. The time had come to take back responsibility for her own life, for better or for worse. She had a lot to think about. Simple things, such as her entire future! Not to mention the small matter of getting out of Spain in one piece. No, Finlay was right. They needed to focus. She could not afford to be distracted by a pair of sea-blue eyes, a mane of auburn hair and a body that Michelangelo himself could have sculpted.

Isabella, her skin glowing from the shower she had taken under the waterfall after he had returned from his own ablutions, her hair restrained in a long wet braid, had a decidedly mulish look on her face. Trouble, Finlay thought, though he couldn't help but smile at this further evidence of the return of the feisty partisan he admired so much. Desired so much. No, he wouldn't think of that.

The sparkle had returned to her eyes. 'We need to talk,' she said.

'We do.' Finlay handed her a cup of coffee, pleased to note the pleasure with which she took it, the admiring glance she gave the small portable trivet he always carried with him to heat the pot on. 'I always travel prepared for anything,' he said by way of explanation, 'although I can think of no item of field equipment that could have prepared me for you.' He was rewarded with a smile. 'Here, take this, you must be hungry.'

'Thank you. I am ravenous.' She took the toasted bread and cheese, sitting cross-legged on the hard-packed mud floor, looking quite at home.

'You'll have found bothies like these useful places during the war, no doubt,' Finlay said.

'Bothies?'

'A hut. A bothy is what we'd call it in the Highlands,' Finlay explained. 'A place for the cattle drovers to rest overnight on their way to market.'

'This land is too mountainous for cattle, but, yes, to answer your question, during the war, such places were often used for storing arms. And hiding partisans, just as this one is doing now.' Isabella finished her breakfast, and set her cup down, obviously bracing herself. 'You were right,' she said.

'In what way?'

'I was never a soldier as you were. I carried a gun, I witnessed some fighting, but I did not fight in the way you did. Estebe was not the first dead man I have seen, but it was the first time I had ever witnessed the barbarity of what a gun can do used in that way.'

'I regret that you did.'

'It is something I will never forget. Never.' She gazed into the fire, blinking rapidly. 'I know I was not wholly responsible for Estebe's death, but I must take some of the blame.'

'Isabella, Estebe was a grown man and he *was* a hardened soldier. He knew the risks and accepted them.'

'Yes, that is true, but I was his commanding officer, Finlay. He died for the cause, but it was under my watch.'

He could not argue with that, and it would be insulting to do so. At a loss, he poured her the last of the coffee.

She nodded her thanks and cupped her hands around the tin mug, staring into the fire. 'How do you reconcile that, Finlay? You must have sacrificed many of your men for the cause, the greater good. How do you do it?'

Her question caught him unawares. 'You do it by not thinking about it and simply obey the orders you are given. It is for others to weigh the moral balance,' Finlay said. It was the stock answer. The army answer. It was a steaming mound of horse manure, and Isabella knew it.

She drained her coffee again, and narrowed her eyes at him. 'You told me that if you had not been so insubordinate you would have been promoted beyond major by now. There are some orders you do not obey. You choose, on occasion, your own path. You follow your own instincts.'

He smiled wryly. 'I've always had a penchant for intelligent women, but until I met you, I never thought there could be such a thing as a lass who was too clever.'

'Don't mock me.'

'Isabella, I wouldn't dare, I was simply— You've a habit of asking difficult questions, do you know that?'

She raised her empty cup in salute. 'I am not the only one.'

'Aye, well, there you go.' Finlay picked up his knife and began to cut the piece of uneaten bread before him into smaller and smaller cubes. 'You're right. Of course I make choices. While there's always someone up the ranks to blame if things go awry, that's not my way, any more than it's my way to ask my men to do something I would not.'

'Such as cross enemy lines to reconnoitre a French arms dump?'

'Ach, that was more a case of my being bored and needing to see a wee bit of action. I'm wondering, though, if you were not in the habit of actually fighting, what you were doing there that night?'

'Ach,' Isabella replied in a fair attempt at his own accent, 'that was a case of my being bored and needing to see a wee bit of action, too. I did not fight,' she continued, reverting to her own voice, 'but I did try to ensure that El Fantasma's reputation for infallibility was preserved, since it was good for morale. It was my father, as usual, who heard the rumours of French activity. He thought that I had others investigate them, but towards the end of the war, more often than not I did that myself.' Isabella gazed into the fire. 'I think—I thought that Papa would be proud of me, of El Fantasma, but Consuela, all the things she said… I don't know, Finlay. I am not so certain now. For Papa, his family came before everything, while I—I think,

I think I have been putting myself first.' She sniffed. 'I am sorry. More self-pity. Excuse me.'

She got to her feet, but before she could move towards the door of the hut, Finlay caught her. 'How can you be so daft?' he said, pulling her into his arms, tilting her face up to force her to look at him. 'You've not been wielding a gun, but you've been fighting for your country all the same. You've put everyone *but* yourself first, Isabella. Selfish—that's the very last thing I'd call you.'

'Daft, that is what you called me. You mean stupid.'

'No. It can mean stupid right enough, but these auld Scots words, they've a wheen of other meanings.'

He was pleased to see that her tears had dried, her lips forming a shaky smile. 'Such as?'

'Such as *brave*, and *bold*. Such as *beautiful* and *bright*. Such as *surprising*.'

'Because I admit I was wrong?'

'Because you question yourself.' Reluctantly, he let her go. She was too distracting, and what was more she deserved an honest answer to her original question— or as honest as he could muster. He sat down on the mud-packed floor once more. 'You asked me how I choose between duty and human life, and I don't really know how to answer that. I've fought on battle-fields where people make their homes. I've staged sieges in towns where women and children and old men and old women are living. I'd like to think that it's been worthwhile. Whenever my men have crossed the line in the aftermath of a battle—and there have been times—I've made sure they faced the consequences.' The memories of some of those times made him wince. Finlay rubbed his eyes. 'I've gone against some orders where my conscience has pricked me, but I've acted on others where I've been faced with the consequences only afterwards.' More images, worse ones, flickered through his mind. He shook his head in an effort to disperse them. 'I'm a soldier. I am trained to obey orders. I'm not supposed to question them. I'm supposed to trust that my superiors will act honourably, in the name of our country, but war…it isn't like that, not all the time. Sometimes the lines are blurred and I—I have not always questioned as perhaps I ought.'

He had not noticed her sitting down beside him until she took his hand in hers. 'But you did question the orders you were given when you came here,' she said gently. 'When I told you who I was, you could have acted then, but instead of taking me by force you waited, tried to persuade me to leave voluntarily.'

'Not very successfully.' Her fingers were long and slender, so small compared to his.

'On the contrary,' Isabella said. 'You have saved my life.'

Gazing at her liquid amber eyes, holding her delicate hand between his, Finlay had the strangest feeling. Heartache? 'Not yet, I haven't. We're not out of the woods yet,' he said, as much to himself as Isabella.

'What is more, you are committing treason to protect me,' she said. 'Your orders from the great duke were to silence me.'

'Aye, well, that was one of those orders I'd never

find it in my conscience to obey, but it's not treason, Isabella, not really. As far as the duke is concerned, El Fantasma will be silenced, just not in the way he's expecting.'

'But surely lying to the Duke of Wellington is as good as committing treason? Finlay Urquhart, I do believe you are a hero. Foolish, reckless, but a hero nonetheless.'

'Stop it, or you'll have me blushing like a wee lassie.'

Isabella's mouth curved into a smile. She closed the gap between them, reaching up to touch his cheek. 'You're no lassie. You're a man, a beautiful man.'

'Well, there, you see, you're wrong. Nobody could describe me as beautiful.'

'Oh, but you are.' She ran her fingers through his hair. 'The first time ever I met you, I thought, there is a man who will attract a second and a third glance.'

Her smile did terrible, wonderful things to him. It stirred his blood, that smile. It made him want to devour her. For she was a feast. A banquet.

Her mouth was only a few inches from his. Her fingers were feathering the skin at the nape of his neck. 'You can't call a rough, burly Highlander beautiful,' Finlay said in a vain attempt to change the subject.

'I just did,' Isabella said with a mischievous smile. 'And I'm not referring to your appearance. You are a beautiful man, Finlay Urquhart, because you have saved my life. You have risked your life—are risking your life for me. I am completely in your debt, as are my family, though they do not know it. You will always have a special place in my heart because of that, regardless of what the future holds.'

'Then, that is all the reward I need,' Finlay said, surprising himself by the depth of emotion in his voice. Forcing himself to get to his feet, he stamped out the fire and began to pack up. 'As to the future, that can keep for later. We've a few more miles to put between us and Hermoso Romero first.'

Chapter Ten

They headed west once more, travelling at a fast pace for some hours, which precluded conversation, before slowing to a walk to give the horses a breather in the late afternoon. 'Tafalla is just ahead,' Isabella said. 'Were you ever there?'

Finlay shook his head. 'No. I think it was used as a garrison late in the campaign, but I was never quartered there.'

'It was one of the towns in the Navarre most heavily fortified by the French,' Isabella told him. 'Our partisan, Mina, he liberated it with the help of some of your British navy guns.'

'I've heard of Mina, though I have never met him.'

'Nor did I.' Isabella made a face. 'He would not have been interested in a mere woman, I don't think. Now, if he had known I was El Fantasma—but no, I will not talk of that. El Fantasma no longer exists. Now I am merely Isabella Romero—whomever she may turn out to be. A woman of means, you need not worry about that,' she said, with what she hoped was a reassuring smile. 'Not only do I have all my jewellery, which will fetch a pretty penny, but I have the bulk of this quarter's allowance. My papa left me well provided for, you know. I must find a way to make alternative arrangements with the bank to have the payments sent on to me.'

'Isabella.' Finlay drew his horse to a halt, leaning over to catch her reins at the same time. His expression was stern. 'You can't touch that money.'

All morning, as they rode, she had been trying to imagine herself in America, but the more she tried, the more terrified she became. She had promised Finlay she would go, she desperately wanted to fulfil that promise, but as the prospect became more real with every mile they travelled—the sheer terror of being on her own, of a future without shape ate away at her resolve. Her courage deserted her. 'Finlay,' she beseeched him now, unable to stop herself, 'is there no alternative to my going to America? May I not remain in Spain and make a new life for myself where no one knows me? It is a big country.'

His expression became grim. 'Not big enough. I thought I'd made it clear—those men will not give up. I know this is hard for you, and I'm right sorry to have to be the one to open your eyes, but you can't carry on living as Isabella Romero.'

'You mean I must take a new name, a new identity?'
'Aye.'
'That is why I cannot claim my allowance?'
'Not the only reason.'
There was a horrible sinking feeling in the pit of her

stomach. Finlay looked like a man trying to swallow poison. 'What are you trying to tell me?' she asked.

He ran his fingers through his hair, then straightened his shoulders, giving her a direct look. 'Isabella Romero has to die. There's no other way to put an end to this.'

'Die.' She clutched at her breast. For a horrible moment she thought he had tricked her and meant it literally. But this was Finlay; he would not harm her, she knew that instinctively. She furrowed her brow. She remembered, vaguely, that conversation on the hillside the day before Estebe died. It seemed so long ago. 'You mean that the world—Xavier, Consuela, my nephew, even the bank—must believe that I am dead?'

'It is the only way to guarantee your safety. I thought you understood that. I thought I'd made it clear.'

'Did you? I don't know. I can't remember. No, that is not fair of me, I know you did, only…' Her voice was rising in panic. She tried breathing deeply, tried to remember. 'I can't go to America, Finlay,' she said. 'Please, there must be another way. I know that's what you said, I know it's what I promised, but I didn't think— I mean, I have not thought— Surely there must be a safe haven somewhere that does not require me to go halfway across the world.'

Her horse was twitching nervously. Finlay dismounted and pulled her unresisting from the saddle, tethering both sets of reins to the stump of a fallen tree before taking her hands in his. 'You can't stay in Spain. You can't come to England with me. I know a wee bit of the ways of these government men, Isabella, from my friend Jack. Their reach is frightening, and those in power across the Continent, they're all in each other's pockets. I doubt very much that there would be anywhere in Europe safe for you.'

'But America!'

'The New World, they call it. Think about it,' he said, with a reassuring smile. 'A place where you can start again, completely afresh. A place where none of the old rules apply, where the restrictions you've been fighting don't exist. They say a man—or a woman— can do anything, achieve anything there, just by dint of hard work. It's a land of equal opportunity, a blank canvas. Isn't that precisely what you've been fighting for?'

'I've been fighting to have such a society in my own country.'

'A country that regards you as a traitor. You could help shape society in America, Isabella, not waste your time trying to dismantle the existing one in Spain.'

'You make it sound like utopia.'

Finlay's smile faltered. His grip on her tightened. 'I'm sure it's not, but there exists the opportunity to make it so. If anyone can contribute to that it's you.'

'You're just saying that to reassure me.'

His eyes darkened. His smile disappeared all together. For a moment, she thought he looked quite desolate, but then he shook his head. 'I'm saying it because I believe it to be true. You're apprehensive, and no wonder. It will be a—a challenge. You'll be lonely. Things will be strange and unfamiliar. But you'll be alive, Isabella. I look at you, and I know you can do anything you set your mind to. Take this chance, lass,

I'm begging you to take this chance, because it's the only one you have.'

He meant it. He was telling her the plain, unvarnished truth, just as he had told her the plain, unvarnished truth about the horrors she'd be subjected to if she was captured. If she did not leave Spain, she would die. If she went to England, she would die. If she travelled to France or to Italy, or to Prussia, or even Russia, they would find her eventually, and she would die. She did not want to die. Faced with the very real prospect, she was filled with defiance and determination, and a very strong will to live, indeed. 'I don't want to die,' she said.

He pulled her into his arms and held her so tight she could hardly breathe. 'You won't. I won't let them get to you. I'll keep you safe, I promise you.'

Her face was muffled against his coat. She could feel his heart beating against her cheek. She knew he would lay down his life for her if he had to. She had already witnessed one life sacrificed for her. She could not risk another. And especially not this one. 'I'm sorry,' she said wretchedly. 'I'm so sorry, Finlay. I will do as you say.'

'Don't cry. Oh, God, Isabella, don't cry.'

'I'm not crying.'

'You've every right to.' Finlay mopped her tears with his handkerchief. 'You're being so brave.'

'I'm not. I'm being—what is it? Feart. I am feart.'

'If you were not, I'd worry about your sanity. If it was me, I'd be feart. If I could find a way to escort you myself...'

'Don't be daft,' she said softly. 'You have to arrange El Fantasma's tragic death, and then you have to go back to England and tell the great duke what has happened, and then you have to go back to the army and once again become Major Finlay Urquhart, the Jock Upstart, and forget all about me.'

'I'll never forget you, Isabella. I will never, ever be able to forget you.'

'I can see how it might be difficult to forget a woman who put your life in mortal danger,' she said lightly, in an effort to lighten the mood.

'It's not that I will remember. I have much more pleasant memories of our time together than that to keep me warm at night.'

Isabella felt herself blush slightly. His visage was no longer grim. His sea-blue eyes were no longer pained. She would have to be very careful not to make him fret for her. She did not want to be a source of worry. She had caused him enough worry. She would do her very best to be the bold, bright, brave partisan he thought her. She would not only comply with the future he had arranged for her, she would embrace it. 'So I'm to sail for America,' Isabella said. 'Should we not then be heading north, for the coast?'

'In good time. They will be searching for us there. It's the obvious place to look.'

'Which is why we're heading west. For how much longer?'

'It's been nigh on a week and there's been no sign of any pursuers. Another day and I think we will be safe enough.' Finlay looked up at the sky, which had turned from blue to grey, with clouds like lumps of charcoal. 'In fact, I see no reason why we should not sleep in a decent bed tonight, partake of a decent dinner.'

'You think that's wise?'

'I reckon you deserve it.' Finlay touched her cheek. 'Not a word of complaint have I heard from you about living and sleeping rough for the past week. You've been a trooper.'

Isabella beamed. 'That is the best compliment you could pay me, but I do not need a feather bed and a proper dinner if you think it is too risky.'

'You shall have both. And a bath, too, in water that's a wee bit warmer than melted ice. It's the least I can do.' He leaned into her. She thought he was going to kiss her, but his lips brushed her forehead, and then he let her go, turning toward the horses. 'To Tafalla it is, then.'

The town was set on a wide cultivated plain, reached by traversing another ancient trail over the Valdorba Mountains. The warren of narrow medieval streets clustered with houses built from mellow honey-coloured stone rose steeply up towards a citadel. The more modern part of the town was built on the flatter land around the Cidacos River, and it was here that they had found lodgings at a small inn, hiring a private salon and two bedchambers. Finlay had made all the arrangements, under the name of Mr and Mrs Upstart, in his halting Spanish. 'Just my little joke,' he had told her with a grin.

Now clean, shaved and dressed in fresh linen, he waited for her in the small salon, gazing morosely into a glass of sherry that he had barely touched. With every passing day she was becoming more precious to him. And yet, with every passing day, the inevitability of losing her forever loomed larger. Their worlds had collided all too briefly, but soon, very soon, they would part forever. Isabella was destined for a brand-new world, and he to return to his old, familiar one, where his career and his family awaited. It made him heartsore to think of it, and pointlessly so. He would not think of it.

Instead, he would make the most of what little time he had in her company. He would make the most of tonight for this bonny, clever, brave lass, who deserved so much more than the hand that fate had dealt her, and who was facing the dangers and the fears of the great unknown with such fortitude it made him want to weep like a bairn.

Fresh from her bath, Isabella wore a pretty olive-green gown trimmed with bronze that made her skin seem golden. A woollen scarf in the same shades was draped around her shoulders. She had braided her hair around her head in a way that reminded Finlay of images of Greek goddesses, though there was nothing at all ethereal in her smile, nor in his reaction to it. 'You look ravishing,' he said.

She blushed endearingly. Such a bonny thing, and yet she had not a trace of vanity in her. Finlay took her hand, pressing a kiss to her fingertips. 'Thank you,' she said. 'You look very...'

'Do not dare try to tell me I'm beautiful,' he teased.

She laughed. 'It's an insult, I remember. May I be permitted to say that you look very dashing instead?'

He grinned, holding out his arm. 'I'll settle for that. Shall we go for a stroll before dinner?'

'I would like that very much,' Isabella said.

Braziers and lanterns were already being lit in the Plaza Mayor. It was time for the traditional evening *paseo* or promenade. They did not join in, Finlay being all too aware that his distinctive auburn hair might draw unwanted attention, so they watched from the shadows. Couples and families strolled, exchanging greetings, passing comment on the unseasonably mild weather, speculating on the possibility of rain. Women compared *toilettes*, children ran laughing round and round the square in excited clusters, while the smaller ones gurgled from their carriages or their mother's arms. Young and old, well-heeled and down-at-heel alike, everyone congregated in the square in the early evening.

'It's a right social mix, isn't it?' Finlay marvelled. 'In London, Hyde Park is where they promenade, but it's more of a fashion parade for the toffs than anything, and you certainly wouldnae get the— I don't know what it is here. There's no sense of people sticking to their own kind.'

Isabella chuckled. 'You have met my brother. There is plenty of that behaviour to be found in Spain, but not for the *paseo*. Do they have such a custom in Scotland?'

'No, we have not the weather for it,' Finlay replied. 'I think I told you we have more than our fair share of rain. Mind you, when there's a wedding, then you'll get everyone out parading in their finery. That's a sight to behold.'

'Tell me about it.'

'Well, now, I'm talking about a kirk wedding mind. The last one I attended was for my youngest sister Sheena—I missed all the others, but I was home on leave for that one. My mother was baking for days before it. My mother makes the best scones in Scotland. They are a sort of cake, though not sweet, like a soft biscuit, and you eat them hot from the griddle with butter or crowdie, which is cheese.'

'What other foods do they eat at wedding feasts? What does the bride wear? And the groom, does he wear the plaid? Me, I like the plaid very much,' Isabella said, her eyes dancing, 'though not, I think, on a man with thin legs. Or fat legs.'

'A lady should not comment on a gentleman's legs,' Finlay said with mock outrage.

'Ah but since you have told me that I am dead, then I am no longer a lady and therefore free to state that I think that you have a fine pair of legs and look most becoming in your kilt,' Isabella retorted with a mischievous twinkle in her eye.

He smiled down at her. 'Then, since I'm not and never have been a gentleman, I'll take the liberty of reminding you that you have a very delightful derrière.'

Colour tinged her cheeks. Her eyes sparkled. Her mouth was curved into the most tantalising, teasing smile. He spoke without thinking. 'If we were not in the midst of half the population of Tafalla, I would kiss you.'

'I don't know if you've noticed, but half the population of Tafalla have just spent the past hour kissing each other.'

'I didn't mean that sort of kiss.'

Isabella held his gaze. 'I know you didn't,' she whispered.

His breath caught in his chest. He had the oddest sensation, as if he were falling head first from a cliff. She was teasing him. Flirting. But as he gazed down at her, his chest tightened, and he knew, clear as day, what it was he felt for her, and it bore no relation at all to what he'd felt for his other flirts.

He would not name it. If he did not give it a name, there was a chance, a tiny wee chance, that it would pass, because what point was there in him feeling... that, when he was about to pack the object of his—that thing, off to America?

'I don't know about you, but I'm ravenous. We should eat. What do you think of that place over there?' Finlay said, steering a slightly bewildered Isabella towards a brightly lit tavern on the corner of the square.

By the time they had gone through the ceremony of being formally seated at a table in the *commodore*, the back room reserved for diners in the tavern, and consumed a complimentary glass of the local aperitif, the awkward moment had passed. The dining room was basic, the food simple but excellent. They ate hungrily, enjoying a range of dishes. *Morcilla*, a variety of spicy blood sausage that reminded Finlay very much of the black pudding to be found back home in Scotland, *me-*

nestra de verduras, a mixture of local vegetables and salty ham, a braised quail with tiny pale-green beans cooked in tomato, simply grilled lamb chops served with potatoes and cabbage, and the famous *pimientos de piquillo*—red peppers preserved in oil and stuffed with salted cod. The wine, Isabella informed him, was not as good as her brother's. Finlay, who had always been a moderate drinker, partook sparingly, but Isabella, like many Spanish women he had met, seemed to be able to consume quite a few glasses without it having any noticeable effect.

They chatted about the food, relishing the first proper meal in over a week. They speculated about their fellow diners. Then, when they had been served an extremely good *roncal* cheese, Isabella raised the subject of his sister's wedding again. Accustomed as he was to having his origins mocked, Finlay automatically embarked on one of his usual, heavily embroidered tales.

'I think you are making this up,' Isabella interrupted halfway through the yarn.

'Not at all. Well, maybe a bit, but not all of it.'

She frowned. 'Why would you do that? I am not a child, to be told stories. I do not want to hear family secrets or—or confidences. I was not prying. I simply wanted to understand you more. You have seen my home, you know so much about me, yet you tell me almost nothing about yourself.'

He had offended her. 'I'm sorry. I'm not used to talking about myself.'

Isabella propped her hand on her chin and studied

him across the table. 'The Jock Upstart,' she said. 'Was that one of the stories you tell in your officers' mess?'

'They would not be interested in the truth,' Finlay said awkwardly, though he wasn't sure, now he came to think about it, that he ever told anyone the truth, save Jack.

'I am interested,' Isabella said. 'What is it like, to have three sisters? Consuela is very fond of hers. She is always writing letters to them. Do your sisters write to you?'

'Aye, once every few months, with news of all my nephews and nieces. I've twelve of them,' Finlay said with a grin.

Isabella's eyes widened. 'Twelve!'

'And counting. Mhairi was expecting another the last I heard.'

'I wonder sometimes what it would have been like, to have a sister.'

'Someone to confide in?' Finlay laid his hands over hers. 'Your mother died when you were a bairn, didn't she? It must have been hard, growing up without any female company.'

'You said that to me that first night we met. I did not think—but now, I don't know. Do you miss them, your family?'

He opened his mouth to assure her that he did, of course he did, then closed it again, frowning. 'Honestly?' He quirked his brow, and Isabella nodded. 'I've been away for so long, that in a way they are strangers to me. They are my blood, I love them, but I'm no more part of their lives than they are mine. Aside from kinship, we have little in common.'

'Though it must be a comfort to know that there are people who care for you, who would be there if you needed them.'

'Aye,' Finlay agreed with surprise, 'that is true. The letters they write, they don't make me want to go home, but it is a comfort indeed, seeing a picture drawn by my nephew, or reading one of my niece's stories. Or reading about the fishing, and the peats and the tattie howking, whatever is the latest gossip my mother thinks fit for my ears,' he said, smiling nostalgically. 'It is good to hear that life can go on in that way, that people can be happy, when you are sitting in a foreign field in the aftermath of battle.'

'What will you do now, Finlay? Now that Europe is at peace, and there are no more battles to fight?'

A damned good question. One of the many lessons this mission had taught him was that he was no peace-time soldier. 'There are always other wars,' he said, thinking, with little enthusiasm, of the rumours he'd heard about India. 'When Wellington hears of my success in silencing El Fantasma, perhaps there will be other such missions, too.'

'You think he will believe you? You have not told me what it is, exactly, that you will tell him.'

'That's Jack's territory.' The light had faded a wee bit from her big golden eyes. She was tired. And he'd been prattling on about his family, and his damned career, when all the while the poor lass had no family now, and much less of a clue than he about her future.

'Let's get you back to the inn,' Finlay said, pressing her hand. 'I'll just go through and pay the shot.'

They were standing at the bar when he opened the connecting door. Two men, dressed in the uniform of the Spanish army, drinking a glass of wine. Not officers, but guards, Finlay reckoned. Their boots were dusty. He heard only one word. 'English.' But it was enough.

Retreating quietly back into the *commodore*, Finlay returned to the table. 'We have to leave. Quietly. Don't panic,' he whispered into Isabella's ear, putting her shawl around her shoulders and throwing some coins onto the table. Fortunately the room had emptied, the few diners left talking intimately over their wine and cheese. Even more fortunately, Isabella asked no questions, doing exactly as he asked, getting to her feet, following the pressure of his hand on her back, to the door that led to the kitchens.

'Soldiers,' he said, as the door closed behind them. 'Spanish army. Two, looking for us. I don't know if there are any more. I'm sorry, but it looks as though you won't be able to enjoy the luxury of a feather bed tonight after all.'

She had not quite believed they were after her. Despite what Finlay had said, despite the urgency with which they travelled, despite the unequivocal evidence of their existence that fateful day at Estebe's house, Isabella had been unable to wholly credit the tenacity of the Spanish government in tracking down El Fantasma, unable to believe that the pamphlets she had written, printed in the cellars of Hermoso Romero, could result in this merciless vendetta. As she scurried along at Finlay's side through the back streets of Tafalla, her heart in her mouth, she no longer doubted. Finlay's concerns were very real. America seemed, of a sudden, a very attractive prospect, if only because it was so very far away. She did not want to be caught. She desperately, desperately did not want them to catch Finlay.

'Should we separate?' she panted. 'Finlay, I don't want them to…'

'Isabella, I'm not going anywhere without you.'

'But they are looking for two of us.'

'An Englishman and a Spanish woman, that's what they said. If anything, it's me who's putting you in danger.'

Isabella's hands tightened on his arm. 'You won't leave me,' she said, before she could stop herself.

He smiled down at her. Even as they fled for their lives, that smile did things to her insides. 'I won't leave you.' His smile faded. 'Not until you're safe on that boat. And the sooner we get you there the better. We'll start to head for the north coast tonight.'

'You said that is where they would concentrate the search for us. But now here they are in Tafalla in the west.'

'They've clearly enough men spare to cover all the options. Ours is not the only army kicking its heels in peacetime. King Ferdinand's men haven't enough to do, either, by the looks of it.'

She was going to be sick. Fear, such as she had

never felt during the war, made her break out in a cold sweat. She stumbled, and would have fallen if Finlay had not had her anchored firmly to his side. 'Courage, lass,' he said.

Isabella managed a weak smile, swallowed the nausea and picked up the pace again. 'I won't let you down.'

'You couldn't.'

His faith, whether misplaced or not, kept her going through the next fraught hours as they hurriedly reclaimed baggage and horses from the inn. They were heading home, east, Finlay told the landlady, a family crisis. He did not pretend that the false trail was likely to do anything other than give their pursuers a choice of three alternative directions. 'And if there's only the two soldiers, we might just get lucky, though we can't count on it,' he'd said.

They rode through the darkness, across the flat land that spread out to Logrono, for the route directly north was too mountainous. Towards dawn, as the horses were flagging and the terrain was becoming more difficult, they quit the main road and stopped to rest in the shelter of a valley where the mountains rose steeply around them. Shaking, exhausted and oddly exhilarated, Isabella sat huddled in a blanket coaxing a tiny fire into life while Finlay tended to the sweating horses.

'We are likely safe enough here for a few hours,' he said, sitting down beside her. 'You should try to sleep.'

'I don't think I could.'

He put his arm around her. 'Try.'

She did because he wanted her to, without any expectation of success.

When she opened her eyes it was daylight, and the smell of coffee brewing on the trivet greeted her. Finlay, astonishingly clean-shaven, his hair damp, handed her a tin mug. 'I have some good news,' he said.

'Let me guess, there has been an uprising in Pamplona and all the soldiers in the area have been recalled to suppress it.'

'Now, that would be remarkably good news,' he said, sitting down beside her and stretching his long legs out in front of him. 'Mine isn't quite in that category. How are you feeling?'

'You let me sleep for the whole night.'

'What little was left of it.'

Noticing that there was only one cup of coffee, Isabella handed Finlay the mug. 'We can share,' she said, when he looked as if he would refuse.

'Thank you.'

He took a sip and handed it back. She took a sip, putting her mouth where his had been. He was watching her. She took another sip. His hand lingered on hers when she handed the mug back. His eyes lingered on her mouth. Her breath caught. Finlay sipped, placing his lips exactly where hers had been. Her heart bumped. She leaned towards him. He leaned towards her. He handed her the mug. His lips brushed hers. He tasted of coffee. She felt the sharp intake of his breath. He kissed her, slowly, his tongue licking along the inside of her lower lip. Then he handed her the mug. 'You finish it.'

At least he did not walk away, or head off to tend to the horses. Isabella finished the coffee. 'You haven't told me the good news.'

'I recognise this place. I've been here before, during the campaign. There's a mountain pass we can follow, well away from the main routes, that will take us towards Vitoria, and from there we can head to San Sebastian.'

'Vitoria. It was a very bloody battle for the English— British, I think.'

Finlay grimaced. 'I confess, it's not a place I've any yearning to see again.'

'You have seen such terrible things. That day, when you opened my eyes to reality, when you told me what they would do to me if they caught me...'

'I'm sorry I had to do that.'

'I know you are,' Isabella said, setting down the mug and touching his hand. 'I know what it cost you to speak as you did, and I am very grateful. If you had been less blunt, I would have been less convinced. How do you do it, Finlay? How is it that you seem so—so divorced from what you have seen, what you have had to do? You are not a savage. You have a conscience, stronger than most, I think.'

'If you're talking about guilt, I have plenty of it.' He frowned down at the dying fire. 'You don't think of it, not when you're on active service. You think only of the next manoeuvre, the next battle. You can't afford to look back. That way can lie madness—and I mean that.' He glanced up at her, his eyes dark. 'You must have heard something of what our men did after Burgos. Some of the atrocities. I was there in the aftermath, Isabella. There was no stopping them. The lust for blood, it wasn't just revenge, it went deeper than that. It was as if some of them—it was as if they were possessed by an evil spirit. I sound like your Inquisition, but it's the only way of describing it.'

'Though, you never took part in such things,' Isabella said. It was not a question. She was absolutely certain of it.

Finlay shook his head. 'No, but my men did. I carry some of the blame.'

'No!'

'I was their commanding officer. I seem to remember you saying some such thing with regard to Estebe.'

'I will always have that guilt as part of me. Is that what you mean?'

'I won't lie to you, that's what I mean.'

'Finlay, one of the things I like so much about you is that you don't lie to me. Not even when you want to.' She touched his hand again, and this time he turned it around to clasp her fingers. 'You treat me as if I have a mind of my own.'

'A very decided one,' he said.

She smiled softly. 'Like the Jock Upstart, I do not take kindly to being given orders. We are very alike in that way.'

'Who'd have thought it?' He raised her hand to his lips, pressing a kiss onto her palm, allowing his mouth to linger for a moment, warm on her skin. 'We must go. We've a few days yet before we reach the coast, and the path is treacherous so we need to make the most of the daylight.'

They travelled all day, leading the horses over the roughest terrain, making slow but steady progress north. It was hard going, but Isabella made not a word of complaint, and though her steps flagged as dusk approached, she insisted on continuing for another mile, until darkness prevented them travelling further. Cheese and stale bread were all they had to eat, but she made no protest about this meagre fare, either.

There was sparse shelter provided by an overhanging rocky outcrop. 'You take the blankets,' Finlay said. 'I'll keep watch.'

'There is no need. No one is following us up here. You will feel better for a sleep, and we will be warmer if we share.' She smiled up at him, her face shadowed by the flickers of the tiny fire they had lit. 'We did it once before, do you remember?'

'I do.' His heart gave a painful twist as he sat down beside her. More than two years ago, it had been. Against all odds they had met in the strangest of circumstances, and here they were again about to huddle under a blanket together for warmth. He hadn't thought himself a man who believed in destiny. He wished fervently that fate had drawn him a kinder hand. Twice, he had crossed paths with the woman who owned his heart, and soon they would be parted forever. He could not resist putting his arm around her and drawing her closer. He loved her. Pointless to deny it any longer. Time to stop pretending it was anything else. He loved her, and he always would.

'It is a strange coincidence, being here like this for the second time, is it not?' Isabella asked.

'I was thinking the very same thing myself.' Finlay shifted on the hard ground, tucking the blanket around them. Her cheek rested on his shoulder. Her hair tickled his chin. He breathed in the sweet, familiar scent of her, and closed his eyes, trying to etch the feel of her body against his, the softness of her, the shape of her, deep in his mind, achingly conscious that he would have so few chances left just to hold her like this.

'We talked of America that night,' Isabella said. 'I never thought I would travel there. I never imagined it would be my home.'

'Isabella, if there was any…'

'Wheesht,' she said, putting her fingers to his mouth, her accent making the word sound like a caress. 'I have been thinking of what you said. America is a new world. A country where ideals are not simply dreams. You are right, Finlay. It is a country where I can start again. I don't know what I will do, but there are so many possibilities. You were right. It is a good place for me to go. Thank you.'

He knew she was trying to make him feel better, but there was a note of real enthusiasm in her voice that was surely not manufactured. She was not simply making the best of things, she was trying her wee heart out to embrace her fate. He loved her so much. *Gràdh, mo chrìdh*, he said to himself, touching his lips to the silky mass of her hair. 'You should sleep now,' he added aloud. 'We've a way to go in the morning.'

'*Buenas noches*, Finlay.'

'*Oidhche mhath*, Isabella.'

'*Oika va?*'

He chuckled softly. 'Not bad. You've an ear for the Gaelic. Goodnight, lass.'

She nestled her head into his shoulder. He kissed her hair again, tightening his arm around the slim curve of her waist. Her breathing slowed. She was asleep almost immediately. '*Gràdh, mo chrìdh,*' Finlay whispered, wanting to say the words to her just once, though she could not hear. 'Love of my heart you are, Isabella. Love of my heart.'

Chapter Eleven

Isabella awoke from a deep slumber to find that her head was cushioned on Finlay's chest. She was lying on her side, with one of her legs wedged between his. His arm anchored her to him; his other hand was splayed across her bottom. She could feel his heart beating, slow and steady, through his shirt. She listened, keeping quite still, to his breathing. Also slow and steady. He was asleep. She did not want to move and risk waking him.

The cloud had cleared while she slept, and the stars were out, huge disks of silver in the inky blue sky, the half-moon glowing milky white. Finlay said the stars in Scotland seemed much farther away. She couldn't imagine how that could be. He stirred, tightening his hold on her. She felt safe here with him. She wished the night would go on forever. She did not want to think of the morning, which would bring her another day closer to the coast, and to the ship that would take her to her new life. If she was not so completely alone, she might be looking forward to it almost as much as she had tried to persuade Finlay she was. A new world. Perhaps there would be an opportunity for a new El Fantasma. Not a partisan, but perhaps— Her mind skittered to a halt. Something. She would think of something tomorrow, and she would tell Finlay, and she would enthuse and speculate, and the guilt he was so patently feeling about sending her off alone to her fate would hopefully abate a little.

She owed him so much. She owed him her life. She couldn't bear to think that he'd be fretting about her once she had sailed. He had his own life to be getting on with. He would be off to fight another war soon enough. Or off on another mission for the Duke of Wellington. She hoped for Finlay's sake that he would be given something constructive to do. Though she hated the idea of him being in danger, she knew he would be miserable kicking his heels in the officers' mess. The Jock Upstart was a man who thrived on action. Her heart lurched at the realisation that she would never know what he was doing, who he was with, what country he was in, even.

Perhaps he would, after all, return to the Highlands and raise a family. She could imagine him, very easily imagine him, with a brood of children—bairns, as he would call them. She could imagine them surprisingly easily. Their bairns. Hers and Finlay's. She had never really thought about children, never imagined herself as a mother. Now, for a fleeting moment, the notion filled her with some soft and warm emotion that she'd never experienced before. 'Stupid,' Isabella muttered to herself. 'Stupid, stupid, stupid!'

She was torturing herself. Better to focus on the real future, whatever that would be. It would be empty of Finlay—that was the only thing she knew for sure. Perhaps she should suggest they correspond, once she had settled in America. But she dismissed the idea immediately. A consolation to her, those letters might be, but they would be a burden to Finlay. The break, when it came, must be clean. In a few more days, only a few more days, they would part, and she must make very sure that the parting was as painless for Finlay as it could be. As to herself—no, truly, there was no point in thinking about her feelings.

She flattened her palm on his chest. He was so solid. She had never lain like this with a man. Slept with a man. It was such a very intimate thing to be doing, despite the fact that they were both more or less fully clothed. Asleep, even Finlay was vulnerable. In a sense, sleeping together was more intimate than making love. Not that anyone would believe that all she had done was slept in his arms. If it were discovered, her reputation would be ruined. If she had any left to ruin, that was. Though her reputation would not matter at all in the New World she was headed towards. No one would know anything about her past history. They would not know that she had spent the night alone, in a Highlander's embrace. It was a terrible pity she had not anything more scandalous to conceal. Almost a waste.

Somehow her hand had slipped inside the opening of Finlay's shirt. The rough hair of his chest prickled her palm. His nipple was unexpectedly hard. Was it as sensitive as hers? When she touched it, did it tingle the way hers did? Was there that shivering connection between his nipple and his—his arousal? There was certainly a connection between his nipple and her arousal. If she turned her head just the tiniest fraction, she could put her lips to the skin of his throat. It was a very, very appealing idea, but she dared not move lest she wake him. Though it was so very tempting. But it would be wrong. He had made it clear, very clear, that he would not make love to her. She was under his protection. She was an innocent. He was not a seducer of virgins.

In a few days' time, she would be alone on a boat, and she would never see him again. No one save Finlay cared about her virginity. She would certainly be more than happy not to have to take it with her. Without her dowry and her pedigree, her virginity was not even a marketable asset. She turned her head a tiny fraction. Just a kiss. But she did not want to wake him. Just one tiny kiss. What was the harm in that?

Her lips touched his throat. His skin was warm. She licked him. He tasted slightly salty. A trickle of perspiration ran down her back. She kissed his throat again. She could feel his pulse beating against her lips. His hand tightened on her rump, and she knew he was awake.

She froze, horrified. She lifted her head to apologise, but Finlay smiled softly. 'Isabella,' he said, 'lovely Isabella. You've no idea how lovely.'

'Finlay.' In the moonlight, his skin was pale, his eyes dark. She reached up to touch his hair. 'The colour of autumn leaves,' she said. 'All that time ago, when first we sat under the stars like this, that's what I thought. That your eyes were colour of the summer sea. And your hair the colour of autumn leaves.'

He laughed softly. 'I wanted to kiss you, that night. Under that blanket. Under those stars. I wanted very much to kiss you.' His hand was caressing her bottom, the flat of his palm smoothing delightful circles. 'I regretted the fact that I didn't,' he said.

'And I, too.' She smoothed her hand over his chest. She felt his heart leap, beat faster than before. Longing, so deep that it was almost painful, overwhelmed her. 'I have so many regrets, Finlay. I don't want this to be another. Make love to me.'

'Isabella…'

'Please,' she interrupted, desperate to quell his conscience before it could put an end to things. 'This has nothing to do with gratitude or guilt, Finlay. I know what I am doing. You will not be stealing my innocence. I am giving it to you. I *know* you want me. I know, too, that it can mean nothing.'

'You're wrong. Isabella, you are so wrong. It means everything. But I can't resist you. I don't want to resist you. I want you more than I've ever wanted anything.'

He loved her so much. *I love you*, he thought as he kissed her. *I love you, Isabella, I love you.* He poured his heart into his kisses. It would be his only chance to love her, to worship her, to show her how he felt. He kissed her hungrily, passionately, then softly, tenderly. 'You are so beautiful,' he said. 'I want you so much.' *I love you so much.*

He rolled her onto her back. He kissed her mouth, her throat, her neck, her shoulders, the mounds of her breasts above the neckline of her riding habit. She tugged at his shirt, slipping her hands beneath the fabric to stroke his skin, making his muscles clench in response, sending the blood shooting to his groin.

He eased her up, sitting her between his legs, and kissed the nape of her neck. Slowly, he began to unbraid her hair, teasing it loose with his fingers. Long, silken strands spread over her shoulders. He pulled her up against him, her back against his chest, cupping her breasts, kissing her neck, then began to unlace her riding habit, taking his time, planting kisses on every inch of skin revealed, slipping the top over her arms, kissing her shoulders, the crook of her elbows, before unlacing her stays and sliding her chemise down. He kissed the knot of her spine. He could feel her breathing, fast and shallow. He cupped her breasts, exposed now, rolling her nipples between his fingers, relishing the small moans of pleasure his touch elicited.

Hot skin, cold air. He pulled his shirt over his head and drew her back against him. The silken touch of her hair caressed his chest. He whispered her name, feathering kisses across her narrow shoulders. She arched back against him, her breathing more ragged. He wanted to see her face. Gently, he rolled her onto her back again. Another long, deep kiss, her tongue on his, making his shaft pulse and throb. He ached to be inside her, but he would not rush this, his one unique opportunity to make love to the woman he loved.

'You are a banquet,' he said, smiling down at her. 'A feast.'

Her response was a sensuous smile that sent his pulses racing. She ran her hands over the breadth of his chest, pressing her mouth to his throat. 'You are not the only one with an appetite.'

'I have never been so ravenous in my life,' Finlay replied, taking her nipple into his mouth.

She gasped with pleasure. He tasted her lingeringly, licking and teasing her, first one nipple and then the other. Her fingers dug into his back. She arched under him. He kissed the delicate line of her ribcage, licking into the hollow of her navel, murmuring her name over and over. Her hands fluttered frantically over him, her untutored touch rousing him, the guttural little moans she made heating his blood, making his pulses race.

He pulled her habit and her petticoats off together. Her skin was creamy white in the moonlight. Her slim beauty, her delicate curves, were almost too much. 'You are so lovely. I have never seen anything to match your loveliness,' he said. He kissed the back of her knee, her calf, her ankle, as he removed her stocking. Then the same for the other leg. Isabella was watching him, wide-eyed, intent. He adored the way she watched him. Not a trace of modesty, as if she, too, was savouring every precious moment, as if she, too, was trying to memorise every inch of him. He could not resist claiming her lips again. She wrapped her arms around him, pressing her naked breasts to his naked chest. Her nipples grazed his skin. He had never felt anything so arousing.

More kisses, far headier than any of the region's wine. He could drink of her and drink of her and never have his fill. Easing her back down, he kissed his way down her body, the valley between her breasts, the dip of her belly, to the apex of her thighs. She was panting now, her fingers clutching at the edge of the blanket on which they lay. The flesh here was sweet, soft, faintly scented with her arousal. He eased her legs farther apart, and slid his tongue inside her. She bucked under him. The taste of her, the heat and wet of her, was heady.

He thought he might come. It took him every bit of self-control he possessed to wait, to get himself under control, but he did it. She was a feast he had waited a long time to consume. He wanted to enjoy every morsel. He slipped his hands under her bottom, tilting her towards him, and licked. She was already tight. Already on the brink. He was careful not to send her over, slowly licking and stroking just enough, then moving away, sliding his fingers inside her, thrusting slowly, carefully. Her moans had become pleas. Her hands were in his hair, on his shoulders, his arms. He licked again. He thrust again with his fingers. She cried out his name, a desperate sound. He licked again, slowly but relentlessly, and she came with a loud cry, pulsing against him, the taste of her so unbearably sweet, so uniquely his lovely Isabella, that he closed his eyes to relish it, telling her again and again, to the rhythm of her climax, whispering so softly that she could not hear him, that he loved her, loved her, loved her.

When the pulses faded to ripples, Finlay looked up to

find her watching him again. He smiled. Isabella smiled back, a slow, sensuous, sated smile. He could call a halt now. He thought about it. But then she reached for him, pulling him towards her, her hands on the waistband of his breeches, shaking her head as if she had read his mind. 'I am hungry, too,' she said. 'Take them off. I want to see you naked,' she said urgently.

He wanted her to look. It was strange, he'd never felt like that before, but he wanted her to see him. He kissed her again before dragging his mouth from hers and hurriedly divesting himself of the last of his clothes. Even in the moonlight, he could see the flush of colour tingeing her cheeks. It was delightful. She was delightful.

'May I touch you?'

'You need to ask? I can think of nothing I want more.' He knelt before her, once more between her legs. She sat up. Her blush was quite distinct now, but she was still looking at him in that intent, sultry way that made him ache with the need to be inside her. She touched his belly. With her finger, she traced the line of hair that arrowed down to his groin. She stroked his flanks. She traced the line of his buttocks. His muscles tightened in response. She reached for his shaft. He inhaled sharply, praying for self-control. Her touch was the faintest feathering, tracing the length of him with her fingertip. 'Dear God,' he said.

She yanked her hand away. 'I'm sorry.'

'No.' He couldn't catch his breath. 'No. I'm just— It is just…'

'You like it?' Her smile became feline. Predatory.

She touched him again, feathering up and down the length of him. 'I think you like it a lot?'

'Aye,' he said, snatching a kiss from her, 'a lot.'

'And this?'

She circled her fingers around his girth. He nodded, gritting his teeth.

'And this?'

A slow stroke of her hand. Finlay nodded again. Pain and pleasure; he'd no idea they were such bedmates.

'And this.'

Another stroke, more sure, but still slow. And another. He was going to come. He would not come. Not yet. 'Isabella.'

She stopped at the warning note in his voice. Then she smiled at him again.

'And this, Finlay?'

Her lips touched the tip of his shaft. He felt her tongue, hot on the most sensitive part of him. With a long, low groan of ecstasy and regret, he pulled himself free of her and laid her down, covering her body with his. 'You are a sorceress,' he said. 'You are the most delightful, delicious, desirable sorceress, and you have me under your spell and I can't wait any longer. Do you still want this, Isabella? Because if you don't, now is the time to say so.'

For answer, she put her arms around his neck and kissed him. 'I want this. I want you. More than anything.'

Her words were no lie. She ached in a way she had never ached before, her body yearning for him in a new way. She wanted him inside her. She wanted that sleek, silken part of him inside her. She tilted herself towards him in open invitation, worlds beyond modesty or embarrassment, caring nothing for her utter lack of experience, surrendering completely to her body's instincts. His kiss was hard and deep. His tongue thrust into her mouth. She was hot, fevered, tense, urgent, but he entered her slowly. She opened her eyes to watch him. His gaze locked on hers as his body became part of her until he filled her. There was no pain. There was only delight. And more tension. Her muscles clenched around him. He pushed higher inside her, and she felt an odd fluttering sensation. Then he waited, watching her. She pulled him towards her for another kiss. 'Yes,' she said. 'Yes.' Permission for anything. Everything. She wanted all of him.

'Yes,' he whispered. 'Oh, yes.'

His first thrust was careful. The effort of control was etched on his face. Another thrust, harder this time. She was learning how to hold him and release him. Another thrust, and she felt the tension inside her building. They were finding a common rhythm now. Thrust, cling, release, thrust. Still he watched her. Still she held his gaze, seeing her pleasure reflected on his face, the power of giving that pleasure making her bolder, making her match his thrust with a tilt of her hips, holding him higher, clinging to him tighter, until her climax took her, sending her spiralling higher than she had ever flown, and Finlay cried out, pulling himself free of her to spend himself with an equally hoarse cry that was her name, and something in his native tongue she did not understand.

Afterwards, she could not sleep. She was afraid to speak. They lay entwined, skin on skin, watching the stars, listening to the whickering of the horses, the gentle burble of a distant stream. Finlay held her as if she was made of glass and he was afraid she might break. She clung to him as if she was afraid she would drown in a sea of emotion. As the waves of pleasure ebbed and the euphoria of their coupling faded, she was left feeling oddly desolate.

She felt the brush of his lips on her hair. His hand tightened possessively around her flank. She moved, burrowing closer. If she could climb inside his skin, she would. If she could live inside his skin, she would. That was when it struck her.

'*Madre de Dios.*'

'What is it?'

'Nothing.' Her heart skipped a beat, then began to beat harder, as if she had been running. *Madre de Dios.* She was in love. Isabella closed her eyes in pain. How could she have been so stupid? How could she have been so blind? Of course she was in love with this man. Had she not just made love to him with her body and her mind, too? She was in love. Of all the foolish things she had done, surely this was the worst.

Finlay's lips brushed her hair again. She found his hand, twining her fingers in his. Tears stung behind her lids. She could not let them fall. He would think she regretted what they had just done. Her heart began to slow. She did not regret it. She lifted his hand to hers and kissed his knuckles. She would never regret it, but he must never find out. She had already given him enough to feel guilty about. This— No, he must not know this. He cared deeply for her, she did not doubt that, but there was no question, none at all, of any possible future for them.

Despite this, she allowed herself to dream for a few precious moments. To imagine that they could lie like this every night, wrapped in each other's loving embrace. That he could make love to her every night, spending himself inside her, in the hope of creating a new human life forged by them both. She allowed herself to dream of a little farm—no, croft—in the Highlands. They would attend the church in the longhouse he had described to her. Their children would play with the children of his three sisters. Everyone from the village would dance at their wedding. She would learn to cook, and to weave, and Finlay would...

Enough of this schoolgirl fantasy! The cold reality was that it was impossible for her to set foot on British soil. Furthermore, if it were known that he was harbouring El Fantasma, Major Finlay Urquhart would be court-martialled and most likely hanged. No, she had to vanish off the face of the earth and resurface in America under an assumed identity, and Finlay had to return to Britain in order to complete his mission and convince Wellington that El Fantasma had been eliminated. Failure to do that would also likely lead to him being hanged, this time for desertion.

Isabella sighed. If only things were different, he

could sail with her to the New World. In America, there would be opportunity for any number of adventures. *Stupid!* If things were different, she would not have to go to America. If things were different, she would not have met Finlay again, and she would not be lying here under the stars, her body still tingling from his lovemaking. Time to stop dreaming and face facts. She was leaving everything behind, including her country and her family, everything she knew and loved. She had kept the pain of this at bay by simply avoiding thinking of it, but she knew, when she was alone, that it would come. She loved Finlay with all her heart. Which did not mean asking him to give up everything, as she had, and come away with her. No, what it meant was to ensure the exact opposite was the case. For his sake. And she'd better make damned sure she remembered that over the next few days.

The stars were beginning to fade. Isabella turned her face into Finlay's chest. An errant tear escaped. She rubbed her cheek against the hard wall of muscle, hoping he would not notice.

He pulled her closer. 'Try to sleep for a bit,' he said softly. 'We've a long day ahead of us tomorrow.'

And a long, empty future ahead of her after that, Isabella thought. But she was not given to self-pity, and would not indulge in it now. 'In less than a week, I will be at sea,' she said with forced cheer. 'If the boat is still waiting.'

'It will be there. Jack gave his word,' Finlay said heavily, unwittingly killing the tiny spark of hope.

'Good,' said Isabella bracingly. 'That is at least one less thing to worry about.'

They were on their way before dawn had fully broken. The mountains to the east obscured the sunrise, and the dull, tarnished silver clouds above absorbed much of the sun's light when it finally did make an appearance. Finlay fought the desolation that threatened to envelop him. He was not by nature morose, nor given to railing against fate, but as he looked at the woman riding by his side and tried to imagine life without her, his rage verged on the biblical.

Why the devil had the fates thrown them together like this, if they were so intent on pulling the pair of them asunder? Bloody fates. And bloody Wellington. The man was power mad. And he was a mite too bloody cautious. What did it matter that El Fantasma could tell a few tales that would embarrass him? True, a few of those tales would stir up quite a storm, but the duke was riding so high on the wave of triumph fuelled by the victory at Waterloo that Finlay reckoned even the revelation that Wellington was in the habit of eating bairns for breakfast wouldn't cost him the political career he was hankering after. Bloody Wellington.

And while he was at it, bloody Jack, too. Jack could have told Wellington to stick his orders where the sun didn't shine. Jack wasn't even in the army anymore. But no, Jack and his principles had to take up El Fantasma's cause, and Jack knew Finlay a bit too damned well, catching him when he was kicking his heels, desperate for orders. Any orders. Some bloody friend.

Finlay's hands tightened on his reins, and his horse started. Quick as a flash, Isabella's hand reached for his rein. 'It's fine. I was dwamming,' he said, getting the horse back under control. 'It means daydreaming.'

She smiled at him. It was a forced smile. Her big golden eyes were shadowed with something that looked distinctly like unhappiness. 'You looked angry. I am sorry if...'

He was immediately contrite. 'Don't apologise. I'm like a bear with a sore heid, but it's not your fault, Isabella.'

'You do not regret last night?'

'No. Dear heavens, no.' He pulled up beside her, and she brought her horse to a halt. 'Isabella, last night was— It was...' *Everything.* The urge to tell her was powerful. 'It was perfect,' Finlay said. 'I only hope that you do not...'

'No, I don't regret it. For me it was also—perfect. Only today, I think that I am a little sad, knowing that soon I will be saying goodbye to you.' Her voice wobbled, but she smiled again valiantly. 'Of course I am very much looking forward to my new life, but I will— I will miss you, Finlay.'

Dear God. There was a sheen of tears in her eyes. She was so brave. He loved her so much. He should thank Jack and Wellington and the fates for throwing them together instead of cursing them for it. If he had not come here to Spain, he would never have known what love was. And if he had not come here to Spain, Isabella would have...

Finlay shuddered. She was safe. They would not

get their hands on her, even if he had to die saving her. She was safe and she was getting the chance of a new life. Without him, but a life. He must remember that. He leaned over in the saddle to kiss her softly. 'I will miss you, too, Isabella. You are a woman like no other. I am glad, and I am honoured, that I have had the chance to know you.'

So much less than he felt, but it was enough, it seemed. She blushed. 'And I, too, Finlay. Glad and deeply honoured.'

Chapter Twelve

They descended from the heights of La Puebla down a steep zigzag path and into the valley below through which the Zadorra River flowed, the site of the bloody Battle of Vitoria. It was a peaceful place, nature having reclaimed the battlefield, leaving little trace of the countless lives lost and the oceans of blood spilled more than two years before. Peaceful now that was, but Isabella sensed a certain melancholy linger in the air. Perhaps she was being fanciful, but she gave an involuntary shudder as she took in the scene.

'It is hard to believe that this particular engagement could have been so decisive,' she said, making a sweeping gesture.

'There were more than ten thousand casualties in total,' Finlay said grimly. 'Our army lost three and a half thousand men. Five hundred Spanish died. Can anything be worth so many lives, so much sacrifice?'

The British and their allies had been positioned on the western banks of the river, he had told her. Isabella stared at the rural scene, trying to imagine the serried ranks of soldiers numbering in the thousands, the field-gun placements firing salvo after merciless salvo, the sound of muskets, the acrid smell of gunpowder as it drifted across the battlefield in a thick pall of smoke. She could not, but Finlay, his eyes blank, staring off into the distance, clearly could. 'They say it was a pivotal moment, the turning point in the war,' Isabella offered.

'Aye. That's what they always say when the body count climbs that high.'

'But in this case, surely it is true. Not long after the Battle of Vitoria was won, Napoleon's army was in retreat. The occupation of Spain was over.'

'And you were free to build a new world, eh? Remind me how is that working out again.'

The bitterness in Finlay's voice took Isabella aback. The viciousness of his barb stung. 'You think it would have been better if the French had won?'

'I think it would have been better if we had not had to fight at all,' he said. 'The French left wagons full of the spoils of war behind as they fled, did you know that? Not just gold, but all sorts. Our men plundered it. They went mad. Discipline broke down entirely. There was no stopping them. Bloodlust, that's what it was. I hope you never witnessed it, Isabella. War can make a man less than human. I saw it with my own eyes but it is only now, with the benefit of some perspective that I begin to see how distasteful the whole bloody enterprise is. An enterprise that I was proud to be part of.'

'But you did not behave…'

'No,' he said tersely, 'I did not. Wellington called them the scum of the earth in a dispatch. The common soldier, who had won his precious victory, who had followed orders that took him hundreds of miles from home, tramped hundreds of miles across this country of yours, starving at times, suffering illness at others, frozen to the marrow often enough. Their wives trailing in their wake, too, some with bairns, having to suffer the same privations. And Wellington rewards them by calling them the scum of the earth.'

'Because they committed atrocities, Finlay.'

He looked at her bleakly. 'What is war itself, Isabella, if not an atrocity, an affront to humanity?'

'No. Don't say that. Don't talk like that.'

'Why not?'

'Because you are a soldier, and fighting wars is what you do. You have spent your life saving the lives of others, forging peace, making the world a safer place, a better place. The wars you have fought have been just wars, Finlay. You are an honourable man, a brave man. You are Major Urquhart, the Jock Upstart. All your life, you have served your country, done your duty. You should be proud of that legacy.'

She finished in a rush, eyeing him anxiously. Every word she had spoken was true, but this rousing little speech had not the effect she intended. If anything, Finlay looked even more bleak. 'In England, all anyone wants to talk about is the great victory of Waterloo. Children re-enact the battle with their little toy soldiers. If you tell a woman you were there, you're guaranteed a grateful embrace. Wellington is toasted at every dinner party in London. Yet the men who won that battle for him, many of them are starving now. So many died or were wounded in all these wars we fought against the French, the country can't afford to pay the pensions they're entitled to. They'll do anything to wriggle out of paying a widow, you know. They'll tell a man it's his own fault that he lost his legs, not the army's. Jack was railing against the injustice of it when we discussed my mission here. I begin to see that he was absolutely right. You are not the only one, Isabella, whose hopes of a better future have been dashed.'

'If Napoleon had not been defeated, the world would most likely be a worse place.'

He smiled at her wryly. 'You don't really believe that, do you? Spain was on the winning side, was it not? And by your own admission, your country has gone backwards and not forward.'

She took his hand in hers, though she doubted the small gesture afforded him a tithe of the comfort she longed to give him. 'You cannot mean that you wish Wellington had been defeated.'

'No, of course not. But I wonder, I am truly beginning to wonder, if I have it in me to fight any more wars on his behalf. Or anyone else's. I am getting tired of taking orders. I'm thinking it might be time I took my life into my own hands.'

'Come with me to America, then,' she said, before she could catch the words.

He touched her cheek. 'They'd execute me for desertion if they caught me, not to mention the shame it would bring to my family and the stain on my character. No, whatever I do, I have to go back.'

'You are not a man to run away from anything, are you, Finlay?'

'You know me very well. Indeed, I am not.'

'I wasn't being serious about you coming with me,' Isabella said, who had actually never been more serious in her whole life. 'The Duke of Wellington might very well be persuaded that El Fantasma has been killed, since it is what he fervently hopes to hear, but his Jock Upstart leads a charmed life. He would know it was a ruse if you did not return.'

'Aye, like as not.' Finlay tucked a strand of her hair behind her ear, and kissed her forehead. 'I'm sorry. This morning I was a bear with a sore heid, and now I'm having a fit of the blue devils. You'll be glad to see the back of me.'

'Aye,' she said, 'like as not.'

He was forced to laugh. 'I'm thinking, once we leave Vitoria, it will be a hard and dangerous push to the coast. The boat will be waiting on standby at San Sebastian. She's a fishing boat. The captain is one of Jack's connections. A fine sailor, he assures me. He'll take you on to Lisbon, where you'll pick up a cargo ship bound for the New World. I'm afraid I don't know the detail—that has been left in the hands of the fisherman. You can trust him with your life, Jack says…'

'Finlay, you need not worry about me. I am perfectly capable of looking after myself. Trust me.'

'I do. I have every faith in you. But I wish…'

'No.' Isabella put her finger to his lips. 'Wheesht, now,' she said. 'You have saved my life. You have given me the chance of another life. That is a priceless gift, Finlay. I promise you, I will make the most of it in return.'

'I know you will.'

'So let us have no more of it.' She looked up at the lowering sky. 'It's going to rain. We should think about finding somewhere to camp for the night.'

'We'll not be camping rough. Tonight you'll have the bath and the feather bed I promised you.' He shook his head when she made to protest. 'It's the last chance you'll get for quite some time. Like I said, the authorities are likely to be hot on our tail all the way to the coast.'

'Then they are likely to be here, in Vitoria, Finlay.'

He smiled at her. 'One advantage I have, of having been in this place before, is that I made a few trustworthy acquaintances, and one of them just happens to be an innkeeper. You shall have a hot bath and a comfortable bed, and you shall be quite safe.'

'Will you share it with me?'

He raised a quizzical brow. 'The bath?'

'I meant the bed, but you are welcome to share both. More than welcome. Very much more. It will be our last chance. I would like…'

'Yes.' He caught her in a tight embrace. 'Yes. I would like that. More than like that. Very much more.'

Alesander Gebara, proprietor of the Hosteria Vasca, greeted Finlay like a long-lost brother, and seemed not at all surprised when informed of the need for discretion. 'They are looking for an Englishman, the soldiers. You,' he said, poking Finlay playfully in the chest, 'are Scottish. So when they come again tonight, I can say no, no, I have seen no English. But it will be best, I think, if I serve you dinner in the privacy of your chamber.'

The inn was ancient, a veritable warren of narrow corridors and rickety staircases, but it had a charm all of its own. The bedchamber Señor Gebara ushered them into was low ceilinged, the heavy, dark oak exposed beams ran at odd angles and a massive stone fireplace dominated one wall, while an imposing tester bed took up most of the floor space, leaving room only for a small table and two chairs set in the window embrasure, and a chest of drawers tucked into a corner.

The innkeeper set about a flurry of activity, summoning a chambermaid to air the bed and set the fire. Another maid was put in charge of the bathing arrangements while Señor Gebara himself brought refreshments from the taproom. 'The finest Rioja in the region,' he said, pouring a glass for each of them.

Isabella took a sip and smilingly informed her host that it was indeed the best she had ever tasted, but she could not help thinking of her brother as she did so. Xavier would be safe as long as the Spanish soldiers were searching for her, but when they were forced to admit defeat, what then? Would the influence her brother wielded really be sufficient to keep him safe from harm?

She would never know. The knowledge gave her a sickening jolt. She would never know. A mixture of panic and fear made her feel faint. She couldn't do this. She had thought herself so strong; she had prided herself on her courage and her daring. What a fool she had been. She was absolutely terrified. She couldn't do this. She simply couldn't.

A warm hand slid around her waist, pulling her up against a strong, solid body. Finlay's smile was warm, too, his sea-blue eyes reassuring. He believed in her. When she had told him how worried she was about letting him down, he'd said she could not. The mist of her panic began to recede. She wouldn't let him down. She would never let him down. Isabella smiled back. Finlay settled her more firmly against him, and returned to his conversation with Señor Gebara.

Isabella listened, sipping at her wine, enjoying the comfort of Finlay's physical proximity, gradually beginning to relax again. It took two maids to carry the enormous copper bath into the room, which they then placed behind screens in front of the now blazing fire. The room was becoming delightfully warm. Steam rose from behind the screens as bucket after bucket of hot water was poured into the bath. The two men were talking of Spain, the changes since the British army and the French had left. The innkeeper sounded very like Estebe. It was not only his accent but the repressed passion that underscored his words. She wondered if he had ever read any of El Fantasma's pamphlets. But Señor Gebara was clearly a prosperous man, his business thriving. He had a wife and a child now, he'd told Finlay. Such a man would not risk all he'd built, would he?

He caught her staring, and smiled warmly at her. He had a very nice smile. He was not much older than Finlay. 'Forgive me, *señora*, I have allowed my tongue to run away with itself, talking of the old days. So many times, I have wondered what became of the Jock Upstart. Not that I doubted he would survive, because— what is it you always said, Finlay?'

'A man who is born to be hanged can never be drowned.'

Señor Gebara laughed. 'That is it, that is it. I am very pleased indeed to see that you are still evading your fate. Those soldiers... If they knew they were chasing the Jock Upstart, they would give up and go back to Madrid. You need have no fear, *señora*. While you have this man to protect you, you are perfectly safe.'

'Ach, you don't know the *señora* here,' Finlay said. 'She's more than capable of protecting herself.'

'A fellow soldier.' The innkeeper nodded. 'I see now why she has your heart, my friend. I am very glad that you, too, have found a woman to share your life.' He turned to Isabella. 'I lost my betrothed in the war,' he said sadly. 'I thought I would never love again, but my Maria, she has shown me that the human spirit is a strong thing, the human heart even stronger. I hope you are as happy with this Jock Upstart, *señora*, as I am with my Maria.'

Isabella did not need Finlay to caution her. She was pleased to be able to maintain the innkeeper's misapprehension, to speak the truth for once. 'I can think of no other man capable of making me this happy,' she said. 'None.'

Alesander left with promises to serve them the best dinner the region could provide in an hour. It was good to see his old friend and ally so happy, but Finlay couldn't help envying the man, too. Alesander had made a new life for himself. Who'd have thought that the wild, bold and fearless guerrilla fighter he'd known would be so content running an inn? Though the way he'd spoken, Finlay would not be surprised to hear that Alesander was still, in his own quiet way, fighting for a better life for his wife and child. Not so very different after all from the man he'd known? Perhaps.

'I like your friend very much,' Isabella said. She was standing at the window, her cheek on the pane. 'Finlay, do you not think that he is in the right of it? The human spirit is a very strong thing. Your friend has made a new life for himself. I would like it so much—so very, very much, if I could believe you could, too.'

He joined her at the window. She clutched his hand tightly. There were tears sparkling on her long lashes. She looked up at him beseechingly. *I can think of no other man capable of making me this happy*, she had said to Alesander. She had said it to maintain their cover, he knew that, but her words had, to his pathetically desperate heart, seemed to carry an undertone of truth. She did care, though. Best not to think about how much; he was heartsore enough.

'Finlay?'

She wanted an answer. She needed the reassurance of an answer. He tried, he tried bloody hard, but he could not imagine what kind of new life he'd forge for himself, and he would not lie to her. 'Isabella,' he said, kissing the tears from her lids, 'we've only got tonight before we spend a lifetime apart. Let's not think about anything else. Not tonight.'

Her lips were soft, sweet, shaped perfectly for his. He ached for her in a new way. The desire was just as fierce, but his need to cherish her, to meld himself to her, to be as one with her, was so much stronger. They would make love, but not yet. He wanted to spin out every single moment of time with her, to be everything to her as she was to him, just for tonight, because tonight was all they would have. He had to make it enough for the memory to last forever.

He had never shared anything so intimate as a bath before. They undressed each other slowly in the fading light, lit only by the glow of the fire, and Finlay discovered that he was wrong about the urgency, the need, the desire, as they touched and stroked, and kissed and licked. The pace was not only his to set. Isabella, his beautiful, feisty Isabella, had a passion to match his. When she pulled him down onto the rug by the fire, he was hers to command. Her mouth, her hands, her hips, captured him as no other had. When she lowered herself onto him, taking him inside her inch by gut-wrenching, achingly delightful inch, he moaned her name, could not resist telling her, in his own language, how much he loved her. They found their rhythm quickly. She seemed to know him instinctively, when to rock on top of him slowly and when to buck and thrust urgently. She came with wild abandon, her climax making him lose control, his own so powerful that he managed, only just, to lift her safely from him at the last second.

She would shed her skin for this man. There was nothing she would not do for him. Lying in his arms, her heart thudding wildly, her body singing with pleasure, Isabella closed her eyes, pressed her cheek to his heartbeat and whispered her love. She had behaved without any inhibitions because, quite simply, she had none with Finlay. He knew her as no one else ever had. Or would.

Pushing this last mournful thought to one side, Isabella sat up. They would have tonight. She was going to make the most of it. 'The bath,' she said, smiling at him. 'You promised you would join me.'

'It will be a tight fit,' he said, smiling back.

It was his wicked smile. It seemed she was not, after all, completely sated. 'I think you have already proved that to both our satisfaction,' Isabella said with a wicked smile of her own.

He laughed then, getting to his feet, his muscles rippling, picking her up and holding her high against him, flesh to flesh, skin to skin, and stepped with her into the bath. He set her down carefully. They stood facing each other and kissed again. The water was still warm. After the icy streams they had washed in of late, it felt hot.

Finlay picked up a tin pitcher and poured water over her. Her skin, alight with his lovemaking, felt every trickle. Another pitcher full. Then the soap. The lather made his hands slippery. His fingers slid over her shoulders, down her arms, back up to her breasts. Her body thrummed with anticipation.

Isabella picked up the jug. There was a delicious ache in postponing pleasure. Water trickled down Finlay's chest, clinging to the rough hair there. Another pitcher full of water. She took the soap from him and began to lather. Her fingers slipped and slid over his skin, finding the ridges of old scars. They were long healed. Some were just the faintest of shadows; others ran deeper.

'Where did you get this one?' she asked, and he told her. 'And this one?' she asked. 'And this one?' There were scars on his shoulders. On his belly. On his thighs. The long, vicious scar on his back was from Corunna, he said. She kissed each one. When her lips reached the base of that worst marking, he turned her round, taking her into his arms. Their bodies slid together, against each other, adhering to each other with the soapsuds, and she forgot about the scars and concentrated on kissing him. By the time they finally stepped from the tub, the water was cold.

Dinner was, as Alesander had promised, excellent. Hearty Basque cuisine, venison in a rich wine stew flavoured with the blood sausages that reminded Finlay of home. They ate at the little table by the window, watching the bustle on the street below, for it was the hour of the *paseo*. Isabella wore one of his shirts. Another first. They'd also managed a couple of other firsts in the bath there, he thought with a grin.

'What are you thinking about?' Isabella asked.

'What do you think?'

She chuckled. 'I think that we are not going to be doing much sleeping in that big comfortable bed.'

'You're not tired, then?'

She shook her head. 'I have the rest of my life to catch up on my sleep.' Her smile wobbled, and his heart lurched in response, but before he could say anything, she had recovered, and took a reviving sip of wine. 'I was thinking,' she said, 'that your scars, they are like a chart of all the places you have been, all the battles you have fought.'

'My body is like a campaign map, right enough,' Finlay said, twirling his half-empty glass around on the table. 'I'm thinking that I've scarcely room for any more entries, nor desire for them.'

Isabella reached for his hand and gently moved the glass away. 'Today, at the site of that terrible battle, and seeing Señor Gebara, too, has brought back horrible memories, things you do not want to think about. I am so sorry.'

Finlay shook his head firmly. 'I'm not.' He stretched his legs out, and pushed his plate aside. 'It's how we keep going, when we're at war—not thinking about it. It's a habit they teach you in the army, not thinking about it, for if you do, you'd not survive. Or you'd run. Or worse.' He glanced over at Isabella. 'Some men can't live with the memories, you know.'

She paled. 'I did not know. Finlay, I…'

'Don't worry. I've no intentions of doing anything daft. Quite the opposite.'

'What do you mean?'

'I told you, it was a good thing, seeing that place again. And seeing Alesander. It's given me pause for thought.' He twined his fingers in hers. 'You've made me question things. Right from the first moment we met, to be honest, you've forced me to confront a lot of unpalatable truths.'

'Me?'

He smiled at her incredulous tone. 'Aye, you. You've a habit of asking the kind of awkward questions that I prefer to avoid. Such as what I'll do now that Wellington has brought us a peace that seems like to last.'

'There will always be other wars to fight, Finlay.'

'There will,' he said sadly. 'Indeed, there will, but I'm done with fighting other people's battles. If this battered body of mine has to be inflicted with any more scars, I'd like them to be of my own devising.'

'What does that mean?'

He frowned, shaking his head. 'I've absolutely no idea, lass. Despite my nickname, I've never really been an upstart, never been anything but unswervingly loyal to my country and my so-called superior officers, but where has it got me? And then there's you. Look at you. Look what a love of your country has made of you. An exile. A traitor.'

'Our cases are not the same.'

'They are more similar than I'd have thought when first I came here. Like you, I'm done with soldiering.'

Across from him, Isabella looked shocked, though when she made to speak, Finlay shook his head. 'I mean it,' he said, and found with surprise that he did. 'I've never in my life thought to be anything but a soldier, but now I'm done with it, and what's more, I'm looking forward to telling Wellington so.'

'What will he say?'

The question gave him pause, for despite his opinion of the man, as a soldier, Finlay had never had anything other than respect for the duke, and—if he was being really honest, which he might as well be now—no little awe. Not that he'd have to actually face the duke if he resigned. But would he feel he'd truly resigned unless he did? Wasn't it his duty, and didn't he always do his duty? He'd not be letting himself down at the last, that was for sure. Finlay shook his head again. 'I don't know what he'll say, though I'll find out soon enough.'

'So you will confront him, then,' Isabella said, with that uncanny ability to read his mind. 'Even though you do not need to?'

'As you said, I'm not a man to run away.' Finlay got to his feet and began to stack the dishes onto a tray.

'No. You are a man who does his duty. Even when he does not wish to.'

Thinking of tomorrow, he thought she'd never said a truer word. He did not want to think about tomorrow. Finlay set the tray outside the door. 'Talking of wishes,' he said, turning the key in the lock, 'I've a few you could help me with, if you're so inclined.'

He was relieved to see the shadow of melancholy

leave her eyes, the sensuous tilt return to her lips. 'Your wish is my command,' she said, giving him a mocking little salute.

Finlay picked her up, setting her gently down on the bed. She stretched her arms over her head, stretching the hem of his shirt she wore up to the top of her thighs. He could see the shadow of her nipples, dark through the white cotton. Her hair was spread out like silk on the pillows.

'I await your orders,' she said.

Finlay pulled his shirt over his head and hurriedly stepped out of his breeches. 'Then, lie back,' he said, kneeling between her legs, 'close your eyes and surrender.'

The following morning Señor Gebara brought their breakfast personally, tapping softly on the door just before daybreak. Finlay set the tray down on the table by the window and returned to the bed, pulling Isabella back into his arms. 'The horses will be ready in half an hour. Alesander has provided us with some supplies, enough to get us to the coast, he says. We'll be two, maybe three days, on the road.'

'Then, we should make haste,' Isabella said, making no move.

'Aye.'

Finlay pulled her tighter. They had lain like this all night, in the sleepy intervals between their passionate lovemaking. Time had seemed suspended; the hours had stretched, seemingly endlessly ahead, until now. Now, as he ran his palm over her flank, as he nestled his chin into her hair, as she pressed herself closer, close enough for their hearts to beat against each other, time began to gallop out of control.

A few more minutes, Isabella thought. She just needed a few more minutes, and then she would be ready. She wrapped her arms tighter around Finlay's waist. She pressed her lips to the hollow of his throat. She felt the stirrings of his arousal and pressed tighter. His erection hardened. She wriggled. She felt his sharp intake of breath. And then his resolute shifting.

'Isabella...'

She leaped from the bed, tearing herself away from him, because the alternative was to cry and to cling, and she would not do that to him. She had promised she would not let him, or herself, down. 'Is that fresh coffee? Would you like some?'

She began to dress. The very thoughtful Señor Gebara had had her undergarments laundered, her habit and boots brushed clean of the dust of the road. She was aware of Finlay watching her as she snatched at clothes and pulled them on, pouring coffee, wittering on about the fresh bread, the salty cheese, the smoky ham, as if she cared about anything other than the fact that every minute, every second, took them inexorably towards their separate fates.

She sat at the table and managed to force down her breakfast without choking. Her smile was manic, she knew that even without the look Finlay gave her, but he said nothing, eating his own breakfast steadily, taking a second cup of coffee, a faint frown furrowing his brow. She had no idea what he was thinking. He had that locked-away look, already putting a distance between them as he shaved. She knew he cared for her—how could she not, after the intensity and raw emotion of their coupling? She suspected he cared more than he would ever allow her to know. But she knew, too, with absolute certainty, that he would not allow himself to care enough, and she knew with equal certainty that she would never wish him to. She was not worth the sacrifice, and he would be sacrificing everything. His family. His career—even if he no longer wanted it. More important, his honour, and Finlay was a man who must always be honourable. A man who would always do his duty. As he was doing now.

As she must do hers. Last night was their goodbye. She had vowed she would make it as easy, as painless, as guilt-free as possible for him. He was not detached; he was not indifferent. He was trying to make it easy for her. Isabella pushed her coffee cup aside and got to her feet. 'Time to go,' she said, straightening her shoulders, head back, like the trooper he expected. 'Time to face the future.'

Finlay stuck to the bargain he'd made with himself for the three days and two nights it took them to reach San Sebastian. He played the soldier, as he had always played the soldier, thinking only of executing his orders as best he could, of protecting and defending Isabella's liberty, wary at every second of potential ambush, dragging his mind back again and again to the task in hand whenever it strayed into dangerous territory. He would not think of their impending parting. He would not allow his heart to ache. He would not wish for anything other than Isabella's safe delivery to the waiting fishing boat, and then his own execution of the final elements of Jack's plan, which would ensure her future safety.

They stood on the final crest above the fortress town of San Sebastian, the scene of the last battle he'd fought in Spain before heading for the Pyrenees in pursuit of the retreating French army. Below, the bay was fringed by a perfect, beautiful crescent of golden sand. A small islet was set like a jewel in the middle of the bay, breaking up the softly rolling waves. It reminded him of Oban bay, in some respects. The distinctively shaped Basque fishing boats, their hulls, to his Highland eyes, so vertiginous and bulky that he found it difficult to believe, looking at them bobbing in the protective embrace of the harbour wall, that they wouldn't simply topple over in the lightest of swells. Isabella was bound for one of those boats. Isabella was bound for that sea, in the directly opposite direction he would take.

Isabella, his lovely Isabella, who had been so brave and so stoic, these past few days. Not a tear had she shed, nor a word of complaint had she uttered. Not a mention of that perfect night they'd shared had she made. No regrets. No looking back. Only onward, forward, to the new life she would forge. A new life in a new world. A world he would not inhabit.

His gut clenched. He thought he might be sick. The breeze ruffled her hair. She dipped her head to make some adjustment to her reins, and he thought he caught a glimpse of tears. Though it might be the wind. His heart contracted. His stomach roiled. It took him a moment to recognise it for what it was. Fear. He was desperately afraid of losing her. He knew at that moment, knew despite all, that he could not let her go.

'Isabella.'

She turned to face him. Tears. They were tears, but she forced a smile. 'I'm fine. I will be fine. It is just— I will be fine,' she said.

She was trying to reassure him. Hope did not spring, it burst forth like the first snowdrop of the year. A fragile shoot, but determinedly pushing itself towards the sun. He hadn't allowed himself to consider how deeply her feelings for him ran; he had been too concerned with damping down his own, but if she cared even a fraction as much as he did…

'Isabella…'

'Finlay, don't worry. I won't let you down. I am—I am ready.'

She straightened in the saddle, determined to play the soldier she thought he expected, and it was his undoing. 'Isabella, I love you so much. My own heart, I love you. I can't let you go without me.'

She thought she had misheard him. She must have misheard him. She opened her mouth, but no words came. She could only stare stupidly.

'Isabella.'

Finlay jumped down from his horse and pulled her from the saddle. These past few days, in their wild race across the mountains, his face had been set, his expression steadfastly distant. He had played the commanding officer, she had played the foot soldier, just as they had agreed. Now the light was back in his eyes. They were the colour of the sea below. Her heart, her poor about-to-be-broken heart, began to beat faster. She couldn't possibly hope. There was no hope. None.

'Isabella.' He took her hands in his. The horses were untethered, she noticed, and then immediately lost interest. 'Isabella.' He shook his head, grinned, shook his head, frowned. 'I've never said the word before.'

Say it again, she prayed, but said nothing, in case her prayers were misguided.

'Never. I don't know if I should… It's—it's likely all wrong, only— Ach, what a blithering eejit I am. I love you. I love you with all my heart, and no amount of telling myself all these other things matter more makes a whit of difference. I love you, lass, and I don't want to have to live without you. I don't know what that means. I can't make any promises, I can't even…'

'I don't care!' Isabella threw her arms around him. 'I don't care what or how or if. All I care about is that I love you, and if you love me, too— Do you? Do you truly love me?'

Finlay laughed. 'Could you ever have doubted it?'

'Yes! You never once…'

'I could not. And you…'

'I could not. Oh, Finlay, how could I tell you that I loved you, how could I ask you to come with me, when it would mean you giving up everything that is important to you?'

'You are everything. You are the only thing that is, or ever will be, important to me.'

'But your family. The army. You will be court-martialled.' Cold reality hit her. She dragged herself free of his embrace. 'Finlay, I love you so much. Too much. I could not do this to you, put your life in danger, ask you to...'

'You haven't asked me,' Finlay said gently, pulling her back into his arms. 'I'm offering. I don't have much, or I won't, not if—when—I leave with you, but without you, I have nothing. I don't know what kind of life we'll make, lass, but I'm asking you for the chance to build it together. Will you give me that chance?'

She wanted to. Her heart cried out yes, but her head...her head needed some convincing yet, it seemed. 'You said it yourself, Finlay, you're not a man to run away. You have a duty to go back, even if it is only to resign. You cannot blight your honour with the shame of desertion, and you cannot take the risk of them catching you, for you will be hanged.'

'I will not lie to you, I would wish it otherwise. I would wish that we could both go to England together, that I could put a clean and honourable end to my career, but I can't. There are some sacrifices worth making. I love you. My duty is to my heart now, and not my country.'

She swallowed the lump in her throat that his words, his beautiful, heartfelt words caused. 'But your family?'

Now he did flinch. She sensed true pain there, but still he shook his head. 'I will be sacrificing no more than you, my love. We will make a new family together. If you'll have me. It won't be easy. It won't be painless.

We'll miss what we've lost, but we won't have lost the most important thing of all.'

'Each other?'

'Each other.'

She could resist no longer. The future, which had seemed like a huge, black abyss, now spread golden before her, not perfect, not rosy or easy, but one redolent with promise. 'I love you, Finlay Urquhart, with all my heart.'

'And I love you, Isabella Romero, with every fragment of mine.'

Epilogue

Oban, Argyll—six months later

The fishing village of Oban reminded Jack Trestain a little of San Sebastian. Funny how things sometimes came full circle. The same horseshoe bay, the island a short distance offshore, the sheltering haven of the harbour, the cluster of white houses lining the front. Admittedly the gently bobbing fishing boats were shallower, longer, the sky was a paler blue and it was significantly colder, but all the same...

Had the similarity struck Finlay when he had sailed for Lisbon with his Isabella all those months ago? He had not mentioned it in his letter, but then he'd had rather more important matters to occupy him. Such as how to arrange his death, along with the death of El Fantasma.

Jack smiled wryly to himself. Who would have thought that the partisan Finlay had encountered all those years ago would turn out to be a blue-blooded Spanish lady? And who would have imagined that the blue-blooded Spanish lady would turn out to be one of Spain's most wanted rebel partisans? 'No one, and it's just as well,' he said to himself as he stepped out of the fishing boat that had carried him here, after agreeing a time for his return journey with the captain, for his visit was a fleeting one with a sole but crucial purpose.

Jack sat on the edge of the harbour wall to garner his thoughts. It had been Celeste's idea that he come here in person. 'For you cannot write such things in a letter, *mon amour*,' she had said. It was true. What he had to say was far too politically sensitive to commit to paper, but that wasn't what his lovely wife-to-be had meant. Finlay's family had already received one tragic letter out of the blue, posing more questions than answers, something Celeste was only too familiar with. On this occasion, he would be there in person to answer all their questions, ease their concerns. This time, they would get the truth. Or as much of it as was prudent to furnish them with.

Finlay's missive had come to him via heaven knew what circuitous route, but by some miracle it had not, to Jack's very experienced eyes, been tampered with. Short and pithy, it had been shocking, but it had also made Jack smile. Clearly, Finlay was head over ears in love with his partisan, though he had naturally said no such thing. Love, as Jack had recently learned, was capable of making a man do all sorts of rash and mad things. Such as ask his best friend to fake his death. *You're a master strategist*, Finlay had written. *I rely on you to give me a suitably fitting end.*

Well, he'd managed that, all right. The fate that had

met the brave Major Urquhart in the remote, rocky mountains of Spain, was deemed heroic when reported in the British press. There had been no overt mention of El Fantasma, of course, but there had been sufficient hints to entice the Spanish chaps to ask the English chaps for more background, and the top-secret information they'd received had convinced them. El Fantasma was dead, and Major Urquhart had died, presumably at the hands of the cut-throat partisan's accomplices, but not before successfully completing his mission. The Romero family were safe from prosecution, just as Finlay had insisted. More important, Wellington had fallen for the story, relieved that a potentially awkward political scandal had been avoided, and had even been persuaded to grant Finlay a posthumous honour.

Jack looked at the medal now, sitting in its leather case. Finlay wouldn't be interested in it, but his father would, and Jack was pretty sure that Mr and Mrs Urquhart would be able to put their son's military pension to good use. It had taken a good deal of strong-arming to secure that pension. Jack had to make an effort to unfurl his fist, thinking about that. It shouldn't have proved so difficult.

He patted his coat pocket, though there was no need. The paper with Finlay's new name and whereabouts in America was safely tucked away there, along with the letter from the bank with the arrangement for payment of the monies due each quarter. It was a risk, telling these strangers that their son was alive, but one Jack was certain to be worth taking. Secrets and lies, he had learned from his lovely Celeste, could tear a family asunder. Finlay's family might never see him again, but their love for him would reach across the oceans that separated them in the letters they could write, and one day, perhaps, Finlay and Isabella's children would be able to visit their father's Highland homeland. That was a thought to warm the heart.

Jack smiled. Mawkish idiot! Love had made him a sentimental fool. His smile widened. No, love had brought him happiness. He hoped Finlay and his Isabella were as happy as he and his Celeste. Reading between the lines of that letter, he'd wager that they were.

* * * * *

Historical Note

The inspiration for Finlay Urquhart, the Jock Upstart, arose when I was reading Richard Holmes's excellent book *Redcoat* while researching my previous book in this series, *The Soldier's Dark Secret*. It was, I discovered, extremely unusual for a man of humble origins to work his way up through the ranks in Wellington's army. He'd have to have been exceptional in every way—brave, bold and bright—but he'd always have remained an outsider to the establishment elite. I do love an underdog, and so Finlay was born.

The main part of my research for the partisan war in Spain came from Ronald Fraser's book *Napoleon's Cursed War*. There were indeed female partisans fighting what was referred to, for the first time, as a guerrilla war—including Catalina Martin, who was promoted to second lieutenant, and Dominica Ruiz, said to have killed three imperial soldiers with her own hands.

Isabella's alter ego, El Fantasma, was a spy rather than a *guerrillero*, her values influenced by what I was hearing in the news—which at the time I was writing, focused on the conflict between matters of state security and freedom of speech and information: the so-called 'enemy within'.

I already knew that Finlay would be disillusioned by the lack of any meaningful change for the better wrought by peace, just as his comrade Jack was. I began to wonder about Isabella, too. My reading implied that in many ways Spain regressed, in terms of social justice, after the end of what they called the War of Independence. I wondered how my heroine would feel, forced to take a back seat in the country she'd fought so hard to liberate.

As always, I've strived to set this story in as accurate a historical background as possible. In July 1813, when the story opens, the French had been driven into the north-eastern corner of Spain after the bloody Battle of Vitoria. Wellington was forced to withdraw from his attempt to storm the fortress town of San Sebastian, and it was not until September that the town finally surrendered, and was immediately sacked by the British—forcing the French to retreat across the Pyrenees. Any mistakes or inaccuracies are entirely my own fault.

Finally, a note on Finlay's accent. He is a Highlander. His family come from Oban, in Argyll, not far from my own home, and he would, of course, have been a native Gaelic speaker. His English would have become fluent in the army, giving him, more than likely, an English rather than a Scots accent. But I wanted my hero to be unmistakably Scots—gritty and a bit rough round the edges—so I'll put my hands up right now and confess that the slang he uses has large elements of straight, modern-day Glaswegian.

Anachronistic, completely historically incorrect, I know, but I hope it works. I leave it up to you to decide.